DAMAGED SOUL

DIRTY SOULS MC - BOOK 4

EMMA CREED

For Andrea,
who has a heart as big as her smile, and never fails to keep me
laughing.
Thank you for being you x

AUTHOR NOTE

Warning

Damaged Soul and all books in the Dirty Soul's Mc series are a work of fiction, and contain adult content. Due to the nature of the series you should expect to come across various subject matter that some readers may find disturbing.

Every Soul has their story and Grimm and Rogue's is DARK...

It contains some graphic flashback scenes that sensitive readers should read with caution. For more details on the triggers featured in this book please contact the author.

Damaged Soul is intended for readers 18+

THE STORY SO FAR

Prez has fulfilled the promise he made to his unexpected ally, CIA agent Helen Scott, and taken down the pedophile ring that she was investigating before her death. Along with his VP Jessie, he finally got revenge on the person who killed his daughter, Hayley. In doing so he has formed a temporary truce with club rivals, the Bastards.

The daughter he had to keep secret for so long, Ella, marrying newly patched member Nyx, and becoming a grandfather has made him more determined than ever to put his club back together again.

Nyx has learnt from his recently found brother, Brax, that ex-club member, Chop, is the person responsible for the death of their mother. He also learnt that his brother carries an unhealthy thirst for justice.

Brax has struggled to adapt to having a family after being a nomad for so long and learned some lessons about love from Helen Scott's daughter, Grace, while he was protecting her. After realizing he couldn't carry the weight of hate he had for Chop if he wanted to keep her, he sacrificed his one chance at vengeance to make her his.

He's since shown his dedication to his family and the brotherhood by becoming a fully patched member of the charter and is filling in for Skid as Road Captain.

Ella's best friend Abby has been working hard to overcome her addiction while waiting for the man she loves to come back for her.

And the club have landed themselves a new hangout after Brax, in an attempt to protect Grace, killed the only man who might know where wild teen, Storm's missing sister is.

Skid is still riding alone, trying to get over his brother Chop's betrayal and the savage loss of his wife, Carly.

While back at the club, someone he deeply cares for is about to land herself in some heat. Now he's going to have to put his faith in the only person who can clean up after her.

'Bound not by blood but loyalty.
We live, we ride, and we die
by our own laws'

AGED 16

"Ignore the staring, sweetheart," Mama whispers to me as we step into the crowded chapel. I do as she says. As we walk to our usual pew at the front, I keep my focus on the floor and count how many tiles I step over. I don't understand why we still have to come here anymore, this is just another one of those things she insists on doing to try to be 'normal'.

Mama holds her head up high, returning the polite smiles and ignoring the sad, pitiful stares being directed at her. Her hand squeezes around my shoulder when we get to our pew, where three spaces have been left empty.

Is everyone else here playing the game too?

I side glance Eleanor Cranum when I hear her tiny giggle. If she had the ability to read the thoughts inside my head, I bet her amusement would slip down her throat and choke her, and I throw her back a look of spite before sitting down beside Mama. She's shifted into her position beside Mary, the preacher's wife, who takes hold of her hand and squeezes it to offer her some strength.

"We're all with you, Anita." Her voice is soft and kind, and it forces another fake smile onto Mama's lips.

Like every other service I've attended on a Sunday, the

preacher's voice is a low hum in the back of my head. I ignore his meaningless words and helpless chants, because I'm far beyond being saved. The thoughts inside my mind don't belong in a sacred place like this, I don't belong in a place like this, and yet I make no attempt to blank them out.

I couldn't if I wanted to because I don't control them. They control me.

I look around at the congregation, and wonder if everything is so perfect for them when they're in the confines of their own homes.

Do any other families sitting here today have their own horror stories? Are the parts of our worlds that we choose to share with others just one spectacular performance that each of us has a role in?

When the service ends, everyone stands out on the perfectly mowed grass, same as they always do. I wonder who would have cut it this week. Church ground maintenance was always a job that Father prided himself on doing. No one else could get the lines as perfect as Peter Carter.

As the sun shines down on all the townspeople that spill out of the church doors and take the time to chat together, all eyes seem to be directed at Mama and me.

Some take the time to come over and express their shock and tell us that we're in their prayers. Others just stare down their noses at us. Somehow through it all though, Mama remains gracious as she thanks them for their kindness.

Eleanor smiles at me from where she stands with her father, as he tucks her under his arm and talks to Mrs. Morton about what colleges he wants her to apply for. It's not an innocent smile she's giving me, it's a seductive one. The kinda one she gave me before I let her suck my dick around the back of the science block last week. I'll bet my fingerprints are still traceable on her shoulders, just a slight yellowish tinge on her skin now, but still a mark of her sin.

When Mama's taken as much as she can stand, she nudges me forward to start walking back home. We pass the same diner that we do every Sunday. When I was younger, I always wished we could be like the other families and stop off for ice cream. I was just never brave enough to ask Father if we could.

But Father ain't here today...

"You wanna get some ice cream?" I look up at Mama daringly, and the smile she gives me back reaches all the way up to her eyes and makes them sparkle.

Opening her purse, she takes out a ten-dollar bill and holds it out to me. I can't remember the last time I had ice cream, and with a slight grin back at her, I take the money from her fingers and head inside. I spend far too long deciding what to choose, and when I finally make a decision, I pay up and take the cones out to her.

She looks happy, sitting and waiting for me on the bench outside. So happy that the hint of a laugh escapes from her lips as she takes her cone from me, along with her change.

Mama then takes a long, contented breath of air and smiles at me again before we continue our journey home in delicious silence.

When we get to the top of our lane, her lips plant a gentle kiss on my cheek, before she wipes the corner of my mouth with her finger.

"Best not tell your father about our little treat," she whispers, as all the light dims from her eyes. "You know how it would displease him."

Her words drain all the warmth from my chest and stop me from moving.

"Sure," I promise her, faking a smile of my own.

I'm confident that it's a secret I can keep because Father is never coming back...

Not from where he is now.

CHAPTER 1

1% MC

GRIMM

TWO MONTHS AGO

"I'm not him... I am not him."

I repeat the words over and over inside my head, but they don't seem to have any effect. The pretty little whore glances over her shoulder seductively as she leads me up the stairs toward the room she knows I have the key to.

It's been months since I allowed myself the pleasure of a pussy. Long enough for this not to be pleasant for her. She smiles at me awkwardly when we reach the door, and it surprises me that she doesn't seem nervous. She can't have been warned about me yet.

Sex is a temptation I rarely give into, but every once in a while, it becomes a necessity. Everyone needs a release sometimes. Mel seems about the only person around here capable of handling the job. She was here way before I came, and I guess all these years hanging out at the club must have grown her an extra couple layers on that thick skin of hers.

What appeals to me about Mel is the fact she never asks questions, more than likely because she senses she wouldn't like my answers but it works for me.

Tonight, Mel wasn't available, and now I'm about to find out if this new club slut is capable of handling me.

I can tell from the dreamy look in her eyes that she's desperate to be claimed. She probably tried it with Troj first, maybe Thorne, they seem the popular choice these days. Now she's desperate enough to be trying that shit with me, and she's about to find out that I'm nothing close to the bad, biker boyfriend dream she's chasing after.

I use my key to unlock the door, it's the only room up here that ever gets locked. Prez gave me this privilege a few years ago because, unlike the other filthy fuckers around here, I'm particular about where I fuck.

This is my space, it may not get used all that often but I take care of it. I know it's clean and I keep the key to ensure none of the others contaminate it.

The girl flashes me a warm, almost kind smile as she shuffles past me to get inside and I take a long, calming breath as I shut the door behind us.

"Where you want me, honey?" She sounds seductive and eager to please, and I have to clench my fists and try to calm the urges inside me. When I open my eyes, I glare them into the thin strip of fabric that barely covers her body.

"Take that off," I instruct, loosening my belt as I step toward her. My cock is hard and hungry, begging for release from the month of torment I've punished myself with.

"My name's Clarissa," she tells me sweetly, as she strips out of the tiny dress she's wearing. When it drops to the floor, she scoops it up and places it neatly over the back of the chair behind her... Perhaps the girls have spoken to her after all.

My eyes scan her bare body, I know some of the brothers can be rough, she's got a couple of marks to prove it. But what I require is on a different level, and as my eyes drop to the floor and I allow my dark thoughts to consume me deeper, I feel the guilt start to build.

"I want you to do exactly as I tell you," I speak through my teeth.

"Sure." She nods her head back at me.

"I won't make this last any longer than it has to," I promise, and she shakes off my words as she closes the gap between us. I haven't even touched her yet and I feel bad for it. Maybe it's because she looks so much sweeter than the others. She's new, fresh, and inexperienced. I could do some real damage to her.

"You got a wrapper for it?" She looks down at the bulge in my jeans and I raise an eyebrow at her. There ain't no way I'd ever forget the fuckin' rubber.

"Course ya do." She smirks to herself, mocking me, and I'll need to make the little bitch pay for that.

I pull a condom out from my back pocket, slipping it between my lips so I can tear it open with my teeth. The girl's eyes widen as she watches me unzip my jeans and take the time to securely stretch the latex over my shaft. Maybe she's not as innocent as I thought, I can tell she likes them big by the way she's lookin' at me.

"Ask," I instruct, pulling my shirt off over my head as I stalk closer to her. The weakness in my voice doesn't fuckin' suit me, and I can hear the sound of *him* laughing at me in my head. He wouldn't need her to fucking ask him, he'd take with or without her permission. But that, right there, is the difference between us. I keep the monster inside me chained. I need to hear that this club whore in front of me, who's probably already taken six dicks and a fist today, wants me.

"I want you to fuck me, Grimm." Her palm stretches over my chest. It makes my skin itch so I snatch her wrist, crushing it with my fingers as I shake my head at her.

She's steady as a fucking rock as I pull her hand away from my skin, which is more than can be said about me. Maybe that's because she doesn't know what's coming next, and I hate myself for desiring it so damn much.

"Ask nicer," I growl, closing my eyes. All that restraint I'm holding on to is slowly draining away, and once it's gone, I know all the empathy inside me will vanish.

My conscience can't save her when it's up and fucked off.

"Fuck me... Please?" She tips her head, giving me a sickly sweet smile that makes me shudder. I step my body into hers, forcing her back against the wall as I wrap my hands around her thighs and lift her up from the ground. When her wet, hungry pussy sits flush with my cock, I hiss through my teeth. It makes my inner demon claw at his cage, screeching at me to set him free.

I feel her heat through the rubber as I enter her, and the rush of the relief scorches at my insides, thick like lava. Each inch she takes from me eats up a little more of the tension. I get my first moan out of her when I've stretched her to her limit. She fidgets to ease her discomfort, but I hold her hips firm and force her to feel the burn.

Her fingers lift up to my face, and I manage to stop her just before they touch me, throwing her arm hard into the wall behind her. I secure it beside her head with one hand, as my other keeps a grip on her thigh. My fingers squeeze into her skin, bruising her body while I hold the little slut where I want her. The force of my body is all that keeps her upright, and I use its power to thrust inside her. Over and over, faster and faster until her screams become deafening.

I make the rules now. Even if it comes with a price. Being this close to another human repulses me, the sensation of her body moving against mine grates on my nerves. When I feel my own scream beginning to build, I overcome it by burying my head into her shoulder and biting her flesh between my teeth. Even when her skin puts a bad taste in my mouth, I force myself to sink deeper. I deserve punishment for giving in to the urges.

I feel her tighten around my cock, constricting, and fucking smothering me. Her soaked snatch leaks all over me and coats my fucking balls with her filth.

I release her wrist to take hold of her neck. My ink-covered hand looks so colorful against her paling skin, and as she throbs beneath my fingertips, I feel my cock get harder inside her. Then clenching my fingers tighter, I listen until she chokes for me.

Her pussy sucks me in deeper, begging for me to offload, but I'm nowhere near done with her yet...

"You're a sick fuck, Grimm," she manages in between the gasps of oxygen I allow her, and instead of panicking as she should be, she smiles. The sadistic little bitch is getting off on my crazy. Handling me way better than I gave her credit for because she thinks this is some kinda kink I got. That it's just a game.

She's wrong.

This is a test.

A test of my self-control.

Can I contain the wickedness inside me? Will I find the strength to release her when her complexion turns too blue?

Her skin is purple under the pressure of my fingers, and my sweat weeps into the pores of her skin as I pound at her pussy and growl like a savage.

She struggles a little, tries to free herself from my hold, but the panic in her eyes only makes me hold on tighter.

"It's okay, baby," she splutters, her fingers grasping around the wrist of the hand I'm stealing her breath with. She's urging me on like I need her fuckin' reassurance. But I'm the one in control here.

My hips smash into hers, and a sweet sound of agonized pleasure releases from her pink stained lips. Her eyes lose their determination, becoming vacant as they roll back.

It's everything I need.

In these moments, I decide if they live or if they die. I have the ultimate power. I'm the dictator. I am in con-fuckin'-trol. Every muscle in my body tenses, my cock throbbing to the point of pain as I fill the rubber that I'm fucking inside her. I waste no more time, quickly releasing the hold I've got on her and taking a step back. Her limp body slumps into a broken heap on the floor. She's a mess, but she's breathing, she's alive.

"Get out," I yell at her, stumbling backward. I need more space between us. My throat's already tightening up and my stomach's starting to cramp.

Somehow, the girl manages to stand, her shaky legs making her stumble toward the chair to snatch up her dress. When she starts to pull it over her head, I decide she isn't moving as fast as I need her to.

"Out," I roar, marching for the door and swinging it open. She's still fumbling with the zip on her dress when I force her out, and she tumbles into the hall.

The room shakes when I slam the door shut, and I only just make it to the basin in the corner of the room before I start spilling my guts up. I can still feel her on my skin, my cock still feels confined by her, even after I rip off the fuckin' condom. I stink of her cheap perfume, it's all too fuckin' much, and I retch over the basin again until there's nothing left to come up.

My skin itches and my head is throbbing because all I hear is his damn voice inside me. I want to tear it out.

I feel blood on my hands, blood that I know isn't really there. Still, it soaks through my skin, leaving a permanent stain on my flesh. It won't wash away, no matter how hard I scrub at it. Because he's inside me, that last scrap of his existence is rooted inside my soul.

As long as I'm alive I'll never be rid of him, and he thrives on my weakness.

The hard thumping in my chest beats to the rhythm of the pounding in my head, and the screeching inside my ears only gets louder. I manage to crawl over to the shower, reaching up to hit the facet. I don't care if the water's hot or cold, just as long as it washes the girl off my body. And that's where I remain, sitting on the floor, with my back resting against the tiles and my hands covering my ears. The water cleansing me while I wait for the calm…

"I'm not him… I am *not* fuckin' him."

"I was wondering when you were gonna show your face," I snap at Skid when he steps inside the office.

"Okay, okay go easy on me." Perching his ass on the edge of the desk, he picks up the spanner that I've just slammed down in a temper and twists it around in his huge hand. I slouch back in the worn-leather office chair and cross my arms over my chest, waiting for an explanation.

Skid's usually all about the fuckin' words, but since his bastard brother took his wife's life, he seems to be all out of them.

"You back for good now?" I ask with a bite of sarcasm. I've heard whispers around the yard that Prez has asked Brax to take his place as Road Captain. The fact that Nyx got hitched to Prez's daughter yesterday is the only reason Skid's come home. I'm not about to pressure the guy into sticking around. Even if he is the only good thing I got.

"I can't, Rogue." His voice is weak, and I hate it. Then he shakes his head like he's disappointed in himself, and it makes me even angrier at Chop. I do my best to hide my disappointment, last thing I want is Skid beating himself up over hurting my fuckin' feelings, especially since I don't have any.

"And what about this place?" My eyes roam around the

garage office, this place used to mean so much to Skid, and I know how important it is to the club.

His eyes glass over as they scan the space around us, the sight seems to cause him physical pain.

"Spoke to Prez, him and Jess are putting a schedule together, they'll get you all the help you need. Thorne's taking care of the books, he'll make sure you get more than your fair share for what you're putting in around here."

I wish he'd have the guts to make eye contact with me, maybe then I might be able to figure out what's going on in his head.

"I thought I might be able to stay here, I even tried moving on, but I ended up making shit worse on myself," he confesses.

"You in trouble, Skid?" I shift uncomfortably in my seat. I may be small, I may be female, but I'd still rip the throat out of any fucker who's causing him to leave me.

"Nah, I ain't in any trouble, just ain't thinking straight no more. Home ain't home to me without Carly here." It's crushing to see Skid, the hardest fucker I know, weak like this.

"I understand." I nod back, hoping it'll ease some of his guilt. I've known the guy long enough to know that he'll be feeling bad for leaving me. We rarely speak about soft shit like feelings, we don't have to. Skid knows how much he means to me.

"I just feel bad for—"

"Hey." I quickly cut him off. "You got nothin' to feel bad for, not when it comes to me. I owe you, remember?" Suddenly I regret that this is the first time I've ever told him that. "I gotta get back to work." I sigh, standing up and moving past him before shit gets too deep.

I don't do deep.

"The boys will look out for you, Rogue." Skid follows me through to the workshop, and when my head spins round to throw him a judgmental look, he holds his hands up defensively.

"I just want you to know, that if you need anything, all you gotta do is ask."

"Skid, you've known me since I was eight years old, you ever known me to ask for help?" Tipping my head to the side, I wait on his response. The low grunty laugh he makes tricks me for a few seconds into believing that I've got the old Skid back.

Seeing a smile on his face feels good, even if it's only brief.

"Guess you're right." His huge callused hand ruffles the top of my head. "I'll be in touch soon." He heads out the roller door toward his bike, knowing he ain't about to get a long drawn out goodbye outta me.

"Hey, Skid," I call across at him, catching him just before he starts his engine. When he looks up at me, I see the immeasurable sadness in his kind brown eyes.

"When you find that cunt brother of yours, you carve a huge chunk out of him for me." I wink, placing my hands in the pockets of my overalls to stop myself from wiping the tear that's about to drip onto my cheek. I haven't shed a tear in fucking years and if I wipe it away it means it's really there.

"You got it, kiddo." Skid nods at me with a sad smile. "You just stay out of trouble, think you can do that for me?"

"Ain't making no promises," I tell him, watching as he kick starts his engine, and his Bobber purrs beautifully.

I feel helpless as I stand and watch him disappear down the track, out the gates, and onto the main road. I have no clue when the next time I'll see him will be, and suddenly I feel lonelier than ever.

THIRTEEN YEARS AGO

"Gotcha, lil' shit." A huge hand grabs my collar, stopping me from running, and drags me backward. My heart is throbbing

from sprinting, and now I wish I hadn't wasted all that energy. Of course, the guy was gonna outpace me.

Stealing in broad daylight was a stupid thing to do, I should have known better, waited until after dark, like I did a few nights ago.

"*Do you know what we do to thieves around here?*" *the huge guy barks at me. My feet scrape over the dusty ground beneath me as he pushes me forward, marching me back toward the garage.*

He's built like a mountain, his eyes wild and threatening, any other eight-year-olds would probably be scared of him.

But I ain't scared of no one.

"*We tear their limbs off one by one, and throw them on the fire pit,*" *he spits, trying his best to draw fear from me.*

"*Let him go.*" *I turn my head toward the voice that's calling from the other side of the yard and see another man jogging toward us. He looks a lot like the man who's holding me and is just as big, just younger.*

"*He's just a kid, Chop, we got the carburetor back, no harm done, right?*" *He struggles with the mean guy's grip as he tries to set me free, but there's no way he's gonna let me go.*

"*I'm a girl, asshole.*" *I scowl at the man trying to help me, and I'm not sure which one of them rips the hood that's covering my head down, but they both share the same shocked look when the long blonde ponytail drops over my shoulder.*

"*Boy, girl, still a fucking thief, and she'll pay the price.*" *Mean guy narrows his eyes at me.*

"*Come on, Chop, she probably doesn't even know what it is she was taking, or who she was taking it from,*" *the younger one says, and it pisses me off that he underestimates me.*

"*It's a carburetor for a Chevy.*" *I raise my eyebrows proudly, and the guy who has me locked tight in his fist, 'Chop', gives his friend a 'told ya so' look.*

"*Jesus Christ, kid, I'm trying to help you out here.*" *The*

15

younger one crouches down to my level, his eyes seem so much kinder than the other guy's.

"What's a little wretch like you doin' stealing car parts from a place like this?" He frowns at me. I shrug and turn my face away from him. I may be a thief but I'm not a rat.

They can throw me on their damn fire, in fact, they'd be doing me a favor.

"Okay, we tried it your way, Skid, now we'll go at it mine. Get the bolt cutters, we'll cut off her fingers till she rats on who she's working for." My feet lift off the ground before Chop even finishes his sentence, and a lump blocks my throat when he pulls me through the garage door and slams my ass onto a stool.

Standing in front of me, he looks so brutal, but I won't give him my fear. So I stare right back at him.

"Was it you that took the battery from the ranger last week?" he asks, and instead of answering, I fold my arms.

"Look at her, Chop, I've seen more meat on a stray fuckin' dog... You can't punish a kid." The nicer guy, 'Skid', steps in front of Chop.

"You hungry, darlin'?" He tips his chin at me, and my stomach grumbling at the mention of food answers the question for me.

"Let me go get someone to fix you up a sandwich, then maybe you might want to tell us who sent you here to steal them parts." He disappears, leaving me alone with the scowling one.

"My brother may be soft as shit, but if you don't start giving me answers, I promise I'll cut 'em out of you, lil' bitch." He looks a little disappointed when my face shows him no fear. But this man knows shit all about me. He won't understand that there ain't much he could do to me that I ain't already suffered.

Skid returns a short time later, carrying a plate in one hand and a soda in the other. I manage to take the time to fake him a smile before snatching the plate off him and devouring the sandwich in seconds. I know it's gonna make my belly ache, and *there's every chance I could throw it back up. But I'm starving and surprisingly, it tastes really good.*

"You know much about cars?" Skid asks, and I shrug my shoulders again, this time it's not because I don't want to answer, my mouth's just too crammed with food... The truth is, I do know about cars, I used to watch my dad for hours when he was working. But he doesn't do that no more. These days I'll be lucky to see him out of bed.

"If you're stealing these parts because you need money, maybe we can help you," Skid suggests.

"What the fuck? Did you hit ya head, Skid? She's a thief." Chop slams both his fists down into the workstation.

"We could use some help around here." Skid ignores the outburst. "Just a few afternoons a week. You could stop by when ya finish school. You might learn something and once you've paid off what you've stolen from us already, we'll start paying you for your time."

His offer sounds appealing. I could sure use the cash.

"Ten dollars, a sandwich, and soda... each day, and I'll be here." I stare Skid right between his eyes so he knows that I mean business.

His lips raise into a smile. "Got yaself a deal, little lady." He spits onto his greasy palm then holds it out for me to shake.

"I never said anything about this being okay," Chop growls.

"Wind it in, Chop, you made me partner remember. I'll take responsibility for the girl."

It's strange, but I like how that sounds. I can't remember the last time anyone had been responsible for me.

"You're getting a good deal..." I spit on my own palm and slam it into Skid's before he can change his mind. "...I already know how to strip an engine."

"This is on you." Chop prods his finger hard into Skid's chest before he storms out and leaves us alone.

17

"Don't mind him, he's always like that." Skid pulls me up off the stool so I'm standing on my feet.

"Here," he passes me a socket. *"I'm gonna filter this out, and you can tell me what you already know."*

"He'll be back," a voice comes from nowhere. And when I spin around, Jessie, the Dirty Souls VP, is resting against the office door.

He's been the one helping me out the most since Skid lost himself.

"In the meantime, you need anything—"

"Just had the same speech from Skid," I quickly cut him off. "I need anything, I'll deal with it myself." Last thing I want is to be in debt to these guys. I've helped them out a few times in the past, but only because I wanted to. I'm not stupid enough to forget how dangerous these men are, or the power they hold over town.

"Skid told me you'd say that." Jessie smirks, pushing his shoulder off the doorframe and grabbing his overalls.

I take a glance across the yard to where Nyx and his brother, Brax, are talking around their bikes. Squealer steps out of the club door, stretching his arms up over his head then scrubbing his eyes like he's seeing daylight for the first time. He's followed out by one of the club's lap bitches, and he slaps her ass before lighting himself up a smoke.

The sound of another bike approaching draws my attention away, and I watch its rider park up beside Nyx. When he gets off, he lifts his head slightly as a greeting to the others before he heads inside.

Grimm's different from the other brothers, his body is more athletic than bulky, but he comes across equally as powerful. His stare leaves a frost where it touches, but just lately whenever I've felt it on me, it's burned.

He keeps his jet-black hair so neat, some days sweeping it to the left, others sleeked right back. I prefer it when it's to the side.

His pale skin and sharp features give him uniqueness. I can admit Grimm is fucking hot in his own edgy way. He's full of darkness, and I can't help feel a little drawn to him.

He's never picked up a shift in the garage before, and words have never passed between us. Maybe that's why he intrigues me so much. Damaged souls can usually mark each other out, and I sense that Grimm is as empty and black inside as I am.

I watch him disappear before I take a deep breath, paste on a smile and get to work.

Skid will find himself again soon, he'll come back to us. And I'm determined to keep this place ticking over until that happens.

"So we all agree, Storm's in." Prez slams the gavel to the table after a unanimous vote, and Storm officially becomes the Dirty Souls new Prospect.

It's been a long time coming, Nyx got his full patch almost a year ago, and although we all tolerate Tommy for Skid's sake, he can't be trusted with anything club related. I know I'm not the only one sick of hearing Squealer bitch about having to do shit for himself.

I follow the guys out of the smoke filled room, through the doors to where the air is much fresher. Storm's waiting, pacing anxiously on the chapel porch, and every brother manages to keep their mouths straight, giving nothing away.

When Storm looks up from the ground, he makes it clear we made the right decision, his eyes show how much he wants in.

It's only been a few weeks since the hot head tore into the clubhouse like a tornado on a warpath for Brax. After taking down the Agency, and saving his old lady, Brax had killed the kid's only link to finding his missing sister. Any fucker mad enough to raise a fist to a man like Brax deserves some respect.

Prez knows potential when he sees it. The boy is lost, he needs guidance and like the rest of us, he needs a channel for all that anger. Now that he's one of us, we can help him with that. We'll also help him find that missing sister of his, at any cost.

The club learned that 'the Agency' were much bigger than we'd originally given them credit for, and we needed to finish them. Prez and Nyx needed it for Ella, finding out the man who'd raised her was one of the sick fuckers, really messed with her head. Brax wanted it for Gracie, whose Mom died while working the case for the CIA. And the rest of us? Well, we just like an excuse to get our hands dirty.

There were some big names connected to the Agency. The fact that our rivals, The Bastards' Prez had been involved has worked majorly to our advantage, we're profiting massively out of the blackening of their name. They claim they had nothing to do with Clunk's actions but unfortunately, their brush has already been tarred, and that shit ain't easy to clean off. No one respectable wants to run deals with nonces.

The only worry we got now is retaliation from Adriano's younger brother, and it appears he's too busy trading women to want to kick up shit with the likes of us.

"You vote?" Storm scratches the back of his neck, and Prez nods for Jessie to put the boy out of his misery.

"We voted," Jessie answers, his face not giving anything away.

"And?" Storm eagerly pushes for more.

"You're in, kid." Brax, who agreed to be his sponsor, tosses him the Prospect cut he's been holding behind his back. When Storm catches it against his chest, his worried face relaxes into a smile.

He wastes no time pulling the cut over his shoulder, then shakes everyone's hand, one by one. When he gets to me, I nod him congratulations as he drops his hand and smiles at me awkwardly. Storm may have only been here a short time, but he's already noted that I avoid unnecessary touching.

"Follow me, kid." Squealer takes our new Prospect under his

arm, leading him toward the club. "Things got a bit messy in room three last night. Bitch is probably still in there. She's gonna need some Advil, antiseptic cream, and a ride home."

I roll my eyes and leave them to it, noticing how Prez hangs back to answer his phone. While all the others filter into the club to celebrate, I stand and watch his face intensify as he listens to the person on the other end of the line.

"Grimm, get over here," he calls across at me after he's hung up. "That was Skid…" Slipping the phone back inside his cut, he checks around the yard for anyone without a patch. "Seems that Rogue's got herself into a situation."

"Rogue?" hearing that name immediately gets my attention. I don't know much about her, just that she works at the garage and that Skid seems to care a whole lot about her. Not that she needs him to. She's always come across to me as the kinda bitch who knows how to take care of herself.

"Yeah, he's gonna message you an address, he wants you to go check it out."

I nod back at Prez. There's only one kinda trouble she could be in if it's me they're sending, and I haven't even made it to the clean-up cage before my phone buzzes with an address.

"You got this covered, Grimm?" Prez calls. "I gotta send five brothers on a run to Utah. Me, Jess, and Troj got a meeting with the Russians. I'm kinda low on hands."

"Sure. How much mess can one tiny person make?" I shrug back, before checking the back of the cage for the basics and slipping into a pair of overalls.

I shouldn't have underestimated that tiny person…

After driving out to the roughest part of town to the address Skid gave me, I grab the baseball cap from the dash and slide it backward over my head. When I let myself into the small but well-kept bungalow, the metallic stench hits me before I've even fully opened the door. I recognize it straight away, it's fresh, barely a few hours, I'm guessing, and I tie my black bandana around my face to cover my nose. When I'm inside, I'm shocked at how much there is of it. Whoever's blood it is, is splattered all over the walls and ceilings, it's soaking into the carpet, and I see no sign of the body it belongs to.

"You're the one who likes cleaning up, right?" The sweet voice distracts me from my assessment of the room, and I follow the blood-smeared trail on the carpet to a set of hot pink painted toes.

I raise my eyes up the slender, milky-colored legs to her cut-off denim shorts and a white tank top that's soaked with blood.

Rogue's pale skin is marred with crimson freckles. There's a long smear of blood on her left cheek which looks like it's been made by a finger, and she's wearing the most haunting smile on her lips.

My cock likes what I'm seeing far too much to be discreet about it.

"I made a start." She runs her blood drenched hand through her ice blonde hair, streaking the strands, before she twists a lock of it around her fingertip like she suddenly became shy or somethin'.

Another look around the room has me wondering if she's seeing the same scene as I am. Shock can do crazy shit to a person.

"Where's the body?" I ask cautiously, she probably ain't in the right frame of mind, there's no guessing what she might do next.

"Grimm, ain't it?" She ignores my question, holding out her blood contaminated hand like she actually expects me to shake it. I stare at it for a while, then look up at her like she's fucking crazy.

"Oops, sorry." Her giggle travels straight to my dick, and I watch in disgust as she attempts to clean her palm by rubbing it on her shorts before she holds it out again.

Her cuteness seems so genuine that I have to question her

sanity. When I shake my head at her, she shrugs and casually steps aside for me. It allows me to continue following the bloody trail to where a body lays.

"Fucker managed to crawl himself that far," she says, stepping over the average-sized male corpse that's lying face down in front of us. A pool of syrup thick blood already congealed beneath it.

I nod my head while trying to pull together a plan of action. I've seen much worse, but never by the hands of someone so small. I can't help being impressed.

"He made the mistake of putting me in a position where it was him or me… I chose me," she explains looking down at him, and when her head tips sideways and she releases that adorable giggle again, my cock twitches.

"I gotta ask you some questions." I pull my bandana down. "I get that you're in shock, but you need to answer them as accurately as possible."

"Sure." Rogue looks up from the body, all wide-eyed and happy to assist.

"Okay…" I clear my throat and try to fucking focus. "Do you know who this guy is?"

Rogue nods, that deadly sweet smile still set firm on her lips.

"Did anyone other than you know that he was here?"

She lifts her shoulders as if I just asked her for the fuckin' time.

Not fucking helpful.

"Did he touch anything while he was here?"

"Yep, me…" She leans her body over the dead corpse that's between us, so I can hear her whisper, "That's the part that got him dead." She winks.

Fuck.

I breathe slowly through my nose, trying to blank all the dark thoughts from my conscience and calm my cock.

"What did you use?" It's getting real hard to distract myself from the tiny red speckles on her tits.

"Oh yeah…" She leaves me standing in the hall, and returns a few seconds later clutching a machete almost the same size as she is.

"Skid gave it me." She smiles proudly as she holds it out to me.

"That what you had on when it happened?" I point my head at the blood drenched clothes she's wearing, pulling out a roll of trash bags from my back pocket. Rogue drops her eyes, assessing the state she's in, and then beams back at me with her crystal blue eyes.

"Okay." Tearing a bag off the roll, I shake it open and hold it out. "You're gonna need to put those, and your weapon in there," I tell her, and when she takes it from my hands, I kneel to the floor and start unpacking some equipment from my duffel.

"These carpets are gonna have to come…" the rest of my sentence gets caught around my tongue when I look up and realize she's standing in her underwear. She must pick up on my shock 'cause she does the fucking giggly thing again, she can sense my awkwardness and she's getting a kick out of it.

"Did you need these too?" Her blood-stained fingers begin sliding into the waist of her panties.

"No! Not right now." I make sure I keep my head down and hold out my hand, hoping I've managed to stop her before she's pulled them off her hips.

"You should go take a shower. I'll make sure to clear up in there after you're done"

"Thanks, Grimm." When I feel her hand touch my shoulder, I quickly stand up. She looks down her nose to my crotch, then licks her lips before she passes through the narrow gap between me and the wall. And all I can do is stand and stare, mesmerized, as I watch her all the way to the bathroom.

I shake myself back to reality, taking everything in around me, prioritizing the list of jobs in my head while figuring what I'm gonna need. Then I take out my cell and dial Skid.

"Talk to me, Grimm, is she okay?" He sounds frantic.

"Um, yeah."

Surprisingly fucking fine, considering.

"I ain't gonna pretty it up, Skid, she's unleashed a fucking massacre on whoever this is." I balance the cell between my ear and shoulder so I can snap on a pair of rubber gloves. Then crouching down, I search the body for something I can use to identify him.

"Jesus Christ, his hips are only still connected by tendons," I tell Skid, before finally locating something in the guy's front pocket.

"Machete?" Skid asks, sounding like a proud father.

"It appears so."

"Told her that thing would come in handy someday."

"You got a name for me, Grimm?" he asks, barely giving me time to open the wallet.

"Yep, we got Eddie Clark." I read the name off the guy's driving license.

"Ain't ever heard of him, you?" Skid sounds curious.

"You want me to get Maddy to look into him?" I suggest, and Skid goes silent on me for a while.

"Yeah, and I want Rogue at the club for a few nights, until we know what we're dealing with here. She can stay at my cabin."

"Sure thing, and, Skid..." I catch him before he hangs up. "Is she always so..."

"Bat shit crazy?" he cuts in. "Yep. Keep me posted, Grimm."

I hang up the phone, just as she steps out of the bathroom. There's only a short towel covering her freshly washed body and she's got her hair wrapped up in another one on top of her head.

The water must have been too hot or her skin's been scrubbed too harshly because it has more color to it now, and she smells deliciously sweet.

I do my best not to stare at her because I'm too fucking afraid of the images she might put in my head.

"Excuse me," she says as she steps past me, making sure the front of her body brushes against mine as she shuffles around the dead man on her carpet.

I wait until she's in the bedroom with the door shut behind her before I let out an agitated breath and prepare myself to get started.

Storm arrives not long after, bringing with him all the supplies I'd texted and asked for.

"The fuck happened here?" he asks, stepping in through the front door and taking a look around.

"Here's my panties, Grimm." Of course, Rogue would choose this moment to step out of the bedroom with her lacey whites dangling on the end of her finger for me. Storm stares between her and me, his eyes bulging from his head.

"She's what fucking happened," I toss my head in her direction. She's wearing jeans now, and a tight as fuck Guns 'n' Roses T-shirt that shows off the bottom half of her stomach.

"Got the Prospect cut, I see. Congratulations." Rogue sounds genuine as she steps over the body in her hall and heads toward him. I follow her with my stare, intrigued by her behavior.

"Well come on, this mess ain't gonna clear up itself now, is it." She shoots me a look over her shoulder. One that could turn Jesus himself into a sinner.

Once Storms brings everything I need inside, I pull out the old iPod from my pocket and scroll to one of my playlists. Rogue is pacing the living room floor now, her phone tight to her ear and I'm just about to put my headphones in when I hear the sudden change of tone in her voice.

"Nah-ah absolutely not," she says sternly. "Skid, I'm fine. I don't need any of your club protection bullshit. I think I've more than proved that I can take care of myself... ask the bone collector to send you some pictures if you don't believe me." She winks at me when she catches me listening in.

I keep my head down and get to work, but I don't hit the play button. I can hear Skid arguing on the other end of the phone from all the way over here. Rogue looks me up and down as she holds the phone away from her ear. I don't know what causes it, but I smile at her. It's strange because actually, I can't remember the last time I smiled at anyone.

"Fine, I'll stay at the club. But just for a few nights," she finally agrees, shaking her head at me while rolling her pretty blue eyes.

"You need any help?" Storm asks, still looking around at the walls in bewilderment.

"Not right now, just need someone to take little Miss Massacre over there back to the club," I point my head at her.

"Gotcha," Storm nods, before heading over to Rogue. "Pack some shit, we leave in five," he tells her before leaving through the front door to wait in the truck.

"Guess I'll be seeing you around." Rogue comes out from her bedroom a few minutes later swinging a duffel bag over her shoulder. I nod her a silent goodbye and then wait until she's skipped out the door, slamming it behind her, before I take her pretty lace panties out of my pocket.

The delicate fabric sits between my fingers, and I give in to the compulsion to bring them to my nose and absorb the scent of her through my nostrils. She smells as sweet as fucking sin, and I wonder if she'd gotten off on taking the life of the man who I'm about to make disappear.

Then I do something really out of character and I break the most important rule of a clean-up. Slipping them back inside my pocket so I can keep them for myself. It's the closest I'm ever gonna come to the real thing. I ignore the fact that that hurts me as I hit play on my iPod and set to work on cleaning up Rogue's mess.

CHAPTER 4
1% MC
ROGUE

I'm pissed at Skid, and if he wasn't going through so much shit, there's no way I would be here riding shotgun with Storm, the new Dirty Souls Prospect.

Kicking my feet up on the dash, I rest my head back and appreciate the breeze coming through the window. Then I close my eyes and go over everything that's happened in the past few hours.

---

2 HOURS AGO

Tossing my plate into the sink, I lick the last traces of the sticky syrup from my fingers then snatch my jacket off the hook, ready to head out for work. I stop in shock when I fling open the door, and someone I'm not expecting is on the other side of it.

"Mornin'." He grins at me coldly, revealing a row of gold teeth that send my stomach rolling with recollection. "You not gonna ask me in?" He stretches up on his toes to peer over my shoulder and look inside.

"No." I smile back sarcastically.

"Is he here?" Before I can make my move, his foot wedges in the door, preventing me from slamming it in his face.

"Oh, that's right." He acts like he's only just remembered. *"Life without parole, wasn't it? I just got out of Pueblo county detention myself."* He takes an unwelcome step closer.

"You've grown up a lot since I last saw ya." Reaching out with his finger, he slowly slides it down my cheek, and the gentleness of it makes me shudder. Eddie always did like to take it slow. He'd treat you like a delicate flower before he crushed you inside his fist.

"Do you know why I'm here, Ev—" I prevent him from continuing, my finger pressing over his lips to silence him.

"Rogue," I correct him, and the asshole smirks at me before slipping his top lip over my fingertip. I snarl when he sucks it inside his mouth but I don't flinch.

"Mmm sweet, just like I remember." His smile is wicked and it seals his fate…

I step aside, allowing him to enter, and the way he reshuffles his cock as he pushes past me makes me smile to myself.

"Wait here." I guide him over to the couch and press my hand on his shoulder until he's seated. Thrill and hunger lurk in his eyes as he rests, and the sick son of a bitch is already stroking himself through his pants. I leave him like that and step through the hall toward my bedroom, where I quietly slide the machete out from under my bed. It's heavy in my hand, so I let it drag behind me, my heart beating fast and spreading the adrenaline to my veins as I make my way back down the hall toward my guest.

"What you got planned for me, baby?" Eddie asks, wetting his top lip with his tongue. His dick is bulging through his pants, and I spend a few seconds wondering how long he'll maintain that stiffy after he's dead.

"Oh, I got somethin' for ya, Eddie." I speak seductively, using all my strength to lift the long heavy weapon up over my shoulder, and without a single moment's hesitation or a teeny tiny scrap of empathy, I hack a deep gash into the side of his

31

body. His blood sprays out in all directions, warming the skin on my face and decorating my walls.

The noise he makes sends a rush of satisfaction through my spine, and I smile at the fucker as I wiggle the handle to free the blade when it gets wedged into a bone.

"Crazy fucking bitch," he yells at me in agony, and I take a little time to admire the mess I've made of him, enjoying the horror turning his skin grey.

I know I haven't got long before he passes out from the pain, so I suck all the fear from his dilated pupils before I strike again.

I don't aim for anywhere in particular, the weapon is far too heavy for me to be accurate with, and the sharp blade ends up wedged in his shoulder. A few more inches to my left and I might have hit an artery, putting the fucker out of his misery far too soon. But that wouldn't be justice, this guy likes to take things slow. Prolonged agony is his thing, so in my opinion, it's the only way for him to go out.

My laughter drowns out the terror ripping from his throat.

I don't have long before the fucker bleeds out on me, and as I look around, I realize there's gonna be a whole lotta mess to clean up when he's done dying.

Taking a few steps back gives me a chance to admire my handy work, and somehow he manages to slide himself off the couch and onto the floor. Sweat dripping from his forehead, and determination seething through his eyes as he drags his failing body toward me. His blood drips in thick splats from the machete blade as I keep stepping backward, making a trail for him to follow. Knowing that each step I take causes him more pain, makes me smile.

He's helpless, crawling at my feet, reaching out his uninjured arm in a pathetic attempt to grasp at my ankles.

"You won't get away with this, Ev—"

I silence him, forcing the toe of my sneaker inside his mouth.

"Na-ah, I told you, it's Rogue now," I remind him, swinging for him again, this time making a deep wound into his back.

His mouth stretches wide, his scream gagged by my foot until I remove it and crouch down to his level.

He chokes, and more blood sprays from his mouth, landing warm against my chest.

I slip my hand between his body and the floor, crushing his crotch in my palm, his dick ain't quite as confident as it had been a few minutes ago.

"Don't worry, baby, it happens," I whisper, gently stroking his jaw with my blood-drenched fingers. He makes an attempt to grab at my face, but his finger slips from my skin weakly. I give him a saccharine grin, before getting up and walking into my room, where I sit on my bed with the door open, and watch him bleed out slowly. Agonizingly slowly, until I can be sure that his hell-ridden soul has crawled itself out of his butchered body.

The feeling is uplifting, a better release than any orgasm I've ever given myself, and I breathe in the silence for a while before I do the sensible thing.

Skid answers almost immediately, and it hurts a little to hear his voice. Even if it has only been two weeks since I last saw him, I miss him.

"Skid... remember you said if I needed anything..."

"Rogue, what's happened?" There's instant concern in his voice.

"Nothing that can't be cleaned up," I assure him

I open my eyes, disappointed when I'm hit with reality again. When I killed Eddie, I never took much, other than making him hurt, into consideration and now I'm being escorted back to the club by their latest rookie. I would have much preferred to stay and watch Grimm clean up my mess. I wonder if he's getting a sick little kick out of it. If when he'd first walked in and seen what I'd done, he'd imagined folding me over the blood-stained couch and fucking me all the way to hell for my sins.

I'd seen a little lust brighten his dark eyes when I'd stripped out of my dirty clothes in front of him, it gave me a rush to receive a reaction from him. Grimm is the only club member that's ever interested me. Probably because he's the only one, except for Skid, who hasn't hit on me at one time or another.

I've always been wired that way, desiring things I shouldn't, yearning for things I can't have. I like challenges. And in my opinion, anything too easily obtained ain't worth having.

I rarely get to see Grimm. I've always assumed that he isn't good with engines because he's never worked in the shop with me before, and there's no way I'd ever be desperate enough to hang out at the club to find out more about him.

Something tells me that even if I did make the effort, he still wouldn't take the time to speak to me. He's got that unapproachable vibe, the kind that makes me curious.

Storm tries his best to focus on the road as he drives us back toward the club, but I notice how his eyes keep flicking sideways at me. He's either thinking about fucking me or trying to evaluate my mental state. I smile at him regardless. He's cute.

"You need me to stop off for anything?" he asks, nervously.

"I'm sure you boys got all I need," I tease, causing him to shuffle awkwardly in his seat.

When we get back to the compound, he drives us straight past the garage, and up the track that leads toward the cabins. It's new territory to me, despite being invited by Skid numerous times, I've never actually taken him up on the offer. I never did buy into the whole family thing the club's got going on. Over the years, I've come to the conclusion that I'm much better off being a loner. That way, I can only let myself down.

Storm pulls to a stop in the yard where all the cabins are, and when he reaches for my bag, I manage to grab it before him.

"Which one of these is Grimm's?" I ask, looking at the long row of cabins, they stretch at least a quarter of the way around the lake.

"Grimm's?" Storm looks at me surprised.

"Yeah, he told me I had to stay with him. Skid's orders." I cross my arms under my tits, forcing them together, the same way the whores who hang around them like needy cats do.

"He did, did he?" Storm shakes his head and his lips raise into an adorable smile. "Fifth cabin down," he tells me, before I hop out and remember to thank him for the ride.

Turns out, everyone around here really does trust each other. I was fully prepared to have to pick a lock to get into Grimm's cabin, but the door is already unlocked. Inside isn't exactly what I expect from a kick-ass biker. The place is spotlessly clean and very minimal. His living room only has a coffee table, a TV, and a couch that is oddly covered in plastic. I guess we could all learn a little something from Grimm.

Over in the kitchen, there's the basics, a stove, a basin, and a refrigerator. Tucked in the corner is a small wooden table and two chairs.

I walk through the cabin into the bathroom, where everything's white and pristinely clean. The towels hanging on the rail in size order even match in color.

I step out and take a peek inside the next room. I figure this one must be his bedroom because it smells like him. The bed in the center of the room is made up to perfection, not a single crease in the sheets and when I open his chest of drawers, I laugh to myself when I find his underwear folded into neat squares and arranged in color order.

The low grumble from my stomach reminds me that I haven't eaten anything since my pancakes this morning, and since ridding the world of its scum is such hungry work, I head back into the kitchen and search through the cupboards for something to eat.

All the cans and cartons are rowed up in size order, I find some bread and take two slices. The inside of his refrigerator is cleaner than an operating theatre. Each shelf is arranged by product type and makes it easy for me to find what I'm looking for. I open one of the plastic containers to get some ham, and with a good slap of mayo, I put myself together a sandwich. After helping myself to a beer, I take a seat on Grimm's plastic-covered couch. Kicking up my feet on the coffee table and picking up the remote, I flick on the TV. I'm not surprised in the slightest when the crime channel comes on.

There's plenty of work I could be getting on with down at the garage, but I figure I'm due a day off. I've worked my ass off lately, I deserve a break. So I stay in Grimm's cabin, binge watching some real crime TV series while downing a few more beers.

By the time it gets dark, I'm bored out of my mind. Grimm still isn't back, and I decide to take a shower in his pristine bathroom. It doesn't matter how hot I'd run the water back at my place, I can still feel that asshole's hands on me. It's been a long time since anyone has been brave enough to touch me like that and I wasn't about to let it happen again. I don't care how fresh out of jail he was, or what he thought he was entitled to. Eddie had no right putting his hands on me, not back then and not now.

I take my time under the warm water, enjoying massaging Grimm's shower gel into my skin, and scrubbing my hair with his shampoo. When I finally get out, I head straight to his room and slowly flick through the clothes in his wardrobe until I find one of his shirts that I like.

Grimm isn't built as big as Skid, his body is much more athletic than muscular but his shirt still falls below my ass cheeks, and I like the way it feels against my skin. Pulling back the covers from his bed, I snuggle myself inside and rest my head on his pillow. I stare up at the ceiling, wondering how many women he's fucked right here in this spot. Does he have a regular whore like some of the others do? For all I know he could have an old lady, just because I haven't seen him with one down at the club doesn't mean she doesn't exist. Then I giggle to myself when I picture him bringing her back here tonight and them finding me in his bed.

I allow my heavy eyes to close and my body to relax with the thought of this world being just a little better because of me. I never did bother to make a list of all the people that had hurt me in the past.

I don't have to remind myself of their names, they're engraved into my soul, tattooed into my memories with poisonous ink. Sometimes when I close my eyes at night, they come back to torment me. But I'm not a scared little girl anymore.

And tonight, there will be one less face to haunt me.

I like the peacefulness here. The old quarry is in the ass-end of nowhere and over the years I've come to know the place well. Bones lay here, secrets lurk beneath the waters, and ashes are merged with the soil. It's the perfect place for me to reflect. I sit here with just the crackle of the fire breaking the silence, colorful flames licking the air, reaching higher, and with the beautiful sky surrounding me, it could be so easy to forget what those flames are destroying.

Fire has always fascinated me, and not just because of its reliability to dispose. Fire works a lot like I do, it strips back layer by layer, taking its time and leaving nothing salvageable.

Getting rid of things this way relaxes me the most, staring at the warm flames, watching their shapes change gives me the time to think things over, a chance to backtrack and make sure nothing has been forgotten.

Maddy got back to me on the ride out here, turns out the guy who was currently feeding my flames was fresh out of Pueblo, and judging from the time of his release and the time it took him to get to Rogue, we figured she must have been the first person he went to see. I don't know who he is to her, but whoever he was, she clearly hadn't been happy to see him.

I'd decided this was the most efficient way to get rid of Rogue's little problem. To obliterate all traces of him. A cover-up or a frame would take planning and detail. I don't have the time or the patience for either.

So, I've taken the easy approach, I wrapped the half-decapitated fucker up in the carpet that he'd bled out on and brought him here. Now that the fire has worked through all the fibers of the carpet, I can smell his skin blistering as the flames eat away at his flesh.

Everyone's different, each corpse has its own unique smell when it burns, and Eddie Clark has a real rotten tinge to him. I got a strong suspicion that he deserved what Rogue did to him. Not that it would matter all that much to me if he hadn't. I'm here to clean up, not to judge.

I wait for hours, just watching and thinking of all the wrong kinda things. Things like how good Rogue looked covered in blood, wearing that sinister smile. The girl didn't show a shred of remorse for what she'd done and I envy her for that.

When the fire eventually dies down, leaving only ash and bone, I head back to the van and take out the sprayer. I drench any embers still glowing and douse the hot ash, soaking it until it's cool enough to pick out bones. When my phone starts to vibrate in my back pocket, I know exactly who it'll be.

"Skid," I answer without even checking, continuing to neatly pack away the charred bones in the cool box that I keep in the cage for occasions such as this one.

"How's it goin'?" he asks, not sounding much calmer.

"Ain't much left of him now," I assure him, checking out the femur bone in my hand, there's a huge chip out of it where the machete must have hit.

"And the house?"

"Every surface checked. Carpets taken care of, walls scrubbed and sanded. I'll have the Prospect do a paint job on the place in the next couple of days." This is all standard shit that Skid would never usually bother to question me on.

"You got any idea what he was doin' there?" he asks.

"Not a clue, but Mads found out he got released from Pueblo county detention this morning."

Skid goes silent for a while, his head probably surveying the same possibilities mine has.

"You think he went straight to her?"

"Mads reckons from the timescale, he must have. Luckily there wasn't much damage to his face, I sent her a picture and she's tapping into some local CCTV to be sure. If she sees him, she'll erase the footage."

"Man on release day only got three things in mind, Grimm. Food, fix, and fucking. And I doubt he'd have been visiting Rogue for food."

"Well, whatever he went there for, he got more than he was expecting." I kick at the damp ash with my boot.

"She ain't happy about staying at the club." Skid sounds worried. "You and the boys just make sure she stays put till we can figure out what he wanted with her."

"Rogue doesn't seem the type to do as she's told." I smirk to myself and start packing away, carrying the empty sprayer and the bones back into the van and lifting out a shovel.

It's already getting dark and I still have to turn over the earth where I had the fire.

"Where you at?" Skid asks before I hang up.

"Sinnerman's quarry," I tell him, knowing he'll approve. Sinnerman's Quarry ain't on our territory, it's secluded and a total ball ache to get to. Which is why I know I can have my fires without being disturbed.

There are plenty of weed patches scattered around here that I'm responsible for.

"Good shout, I owe ya, brother," he tells me before hanging up.

I put my phone away and head back to the damp earth, smashing the shovel into the dirt and turning it over. After mixing the ash into the dirt, and when the patch is fully upturned, I take a sachet of seeds out of my pocket and spread them over the patch, stomping them into the ground with the heel of my boot.

I make sure I destroy any traces of me being here before I drive the van back to the club.

Instead of heading straight to my cabin for a shower like I want to, I stop by the club and take the cool-box down to my basement. Doesn't matter how shattered I feel, I never leave a job unfinished and I won't be able to switch off until these bones are ground to dust.

Jessie and Brax each have their own room beneath the club, and I have mine. It goes without saying that the people who find themselves in Jessie and Brax's rooms often become my problem.

Pulling a dust mask over my face, I set to work, adding all that's left of Eddie Clark into my custom-made grinder.

It's late by the time I'm finished, and once the remains are sealed into an airtight bag and locked inside the safe that's built into the wall, I decide I'm done.

It's never the physicality of a clean-up that drains me, more the constant thinking it requires. That isn't to say I don't enjoy doing it. Everyone around here has their role, mine has always been fixing up the mess others leave behind.

I stop by the main bar room before heading up to my cabin. And when Tommy sees me coming he pours me a bourbon, he's getting better at this shit, so I tip my head at him as a thank you before knocking it back.

"You want me to line you one up, kid?" Tac asks, his thumb dusting the tip of his nose after he's done hoovering a long line off the bar.

I decline, last thing I need right now is a fucking buzz, not when I intend on getting an early night. I've already made up my mind that I'm going back to Rogue's place tomorrow to paint her walls myself. I need assurance that the job gets done properly and Storm is still green. That, and the fact I have a strange impulse to be in her space again.

"Early night then, Grimm?" Storm winks at me like we're sharing some kinda private joke. He saw the state of Rogue's place, so he gets why I'm so whacked.

"Yep." I down the next shot Tommy puts in front of me, then stand up. "Wash the cage down, inside and out, pay close attention to the wheels." I toss Storm the keys as I make my way out to get on my bike. Seeing how thorough he is with the cage will give me a good indication of how much I can trust him with. I already know I'll go over it myself in the morning. I'm a control freak. I own that.

Riding up to my cabin, I struggle to get the image of Rogue standing in front of me, her pretty skin tainted with blood, wearing just those white fucking panties and a bra out of my head. The same panties that are burning a hole through the back pocket of my overalls, reminding me how weak I am for taking them.

It crosses my mind to knock on Skid's cabin door, it would be perfectly reasonable of me to tell her that everything's taken care of, leaving out the fact I've been fucking hard for her since I saw her standing among the massacre she created.

Shaking that thought out of my head, I park up outside my cabin. I can't wait to get inside to get myself clean, and I'm gonna have to release the heavy ache Rogue's put in my balls by bashing one out in the shower. I'll visualize the crazy little bitch on her knees in front of me, mouth wide open and tongue stuck out, waiting for me to blow all over it.

The thought alone almost has me comin' inside my jeans.

I burst through the door and flick on the light, straight away I can sense that something's off. The room has a different scent, a sweet one. The coffee table isn't in line with the bathroom door, and there's shit littering the top of it. My eyes move over to the kitchen where there are crumbs scattered all over the work surface and an unwashed plate and a knife in the sink.

I'll bet this is Squealer's idea of a sick joke.

I storm through to the bathroom, shuddering at the soaking wet towel that's been left on the floor. The shower curtain is hanging out over the bath and there's a wet patch where it's been dripping. I pick up the towel and put the curtain right. Then tighten the tap that isn't aligned to match the other one properly, before following the watermarked footprints on the wood floor that lead to my room.

When I open the door, I immediately get to the root of the fucking problem when I see the blonde-haired, tiny little hellion that's all twisted up in my sheets.

I turn around and get out of there, closing the door behind me and trying to breathe. My neck feels constricted and my chest seems too heavy to lift. What the fuck is she doing here... in my cabin... in my space? She's supposed to be at Skid's.

Moving away from the door, I rush to the kitchen and start to clean her mess before I lose my head to compulsion. I wash and dry the plate and the knife, before putting them in the right place. Then I clear the coffee table, wipe it over and take out the trash. Once I've straightened out the plastic on the couch and sorted the bathroom, everything is back to how it should be. Well almost, there's nothing normal about the fact there's a fucking girl in my bed...

I lock myself in the bathroom, and rest my ass on the edge of the bath, taking long, steady breaths while I figure out what to do. What is she even doing here? She can't stay here. Why would she even want to when she has a perfectly good space of her own over at Skid's?

I put my overalls and clothes in the wash and shower myself

off, my body smells like bleach, bonfire, and chargrilled corpse. And I take my time making sure I rinse away every trace of the day, I scrub beneath my fingernails with a nail brush before I scrape it all over my skin and lather myself in suds. It usually takes this and a hot Dettol bath for me to feel normal after a clean-up, but tonight a scorching shower will have to do. I still have to figure out what I'm gonna do about the cold-blooded killer that's sleeping in my bed.

Slowly creeping into my room, I take some underwear out my top drawer and pull them up under my towel. I flick on the bedside lamp and take a good, long look at her. Asleep, she looks so different, almost peaceful. Her soft blonde hair is splayed out all over my pillow while she hums sleepily, and I don't know what possesses me to do it, but I end up stepping forward and sliding in beside her.

I lie beside her, frozen, the feeling of having someone in my space is unfamiliar. The closeness between us overwhelming, and I wonder how long I'll stand it for. This is a whole new kind of test for me and I feel fucking everything. Her heat radiating close to mine, the sound of her sleepy breaths, and how it touches the side of my cheek every time she exhales. But somehow, the longer I lie here, the calmer I become. Having her here is nothing like I imagined it to be, nothing at all.

"Does it freak you out that I'm here?" Rogue's lips move, but her eyes remain closed.

"No," I lie, because I've come this far and for some strange reason, I really don't want her to leave.

"Good," she whispers, turning her head away from me and shuffling her ass a little closer to my thigh.

How has it taken me this long to realize that she's wearing my fuckin' shirt?

"And don't worry, I ain't gonna kill ya in ya sleep," she adds in a sweet sleepy voice that contradicts her words.

"That's reassuring," I manage, reaching my arm back to flick off the light. The room fills with darkness, and her soft breaths and the thudding in my chest are the only sound I hear.

But there's something about having her close that pleases me… and for now, I guess it's okay that she's here.

CHAPTER 6

1% MC

ROGUE

When I wake up, Grimm is still sound asleep. Somehow, he managed to spend the whole night in bed beside me and avoided making any form of contact, despite me silently yearning for him to slip.

I use the time to appreciate him while he sleeps, he actually looks kinda cute with his long eyelashes and the tiny cross tattoo that's inked just under his left eye. There's no denying that Grimm is beautiful, with his prominent features and chiseled jawline he almost doesn't seem real. And looking at the silver ring through his slender nose makes me really want to get one too.

His lips look as though they'd feel soft; they're deep, pink and so fucking tempting. It would be so easy to reach a little closer and touch them with mine. But I don't want to freak him out. Something tells me I've already pushed Grimm's limits far enough, and it surprises me what efforts I've put in to get his attention.

I move quietly, tiptoeing my way out to the kitchen, and helping myself to what I need from the refrigerator to make breakfast. Grimm shows his face a little later, standing in the bedroom doorway wearing just his underwear and a tee. His arms are crossed over his chest and his tongue rolls inside his cheek as he watches me moving around his kitchen.

His hair is unusually messy, and sexy as fuck.

"Tough night?" I ask, my cheeks automatically lifting into a smile for him. This doesn't have to be weird, people eat breakfast together all the time.

"Well, someone gave me quite the mess to work on yesterday." Grimm rubs his eye with the heel of his palm as he steps closer.

"Take a seat, I made us breakfast." I point the spatula I'm holding toward the table and notice how he looks over the kitchen counter behind me. His eyes stretching wide when he sees the empty shells and spilled egg whites.

"I'm totally gonna clean that up when I'm done," I promise, lifting up my shoulders and offering an innocent smile that I'm hoping he won't be able to resist. He does nothing to hide the look of disgust on his face, but he does pull out a chair and sit at the table.

I place a full plate in front of him before taking the seat opposite. Grimm's eyes fall onto the plate of food, then travel back up to me again.

"Sorry, do you like, say grace or summat?" I don't have Grimm down as a religious guy, but when it comes to him, nothing would surprise me.

"You don't wanna talk?" he asks, still looking shocked. Jeez, I've only made the guy a breakfast, isn't like I've used his toothbrush or anything.

"Sure." I shrug. "What's your preference, piston head or cylinder? If I had a bike, I'd definitely go for a piston—"

"I meant about yesterday," he interrupts me, I hate it when people do that.

"Not really." Shaking my head, I lift up my fork and pop a slice of crispy bacon inside my mouth. In my opinion, yesterday is done with, Eddie is dead, there's no reason to let him ruin today.

"You don't wanna know what I did with him?" Grimm looks confused, and it's a cute look on him.

"No," I answer, before a thought suddenly creeps inside my head. "...Unless you wanna tell me about it." I bite my lip seductively, maybe this is the kinda shit that gets him off.

Grimm slowly shakes his head before he gets back to finishing up his breakfast, then he nods me a thank you before carrying his plate over to the sink. I watch him wash it up along with everything else I've used, and when I offer my help, he refuses with a shake of his head. Soon as he's done, he silently makes his way toward the bathroom.

A while later, he comes out with a towel wrapped around his waist. Grimm may not be as big as some of the others but he's cut like a work of art. It looks like shifting dead weight around really works those muscles for him, and he has way more tattoos than I imagined. In fact, his body is covered in them. He gives me an awkward kinda smile when he catches me staring and disappears into his room. When he returns to the kitchen a few minutes later, he's dressed in black jeans, a white tee, and his cut, and his hair is combed over to the side... just how I like it.

"I gotta go talk to Prez, he'll wanna know everything was taken care of yesterday." He picks up his keys and cell from the table.

I quickly cover his hand with mine, pinning it to the table and preventing him from leaving. I don't even know what causes the reaction from me, but the way Grimm stares at my hand like it's made of acid, and is burning through his skin makes me jolt it away.

"Thank you, this wasn't your problem. I appreciate the help," I tell him.

"Yeah well, your problem's Skid's problem, and that makes it mine," he says a little harshly before stomping toward the door.

"You wanna know why I did it?" The words blurt out, because for some reason I'm desperate for a little more of his time, and I chew down on my bottom lip and twist on my heels, feeling strangely nervous while I wait for his response.

His nostrils flare out, and his jaw tightens like he's suddenly become mad at me, and it makes my pussy weep into my panties.

"Did he deserve it?" Grimm's brows hood over his eyes, and something inside them warns me that if I lie to him, he'll know about it.

Nodding my head, I show him no hesitation. Eddie deserved to die, if I could do it over again I would.

"Then I don't need to know." Grimm's face remains deathly serious as he turns away from me and closes the door on his way out.

I release a frustrated breath once he's left. Being around him is a lot harder than I anticipated. He's standoffish and uninterested, but it does nothing to deter me from wanting to jump his bones. It actually makes me want him even more desperately.

I wait until his bike rumbles out the yard before I make my way back to his bedroom. It's no shock that he's made the bed, and I crease it up by lying spread-out on top of the sheets. Sheets that now don't just smell like him, but like us.

My hand slides inside my panties and I close my eyes, letting my finger stroke between my pussy lips. I welcome the excitement that builds in my lower belly and threatens to turn into something much more intense. Circling the tip of my finger around my clit, I imagine the chill of Grimm's nose ring touching me there, his warm, wet tongue lapping at me. Fingers digging deep into my thighs as he holds them open and licks me while those dark eyes watch me come apart.

He'd start off slow, wanting to taste me, but it wouldn't take long for him to become fast and uncontrolled, forcing me to come all over his tongue and soak his black bed sheets.

I lay staring at the ceiling for a while after I've come, feeling a little bit foolish, and a whole lot relieved. Then eventually I pull myself together, get up and head to the bathroom for a shower.

When I've put on some fresh clothes from my duffel bag, I set off for work. As I step onto Grimm's front porch, the first people I see are Jessie and his old lady at their door, both looking equally shocked to see me.

"Mornin'." I hold up my hand and head straight past them, acting like it's no big deal. Last thing I want is questions.

"Rogue?" Jessie calls after me, and I begrudgingly stop in my tracks, rolling my eyes before turning around to face him.

"You 'kay, I heard you had a pretty rough day yesterday?" I can tell from the way he's looking at me that he's trying to figure me out.

I'm not an idiot. I know what Jessie's role is around here. The guy knows a lie from the truth. It's just as well I got nothing to hide.

"Rougher for some," I hit him back sarcastically, wanting to hurry up and move on.

Jessie sniggers before turning his tone serious. "Skid's real worried about ya. We're all worried."

"I'm sure you got bigger things to worry about." I look over his shoulder toward his old lady. The girl is as damn near perfect as you can get, in a wholesome, churchy kinda way. She's around the same age as me, but that's all we got in common.

"We take care of each other around here, Rogue, if you're in trouble, the club can help you."

"I ain't in any trouble, and the club has already helped me enough. I'm fine," I assure him, flicking my hair over my shoulder before I carry on down the track to the garage.

Jesus, this place is suffocating, everyone in each other's business. Looking for problems to solve. It's exhausting.

I roll up the garage door and inhale a long, deep breath, there's nothing quite like the smell of engine oil in the morning. I notice that someone's made a start on Roswell's truck, whoever it was must have picked up some of the slack around here yesterday. I move through the workshop into the office to hang up my jacket. Marilyn must have come over yesterday to take everyone's overalls over to laundry, because the only one here is my spare one. When I pick it off the hook, I immediately smell peaches, which makes sense when I see Carly's denim jacket hiding beneath. She always used to keep it down here for the nights she spent talking to Skid while he worked late, and a memory hits me, one that I haven't thought about in a real long time.

AGED 14

"Hey, darlin'." Carly kisses Skid on his cheek and when he grabs her ass with his greasy hand, she swats it away.

"I brought you some leftovers back from the diner." She smiles at me, placing a takeaway container on the workstation in front of me where I'm cleaning up the carburetor Skid's just taken out.

"Well, don't sit there staring at it, go wash up before it gets cold." Skid smiles at me, wiping his hands with a rag and then scooping his girlfriend up by her waist.

I like Carly, she's pretty and kind. She's the perfect woman for Skid. I know he wants to ask her to marry him. I heard him and Chop arguing about it when I arrived here earlier than usual this morning.

"You're gonna make an incredible daddy someday, you know," I hear Carly tell him as I dash off toward the club to wash up my hands. She's right. Skid will make a great dad. I've often wished he was mine, but then I feel guilty because I know my own daddy loves me. He's just hurting real bad.

I head over to the club to use the restroom in the foyer, and quickly set to work scrubbing the grease and oil off my hands. When I'm coming back out, I make sure I pull my sleeves down over my arms before I get to the garage. "What are those?" *A deep voice comes from the firepit and when I follow it, I see Chop sitting there, watching me.*

"Just scratches." *I tug at my sleeve, but it's too late, he's seen and he tosses his empty beer bottle in the fire as he comes at me. Snatching my wrist in his hand, he pushes up my sleeve roughly, growling when he inspects my arm and sees all my scars. I must be imagining it, but he actually looks a little hurt.*

"You do this to yourself?" *he asks, keeping his hold on me firm.*

"No." *I brush it off, I don't want him to make a big deal out of it.* "Just caught myself on some brambles, playing with some friends in the woods."

"You don't got no friends, and brambles scratch, they don't slice. Cut the bullshit. Did you do this to yourself?" *he asks me again.*

I look at the floor and nod because I know it's wrong. I've made a real mess of myself, but when I do it, just for those few seconds it feels right, it's something I have control over and when things get bad, I really need that.

"Skid know about this?" *he checks.*

"No, and he can't." *I quickly look up at him, I really can't have him say anything. Skid's always asking me questions about my life at home and I hate lying to him. If he knew about this he'd want to speak to my dad, he might report him and I'd get taken away from him. He'd never survive losing me too.*

"I'll keep your secret for you." *He narrows his eyes at me.* "But I want you to tell me who gave ya those marks on your neck, and who beat your ass so hard last week that you couldn't sit down."

"What marks?" *I play dumb because it's all I've got, there's no way I'm telling Chop the truth.*

"Skid's head is full of dreams and pussy shit right now, he's not noticing stuff. But I am. I know you got secrets, we all have, and we all got every right to keep 'em. I'm just telling ya that if you had someone hurting ya and you wanted it taken care of..." He releases me from his grip and shrugs.

I've often wondered if Chop ever killed a man, I know the men that hang around here do bad things, and the way he's looking at me now leaves me with no doubt that Chop has ended a life.

"Why would you do that for me?" Sure, Chop thawed a little over the years I've got to know him. He's even taken the time to show me some pretty cool stuff. I'd never admit it to him, but he's an even better mechanic than his brother.

"You're a good girl, you learn fast. Maybe I'm starting to like you," he snarls at me, then the smile he gives me actually feels genuine.

A loud squeal comes from the garage that steals both our attention for a second.

"Think about what I said." He nods me away, and I quickly rush back to the workshop hoping my food's still warm. When I walk in, Skid is busy making out with Carly.

"Ewww, that's so gross," I mutter at them, taking a stool and lifting the lid on the food Carly brought for me.

"You make the most of that food, because you won't be getting free leftovers for much longer," Skid warns me, spinning Carly around to face me and hanging his huge arm across her neck.

"You're looking at the future Mrs. Tanner." With a huge beam on her face, Carly lifts her hand up to stroke his forearm, revealing a sparkly ring on her finger. "And no old lady of mine is gonna be working night shifts at a truck stop." He smacks a kiss on her cheek.

"I think you'll find that this is the twenty-first century and *that I'll do as I damn please." Carly twists her neck to look up at him and smirks.*

"Darlin', you're gonna be far too busy taking care of all them kids we're gonna be makin' to work." He buries his head into her neck, and as I roll my eyes and tuck into my food, I can't help thinking about how lucky those kids are gonna be.

The expression on Carly's face suddenly changes, and when I notice Skid tense too, I look over my shoulder and realize Chop's standing in the entrance. He doesn't look happy, but that's no shock since he made it clear what his thoughts on the whole marriage thing were earlier when they'd been arguing.

"She said yes," Skid tells his brother the good news, keeping his mouth straight and his tone serious.

"Congratulations." Chop dips his head, and I can feel the tension coming off him like steam off fresh shit. I don't know why he hates Carly so much. She's impossible not to like.

Carly turns her body back into Skid's, and the hand her new shiny rock is on slips through his beard. And when I notice the hatred in Chop's eyes turn to hurt, I suddenly figure it all out.

Chop doesn't hate Carly at all. He loves her…

CHAPTER 7

1% MC

GRIMM

I get back to the club around five, I've spent most of the day painting Rogue's living room and hall. The place still smells like cherries and syrup to me, despite the massacre I'd cleaned up yesterday and the lingering smell of cleaning fluids and fresh paint.

I park up outside the clubhouse and notice that the garage door is still up. I can just make out Rogue's pink overalls. She's folded over the hood of a Chevy, her ass wiggling as she struggles to loosen something inside. She must sense me watching her, and my cock turns stiff when she looks over her shoulder and winks at me.

I've spent all day trying to get my head around what she was doing at my cabin, wondering if she's gonna come over again tonight. The whole situation is really fucking with me. I don't think I can handle another night lying next to her with a rock-hard cock, trying not to give in to the temptation to touch.

"Heard she's staying at your place." Troj appears from behind me, holding out his cigarette pack for me to help myself.

"She kinda invited herself," I tell him, sliding out a smoke and balancing it between my lips.

"And does Skid know about your little slumber party?" He flicks his Zippo open and after lighting me up, he sparks up his own.

"Ain't nothing for him to know about." I shrug. It's the truth, and that's exactly how it's gonna stay. Whatever weird situation this is between me and Rogue, it's innocent. I just wish I could say the same thing about the thoughts in my head.

"Is it true she took the guy's leg off?" Troj smirks.

"There wasn't much holding him together," I answer, too fucking mesmerized by her to take my eyes off her. I've always noticed her. It's impossible not to. But now I find myself noticing everything.

"Girl ain't right in the head." Troj joins me in watching her bobbing her head to the up-tempo music that's blasting from the garage stereo, her hips shaking as she switches tools.

"Can't deny she's a hot piece of ass, but hell, Grimm, that's a whole lotta crazy to be keepin' a handle on."

"Like I told ya, Troj, ain't nothin' goin' on." I flick my finished smoke onto the asphalt and scrape it out with my boot before heading inside the club.

Taking a stool at the bar, I nod for Mel to get me a drink. She reads me well, pouring me out a scotch, then smiles like a temptress as she places it in front of me.

I knock it back, slamming the glass on the bar and pushing it forward for another, then she makes an even better call and fetches me the bottle.

"Hey, man." Jessie takes the stool beside me, and I can tell by the tone of his voice that he's looking to have something out.

"Look, if it's about Rogue stayin' at mine, we don't need to talk about it." I rotate two fingers into my temple, I can't deal with this conversation again, how the fuck am I supposed to explain something I don't understand myself.

"What I was gonna say..." Jessie looks at me sternly, "...is that the longer we can get her to stick around here, the better. Maddy pulled up some pretty shady shit on the guy she hacked up." He raises up a hand to Mel, who sneers at him when she snaps the lid on a beer and slams it on the bar in front of him.

Guess she still hasn't forgiven him for getting himself an old lady that wasn't her.

"What kinda shit?" I ask, trying not to sound too invested, despite the fact I'm burning for more information.

"Well, she picked up some CCTV of him leaving a bar over in Pueblo. And yes, before you ask, she took care of it. All that shit's been wiped. But we still don't know who he was meeting there or if they knew where he was heading after he left."

I nod slowly, taking in everything he's saying. None of it sounds good for Rogue.

Since Maddy came to the club, she's been a huge asset. Cleaning up usually goes far beyond the actual crime scene, and her hacking skills help us be real thorough.

"Look, I got no idea why but Rogue seems to have 'attached' herself to you," he starts, and I raise an eyebrow at Jessie's observation. His arms go up defensively when he notices how pissed it gets me. "We need to keep an eye on her, and if you're what's gonna keep her around here for longer, roll with it. Skid can't lose anyone else close to him, brother."

Jessie has a point, and although I call bullshit on the whole attachment thing, I agree that it's important for us to keep her safe... For Skid.

I throw back another shot, and Jessie reaches into his cut, pulling a baggy from his inside pocket and placing it on the bar in front of me.

"Guess you'll be needing something a little stronger." He chuckles to himself as he walks out. VP's right, ain't nothing right now I need more than to get out of my own head for a few hours.

"You want me to rack that up for you, honey?" Mel offers, holding a plastic card between her fingers.

"I got it." Taking the card out of her hand, I tap out a small amount of the bag's contents onto the arch of my hand, forming the perfect line. I then press one of my nostrils closed with my finger and inhale the line in one long swoop with the other. It burns as it travels through my airways, and an instant rush shivers down my spine.

Then taking the bottle from the bar, and the baggy, with me I get myself comfortable on one of the leather couches in the corner.

It's quiet here now, but the room will slowly fill as the night passes, my brothers will come, some will get high, some will get drunk, or both. The single ones will pick themselves a whore to entertain them, while Jessie, Nyx, and Brax will go back to their old ladies. And me? I'll sit back and I'll watch them.

I'll torment myself by letting my imagination flow freely.

Because when I'm buzzed, it's easy to pretend that my requirements from a woman aren't fucked up and that I'm a better man than the one I loathe.

My father.

Brax and his old lady come in together about half an hour later. They both say hi, and I nod back at them, watching as he sits her on a stool at the bar and kisses her neck like she's the most precious thing in the world. I wonder if he's ever thought about slicing her open and watching her blood spill over her skin. Probably not.

Brax was a nomad for years before he committed, and not just to her, but to our Charter. Anyone can see how much he worships her. He wouldn't want to cause her pain.

I always thought Brax was more like me than any of the others, that he was numb to all that kinda shit. Turns out I was wrong and I'm a lone wolf living among a pack. The one that will never really fit in, but will always have his place. That being said, this is my home and these are my people. They always have my back, they never judge, and I've been here long enough now to never imagine being anywhere else. We may be outlaws, but at least the people who suffer by our hand deserve it. We don't prey on the weak and vulnerable.

AGED 6

"Quickly, Richie, pick those trains up off the floor." Mama starts breaking up the track that I've just put together perfectly, I even managed to make a junction all by myself.

"But I'm playing," I moan back at her, and she stops flapping to look at me, guilt and sympathy taking over her panic.

"I know, darling." She crouches down to me. "But you know how your father feels about unnecessary clutter, we don't want to upset him, do we?"

Taking two tissues from the box on the table beside her, she rubs the chocolate from the corner of my mouth then stands back to admire me.

"Come on, Richie, we'll get them back out for a few hours after school tomorrow."

She squares up the tissue box and makes sure the next available tissue is standing up at the perfect point. Then she helps me break up the track and put it back in the box.

I come back down the stairs from putting the box away, just as Father's car pulls up in front of the house. Mama's eyes dart nervously around, checking for any imperfections or flaws that she might be punished for.

Most kids my age idolize their fathers. I hate hearing the kids at school talk about the plans they have with them at the weekend. I detest mine, and I hate even more how he makes Mama scared of him.

He barks at her like she's his servant.

He takes pleasure in how scared of him she is.

And if she doesn't do things perfectly, he hurts her with his fists.

Mama quickly tucks the back of my shirt into my pants and pushes back my shoulders so I'm standing straighter. Then dusting off her apron, she takes one final glance at her hair in the mirror before the door opens. Her "everything is wonderful" smile takes over as she moves toward him. I can tell that the kiss she places on his cheek isn't welcomed, and I shudder when his eyes narrow in on me.

"You do your homework, boy?" he asks, disregarding Mama so he can hang up his jacket.

"Didn't have any, sir," I reply. It's the truth, I'm much smarter than the other kids at school and sometimes my teacher lets me do my homework in class while they catch up.

"Then I'll set you some sums after dinner," he tells me, walking past to inspect the living room.

His shoes tap against the immaculately polished wood floor. He checks the windows first, running his fingers across the sills and rubbing imaginary dust between his finger and thumb. Then he inspects the bookshelf, where his books stand in the exact neat order that they were in when he checked them yesterday. There won't be a speck of dust found. Mama spends her entire day making sure of it.

I hear the relieved breath Mama lets out when he passes us in the hall and makes his way into the kitchen. The room is faultless as always. The table is already laid for three, with each item of cutlery having the precise amount of space set between them. Mama uses a ruler to be sure.

When he makes his way over to the stove, I notice how Mama tenses like she's bracing herself for something.

I brace myself too.

Reaching for a towel, Father lifts the lid off the pot that bubbles on the stove.

"What is this?" he asks, looking down into the pot with disgust.

"Dinner." Mama smiles as if there's nothing wrong, yet I notice how her hands are shaking behind her back.

"Dinner." Father nods his head as he puts the lid calmly

back in place. I swallow thickly, knowing from his tone that he isn't satisfied. He takes the eleven steps between the stove and Mama agonizingly slowly, like a predator ready to pounce its prey.

"Tell me, Anita, is today a Thursday?" His nose touches the end of hers.

"No, Peter, it's not." Her eyes fall to the floor regretfully.

"What night is it?"

"It's Wednesday." Her voice is just a shaky whisper, barely audible.

"And what do we eat on Wednesdays?"

"B...Beef b...b...brisket." I see the tears starting to form in her eyes and I wish I could stop the inevitable from happening for her.

Mama yelps like a puppy being kicked when Father fists her perfectly set hair, and marches her into the kitchen. She begs him to stop when he forces her face toward the boiling hot pot.

"Is this beef fucking brisket, Anita?" he shouts at her, and her cheek is so close to the hot metal that she must feel like it's melting.

"No," she cries, the fear in her eyes reflecting back at me from the shiny pot.

I manage to catch a breath when he finally releases her, and she slumps to the floor helplessly, breaking into tears.

"Explain." He starts pacing the floor in front of her. Backward and forward over the same spot, with his hands crossed behind his back like a Sergeant Major.

"I... I went to the butchers to get the brisket but they were out."

"Then you should have gone earlier," Father responds, trying to find his calm.

Mama nods her head back at him. "I should have. I'm sorry," she agrees submissively.

"Get up off the floor." He stops pacing and stands over her,

and when she manages to drag herself up onto her feet, she screeches when he swipes the back of his hand across her cheek.

"Do not let me down again," he warns, marching out of the kitchen and past me like I'm invisible.

He takes his chair in the living room and opens the paper— that Mama had made sure is placed ready for his evening read— like nothing's happened, and I turn my head to look into the kitchen where Mama has already started pulling herself back together again. Wiping the back of her hand over her cheeks to brush away the tears, she looks up at me with a brave smile and winks to let me know that she's okay. It's our secret signal.

I look back over at my father, and my hate for him burns through my veins. It heats through my skin, making it hard for me to control. But I breathe, slowly. In and out while I count to ten in my head. One, two, three…

I stumble back inside the cabin a few hours later, my buzz is starting to wear off and I'm fed up of watching the others getting their dicks polished.

I've spent all night wondering if Rogue has let herself back into my cabin, and even though I know it's a real bad idea. I had to come home and check.

The cabin is silent when I walk in, and I try to ignore the stab of disappointment I'm feeling as I take off my cut and hang it on the hook behind the door. I should have fucked Mel, released some of the fuckin' tension inside me. It's been far too long since I gave into my sick urges, and for the last twenty-four hours, Rogue has been putting thoughts in my mind that are impossible to ignore.

Keeping the demon caged is really starting to drain me.

I freeze when I open my bedroom door and find her sitting in my bed, casually flicking through a bike magazine.

"Good night?" she asks, looking up at me and smiling like it's perfectly normal for her to be here. In my bed. Wearing my fucking shirt again.

"Yeah." I nod, still adjusting to her being in front of me. How much longer can I ignore how fucking weird this is?

"I'm taking a shower," I mumble, turning around and marching straight to the bathroom where I can lock myself away from her.

She doesn't belong here, why is she trying to push my limits? It's too much. I'm not strong enough. Her being here is bad for me, bad for her, bad for fucking everything.

I stay in the shower for as long as I can, the warm water spilling down my back, and doing fuck all to calm me the way it usually does.

Eventually, I drag myself out, dry off, and wrap the towel around my waist before taking a breath and heading back to my bedroom.

The way Rogue's eyes skim over my body when I enter sends sparks over my skin. I turn my back to her to sit on the edge of the bed, trying to adjust to the way my body's reacting, the way it craves contact with hers feels strange to me. I shiver when her fingertips gently touch the skin on my back, lightly trailing across my shoulder, but I don't flinch. I remain still, and I'm confused by the warmth that suddenly fills my chest.

"Storm told me you spent the day at my house today." Her body crawls closer to mine, and I grip at the sheets when her arms wrap around my neck, her chest pressing against my back.

I'm too weak to fuckin' speak, so I nod my head. I have no idea how I'm dealing with this so well. How my breaths are still forming so easily.

"Guess I owe you a hug." Her soft breath tickles my skin as she whispers inside my ear and it makes my cock rise beneath the towel.

I shouldn't allow her to be so close, not while I'm visualizing her pinned to my bed by her wrists, and owning the fuck out of her sassy little cunt.

When that delicate hand of hers starts to creep down my chest, I damn nearly turn around and flip her on her back to let my cock have its way.

"Bring your bike by the garage when you've got time, and I'll work on that crank you get when you shift into second."

I don't have the chance to ask her how the hell she knows that, because the bitch's teeth sink into my lobe and all my focus diverts to not blowing my load.

She goes back to her side of the bed and lies back. And I lie out beside her, keeping a safe amount of distance between us as we both silently stare up at the ceiling.

Her hand slowly creeps over mine, and I don't know what the fuck's come over me when I slip my fingers between hers, and squeeze her inside them.

"I don't say this to many people, Grimm, but I like you," she confesses, and when I roll my head to the side to look at her and those big blue eyes are staring back at me, I feel myself weakening.

"I think I like you too," I whisper, petrified at how those words sound coming out of me. I watch a satisfied little smile decorate her face before she closes her eyes, and it makes it impossible to believe that she could be the creator of such chaos. Then I wonder if she is it... my ultimate test. I can't deny it to myself any more, Rogue has become the darkest of my desires, and if she's what Satan has sent to test me... I'm completely fucked.

CHAPTER 8

1% MC

ROGUE

Four whole days pass, and Grimm still hasn't asked for an explanation for why I'm staying at his place. It's obvious that he's trying to avoid me. He leaves the cabin early and he gets back late. But every night after he gets home, he gets into bed beside me and lies awake with me in the darkness for a little while.

He wants what I want, I can sense it. The pull between us is undeniable, and if Grimm was any other man he'd have taken what he wanted from me by now.

I think that's why I crave him so much, because I know that beneath all that coldness toward me, there's a trace of a conscience there. Instinct tells me that Grimm senses all the emotions inside me that I fight to keep hidden and that he's protecting me from all of his. Either that or he thinks my head isn't screwed on right and worries that if he fucks me, he'll end up like Eddie.

It's a Sunday, but I have every intention of catching up with some work at the garage... Until I see him step out of the bedroom.

He looks different today, instead of his usual ripped jeans and black T-shirt, he's wearing smart black jeans, an immaculately pressed black shirt, and, even more shockingly, a thin black tie.

He takes the seat at the table and concentrates profoundly on polishing his black shoes

"Who died?" I ask, leaning my ass against the kitchen counter and sipping my coffee.

Taking his attention away from his shoes, he stares back at me coldly, it's a warning for me not to continue my questioning, and it's also hot as fuck.

"I'll be back later," he tells me, slipping them on and tying the laces. I don't know how he does it to me, but watching Grimm doing simple, everyday tasks gets me real flustered.

When he stands up, he tips his chin at me and heads straight out the door, leaving his cut hanging on the hook.

I wait until I hear his bike leave the yard, then knowing I only have a few seconds to make the decision, I weigh up my options.

Naturally, I go with the one that's gonna get me in trouble, and I snatch up my purse as I rush out the door.

The yard is empty and I quickly hop inside the car parked outside Skid's cabin.

I feel under the wheel and tug on the plastic casing. Hot wiring a car was one of the first things Chop ever taught me. I may have gotten a little rusty, but I shouldn't have any trouble. Turns out my skills aren't required, the keys are still hanging from the ignition. So, after starting the engine, I quickly reverse and make my way down the track toward the clubhouse in pursuit of Grimm.

I spot him at the bottom of the track, heading out onto the main road. After pulling out myself, I make sure I keep a safe distance as I tail him through town, and up past Pines Peak.

The thought comes to me that he might be meeting a female. He's sure made an effort to look good this morning. The thought of all that being for someone else makes me squeeze the steering wheel tighter in my palms.

At the very least, if that's what he is doing, I can see what the bitch has that I don't.

Grimm eventually pulls off the main road, and I slow my speed down, giving him a chance to get ahead before I take the same turn myself. We're in a much quieter setting now, and it's getting real hard not to be noticeable.

When he rides his bike through a tall set of gates that lead to a huge mansion-style property, I have no choice but to keep driving past. A few yards up the road, I find a place to pull over, ditch the car, and jog back toward the gates.

I keep myself shielded behind the stone pillar and watch him making his way through the front entrance before I read the plaque on the gate.

Forestbank Care Home.

Grimm must be here to visit someone, and I really want to know who it is.

It's not like I can just ask him when he comes home, me owning up to being desperate enough to follow him isn't gonna happen. Besides, even if I did, I doubt he'd tell me.

There's only one option if I want to find out. I'll have to go undercover.

With Skid away, and me being stuck at the club, a little project to keep me occupied will do me some good. So I make a mental note of the time, before going back to the car and heading back to Manitou Springs.

I stop off at the drive-and-buy to pick up some chicken for dinner. Cooking's never something I made a lot of effort with. I always figured it was kinda pointless cooking for one. But just lately, cooking for Grimm has given me fulfillment.

I kinda like how it feels to take care of him.

Instead of rushing back to the club, I decide to take advantage of my freedom and stop off at my place to get some fresh clothes. The smell of fresh paint hits me as soon as I open the door, and when I look around there isn't a single trace of what happened here a few days ago.

I guess Grimm really is as good as they say he is.

New carpets have been laid, and the place has been left immaculately clean. He's even done the dishes that had been left in the sink that morning. It makes me wonder how long it'll be before I get to come home. I'd never admit it to anyone other than myself, but I understand why Skid wants to be cautious. That being said, I still don't think he gives me enough credit. I'm nothing like the other girls he knows. He should realize that by now.

I've been through enough to know how to take care of myself.

Shoving some clean jeans and a few shirts into a bag, I pick out a few more sets of matching underwear to taunt Grimm with, and then I leave.

I don't know why I'm so attached to the house. The place holds nothing but horrific memories for me. But this little bungalow on Oakwood Terrace feels like a part of me. We've been through a lot together, and yet here we are, still standing strong.

Grimm's new carpets and the fresh paint on the walls may cover the surface damage. Same as my fake smiles and callous attitude does.

But under that surface, we're dry rot, irrepairable, and decaying from the inside out.

I've never left this place because I want them to know where they can find me, just like Eddie did. I want them to see the same person that everyone else does. A strong girl who is full of fight and takes no shit. I want them to see for themselves that each one of them got me wrong.

Evangeline, the weak little girl, doesn't exist anymore.

Rogue is tough.

Rogue got her life straight.

No one fucks with her, and no one can hurt her.

These walls may be clean now but I still see the stains on them. They're marked in my memories and there isn't anything Grimm can do to clear that up.

I don't know if I'd want him to... those memories are what feed my strength.

Locking the door behind me, I head back to the club and somehow manage to drive up to the cabins without anyone in the yard seeing me.

It's still only 1pm, so after parking Skid's car back where I found it, I decide to head down to the garage and do some work.

Jessie and Troj are both here working when I arrive.

Jessie's a natural mechanic, he started off the same as I did, hanging out at the garage every moment he could and watching Skid and Chop work.

Now, without Skid here, I know I wouldn't be coping without him.

Troj, on the other hand... Well, he looks good in the overalls. Today he's excelling the shit out of that with his long hair tied up and the top half of his overalls rolled down and wrapped around his waist. It's mild outside but the temperature in the workshop is high, making his skin glisten with sweat, and the white tank he's wearing is providing some serious arm porn.

A person could underestimate Troj, he isn't the biggest guy around here and he's got a real pretty face, but I've seen the guy fight and know the damage he can do.

Between him and Jessie, they seem to have everything under control, but I get in my overalls and get my hands dirty anyway. Distracting myself for a few hours isn't gonna do me any harm.

I never know what Grimm is planning in the evenings but the one thing I can always be certain of is that he'll be home late so he can avoid me. We haven't talked about how long I'll stay here with him, or why I didn't move into Skid's empty cabin because we both seem to avoid serious conversations...

In fact, Grimm avoids any conversation.

He comes through the door about half an hour after I do, taking one of those long, thoughtful glances at me that makes me wish I could read his mind, as he loosens his tie and heads straight to the bathroom.

A while later, he comes back out with a towel around his hips, giving me another glimpse of the top half of his body.

I never hide the fact that I look, maybe it might help him get the hint, and I like the way his eyes scold me for it.

His fingers sweep through his ink-black hair on the way to the bedroom and I smile at him a little shyly when his forehead creases like he's trying to figure something out.

He's still buckling the belt of his jeans up when he comes out of the bedroom, and he's looking like he's got something on his mind.

"Whose jeans are those?" he asks, his eyes focusing on my legs. They're nothing special, just a pair of old Levi's that I picked up at a thrift store and ripped into myself.

"They're mine," I answer, wondering where the sudden interest in my clothing's come from.

"Ain't seen you wear them before." I watch his eyes narrow suspiciously, and my stomach does some weird-ass flutter that I figure comes from the fact he's noticed such a small detail.

"That's because I stopped by the house and picked up some stuff when I went out for groceries." I shrug, serving up the grilled chicken I've cooked onto some plates. It will make a nice change for me to not put his in the microwave and eat alone.

I ignore the way his nostrils flare, and the furious look he's giving me.

Instead, I smile and place his plate on the table. I've even gone through the trouble of making sure the different foods aren't touching to save him sorting it out himself.

"You left the club?" he prowls toward me, sparking another reaction outta my pussy.

He looks crazy mad, and the way he wets his bottom lip with his tongue, suggests he's about to devour me.

Slowly, I nod, guessing that he won't approve of my answer. I'm provoking him, and really enjoying the reaction I'm getting.

"Why?" he asks, his voice soft and curious despite his anger.

"I needed to get groceries, and I needed to get more clothes." I speak slowly, savoring his attention.

"Someone could have picked that up for you, you heard what Skid said about leavin' the compound." There's still distance between us. Far too much of it. And suddenly it feels like a punishment.

"Yeah, I heard him, but I decided to break the rules," I admit unapologetically, waiting for him to respond. I reach my finger out and run it across the top of Grimm's belt, my nail scraping along his skin. I've never craved anything the way I do him and I'm sure it's because he seems so out of reach.

"It ain't safe for you to be roaming around by yourself," he growls, and I can tell it's taking all of his effort to remain calm.

"You underestimate me, Grimm, you had to scrape the last man who did that off my floor." I tilt my head and reach for his hair. Taking a few strands of it from the front and playing with them in my fingers, before sliding it over to the left.

Grimm doesn't like being touched, I've learned that from watching him. And the fact he doesn't flinch at me makes me feel special.

"Skid told me to keep you at the club, and to keep you out of danger," he reminds me, his black pupils swelling.

"It's a shame I'm nothing like the bitches around here you boys are used to taming, Grimm. I ain't a fucking pet. I don't do as I'm told. I *am* the danger." There's silence and a long stare off that neither of us is gonna back down from.

"If you need to leave the club. You ask. I will arrange for someone to go with you," he tells me, stepping into my space so his body is flush with mine and his eyes are peering down at me. The tension coming off him is thrilling, and I know that despite all his efforts, I'm under his skin now.

"I never ask permission," I whisper, letting my hand slide across his jaw. I've been tempted for so long to know what his lips feel like, so I let my fingertip trace along his bottom one. It's soft, nothing like the harshness of those eyes that are firm and unmoving as they focus on me.

"You better eat up." I decide to release the tension, picking my lips up into a smile and breaking our eye contact to look at the food on the table.

I'm pleasantly surprised when Grimm roughly pulls out the chair and takes a seat. Then even more shocked when he's finished clearing up the mess I've made, and takes a seat on the couch instead of leaving for the club.

Pulling two beers from the refrigerator, I dangle one in front of him.

"Not going down to the club tonight?" I ask.

"Don't feel much like company," he snaps back at me, and like a teenage girl I actually fucking blush. I really need to do a better job of hiding my emotions, and why am I suddenly incapable of coming up with a snappy remark like I usually would.

"You don't count," he adds, glancing up at me through those thick lashes and making me feel weak. He snatches up the remote and turns on the TV. The crime channel is on again and he seems content watching what's on that. Twisting the top off my beer, I sit down beside him, making sure there's a decent-sized gap between us. And I ignore the look of disgust in his side glance when I tuck my feet up.

"Do anything good today?" I ask. A shake of his head is the only response I get. It's a good job I'm not one to give up easily. "You did a great job of the house, wouldn't even know anything had happened there," I add, trying to lighten the atmosphere. Grimm looks uncomfortable, tugging on his jeans to straighten them out as I edge a little closer and let my hand rest on his thigh.

He makes me jump when his hand slams over mine and he crushes me under his palm.

"Don't get the wrong idea about what you're doing here, Rogue," he warns, slamming down his beer on the coffee table and getting up. He grabs his cut on the way out the door, slamming it behind him.

I've spent the past few years growing extra layers on my skin, and in just a few short seconds, Grimm just managed to claw straight through them. I'm real fucking mad at him for that. But instead of getting angry, I decide to channel my energy in another direction. One that I'm gonna need the sweet girl a few doors down to help me with.

CHAPTER 9

1% MC

GRIMM

Prez calling church this early on a Monday morning can only mean one thing. Trouble... and once everyone's in their places, his eyes land directly on me.

"Girl picked the wrong guy this time." He tosses a brown folder across the table. Since Maddy arrived at the club things aren't only more organized, they're better presented too.

I like it.

I reach out for the file, and as I flick through the CCTV stills inside, I notice that they're of the guy Rogue massacred, and he's wearing the same clothes he was in when I got there.

"These were taken at a bar in Pueblo about an hour before he arrived at Rogue's place," Prez informs.

"And the others?" I question when I notice the still of him talking with a few other men outside. The camera angle isn't allowing us to see two of their faces but at least we can see one of them.

"Mads is working on it." Jessie leans forward to stub his cigarette out in the ashtray then slides it down the table to Brax as he exhales the last of his smoke. "Whoever they are, there's a strong chance they knew where he was goin'."

Shit.

"We could do without this kinda shit." Nyx shakes his head, and for some reason, it really fucking riles me. I stand up to go at him and feel the weight of Squealer's heavy arm slam across my chest.

"Chillax, kiddo, we'll take care of it," he tells me from the corner of his mouth, as he eases me back into my seat.

"The girl means summat to Skid," Prez explains to Nyx who's being held back by his brother Brax.

"Yeah, and it seems like he ain't the only one she means summat to," Nyx's smart trap opens up again as he gets forced back into his chair, and I respond to his cocky smirk with a cold stare.

"Rogue's helped the club out on more than one occasion," Prez reminds him, stroking his hand through his beard, the way he always does when he's thinking on something.

"Jessie, get Maddy and go with Grimm to speak to Rogue, we need her to take a look at those photos and see if she can tell us anything about the men he's with. The fact it's been over a week and there ain't no missing person report on Eddie is a good sign, but it's always better to be safe."

I nod my agreement back at him.

We all leave church a while later, me and Jessie heading up to the cabins to speak to Rogue. Maddy meets us at my place with her laptop and we all wait for a response from Rogue while she looks at the photos.

"Ain't never seen them before in my life." She smiles, grabbing her jacket and heading for the door. Something about the way she smiles is off, and I quickly step in front of her before she can make it out.

"Look again," I order her firmly.

"Grimm, I already told you, I don't know who those guys are." She tries being cute, but it ain't gonna work with me. I stare her down, letting her know that I ain't gonna budge until she's taken another look at those photos.

"They were with Eddie before he came over to yours that day," Maddy interrupts, her soft voice sounding sympathetic. She didn't see what was left of the guy, she doesn't know what Rogue's capable of.

"Pretty soon, people are gonna start wondering where he got to. It could really help us make sure there was no trail back to you if you recognize them," she adds.

Rogue rolls her eyes at me before she turns back around to face Maddy and Jessie.

"You ever heard of a bar out in Pueblo called Pitchers? It's where these were taken, you ever been there?" Jessie asks.

"Jesus Christ. It would be easier to just hand myself into the cops." Rogue snatches the photos back off Maddy and flicks through them again.

"I ain't never seen the men. I ain't never been to the bar. Now if you'd all let me get back to work, I got a fuel injection system on a Honda that ain't gonna fix itself." I step out of her path as she storms out.

Maddy and Jessie are both staring at me when I turn around. I shrug back at them to disguise the fact that I want to chase after her, smash her into the wall of my cabin and fuck the stubbornness out of her. Instead, I head out back to cool off, onto my deck that overlooks the lake, and light myself a smoke.

There's a fucking trail... This shit is a lot more complicated than we hoped and Skid doesn't need anything else to stress over.

With any luck, Rogue working at the garage all day will enable me to get some thinking done and put some kinda plan in place.

I still got the dust that's left of Eddie's bones to get rid of, so when I'm sure Jessie and his old lady have let themselves out, I grab my keys and head straight down the club to my basement. I grab the sealed plastic bag from my safe and leave the compound, without bothering to look over at the garage. I'm still pissed at Rogue for being so fuckin' awkward.

How the hell are we supposed to help her if she refuses to cooperate?

Rogue knows who those men are, it's written all over her face, and for some reason, she feels the need to lie to us about it. That puts her and the club at risk.

The girl thinks she's fucking invincible.

I'm not thinking straight while I'm riding, and I surprise myself when I realize which direction I'm heading in. It isn't often I make a trip back to my past.

The small town where I used to live never changes, and the low rumble of my bike turns the heads of everyone I pass as I head through the main street. I don't have to worry about being recognized. No one here would recognize me now. I'm not the same boy that left here all those years ago.

I take a left at the old gas station, then after a few more yards, another left down the long track that leads to the house where I grew up.

The place looked so much grander when I was younger. So perfect. Now the paint on the cladding is faded and chipped, and tall weeds grow up the guttering and poke through the roof tiles.

My foot creaks on the porch step, and the stench of rotting wood makes my lips curl into a snarl. I remember sitting on the porch swing and waiting for dad to come home. The swing's broken now, the chain on one side seized by rust and causing it to hang unevenly. I should feel the urge to fix it, but this place is beyond repair to me.

Bad memories can't be cleaned up. No one has control over them.

My hand reaches for the handle of the front door, and just like every other time I've come back here, something stops me.

I don't need to be reminded of how alike we were, I see the resemblance every day when I look in the mirror. I hear his voice inside my head and feel his sins on my hands.

His thoughts are forever polluting mine, there's no escaping from him, and being here isn't gonna help that.

Backing away, my foot lands heavy on one of the decaying steps and I stumble when it snaps beneath me. I waste no more time and get back on my bike, kicking up the dust on the long narrow track that leads me back to the road.

Before I leave town, I stop by the chapel. I look out of place here now, but when I was a boy, me and my parents would come here every Sunday. We had a car, but Father preferred for us to walk. He liked to parade us through town, to show off his biddable wife, and well-mannered son. His perfect family.

I push through the chapel doors with Eddie Clark's bone dust burning a hole in my pocket and as I step toward the altar, my head turns to the pew where we used to sit. I picture her there wearing the baby blue dress that rests just below her knee, and her matching jacket. Her smile so beautiful, no one would have ever guessed it was fake.

Age 8

The water scalds my skin, and the bleach stings my eyes but I don't cry. If I show Mama that I'm hurting it'll only make her more upset.

"That's enough, he's clean, let him get out." She's begging Father now, and I hate the satisfaction it brings him. He's feeding on her weakness, sucking it out of her like a leech and I wish she'd stop giving him more power.

"I told you he wasn't to play with the Hopewell boys, Anita, the family are unholy and have no hygiene standards."

"I didn't know he was playing with them, I would have told him not to if I'd have known. He was just being a child, Peter. Please, he's suffered enough."

"You allow our boy to roam the streets, not knowing where he is?" He looks furious but I have to focus on breathing. I can

feel my skin starting to blister and as badly as I want to scream, I know it won't do any good, it will just make him madder and then he'll hurt Mama too.

"Scrub him clean, Anita, wash the sins away from him. Who knows what he's touched while he was with them, or the thoughts they might have contaminated his mind with."

Mama mouths me a sorry as she grabs a bar of soap and starts to rub it over my skin, the bleach and hot water make it super-sensitive and each of her delicate strokes feels like a talon ripping through my skin.

"Not like that, Anita. Harder." Father snatches the soap out of her hand and scrubs it against my back. This time, I fail to stop the painful yelp from crawling out my throat.

"Shut up," he snarls at me, his hand moving faster, as Mother's sobs get louder.

"No use crying, you stupid bitch, this is all your fault," he yells at her. I feel like my skin is going to split under his friction, but I have to hold in my tears. Mama's already broken, I need her to see that I can be brave.

"Maybe next time you will think before you let our son roam the streets like a reprobate." He throws the cloth hard at the water, making it splash into my eyes and sting them, before he storms out of the bathroom. Mama waits until his footsteps fade before she quickly tugs me out of the water.

My body shakes uncontrollably from shock but I still don't cry. Mama needs me to be strong.

She wraps a towel around me and I flinch when it scrapes my skin.

"I'm sorry, Richie," she whispers, patting me dry as carefully as she can. "I'm so sorry." She kisses my head and sobs into my hair. "I should never have let you out alone, look at your skin." Her fingers tremble as she touches them to my red raw shoulder.

"It's okay, Mama." I place my hand over hers to try and

make them stop.

It's an hour later when Father calls me down to do my homework, Mother is sitting and sewing, and Father is reading. My skin is still inflamed and sore from the boiling hot water and when he looks up from his page so calmly, I have the undeniable urge to make him hurt.

Mama must notice because she shakes her head at me subtly in warning.

"You will read from the Bible until bedtime, son. After being in the company of the Hopewell boys, you must be cleansed. Their father is a crook and their mother is a whore, we will all pray for those poor boys' souls tonight."

I don't feel I need to pray for them, their mother may be a whore and their father a crook, but Todd and Kaleb smile and they play. They scrape their knees and get mud on their shirts.

What I actually pray for that night is for God to strike my father and free me and Mama from his hell.

On the ride back to Manitou Springs, I stop at a different gas station and use the restroom to flush the remaining particles of Eddie away.

It's dark when I get back to the club, and I ride straight past the clubhouse where the music is thumping and the firepit is blazing.

Inside my cabin is pitch black, but I can sense that she's here. Her scent lingers in the air around me.

I find her in my bed, and I want to tear out the comfort that seeing her there puts inside my chest. But something else tears it out instead, and my forehead creases when I realize she isn't lying as peaceful as she usually does.

Her face looks disturbed, and her blonde hair sticks to her

cheeks. She's struggling to breathe and I find myself crouching beside her, so my hand can cradle her head.

She's dreaming, and I'm gonna have to wake her from her nightmare because her torment is slicing through me like daggers.

"Rogue," I whisper, not wanting to shock her. Her head shakes and her body tenses.

"Rogue." My voice gets louder and sounds a lot more desperate.

She's panting now, trying to draw breaths that her lungs can't quite reach.

I lean in closer, my lips almost touching her clammy skin as I whisper her name into her ear.

"Grimm." Her head turns toward me and her eyes open wide. Big blue crystals lighting up the dim room surrounding us.

"It's just a dream," I tell her, but my words don't take the fear from her face. Vulnerability doesn't suit her, and it pains me to see.

My hand moves to her mouth and I swipe my thumb across her lips, hoping it will stop them from trembling. Her pupils are fixed on mine, drawing me in with a force that I'm powerless to.

"Stay with me," she begs, and just the weakness in her voice has me moving, my body slipping onto the bed to rest beside her. I wrap my arms around her shoulders and hold her tight to my body.

The closeness doesn't seem to affect me. It never does with Rogue. With her, I never seem to be close enough.

Lying beside her still fully clothed, with her flustered cheek resting against the leather of my cut, I breathe her in through my nostrils and let my lips press into the top of her head. There's no space between us, and I like that. It makes me feel whole.

"Promise me you'll stay," she says sleepily, her hand clutching at my T-shirt.

"I'll stay," I promise, feeling her body relax a little. It makes me panic that she's giving me that control. Rogue is so strong, so independent, and yet here she is needing me.

Hell knows why.

And it doesn't matter how much that thought suffocates me. I ain't going nowhere.

I wake up smelling leather and cigarettes, with Grimm's arms wrapped around my body. He must have fallen asleep sitting up with his back propped against the headboard, and I can tell he's not awake yet by the way his chest is lifting my head up and down, his heart beating steady against my ear.

I'm frustrated that I can't see his face. But I don't want to risk waking him, not while he's so peaceful and making me feel protected.

"I got to go." His panicked voice startles me awake. I must have drifted back to sleep. Sitting up, I take a look over my shoulder, and Grimm's eyes dart wildly at the space around us before he leaps off the bed, running his hands through his hair.

"You were… you had a…" he starts explaining like he's just been found guilty of something sinful. I can't help but find his embarrassment amusing.

"I know." Shifting up on my knees, I shuffle closer to the edge of the bed where he's standing. He doesn't move, just stares back at me with those cold, dark eyes.

I bring my face closer to his so our noses are almost touching, and he closes his eyes and breathes me in.

I want him to kiss me, I want him to give in to whatever's holding him back.

"I gotta go." He rushes out the door and I let my body flop back onto the mattress.

It's the same every time with him, just when we start to make progress, he has to pull a little more out of my reach.

Seeing the men in the picture Maddy showed me yesterday stirred up memories, ones that I've spent a lot of time trying to forget. Last night, I let those memories defeat me. And now I've woken up hungry for their blood.

I don't have time for those kinda thoughts today though. Today I'm gonna do something a little different, and it's gonna require all my patience...

"Hi." I smile sweetly at Jessie's old lady when she opens the door of their cabin.

Maddy looks a little shocked to see me, but she soon covers it up with a welcoming smile.

"Come on in." She steps out of the way so I can pass and when I take a look around the cabin, I realize how different it is to Grimm's place. The layout is the same, but here it's much cozier.

"You thought any more about those pictures?" she asks, making her way over to the coffee machine and taking two mugs from the cupboard above it.

"They don't matter." The lie rolls easily off my tongue.

I'm not here about the fucking pictures.

"Rogue, if those men knew where Eddie went that day, they might come after you."

"Oh, I'm counting on it," I blurt out, immediately regretting my words when I note Maddy's confusion.

"I need to borrow some clothes." I quickly change the

subject, mimicking one of her friendly smiles. I've been studying her movements for a few days now, paying close attention to her body language and the different types of smiles she uses for different situations.

"What sort of clothes?" Handing over a mug of steaming coffee, the confusion remains stuck to her innocent-looking face.

'Something…" I glance over the colorful dress she's wearing, "…pretty." I settle on a word I think politely describes her dress sense.

"Is it for a special occasion? Because Jessie says you're not supposed to leave the club without someone with you. I don't want you to get in any trouble." I can tell that her confusion has quickly turned into suspicion and I'm gonna have to up my game.

"Relax, I just want to try out a few new styles. You know, make a change from the overalls and jeans." I shock myself at how genuine I manage to make myself sound.

"Follow me then." Maddy's mood flips to excitement as she grabs my hand and tugs me toward her bedroom. The prospect of styling me up must be too tempting for her to resist.

I'll bet she was one of those girls that wasted hours playing with dolls when she was younger.

I spend the best part of half an hour going through her wardrobe and shoe collection. A lot of it is the same kinda shit. Pastel colors and floral prints, and eventually I find something tolerable. A denim dress with spaghetti straps.

As it can still get 'a little chilly' out, she suggests I wear a button-up sweater on top, which I figure will do a good job at hiding my tattoos, they don't exactly match the image I'm trying to portray.

We team it up with some black pumps, and when we're done, I barely recognize the reflection that stares back at me in Maddy's bedroom mirror.

"You look great. I think Grimm will really like it." She stands back and admires me proudly.

"This ain't for Grimm," I snap.

"Sure." She holds up her hands defensively. "You keep that one if you like, I hardly ever wear it."

"Appreciate that." I nod at her. "I should get going." I try recreating the grateful smile I'd watched her exchange with Ella outside the garage a few days ago after she'd picked her up some milk on a trip to the store. Then I move quickly toward the front door, ready for phase two of my plan.

"Rogue," Maddy calls out after me, and when I spin around to face her I notice that she's suddenly looking serious.

"People around here want to help you. If you know who those guys are you should tell us. It's what Skid would want."

"I don't know who those men are," I tell her once again. Keeping my face straight and hiding the repulsion I feel when I think about their faces.

"If you ever get lonely, just call by." Maddy seems to accept my answer as she waves me off.

"I don't get lonely," I assure her.

Back at Grimm's, I go straight to the bathroom and do my best attempt to recreate the cute plaits that Maddy sometimes styles her hair into, and I go a lot less heavy on the eyeliner when I do my makeup.

The plan is to go back to the care home that I followed Grimm to last week, and sweet little Maddy a few doors down is the character I'm gonna play to get the information I need.

When I'm ready to leave, I take a quick glance out the window to make sure no one is around, before walking out onto the yard. Then I hop inside Skid's car and start the engine.

I buzz with adrenaline as I drive past the clubhouse. Something is thrilling about breaking rules, but it's a little underwhelming when I figure I have nothing to worry about, the yard is dead. There aren't any bikes parked outside the clubhouse, and I've hung around here long enough to know that means shit is going down somewhere.

I arrive at the care home a little while later and park on the gravel beside all the other cars. Checking myself in the visor mirror, I rehearse that wholesome, friendly, Maddy smile one last time before I get out of the car and make my way inside.

The foyer isn't what I expect. Much more like the reception of a swanky hotel than a care home. Not that I've ever been to any I can compare it to, but I've seen plenty on TV. There are elaborate fresh flowers arranged in antique-looking vases, and the marble floor is polished so shiny that I worry I might slip.

When I approach the mahogany desk, a man wearing a white tunic smiles me a warm greeting.

"Morning, can I help you?"

I hadn't quite thought this part of the plan through, I have no idea if the visitor log is computerized or handwritten. My eyes quickly scan the desk and when I notice the thick leather-bound book with a black fountain pen laid beside it, all my prayers are answered.

"I'll just sign myself in, shall I?" I respond as if I'm familiar with the procedure. The book is open on today's date, ready for the next visitor's signature. Tunic guy doesn't question me, and as I reach forward, I purposely flick the book off the edge of the desk so it falls to the floor.

"Oops," I giggle, crouching down out of sight to retrieve it. I work fast, flicking back a few pages to Sunday's date. My fingers and eyes scrolling down the page to the time Grimm had visited. There's a squiggle for a signature that matches beside the name Anita Carter.

It's all the information I need for now. I could leave, go back to the club and do some research on my phone. It would be easy enough to manipulate Maddy into helping me. She's apparently good at this kinda shit.

Instead, I place the book neatly back on the desk and find

today's page again. Then treating the man behind the desk to another smile borrowed from Maddy, I pick up the pen and write Anita Carter in the patient box, then sign my name beside it.

My real name…

The man in the tunic nods his head like he's expecting me to move along, but I have no idea where I'm going.

"It's been a while since I last visited," I laugh flirtatiously and lick my lips at him. It gets 'em every time.

"Anita's still here on the ground floor. Room 3, just down the corridor to the left." He directs me with his hand, and knowing that what I'm about to do is a terrible idea, I thank him and make my way toward the room.

Standing in front of the door before I enter, I give myself a chance to back out. I have no idea who will be on the other side of this door, No plan. This could potentially go horribly wrong. But curiosity gets the better of me and I quickly tap my knuckles against the dark wood before I change my mind.

Whoever is behind this door must be important to Grimm, and for that reason, I want to meet them. When no one answers, I slowly push the door open and peep my head around it.

The room isn't too shabby, there's a crystal chandelier hanging from the center of the high ceiling. A huge king-size bed on one side of the room and a comfortable-looking couch in front of a large flat screen TV on the other. The sound of water comes from a door a few meters away and it starts to open.

"Richie, is that you?" a chirpy female voice chimes, and a middle-aged woman steps out in front of me. She's tall and beautiful, with long dark hair that's immaculately styled, and she's wearing a lemon-colored a-line dress with a jacket that matches perfectly.

She must be the manager, and I suddenly start trying to pull an explanation together in my head.

"I'm sorry, I thought you were my son," she says, stepping toward me. "Do come in and make yourself at home." She takes my arm in hers before I can respond and leads me toward the couch, urging me to sit.

"Anita," she holds out her hand gracefully for me to take.

"Evvv...angelene," I stutter, still unsure sure what's going on. Whoever this woman is, is definitely the person Grimm visited, her name was logged as a patient. But she doesn't seem like a patient in need of care. In fact, she seems much more like the caregiver, with her warm, welcoming manner.

"What a beautiful name." She smiles. "Tell me what brings you to me today, Evangeline?"

The woman looks at me, expectant of an answer, and I see a resemblance to Grimm in her perfect cheekbones and slender nose.

"Did my husband send you? He's always worrying about me being lonely while he's away?" She smiles proudly and when I look down, I realize her hand is still holding on to mine.

"Yes." I nod cheerfully because I'm all out of options.

"Well I hope he's paying you for your time." She laughs.

"Of course." My lips hitch up, in the way Maddy's had when she'd opened the door to me earlier, then as my eyes roam around the room, I spot a silver-framed photograph beside the TV.

"That's Richie," Anita tells me, standing up and taking the photo in her hand. She stares down at it adoringly before making her way back over to me and placing it in my hands. It's obvious the little boy in the picture is Grimm, he has the same ink-black hair and sad eyes.

"Of course, he's not a little boy anymore. He's a man now."

"He's lovely." I hand back the photograph, and she takes another look at it before placing it back in the exact same spot she took it from.

"He only manages to come home once a month, he works away on business."

Home?

"You have a lovely home," I tell her politely, looking around the room and taking note of all the elaborate things. None of this is what you'd expect in a regular care home. I can't imagine how much it must cost to keep someone here."

"Evangeline, do you sew?" Anita asks when she sits back down beside me,

"I'm afraid not."

"If my husband wishes for us to spend time together, perhaps you'd allow me to teach you."

"I would like that very much, Mrs. Carter," I nod.

I've already decided I'm gonna be visiting again. I get the feeling I could learn a lot about Grimm from being here. I've only been here five minutes and already I know his real name.

Anita claps her hands together excitingly.

"Excellent. And maybe next time you visit, you might get to meet my son. I think he'd like you."

"I'd like to think so." I smile back at her, making myself a little bit more comfortable before I ask where she got her beautiful cushion covers from.

CHAPTER 11

1% MC

GRIMM

It's been a long assed day, and it's dark when I finally get back to the cabin.

Some shit went west for our Utah Charter, one of their club whores got her tiz on and was threatening to rat. Since Declan and his boys have about as much control over their sheriff's department as they do their bitches, we had to step in and help out.

We rode out and brought back the majority of their guns and stash.

Prez already has a buyer lined up for the guns, and blow never lasts long around here.

Rogue looks guilty as soon as I walk through the door, not to mention a hella lot different to usual. The cute denim dress she's wearing is showing off her well toned legs too fuckin' well.

"Good day?" she asks, opening the oven and taking out something that smells delicious.

"Had to ride out to Utah," I tell her, hanging my cut up on its hook and making my way over to the table where she's set up two spaces.

"What went down in Utah?" She places a loaded plate in front of me. I've never eaten so well in my life.

I look up from it to nod her a thank you.

"Sorry, forgot, brothers don't talk club business with their bitches, right?" She makes that sweet little giggle as she takes the seat opposite.

"You ain't my bitch," I correct her, sternly.

"Well then, I guess that means you can tell me." With her elbow on the table, she props up her chin in her hand.

Bad fucking manners.

"We don't talk club business with anyone." I'm blunt with her, picking up my fork and digging into the pasta. Rogue is surprisingly an exceptional cook.

"How about we don't talk club business, and you tell me about you, did you grow up around here?" The way she's acting is off. I know Rogue's habits well enough to know when she's performing.

"How about we just don't talk?" I suggest. Her prying is making me uneasy and I sure as hell don't wanna discuss my fucking childhood with her.

"I just thought it would be fun to get to know each other better." She gives me her wounded puppy eyes, but there ain't no chance I'm falling for it.

Ignoring her, I finish up my plate. Sure, I feel like an asshole for ignoring her efforts, but not badly enough to want to talk about the past. I ain't used to people asking questions, I've adapted to solitude.

When we're done eating, I clear up while Rogue takes a shower. A call comes through from Skid, and I take it outside so she can't hear.

I assure him that everything's under control, and that she isn't causing too much trouble. Again, he doesn't ask me where she's staying, so I don't tell him. Though the fact he's calling me makes me suspect he already knows.

She comes out of the bedroom just as I step back inside, dressed like herself again in cropped denim hot pants that sit just under her ass cheeks, and a short sweater that shows off her flat stomach.

She must know I've had a tough day from how I've treated her. But then Rogue seems to have a way of sensing my mood, she's been doing it since the day she'd invited herself to stay with me.

Coming toward me, she takes my hand in hers and leads me over to the couch, and when I sit down she nudges my knees apart so she can stand between them. Her eyes stay on mine as she pulls her sweater up over her head and lets it drop to the floor. My gaze goes straight to her round tits. They're fucking perfect, topped off with hard pink nipples that I want to sink my teeth into.

I lower my vision over her tight, well-toned stomach to where her fingers are popping open the buttons on her shorts, and watch as she shimmies them off her thighs, rolling her panties down with them over her long legs until they fall at her ankles.

I should stop her, especially when she moves to climb on top of me and straddles my lap, but I don't. I even let her slide her hand through my hair and position it how she likes it.

Her fingertips trace over my temple, stroking over my jaw line then making a long tingly path down my neck and through my chest. The whole time her eyes remain focused on mine. Daring for me to stop her, and pleading for me not to all at the same time.

This is what I'd usually deem as torture, but somehow, Rogue and her hot as sin body are an exception to all my rules.

I like her hands on me. Having her close feels like the only time I'm getting to breathe these days.

Her hips shift, rubbing her pussy against my dick through my jeans. I'm tempted to snatch up her blonde hair, wrap it around my fist, and drag her closer so I can bite into her neck. To mark her, and make her cry out with pain. But somehow, I still have control of myself... I wonder how long it will last?

Her touch moves lower, finding my belt, and when she

begins to slide the leather through the buckle, I have plenty of time to stop her.

I need to fucking stop her.

But she's becoming harder and harder to resist.

When she opens the front of my jeans, my rock hard cock springs free for her. Seeing it for the first time makes her tongue trail around her lips. She slides down my body, onto her knees, those big blue eyes still fucking with me, daring me to tell her to stop.

Her warm breath touches my tip, and it makes me crave her mouth even more. I can just imagine how perfect she'd look with her cheeks hollowing as she sucked me.

But it wouldn't be enough.

I'd need to feel her throat tighten as she gagged. I'd have to grip her hair and control the way her head moved, guide it up and down my shaft and hold her steady while she chokes on me.

Then I'd demand her to promise me that she'd never take another man's cock to her mouth so long as she lives before I permitted her any air.

I can't let it happen. Not now, not ever.

"Get up," I growl at her, and I can't decide if it's confusion or disappointment that she stares back at me with. When I stand up, it's with so much force that I almost knock her off her knees, and quickly I shove myself back inside my jeans.

"What the fuck is wrong with you, Grimm?" She yells at me like she's hurting, and it's impossible to ignore the stab it causes deep in my chest. Still, it's a damn sight better than the alternative. That shit could be irreparable.

Rushing for the door, I leave before the pain consumes me. There's no way I can give into temptation, not with her. She's not just some club whore. I care about her. In my own fucked up way I like her, and this is the only way I know how to save her.

I ignore her angry demands for me to go back to her as I storm out onto the yard, jump on my bike, and ride down to the club. I pay no attention to who's hanging round the firepit, or the fact that Roswell the local sheriff is being led up to one of the rutting rooms by Haven, Prez's number one girl. I just slam through the doors to the main bar room, and snatch the bottle of Jack from the end of the bar, wiping off the top with my shirt before I throw back a huge mouthful.

It's not e-fuckin'-nough to calm me down, and it won't be enough to forget.

AGED 11

"All your chores are done, why don't you go get some fresh air, sweetheart?" Mama's ironing again, all her concentration is on getting the creases just right. "Maybe you could go help your father over at Mrs. Pinkerman's place?"

Dad always does charitable things on a Saturday. He likes to give back to the community.

"Sure," I agree, pulling on my jacket and heading out the door. It's about a twenty minute walk to Mrs. Pinkerman's place and there's always loads to do there. Her husband died last year and she refuses to move from the homestead.

I pass the Hopewell's bungalow on the way, and notice something that makes me stop. My father's car is parked on the drive, which is strange considering what he thinks of them. I hope he's not here because he knows I snuck out with them last Tuesday, or to preach, I hate it when he does that. The Hopewell's may not attend church but Todd and Kaleb are the only kids at school that speak to me. Everyone else thinks I'm weird. I can't exactly blame them for it. While all the other kids turn up to class in jeans with T-shirts of their favourite cartoon characters, Mama insists I wear a shirt and tie.

"You represent our family when you go to school, Richie. Your father would want you to look smart."

I should keep walking, go to Mrs. Pinkerman's like Mama told me to, but curiosity gets the better of me and I decide to sneak around the back of the house. There's no sign of the boys or Mr. Hopewell, and as I creep up toward the back door, I hear a choke come from one of the windows.

"Take it, you fucking slut." The voice I hear belongs to my father. I move quietly toward the window to get a better look and my eyes widen when I see what it is that he's trying to give her. Mrs. Hopewell is on the kitchen counter, with my father between her legs. He's rubbing his body against hers and pinning her to the kitchen cabinet behind her by her neck.

"You're hurting me, stop," she begs, but he keeps on moving his body against hers.

"I'm gonna fuck the life out of you, whore," he grunts cruelly,

"Please stop. I won't te—" Father silences her, and shocks me when he presses a knife against her cheek. "You've been asking for this for months. I see the way you look at me when I come in the store. You've been begging me to fuck you with those eyes of yours."

"Pl..." she chokes as his fingers press harder into her skin, he's squeezing the life out of her body. I should help her, I should run and get someone, but I can't stop watching him. I may not listen all that much at Bible class but even I know that what I'm witnessing is sin. My father is giving himself to another woman and worse, he's making her suffer.

I should stop him. But that would make him angry. He'll beat me in front of Mama again and that'll make her sad.

I look at Todd and Kaleb's Mom. She looks so scared, and Father is absorbing it, pulling strength from her weakness the same way he does from Mama. But Mama is safe, she's back at home, ironing his shirts and making sure the creases in his pants are perfect.

The Hopewell's house is filthy, Mrs. Hopewell doesn't keep herself as clean as Mama does. Maybe that's why he's punishing her.

I can't watch anymore. I hate him for doing this to Mama. I hate him for hurting Mrs. Hopewell, but I hate myself more for being grateful that Mrs. Hopewell is the one suffering instead of her.

Maybe he'll come home in a better mood. Maybe he will be nice to Mama like he was last Thursday night when he come home from work and took us all out for dinner.

I leave, and go to Mrs. Pinkerman's like Mama told me to. I'll let my father keep his filthy secret, and next time I sneak out at night to catch fireflies I won't feel like such a sinner.

Father never showed up at Mrs. Pinkerman's that afternoon, but neither of us discuss that when I get home later in the evening.

Instead, he just stares at me across the table waiting for me to slip up and forget my manners. He seems happier than usual though, he even places a kiss on Mama's cheek when he gets up from the table to move into the living room. It makes her happy, I can tell by the way she touches her hand to the spot and smiles to herself before she cleans up the plates.

Squealer knows exactly what I'm looking for before I've even opened my mouth. He slides me a baggy of white powder across from where he's sitting and I chop it out on the bar, my hands shaking, but still making sure the line is even in width and dead straight before I take it.

Swiping my thumb under my nose to catch any residue, I

head toward the back of the room, tapping one of the new club bitches on her shoulder as I pass her on the way.

Who she is, is insignificant. The girl is new, I've never used her before, and I hope she isn't gonna hesitate or ask dumb questions because I ain't in a tolerable fuckin' mood.

She smiles at me like she's just been picked first in gym class when I point to the floor in the corner of the room.

"Take off your panties," I tell her, relieved when she does as she's told immediately, bitch is gonna do real well round here with that kinda attitude.

She lets the tiny strip of fabric dangle off her fingertip like she's expecting me to take them off her.

"Sit." I move my eyes to the space on the floor where I want her, and with a slight apprehensive glance around the room, she sits down for me.

"Finger fuck yourself," I order, knocking back another mouthful of Jack.

"Pardon?" Her eyes widen. There aren't many people in here, the music ain't that loud, she fucking heard me the first time.

"Your finger... I want you to use it and fuck yourself," I repeat myself, this time slowly so she won't misunderstand me.

"But..." The pathetic giggle she makes irritates the shit out of me.

"Do it, or fuck off," I snarl. Then watch as she sucks her finger inside her mouth, lowering it to her pussy and begins rubbing it back and forth over her clit.

It doesn't take long for her to soak her own fingers. Like most whores round here, she's getting off on undivided attention.

I focus on her finger as it moves lower, teasing at her entrance.

"Take two of them," I instruct, my hands twitching to reach out and show her how it should be done. But this is all part of the test. I am strong enough to beat the demons.

I have self preservation. I can control myself.

And this way, no one gets hurt.

Her pussy takes her index and middle finger all the way to her knuckles, and she works herself hard, straining her head against the wall behind her. "Don't stop until you come." I cross my arms over my chest and watch her, wondering if I'll ever find enough restraint to test myself like this with Rogue. I'd really like to. The thought of commanding her gets me hard and fucking furious with myself all at the same time.

I'm not him... I'm not fucking him.

My need to control is a sickness, passed down through the generations. But I've got a handle on it. I just can't trust myself around Rogue, if anyone is liable to break me, it's her

I won't become him.

I won't ruin.

I won't destroy.

I desire women, same as any other guy around here. But I need more than just a bitch's pussy. I crave control, I need them to follow whatever I instruct them to and to do it perfectly. And once my urge takes over there's no going back. I can't shut out the thoughts in my head. I can't make the images vanish.

I figured out a long time ago that I was incapable of normal and, up until now, I've been prepared to live with that.

Rogue makes me want what everyone else around here seems to be getting. I want her in my life. In my cabin, in my bed. On my fucking bike. I want her wearing my clothes, eating off my cutlery, and touching my things... I even want her touching me...

But just as much, I want her under my control. I want to own her, and Rogue isn't the type of girl to be owned by anyone.

The girl in front of me is close, I know the signs, loss of coordination to the hand, uncontrolled thrashing of the hips. She's gonna come all over her fingers and then eat up her mess just like I tell her to.

But something makes me pull my eyes away from her. A

sudden sixth sense that I never knew I possessed burns into the back of my skull and forces me to turn around. And I see her standing in front of me, eyes that are too angry for tears, wild and looking at me like she's about to pounce. But what she does is much worse.

She runs.

CHAPTER 12

1% MC

ROGUE

I should never have followed him down here. I knew I'd made a mistake the second I saw him, fascinated by the whore on the floor in front of him. The one who's playing with herself and lapping up all his attention.

It stokes at the already lit fire in the pit of my stomach, and when Grimm turns around and catches me watching him, I try so hard to hide my hurt that my teeth feel like they might snap from the strain in my jaw.

I've dealt with many things in my life, but I don't know how to handle this. Rejection from Grimm feels like a punch to the cunt, so I do what's safest for everyone and get the fuck out of there.

I hear him calling after me, but it only makes me quicken my pace. I've been so stupid offering myself to him, practically begging him like a needy fucking puppy. Grimm doesn't fucking want me, if he did he would have had me by now.

Turns out he much prefers to get his pleasure from the whores who get passed between brothers like a lit joint.

I hide behind the garage, watching him run up the track toward the cabins. He's assuming that I've run home, and as soon as he's out of sight I jump inside the jeep I've got booked in for a service in the morning, and drive off the compound.

I drive out of Manitou Springs, wiping tears from my cheek

with the back of my hand. I can't handle feeling this weak, I have to remember who I am now, and I know exactly where I can go to remind myself.

It's risky, especially after hearing Maddy's warning. But I need an outlet and I need to regain some of my pride.

The Orchid Lounge is on Bastard territory, and when I first came here a few years ago, that's exactly the reason I chose it. Skid would never show his face around here, and neither would any of the other Dirty Soul members.

It's been a while since I last came here. Months in fact, but tonight, this is just what I need.

"Rogue?" The guy on the door does a double-take as I strut toward him with no intention of stopping.

"Living and breathing," I sigh, and he pisses me off when he puts his large frame in my path.

"Is Adrian expecting you?"

"I didn't realize I needed an invitation these days?" I bite back sarcastically.

"You never need an invitation," he smirks at me, stepping aside and opening the door for me.

The club is busy tonight. All the front row tables are fully occupied, the men ogling the stage where a naked woman swings herself athletically around the pole. I stand and watch her for a moment, she owns the eyes of every man in the room, just like that little whore back at the club had owned Grimm's. Every man in here wants her, in their perverted little heads, they're deciding what they'd do to her if they ever had the chance. But here they can't touch her. Whatever their desires are will remain fantasies.

She has all the power.

"Gio told me you were here." I turn around when I hear his voice, and Adrian looks happy to see me.

"I wondered if you had a slot on stage for me tonight?" I ask sweetly.

"I always got a slot for you on stage," he chuckles back at

me. "I'm in the middle of some business, go backstage and get yourself ready, you can come on after Rhonda. Hopefully, I'll catch up with ya after."

I wink at him and turn on my heels ready to head for the dressing room.

"Hey, Rogue, what's this setting me back?" Adrian calls after me, and when I turn around, his letchy eyes are rolling over me slowly.

"Old times sake."

"I'm not about to argue with that." Looking pleased with himself, he leaves to go back to his office.

Backstage is chaos. Women are leaning over the top of each other trying to get ready. Not one of them looks pleased to see me, but then I've never been one for making nice. All the faces seem new since the last time I came here, but I don't give a shit. I'm not here to make friends. I'm here to heal myself.

Flicking through the rail of clothes, I find an outfit I like the look of. A black leather dress with a double-ended zip that runs straight through the middle of it.

"You can't wear that one, it's Sarah's," one of the girls pipes up and, keeping the dress in my hand, I slowly make my way toward her.

"Did you say something?" I ask, trying to keep some calm in my voice.

"Yeah." She looks down her nose at me like I'm a piece of shit on her fake Louboutin. "I said, you can't wear that one because it's Sarah's." She talks back at me like she's talking to a child.

Some bitches can be so fucking dumb.

I grin back at her, watching the way she looks around the room at the others. I'll bet this bitch was captain of the cheerleading squad and leader of the mean girls' crew back in high school.

"Not tonight it ain't," I tell her. "Sarah," I call out the girl's name, without taking my eyes off the bitch in front of me.

"Yes?" a weak voice comes from the back of the room, and I flick my eyes to the mirror until I locate her in its reflection. Sarah is shiny and brand new, anyone can see that. Timid, shy, she's here because she has to be, not because she's an attention whore like some of the rest of us.

"Got a problem with me wearing your dress, princess?" I ask politely.

She shakes her head, and I smile back at her through the mirror.

"Glad we cleared that up."

"As for you…" My eyes fall back on the queen fuckin' bee and I grab the back of her hair, tugging her shit extensions away from her scalp and making her yelp. "Stay out of a bitch's business." When I slide my tongue over her cheek, I hear the other girls gasp and I snarl her one last warning before I release her.

I gotta get ready to go on stage.

AGED 11

"You like it?" Daddy's friend asks as I pull the frilly dress out from the bag.

I nod my head but don't give too much away. Eddie always makes me feel nervous. I don't understand why my dad is friends with these people.

"Well, put it on then." He smiles at me, revealing his golden teeth.

I take the bag and turn to go to the bathroom but his hand pulls me back, and he shakes his head at me

I swallow down the nasty taste in my mouth and try to shake off the unnerving feeling that's building in my chest.

"I want you to take off your clothes, very slowly for me. Do you understand?" he whispers, his voice sounding so much kinder than it does when he talks to the others. When Daddy left him in charge of me, he told me I had to do whatever Eddie told me to. So I nod. I already know the consequences of not doing as I'm told for Eddie, I still feel the pain when I sit down from last week when I got smart.

I start with my blouse, my fingers shaking as I slowly undo the buttons, and I put all my concentration into each one I open.

Eddie's finger hooks under my chin and forces my head up to look at him.

"Smile," he encourages me, his finger sliding through the trail of open buttons, and feeling like glass cutting through my skin.

When I take the blouse off completely, he slouches back on the couch and buries his hand inside his pants. Rubbing between his legs, and making low grunts as I reveal more and more of my body to him.

When I'm completely naked, I stand in front of him, while his hand works much faster and harder.

"On your knees, Evangeline," he orders, and I breathe a sigh of relief when I realize he isn't going to hurt me this time.

Using the hand he isn't rubbing himself with, he places my head into position. Exactly where he wants me, maneuvering me like I'm his puppet.

"You want your reward for being such a good girl for me?" he asks, his hand moving faster and making a loud slapping sound. I hate that my fear can be used to control me. I wish that I could take his filthy, stenching reward and spit it straight back in his ugly face.

But that's all I can do. Wish, imagine, fantasize. Because I'm not strong enough yet, but one day I will be.

I'll make him regret praying on my weakness.

I'll make them all pay.

I open my mouth and I take my reward, swallowing it down like a good girl. Then I pick up my new dress from the floor, take it to my room, and use it to wipe my mouth before I throw it in the trash.

The music starts and I step out onto the stage where greedy eyes letch at my body as I begin to move to the music. I'm in control here. They can look as much as they like, but they have to keep their hands to themselves. Their cocks can be hard for me, but they'll never get to touch, they won't even get close.

There are no rewards here.

Not for them anyway. All these men will get here tonight is an achy dick, a serious case of blue balls, and a fantasy to take back home.

I'm having fun, dancing for the rows of faceless men. Until I see a face I recognize. One whose eyes peer into my soul and make me freeze.

Grimm is standing at the back of the room, arms folded over his chest and teeth biting on the knuckle of his right hand. I can't seem to move, my feet feel rooted to the stage and the look in his eyes is so haunting I feel it chilling my skin.

I stand still, waiting for his next move, and ignoring the jeers and complaints from the crowd. He's expressionless and I watch him nervously as he unfolds his arms and rubs his lips together. His eyes close while he takes a breath and it reminds me that I should take one too. Thrill sparks at my core when he starts to march toward me, ignoring the heckles from the crowd as he steps up onto the stage.

The rules suddenly change, Grimm is touching me and no one is attempting to stop him. Security is nowhere to be seen as his hands wrap tightly around my waist, crushing my bones as he throws me up onto his shoulder.

"What the hell are you doing?" I scream over the music. My fists banging hard into his back.

"I'm taking you home," he growls back at me, and I can hear all the tension in his tone. I feel it in his fingers, and instead of fighting against him, I let him take me.

CHAPTER 13

1% MC

GRIMM

S he isn't at the cabin, she isn't with Maddy and she isn't at Skid's place either.

I can feel myself starting to panic because I have no idea where she is and no control over the situation.

Judging from the look on her face, what Rogue just saw upset her, and something in my gut tells me that Rogue upset, is a whole lot worse than Rogue mad. She could be anywhere, and knowing there might be people out there who would want to hurt her has my anxiety worked up into overload.

I rush back down to the club, checking the garage, and come up with nothing.

I even check the lounge bar, where only members are allowed just in case, but all I find is Tac, Thorne, Nyx, and Brax playing poker.

"You want in?" Brax asks, raising his eyes up from his hand. I shake my head, in any other circumstances I'd clean these fuckers up, but I have bigger things to worry about.

"Where's Prez?" I ask, hearing the panic in my voice.

My phone starts ringing in my pocket, I can't recall Rogue having my cell number, but still hope it might be her.

It fucking isn't.

"Troj," I answer, hoping to fuck this isn't a clean-up they

want me to deal with. I'll never be able to think straight knowing she might be in danger.

"You're looking out for Rogue, right?" he checks.

"Yeah," I snap back.

"Then you should probably get down to the Orchid Lounge."

The Orchid Lounge is a strip bar out at Fountain, the owner used to deal with the Bastards, but their numbers have dropped dramatically since their ex Prez got called out as a nonce. Nobody wants to work with them anymore.

Dirty Souls have been looking into expanding our territory so we can benefit from their misfortune, and Troj rode out there to make the owner our offer earlier tonight.

"I figure you got about twenty minutes before she goes out?"

"Goes out?" My stress levels reach boiling point.

I hang up the phone and check I still have the cage keys in my pocket, but they aren't there. I must have taken them out earlier and left them at my cabin.

"Brax, give me the keys to your truck." I hold out my hand in front of me. I haven't got time to go back to my cabin.

"What you need my truck for now?"

"I haven't got time for explaining, just give me the fuckin' keys."

He gives me that hard stare back, one that for most would end with pain. Then balancing his smoke between his lips, he stands up, digs his hand into his pocket, and tosses me his keys.

"Bitches, they get to us all eventually." He shakes his head and smirks at his brother, Nyx, before sitting back down.

"Not me, you won't catch..." I don't hear what Tac has to say for himself 'cause I'm already out in the foyer, the door slamming behind me.

I get in Brax's truck and start up the engine, then with a screech of the tires, I speed out of the compound toward Fountain

Troj is waiting for me at the entrance and explaining to the big guy on the door that I'm with him.

"I was in Adrian's office giving him Prez's offer. He came out to talk to a girl, then I saw them on the CCTV. I know Skid didn't want her leaving the compound. Thought you'd be the best one to come take her back. I can't deal with that level of crazy." Troj shakes his head at me.

I move past him, slapping him on the back in gratitude. The room is full of men, some old, some young. Some rich, some counting out their cents on the table. But all of them are enchanted by the girl who is dancing on the stage.

Rogue is wearing a leather dress with a zip straight through the middle. It clings to her body like she's been sewn inside it and my cock strains against my jeans when I think about ripping it off her. I really don't have time to stand and fuckin' admire but I can't help myself. She's fucking stunning, and I'm fucking furious.

She knows the implications of leaving the club. And for her to come here of all places, letting these men feast on her body like maggots on rotting flesh, has me chewing on my knuckles.

Rogue remains still when she sees me, her eyes planted into mine and waiting for my reaction, and I take a long, deep breath. I don't want to react, but she's left me with no choice. I storm forward, standing up on an empty chair and hopping onto the stage and before she has any time to protest, I got her wrapped in my arms and over my shoulder.

She doesn't fight like I expect her to, and despite me being unable to see her face I almost imagine her smiling at her victory. The hot little bitch wanted my attention, and now she fuckin' has it.

I see you, Rogue, I fucking see you....

When she asks me where I'm taking her, I tell her I'm taking her home. Whether she likes it or not the club is her home now, at least until we know that she's safe.

I nod at the doorman as I haul her outside, and then I throw her into the passenger seat of Brax's truck. When I slam the door, trapping her inside, I take a long, steady breath to try and calm myself.

This is her way of provoking me, she's coaxing the monster inside me to rear his ugly head and I have to fight to keep him contained.

Pushing my body off the door, I stalk around the hood to the driver's side and get behind the wheel ready to start the journey home. I'll have to send Storm and Tommy out here to pick up the jeep I recognize from the garage that's parked on the opposite side of the parking lot.

"Why did you do that, Grimm?" she asks when I get on to the interstate. I don't answer her, just keep my focus on the road ahead. Still trying to tame my fury.

"Grimm, why did you do that?" She's yelling at me now, I know how much she hates to be ignored and so I punish her with my silence.

"You had no right coming to the club and hauling me off that stage like I'm your property. I don't belong to you. I don't belong to anyone." She crosses her arms defiantly. She's right about that much, and I feel it burning up the fury in my veins. She must notice how my muscles twitch because I see her satisfied smirk from the corner of my eye.

"You wanna control me, Grimm?" she asks like she's got me all figured out.

I don't respond to her question, just let flames flick in the pit of my stomach at her accuracy. She's reading my mind and using my own thoughts to taunt me.

I pull off at the exit for Manitou Springs, desperate to be back at the club and out the confines of this damn truck.

"You want to watch me get off... Like that whore?" Her tone changes, like she's afraid of my answer. And my hand grips at the steering wheel tighter.

"Wanna watch me flick myself off for you, Grimm?" she asks again, unzipping the bottom of that fucking dress and revealing her black-lace-covered pussy to me. I quickly flick my eyes back to the road. This bitch is asking for trouble, but she thrives on that shit.

One more glance to where her palm presses between her legs, and I lose all willpower. Slowing down the truck, I steer into a lay-by.

Thrill hums all over my skin as I twist in my seat and rest an elbow on the steering wheel, giving her my full attention. I watch her eyes glisten as she soaks up every second of it. Then reaching over my head, I flick on the interior light to get a better look, and the satisfied smile that rests on her lips confirms everything.

Dipping her hand into the waistline of her panties, she skims her finger through her pussy lips. My fingers twitch to rip the lace from her skin and watch her cunt cream all over her fingers. I even feel tempted to put my fuckin' mouth on her, to eat her out until she screams my name and I taste her pleasure for myself.

But I hold back, managing to focus on her hand and how she's working herself. I ignore how her eyes burn into my head, feeding off my attention.

Again, she must read my fuckin' mind because she rolls her panties off her hips, all the way down her legs, and tosses them onto my lap. I have the perfect view of her like this. Her knees risen to her chest and legs spread wide, her fingers making slow strokes that circle her clit.

"Touch me, Grimm," her lips move slowly as they whisper to me, she doesn't see me shake my head because her eyes are closed, her head hanging backward exposing that long, slender throat to me.

It would be easier than breathing to reach forward, to give her needy pussy exactly what it wants, to have her soak my finger instead of her own. But where is the self-preservation in that?

This, right in front of me... she... is my ultimate test, and I need her to hurry the fuck up and come before I fail it.

"Don't come until I say you can," I warn, and a tiny, helpless whimper feeds me a little of my fix. She's responding to me, abiding by my words. Without even touching her I'm commanding her body, and it gives me a sick satisfaction that I don't even try to deny myself.

"Please, Grimm," she begs so sweetly, so desperately that I have to clench my teeth together to stop myself from giving in to her.

Her hand hits the roof of the truck and her body tenses. I sit and watch her hips roll.

"Not until I tell you," I remind her.

"Touch me?" she whispers, she's past the point of having any pride. So desperate to come that she'd beg for it.

"You wanna come for me? Do you want to put a finger inside yourself?"

"Yes," she breathes, her teeth sinking deep into her bottom lip. I lean forward, close enough for the tip of my nose to brush over her cheek.

"Then do it," I whisper, "wet those fingers, and make yourself feel good for me."

Rogue's hips lift from her seat as she speeds up her rhythm and intensifies her pressure. My cock is solid, and my heart races with both thrill and anger combined as I watch her give herself a punishing orgasm. I lean away from her again so I can admire how beautiful she looks when she comes, my fist clenching at the wheel as I imagine how good feeling her pussy pulse would be.

She slowly brings herself down, her head falling sideways on the headrest and her eyes finding mine again. Big, bright crystals that strike so fucking hard I feel them bruising me on the inside.

"That better, Grimm?" she asks me seductively, still trying to catch her breath.

"Not at all," I admit spitefully, turning my head away from her and starting up the engine.

CHAPTER 14

There's silence for the rest of the journey, and Grimm acting like what just happened had no effect on him has me furious.

I know I made him feel something. The way he'd marched on that stage and dragged me off it proved it.

When we get back to the cabin, he remains in the truck after I get out. Then as soon as he sees that I'm inside, he drives away. Part of me wants to run away again, but I'm exhausted, both mentally and physically. Meeting Grimm's mom today confirmed my suspicions. There's so much more to his story. Seeing him watch that slut at the club made me envious enough to kill a bitch. It's both ironic and fucked up that I found it kinda comforting when he threw me over his shoulder and dragged me off the stage.

It felt like he cared. Like in his own fucked up way he was saving me from myself.

Up until now, I've never thought I needed rescuing.

I slip the leather dress off and take a shower, and when I'm finished I leave the bathroom exactly how Grimm likes it. I even line up the towels on the rail before I take myself to bed.

Lying in the darkness, I wonder what Grimm is doing now. Will he finish what I'd interrupted with that pretty little whore bag down at the clubhouse?

I can't think about it, not without wanting to cause havoc. So I close my eyes to try to get some sleep, and as they start to get heavier, I feel myself drifting to a much darker place.

AGED 12

"Shhhhh." I feel his heavy weight on top of me, and his stale beer breath lingering over my mouth. There's no point screaming. Screaming never does any good. He'll cover my mouth with his hand if I do, then each breath I take will have to be through my nostrils and I'll be forced to smell everything so much more.

Derek is by far the worst of Daddy's friends. He's almost kind when he takes me, and so much gentler than the others. He told me once that all he wants is me to love him. But I could never do that.

His huge dirty hand brushes my freshly washed hair against the pillow, and I squeeze my eyes shut tight.

"Let them fall for me, princess," he tells me, soothing his thumb over my eyelids. Derek gets a sick kick out of my tears. I don't want to give him them, he doesn't deserve the satisfaction they bring him. But I know he won't finish until I do.

To keep them from him will only prolong MY torture.

"That's it, angel," he whispers when he finds his rhythm.

I'm sure he has a wife and children of his own. That's what I don't understand, if he already has someone to love him, why does he keep coming back to me. My tears come without effort, streaming from my eyes and running past my cheek.

"That's right," he praises me, his sloppy tongue sliding over my skin and lapping up my tears like they're holy water.

While he salivates on my misery, I distract myself, thinking about how I'd like to rip that tongue right out of his mouth.

There's a steak knife in our kitchen drawer that I figure would do the job. And after I've taken the tongue from his mouth, I could use that to slice through his cock too. Making sure he never hurts me again.

My thoughts dry out my eyes, just as his heavy cock lands on my stomach and leaks onto my skin. He catches his breath, his body limp and vulnerable. If I had that knife, now would be the perfect time to slit his throat and end him.

Maybe one day I will.

"Good girl," he huffs, pulling my nightdress neatly back into place. His finger runs over my cheek and he collects a stray tear with it. "One more for the collection." He smiles at me before he licks over the collection of tiny teardrop tattoos he has on his hand.

When he leaves, I want to wash him off my body, but to go to the bathroom means walking past them all. The last thing I want to do is provoke the others. So I lay in bed, listening to the sound of their laughter, and hearing the steady hum of Derek's tattoo gun, knowing that he's marking himself with another victory.

"Ssshh." I wake up with a start, worried that I'm starting the same dream over again, but instead of the nasty brute on top of me, I feel a hand that trembles against my cheek.

Grimm.

"You were dreamin' again," he tells me in a whisper that instantly soothes me. "You're safe." His thumb moves across my cheek to wipe away my tears. I must have been crying in my sleep, and I feel a little less tainted now he's touched me there.

"You're okay now," he reassures me again.

But I know that I'm not, how can I ever be if I keep going back there?

"He tattooed himself each time." The words tumble out of

my mouth without my permission and Grimm scrunches his forehead at me, confused by my rambling.

"Twelve reminders, twelve tears, all tattooed on his hand." Grimm's eyes grow fierce.

"Who... who did this to you, Rogue?" His voice is soft, but his body is tense and I hate that I so desperately need him to hold me.

I can't need anyone. I don't function that way

"It doesn't matter now," I tell him honestly, because having Grimm close, the way he's touching me so gently seems like the only thing that does. The horrors of my past don't seem nearly as bad when he's comforting me.

"No one will ever hurt you again," he promises. And although I made that promise to myself a long time ago, Grimm saying it makes me believe it could be true.

His head moves a little closer to mine, and his teeth dig into his bottom lip like he's holding himself back. They're so close to mine I can almost feel them.

"Sleep," he whispers, pulling away from me again. But instead of leaving completely, his arms wrap around me and his hips nudge me to make space for him beside me.

"I was jealous, earlier at the club, seeing you with that girl. I hated it," I admit. Jesus Christ, my mouth has a mind of its fucking own tonight.

"I know." His sharp answer doesn't even make me mad, how can it when drifting off in his arms makes me feel invincible again?

CHAPTER 15

1% MC

GRIMM

I manage to slide out of bed without waking Rogue, and after a cold shower, I head straight down to the club.

"Mornin," Troj nods his head at me as I pass him in the foyer. He's got some bitch following him down the stairs and he's looking pleased with himself.

"You know where Prez is?" I ask.

"He was in one of the rooms." Troj peers upwards to the landing. "You sort that shit out with Rogue last night?" he checks, with a smug grin on his face.

"I took care of it."

"Adrian was telling me that she used to be a regular," he informs me, and I try my best to keep my reaction off my face. Thoughts of Rogue letting other men look at her like that makes me fucking crazy mad.

"Like I said, I took care of it, she won't be giving us the slip again," I assure him, though I ain't convinced of that myself. Rogue is an untamable creature. One I fear I'll never understand.

I find Prez upstairs in the dining hall, eating a breakfast that Marilyn must have cooked up.

"You hungry, darlin'?" she calls out to me from the hatch of the huge industrial kitchen, and I shake my head back at her.

"Grimm." Prez wipes his mouth with a paper napkin and waits for me to speak.

"You got anything for me?" I ask before he has the chance to bring up last night too.

"Nah, we're on top of everything for now." He takes a sip of his coffee.

"It doesn't have to be a clean up, I'll take anything. I just need to be outta here for a day or two." Prez was the one to tell me himself that I should take a break. Well this is me askin'.

"The girl's gettin' to ya, huh?" He makes a gravelly laugh before taking a sip from his tiny espresso cup.

"I just ain't used to sharing my space, and she isn't exactly cooperative on my boundaries," I explain.

"I get she ain't easy. Troj told me 'bout last night. I got a couple of brothers heading outta state later this mornin'. It's an overnighter at Lincoln to meet a buyer for some of the Utah supplies we're storing, if you want in?"

"Sounds good." I nod. "What about Rogue? She's a flight risk." As much as I need some space, I can't risk her leaving the compound again, especially with me not here.

"I'll put Thorne on to her, ain't much gets past him. Go pack a bag, Brax is leading the boys out around eleven."

I know she's gonna be mad at me for running away from her again, but I have little choice. I can feel all the bad brewing inside me. It's only a matter of time before I crack and the evil seeps out of me. I can't have Rogue know what I really am.

AGED 14

"Shit." Mama cursing must mean something bad happened, and when I rush down the stairs, I find her in tears.

"What's wrong?" I ask, it's unlike her to cry when Dad isn't around

"Your father will be home in ten minutes and I haven't lit the

fire. I cut my finger while I was chopping the vegetables for dinner and it set me off schedule. I haven't even split the logs for tonight."

"Relax, I got it," I assure her, picking up the wood basket and making my way out the back door. I place the basket on the floor and look for the ax, but it's not in its usual place and after a good search around the yard, I realize it's nowhere to be seen. I turn my head toward Father's shed when a thought comes into my head. He forbids anyone from going in there, and it's been at least a week since he's had an excuse to reprimand Mama. I wouldn't be surprised if he's put it in there on purpose. So he can punish Mama for either not having the fire ready or for invading his 'privacy'.

I rush over to the shed, I'll take the consequences if I have to. He'll have to beat me for breaking the rules and, as much as Mama will hurt, at least she won't be the one who gets pounded. I feel around under the plant pot for the key that I know he keeps hidden there, and when I locate it, I open the door and let myself inside.

I set to work looking for the ax but get distracted when my eyes catch the red toolbox on the floor, tucked under his workbench. It's shiny and immaculate, and considering all Father's tools are hung in size order, I wonder what he has inside it. Checking over my shoulder for any sign of his car coming up the lane, I quickly pull it out, lift the lid and peek inside. There are dozens of polaroid photographs, I didn't even know we had a polaroid camera, and as I flick through them my fingers shake when I realize what these photographs are of. They all contain women. Some clothed, some not. Some are bound and gagged while others have their arms free. But they all share one very crucial thing in common.

They are all lifeless.

My breath feels trapped in my chest as I continue to stare at the photographs, and when I come to a face I recognize, the suspicion that I've carried around for almost a year is confirmed.

Two days after I caught my dad screwing Mrs. Hopewell into her kitchen worktop, our town held a vigil for her. When Mr. Hopewell, Kaleb, and his sons returned from their fishing trip that day, she had vanished without a trace.

Of course in a small town, there were many rumors. The most popular being that she ran out on them to be with another man. Nobody talks much about her now. But I've always wondered if my father had something to do with her disappearance.

I look at the photo in my hand and as her wide, soul-empty eyes stare back at me, I realize I'd been right. I drop it back into the box, slam the lid shut, and kick it back under the workbench.

There can be only one reason why my father has these photographs. He did this to these women. He hurt them and this is the evidence of it. This could put him away. This could save Mama and me from his evil hands.

"What are ya doing in here, boy?" My body freezes when I hear his voice and when I slowly turn my body around to face him, he's looking furious.

"I was… I need the ax to chop the wood." I quickly pull myself together.

He reaches his hand down beside the door where the ax is propped and picks it up. Staring at me coldly as he passes it to me.

"Did you like what you saw?" he asks casually. I can't remember a time when he's ever sounded so interested in me.

"I don't know what you're talking about, sir." I keep my eyes rooted to the floor.

"The women in the box, the photographs you were looking at. Did you like them?"

I shake my head in response, feeling the tears in my eyes building when I think about Todd and Kaleb. Their mama didn't deserve what happened to her. I could have stopped it. I was there that day.

"We all have our reason for being here, Richie. God has a purpose for all of us. This is mine." I remain still as he moves toward me, bracing myself to take the repercussions of being caught. But instead, he reaches down beside me and pulls out the box, placing it on his workstation and carefully opening the lid.

"This one," he picks up one of the photos, the woman in it is scrawny and covered in bruises. "She worked the streets, solicited herself. She had no respect for herself or her body." He places it down and pulls up another one. "Henrietta, she used her beauty to manipulate men into giving her what she wanted. A grade-A student, who couldn't even file a document in the correct drawer." He laughs to himself as he reaches for another photograph, the one of Mrs. Hopewell. "Ahhh, Julia Hopewell. You remember her. She was a temptress who used her eyes to lure good, honest men like me into temptation."

I don't say a word. I couldn't if I wanted to. Why is he doing this, why is he taunting me with these photographs like I should be impressed by them?

"God placed a little evil into all of us, it's there to tempt and test our restraint... But for some of us, it's there to do his work." He snaps the box shut and clears his throat. The ax is slipping through my sweaty palm, and I swallow down the urge to swing it at his head.

"Go chop the wood, boy, then clean up for supper. It's pot roast night." He smiles at me, he actually smiles, and I clutch the ax handle in my hand and quickly make my way back to the log pile. The air in the shed was so stuffy I could feel myself choking on it and when I get out into the fresh air, I try to fill my lungs with fresh, clean oxygen.

"You can start with Mark 11:25." Father hands me the book after supper and I resist the temptation to snatch the thing out of his hands.

"And when you stand praying, if you hold anything against anyone…" I look him square in the eyes. *I don't need to look at the words. This is a passage Father has me read often "…forgive them, so that your Father in heaven may forgive you your sins."*

The prayer I'll be saying tonight will ask that if there is a God, and He really has the power that His book says He does, then may He strike my father dead on the spot for being evil. For killing those women, and for making Mama suffer. And if God doesn't act, then I'll have to use the little bit of evil that He put inside me.

I'll become a sinner, and send my father to his judgment.

I will end him if I have to.

"Thanks for bringing me here." I bat my lashes at Thorne when he parks his truck outside my house.

"Ain't no bother. Skid don't want you goin' out alone, that don't make you a prisoner. You want me to come inside with ya?" he checks.

"I think I got it." I wink, hopping out the truck and making my way across my front lawn.

I'm sick of getting by with the bare essentials in Grimm's kitchen, and I need to grab some more clothes.

Unlocking the door, I toss the keys onto the side table and flick through the mail I picked up from the mailbox for anything important, and I stop when I see a postal stamp that I recognize.

The one that always drags the guilt out of me.

I've had a number of these over the years, only ever when he needs something from me. He'll either want me to smuggle something in, or to get in touch with someone for him. Whatever it is, I've never let him down. Tearing open the envelope, I'm not surprised to find that it's a visiting order.

I quickly shove the letter into my back pocket and move to the kitchen. I can worry about it later.

Packing up what I need, I move through to my bedroom and grab myself some more clothes.

For some reason, I stop and take time to look at Mama's

photo as I pass it in the hall. I see a resemblance between us. I wasted a lot of my childhood hoping she'd come back and rescue me. Now, I detest her just as much as I do them.

AGED 8

"Go to your room, honey," Mama tells me. I've woken up and walked into the living room after a bad dream. I just want her to come and lie with me until I fall back to sleep again.

The room is clouded with smoke, and Daddy and his friends are drinking beer. One of them is drawing something on Frank's forearm with a loud machine that's making my head buzz. My mama looks nervous and urges me away with her eyes.

"She's okay, ain't ya, sweetheart?" Daddy's friend holds out his arms for me to go to him.

"Come give ya uncle Nick a hug." Daddy pats me on the head as he gets out of his chair and heads into the kitchen, probably to fetch more beers.

"I really think she should be going to sleep." Mama takes my hand and drags me away, but Uncle Nick's arm is wrapped around me tight, crushing me into his lap.

"She's beautiful just like her mama, ain't she, Frank?" I don't like the way he's stroking my leg, but I like that he thinks I look like Mama. She really is beautiful.

"Bed, Evangeline." I look over to my dad, and he doesn't look happy, maybe he doesn't like it that Uncle Nick likes Mama so much.

I get up off Uncle Nick's lap and go back to my bedroom. I try to sleep but the men are being so loud that their laughter vibrates through the walls of my room. It's always like this when they come over. It started out just being weekends, but now it's every night and I know Mama doesn't like it. She just loves Daddy too much to stop him from having fun.

Eventually, the noise dulls down and is replaced with snoring. Daddy is always the first one to pass out. He gets real tired these days, and his eyes are always so sad and distant.

When my door creaks open, I freeze until I feel a warm hand rub gently over my back.

"Sleep, honey," Mama's calming voice whispers to me. She's come to me at last and now she's gonna lie with me until I fall asleep, just like I want her to.

"I love you so much, Evangeline," she tells me, and I don't mind that her words come out a little slurry, or that she smells of the strange stuff they all smoke from Daddy's pipe. Just having her close is a comfort.

"I'm sorry that this is the life I've given you. It wasn't supposed to be like this." I close my eyes and relax with her words. I don't bother to tell her that I'm just happy to have her with me. That it doesn't matter that she sleeps most of the day and I have to get myself up for school. I love the time we spend together even if it's just watching TV while we wait for Daddy and his friends to get back from the bar.

"One day I'll make all this right," she promises.

I nod my head sleepily, I believe her, and I can't wait. Maybe I can help her make things better. I'm already big enough to do chores around the house.

I let my eyes close and my mind be free because I have my mama here with me and one day, she's gonna make things better for us.

That night was the last time I ever heard her voice. The next morning I found her note. It said that she didn't love Daddy anymore and that one day she'd be back for me.

But she never did come back, and Daddy lost his mind.

He got worse. Stopped going to work, his friends came over more often and he took more of the stuff that makes him sleep. Uncle Nick told me that Mama had a sickness. That what she needed, Daddy couldn't give her any more, and not to get my hopes up on her coming back for me.

I should have listened to him because he was right. I did some research a few years ago. Police had found her body when they raided a crack den a few miles outta town. I hadn't seen her in eleven years, and all that time she'd been so close. Not once had she ever thought to check in on me.

Sure, my dad may not be perfect, but at least he didn't abandon me. Not by choice anyway.

I pull the letter outta my pocket and take another look at it. I could ask Grimm to take me, but that would raise questions. It's kinda ironic that I don't like the idea of that, considering the lengths I'm going through to uncover his family secrets.

Everyone has skeletons in their closets, last thing I want is to be letting him in on any more of mine.

"What's taking so long?" Thorne's voice comes from the front door. I spin around, quickly shoving the visiting order back inside my pocket.

Thorne's looking impatient. It's a good look on him.

"I'm all done." I lift my bag of clothes off the floor, and give him a wide smile as I walk past the kitchen and grab the box of kitchen equipment I'm taking back.

Being the gentleman that he is, Thorne takes the box out of my hands and looks a little surprised after he's looked at its contents.

"You try mashing potatoes with a fork," I tell him, and he shakes his head and huffs a laugh at me.

"What's so funny?"

"Just never had you down as the domesticated type," he grins.

Thorne's a real handsome guy, in a hot, daddy fetish kinda way. With his grey hair and matching stubble, I imagine he could do some real damage to a girl's heart.

"Far from it. But a girl's gotta survive." I lift the wooden rolling pin out of the box and hold it up in front of him. He stares it up and down with a smirk, and after I drop it back into the box, he follows me back out to the truck.

"Skid, you're on speakerphone." Prez places the phone down on the table in front of him while we all sit in our seats and listen.

"Good, Jessie, I got another job for your girl," Skid's voice booms out from the speaker. "I've done some digging of my own on the guys in the picture. Turns out they're cookin'. Not in Manitou Springs so technically it ain't our business. But I figure since one of them showed up on Rogue's doorstep…"

"It makes it our problem, brother," Prez interrupts, to remind him that just because he ain't sitting in his chair, doesn't mean he ain't still a part of this fucked up family.

"She ain't helping though, Skid. Whatever her involvement is with these men, she's keeping her cards tight to her chest."

"Talkin' ain't her style." I hear the snigger in Skid's voice, and not one of us sat around this table don't wish he weren't here so we could see it.

"Jess, can you ask Mads to check out the address for me? I also got a cell number on one of their dealers. I'll message it though," he adds.

"On it," Jessie promises. "We'll be in touch soon as Maddy has more information. In the meantime, if you need anything…"

"I know, and I appreciate," Skid says before hanging up the phone.

"Jessie, you stick with Maddy, I wanna know as soon as she gets a trace on that cell number. Grimm, you did good on that job for the Russians yesterday. How did our new Prospect deal?"

"Let's just say shiftin' stiff ain't his forte." I light up a smoke and smirk to myself when I recall him throwing up on the whole journey back from Denver. I never did make it to Lincoln with the others, a job came up that required my expertise and since we're all about keeping the Russians happy these days, it took priority.

"Somebody must have really fucked you up." Squealer looks at me and shakes his head just before Prez slams down the gavel.

We all make our way outta church, and straight to the bar. I notice that the garage is closed now, and I hope Rogue is in my cabin. I take a seat beside Tac and Thorne at the bar and Storm places a bottle of bud in front of me.

"You feeling better, kid?" Tac reaches over the bar and ruffles his hair.

"No, shit was nasty. Remind me never to fuck off a Russian." Storm pours them both a bourbon and then heads off to serve Troj. The club gets busier as the night goes on. It's too crowded, and there seem to be a lot more hangouts than usual here tonight. I'm starting to feel suffocated.

"You need a hand?" I hear her voice before I see her and when I turn my head, I realize that she's talking to Storm. Rogue rounds the bar and lifts up the hatch, starting to serve drinks like she's been doing it her whole damn life. She's a natural, and I hate the way every man in the fuckin' building is eyeing her up like fresh fuckin' meat.

"You tapped it yet?" Squealer creeps up behind me, and when I look over my shoulder and see the way he's looking at her, it makes me wanna cause him physical fucking pain.

"It ain't like that, I'm just taking care of her for Skid." I clench the bottle tight in my hand.

"Just how well you takin' care of her...? You know, the way

she's shaking that cute little ass behind that bar is gonna give brothers the wrong impression on why she's here," he taunts.

"What was that, Squeal?" Rogue comes over right on cue, looking him over and rolling that tongue of hers on the inside of her cheek.

"Just speakin' to Grimm here about you helping out."

"Storm was struggling, so I'm helping. That ain't an issue, is it?" She widens her pretty blue eyes innocently. I still don't know why she came down here in the first place. Rogue never hangs out at the clubhouse. I don't like her down here. She doesn't belong among these people. I want her back in my space, where no one can be thinking about her with their dirty, decrepit thoughts.

"Ain't no issue. You're free game, darlin'. No claim, no blame…" The way Squealer looks at me when he says that throws down a challenge, and I snigger and look away, refusing to give him a rise.

"I'm not game, and I'm certainly no one's to claim," Rogue snaps back at him.

"Prove it," he dares her, his huge tattooed arms leaning forward to rest on the bar and his nose just inches away from her chest. He looks up at her seductively and the smile she gives him back is darker than the devil's asshole.

"Oh, I'll prove it, to all of you." Rogue's attention is directed at me now and her eyes scorch, stirring up all the temptation inside me to rein her the fuck in from whatever it is she's thinking about doing.

She moves out from behind the bar, swaying her hips as she makes her way toward the stage. No one ever really uses it anymore, it's just something that's always been here. Years ago, this place had been a vacation site and this had been the entertainment hall. Now, it looks like Rogue is about to make herself the main event.

I watch her pull herself up onto the stage, ignoring the way

Squealer smiles victoriously beside me.

She isn't exactly dressed for the occasion, but she still looks hotter than sin. In a pair of cut-off jeans and the shirt of mine that she's got tied up around her waist.

I'm not sure who's in charge of the music, but I'm about ready to slit their fucking throat when the track playing changes to something more seductive and moody.

Rogue begins to move, in the same way she would have at The Orchid Lounge if I hadn't been there to stop her. But Rogue isn't there now. She's on our territory. She's safe and I have no reason to stop her from shaking that ass of hers, other than my own selfish ones.

The girl knows how to test me, she wants me to give her the same reaction as I had then and I can feel my restraint snapping when I sense the eye of every fucker in the club on her.

She moves slowly, untying my shirt and creasing it up in her hand. Then teases when she fists it between her legs. I lean forward and rest my elbows on the bar, watching her undo the buttons on her bottoms. She's waiting for me to stop her, she wants me to break and admit that I don't like what she's doing. Part of me wonders if she wants me to prove her wrong, and claim her, here and now with everyone watching.

But I won't break. I can't break.

She tosses the shirt off stage and runs her hands over her body like she's getting herself off. Then when she slides her hand into the waist of her denims, it earns her a roar from her audience.

Squealer looks like a fucking kid at Christmas, and I lean in just close enough for him to hear me.

"You may be a fuck ton bigger than me, but I'm smart, Squeal. You kill those thoughts from your head or I'll make sure your dick goes into retirement way before it's fucking time," I warn him.

"Calm down, kiddo, let's just enjoy the fucking show." He

winks and nods his head toward the stage where Rogue has pulled open her shorts, revealing her hot-pink panties.

"If I were you, I'd be focusing all them smarts you got into reining that little cray cray the fuck in." He smacks me on the back before leaving me to join his brother, who's also watching the show intently, getting his cock sucked by Paige.

It's a slow, torturous three minutes before the song ends. Thankfully, Rogue doesn't strip down any further than her underwear, which I guess is a small mercy.

She's still tying my shirt around her waist when she comes back to the bar looking mighty proud of herself.

"Can I get ya something, Grimm?" she asks with a sarcastic bite that has me biting on the inside of my cheek.

I ignore her and do the only thing I can think of that's gonna take the edge off. Pulling the baggy out my pocket, I shake out a small line on the arch of my hand, then inhale.

Feeling the rage calm, and my body take on a new kinda buzz, Rogue watches me from the end of the bar. Clearly getting her own high out of the effect she's having on me.

The night goes on and I drink more whiskey and snort more blow. Rogue purposely makes nice with all the other brothers, glancing over at me every once in a while, waiting for me to snap. She doesn't know that I'm the master of my control. That I've spent the past nine years practicing self-restraint.

"Hey, don't I know you from somewhere?" one of the hangouts calls over at her from across the bar, and I notice how she looks a little less confident when she sees him.

Shaking her head, she quickly gets back to serving.

"Yeah, I do. You used to work out at The Orchid Lounge." The guy isn't giving in, and I can see Rogue getting increasingly frustrated. She leaves the bar to go pick up some glasses, and when she comes back and places a load on the bar, the fucker goes too far and puts his hands on her.

His hand wraps around her wrist, forcing her back tight onto his body. The glass I'm holding is close to shattering in the fist I make around it, and my blood flushing past my ears dulls out any music. She struggles to get free from him and shakes her head at whatever he's whispering inside her ear. When she does manage to wriggle herself free, she immediately gets back to work.

"Ain't nothing but a cheap slut anyway," he yells out at her, and the insult forces me up off my stool.

The cunt doesn't see me coming, and I grab the back of his head and slam it down hard into the bar, all the empty glasses Rogue has picked up smash, and I feel their sharp shards cut into my knuckles. When I pull his head back up, I decide he isn't bleeding enough, so I slam it back into the bed of broken glass. I hold him down until he begs, then I add a little bit more pressure to the palm that's keeping him pinned before I wrench him back up again.

"Apologize," I order. Rogue is staring right at us, her mouth open, and her pretty blue eyes wide.

"I... I'm sorry," he stutters, sounding as sincere as a man can when his face is shredded to pieces. Releasing him, I look around at the mess I've made, then narrow my eyes at Rogue before I get the hell out of there.

Once outside, I suck in the fresh air, hoping it might extinguish the fire in my chest. My fists are stiff balls of tension. I'm not nearly finished with that asshole back inside but I also suspect that had I stayed any longer, I would have killed him.

"Hey, what was all that shit about?" Troj chases out after me, and I shrug him off when he places a hand on my shoulder. I don't offer him any answers, just stare into the flames that are dancing from the fire pit. Troj joins me in the silence. Patiently waiting for me to be ready with an explanation.

"He called her a slut," I growl after some time has passed. "Rogue ain't no fuckin' slut. I don't know who he is, but I never wanna see him around here again."

"Chill, man, he ain't no one, just a dumb hangout. Squealer and Screwy are seeing him on his way now."

Right on cue, the club doors burst open and the mouthy prick's body gets launched outside, followed by the temper twins who each take their turn to kick him in the ribs.

"Don't think he'll be showing his face around here anytime soon." Troj laughs as we watch the fucker scurry onto his feet and get into his car. I doubt he's in any fit state to drive, I really fucked up his face. I'm surprised he can even see. Still, I guess he'd rather take his chances than stick around here, and his wheels skid up the gravel as he speeds off.

"Take it easy, brother." Troj pats my back, before heading back inside and grabbing himself one of the girls that are hanging around by the door watching the latest drama. He drapes his arm over her shoulder and whispers something to her that makes her giggle.

The flames enchant me, somehow managing to ease the loud thumping in my head. I watch the hot flickers grow, thinking how they have the potential to do so much damage if uncontrolled.

"That was really sweet, what ya did back there," Rogue's voice interrupts my thoughts, causing my heart rate to automatically pick back up again.

"I wasn't gonna have him talk to you like that." I keep my focus on the flames and the pile of ash that's building beneath them. Too fucking scared to look at her.

"Take me home, Grimm." She stands her body in front of mine and holds out her hand. I dare myself to look up at her, and when I do, I realize she's lost all her sass. Her eyes hold a calm I've never seen there before, and taking her hand in mine, I let her pull me onto my feet, really enjoying the smiles she makes for me. When I lead her over to my bike, I don't give a fuck who's around to see when I put her on the back of it. Then I take a steady ride back up to my cabin, where I know I can have her all to myself.

"You want something to eat?" she asks me, heading straight for the kitchen. I ignore her question, sliding a hand through my hair and taking a seat on the couch. I can't fucking eat, not while I'm so wound up. I'm far too angry to think about food. She shrugs back at me and potters around my kitchen looking for something to do with herself.

"Why d'you do it?" I speak the question that's in my head out loud. Then I turn my head to look at her when I realize that I have to know the answer.

"Why?" I repeat.

She raises her shoulders like it's no big deal. But it ain't good enough.

"I saw that what that guy said hurt you... But the way you act, the way you crave attention, Rogue... Guys are gonna be thinking they can treat you that way."

"Were you jealous of the way they watched me?" She ignores my question and steps closer. Starting to sway her hips the same way she had on the club stage, her focus is all on me and I like how it feels, even if it is a torture. She slowly undoes the buttons of my shirt that she's wearing, and after she takes it off, she tosses it onto my lap. I grab it in my fist and stand so my body is flush to hers, and then I look down my nose into those desperate, pretty eyes.

"Maybe if you stop acting like you're worthless, Rogue, you might start to see yourself a little better." I crush my shirt tight into her body, then back away from her and head to the bathroom. I need to lock myself away from her. Her naked skin is far to fuckin' tempting.

"And what if that's exactly what I am, Grimm? Worthless," she calls out after me,

"We both know that ain't true..." I don't turn around, just slam the door behind me.

CHAPTER 18

He isn't in the cabin when I wake up, and I know that he'll spend the day trying to avoid me after what went down last night. I can't face another day of that, so I decide to go somewhere where I can be close to him... without him realizing. I open his wardrobe and flick through my clothes for something appropriate to wear.

I don't want to be Maddy when I visit Anita today. I want to be Evangeline, or at least the girl Evangeline might have been without all the fucked up shit in between.

Deciding on a pair of jeans and an oversized sweater, I leave the cabin and take Skid's car again. This time when I drive past the clubhouse, it's bustling with people. Everyone seems to be getting their instructions from Prez and are so wrapped up in what he's saying that I manage to sneak out right under their noses.

I drive to the care home, wondering what today's visit will reveal about Richie Carter. Will I ever learn what happened to turn the sweet boy in the picture into the disturbed version of himself I'm becoming obsessed with?

Smiling at the woman behind the desk, I sign myself in and make my way to Mrs. Carter's room. She beams when she opens the door to me and pulls me in for a long hug that proves she's happy to see me again.

"I'm so glad you came back, Evangeline." She takes my hand, leading me over to the couch. "Shall I get someone to bring us some drinks, it's quite warm today. Perhaps some lemonade?"

I nod my head and watch her lift the receiver from the phone beside her.

"Two glasses of lemonade please," she requests, politely. Then after hanging up, she takes both my hands in hers.

"You must tell me what you have been up to," she asks excitedly, and my heart breaks for her. Whether this was an act for me, or a mental state she's trapped in, anyone can see that Anita Carter isn't living in the real world. I envy her for that a little bit, and I wonder if Grimm plays along with it when he visits?

"I've been busy with work."

"You didn't tell me what you did when you were last here," she reminds me.

"I fix up cars."

Mrs. Carter throws her head back and laughs. "A pretty girl like you, fixing cars. That's quite the vision." She chuckles, and I like that it amuses her. The smile she's giving me back is genuine.

The door knocks not long after, and a woman wearing a white tunic like the rest of the staff steps in. It must cost a fortune to keep someone in a place like this, where residents get to make such demands.

"Thank you," Anita smiles at the carer before she leaves. Then passes me a tall glass of lemonade from the silver tray.

"So how long have you been fixing cars?"

"For as long as I can remember, I used to watch my daddy when I was small." Saying his name reminds me that I still have a visiting order that needs to be dealt with.

"My husband doesn't have much time for Richie, I'm afraid, he works too hard. Sometimes I think Richie would like a father who shows him how to do things like that." Her mind seems to wander off, but I need to keep her on the subject of her son.

"And do you see Richie's father often?" I take a sip of the fancy lemonade.

"He was the first man I ever loved. The only man I've ever loved." She's becoming distant now. Like she's trying to recall memories.

"Do you have someone, Evangeline? I see you're not married." Her eyes fall to my hand and I laugh.

"No, I'm not married."

"But there is someone, no?"

"There's someone," I admit. "I'm not all that sure how he feels about me though."

"My dear girl, you're beautiful, he'd have to be blind not to be over his heels in love with you."

"It's complicated." I smile back at her, if only she knew how fuckin' complicated.

"Well, if you're unsure, you must ask him. My guess is that he feels unworthy." Her hand strokes over my cheek and I find myself leaning into it.

"I wish my son could find a girl like you, I sometimes worry that he'll never find his happiness." My heart leaps at the opportunity to talk about Grimm.

"What makes you think that?"

"My Richie's a quiet boy, he doesn't have a lot to say, and he likes things a certain way. There aren't many that would accept him the way he is. But if someone gave him that chance. They'd see what I see."

"And what do you see?" I can feel my pulse beating faster as I wait for her to tell me.

"Fierce loyalty. A loving heart that has hardened but is still repairable. If he found the right person to heal it." She looks at me in a way that has me worried, like she's somehow figured me out, but then her eyes turn vacant again.

"You must tell the person you like how you feel. Life's far too short for complicated, Evangeline." I nod her a silent promise and decide that I have every intention on keeping it.

I spend the next hour enjoying Anita's company. Surprised when she freely opens her patio doors and leads me out onto the well-presented lawns. She ignores the other patients that roam around us like her mind blanks them out. I admire the flowers that she proudly tells me she's grown herself because they're her husband's favorite. I even compliment the vegetable patch that she tells me he spends all his spare time working on.

When it's time for me to leave, she kisses me on each cheek and makes me promise to visit again soon. I've almost made it out of the reception door when a female voice calls after me.

"I'm sorry… Evangeline." She checks the logbook in her hand.

"Yes," I give her a Maddy smile in the hope she'll buy whatever lie I'm about to tell her.

"Your relationship to our patient hasn't been logged for either of your visits. Are you a relation of Mrs. Carter's?" She seems unsuspecting, so I play along.

"I'm Anita's niece."

"Of course." The woman fills in the blank and closes the book. "You have a good day, and we look forward to seeing you again soon. Your visits have a very positive effect on your auntie."

I take the compliment like any loving niece would, and be on my way.

There are no bikes parked up outside the club when I return and I head straight up to the cabin. My mood bouncy as I listen to the radio and dice up some chicken for later.

I'm sitting out on the deck enjoying a well-deserved joint when I hear the cabin door slam shut. Grimm looks tired, his hand rubbing over his face and unsettling his fringe makes me want to fucking jump him.

He steps out to join me on the deck, and I'm surprised when he actually takes the joint out my hand when I offer it to him. Drawing back hard, he releases the smoke from his lungs in a long, satisfied breath that makes my pussy tense.

"Tough day, honey?" I ask cheerily as he passes it back to me, sitting his ass on the floor and leaning his back against the wooden railings.

"Just club shit," he says, letting his head fall back.

"You wanna talk about it?"

"No."

"You wanna eat?"

"Yeah." When he looks back at me, his lips pick up into a lopsided smile, one that makes me so fucking happy I feel my heart skip.

"Well come on then." I stand up in front of him and hang my hand in front of his face, and he snorts a cute little laugh before taking it.

I don't know what I've done, but I've somehow managed to change his mood. I made him smile, and I can't remember ever being happier about something.

We eat our meal in silence, I can see how tired he is from the dark rings under his eyes, and I wonder what's been going on with the club that's taking so much out of him. When we finish eating, he clears up our plates and I let him do his usual routine, despite the fact I'd made sure the kitchen was spotless before he got home so I'd get more time with him.

"I got to go back down to the club, we got church before Prez and Jessie ride out," he tells me, pulling his cut back on.

"Grimm..." It's now or never. I'm about to make good on that promise I made his mama.

"Do you like me?" I hate how pathetic I sound, like some needy eighth-grader talking to her crush. Grimm scrunches his forehead at my question.

"You wouldn't be here if I didn't like you," he answers, looking as serious as a fuckin' heart attack.

"Then why don't you want me?" The question tumbles from my lips and I regret it immediately. Even if I do really want to know the answer.

"I'm doing you a favor," he tells me, then quickly turns and walks out before I can question him any more. His response gives me a tiny glimmer of hope, but at the same time, it crushes me.

I get home late and wake up early. Lying beside Rogue all night takes a lot of self-control. I already had to get up at 3am to beat one out in the bathroom.

But I know I'm doing the right thing. She needs to be protected from me.

AGED 15

"I've got plans for us today, son." My father stares at me over the breakfast table and I watch a look of contentment creep onto Mama's face. "Go get yourself ready," he orders, and I quickly get up from the table and head straight for my room. It's probably going to be more chores, perhaps the fences over at the farm need fixing up again. So I throw on a pair of jeans and an old T-shirt then lace up my boots.

Father remains silent as we drive out of town and arrive at an abandoned scrap yard. The gates are rusty and I watch Father get out the car and take some keys out of his pocket, he unlocks the chain wrapped around them and drags them open, before jumping back in the car and driving through. I want to ask him why he's got the key to this place. It's full of old cars and scrap metal, and there's a tire pile almost as tall as our house. The whole place is so disorganized it makes me twitchy. I can't imagine what it must be doing to him.

I remain quiet, this is probably his latest project. Another opportunity for him to appear a pillar of the community.

"Do you remember your grandad?" he asks me after he parks between two of the storage containers.

"Barely," I answer, the air fresheners in the car are so strong they make me feel sick.

"This place used to belong to him and his brother," he explains, his fingers tapping at the wheel. "It got left to me after they both died."

This is news to me, Father is a broker. I could never imagine him working at a place like this.

"I worked a few summers here when I was a kid, but I hated it. I was angry at them for leaving me the burden of the place." Hearing Dad open up like this is odd, he never talks about his family or his feelings. "But I made the best out of the situation, as I do with all eventualities, Richie." He stares out through the windshield and when he goes to speak again, he hesitates.

"Those women in the photographs..." he starts, and the images flashback into my mind. I've thought about them a lot since seeing them. In fact, I've even let myself into his shed to look at them again a few times. Call me sick and twisted but there's something beautiful about each and every one of them. Something that entices me back. I wonder what their stories are, where they came from, how they sinned. I wonder if Father fucked them all, the way he did Mrs. Hopewell before he ended her.

"I know you think bad of me, but that's because you don't understand. The Lord gives me this strength, He allows me rage and when that happens, I have to lash out. I don't want to hurt your Mom. She's a good woman, a good wife. She's worthy. So to protect her I have to use the power He gives me to do good. I

rid the world of those that taint it." He takes a deep breath through his nostrils. "And once I'm gone, Richie, it's going to be your responsibility. God has chosen you like He chose me. I already see it in you. You hold that anger inside you. I hear it scream to come out. I saw it in the way you looked at the women in those photographs. You won't be able to hold it in forever, and if you're not careful you will cause the wrong people pain. I can help you control it. I can help you hide it… Because those that aren't chosen don't understand." He looks at me now, his eyes focused.

"We'll do this to protect your mother, to protect ourselves, and to save our souls." He gets out of the car and comes round to open my door. I keep my eyes on his as I get out and follow him toward the storage locker. He takes the keychain out of his pocket and opens the huge steel door. And when I see what's inside, I don't know how I manage not to gag.

Lying on the floor is a woman, a beautiful woman with her arms and legs bound. She's naked, and her body is cut and bruised. Father kneels down in front of her and strokes his hand through her curly brown hair. "Evil always finds the most beautiful of vessels."

"You did this to her?" I ask, looking down at the ruined body. Her throat's been slit and she's lying in a pool of her own blood.

"In the Lord's name, son. This woman may have the look of an angel but she carries the devil's soul."

"You can't… You can't do this to people." I shake my head as I watch him.

"I don't have a choice, Richie. The power's inside me, God gave it to me for a reason. I'm going to help you control yours. I'm going to teach you." He stands up and steps toward me. His hands are bloody from touching her and I take a step back from him.

"No… I don't have whatever it is. I don't want to hurt

anybody." That's a lie, because I've thought plenty about hurting him.

"Not yet, but you will and I, as your father, must teach you how to deal with these situations efficiently."

"In the other storage container, you will find everything we need to clean any traces of the girl being here away. We will dispose of her body and then we'll be home in time for supper."

"I don't want to do this." I can feel my body shaking, why do I find the girl so pretty, even in death. I'm sick."

"You haven't got a choice. This is God's gift. What I do to these women keeps your Mama safe. Because the power is strong. So strong that it can strike at any time. This is how I control it. Now, we are going to need to wrap her body so we don't get blood in the trunk. There's a roll of black plastic in the other lock-up."

He hands me a key with his clean hand and I take it. It's contaminated with his germs and I can feel the grime of it on my skin. I want to scream. I want to throw the key at the steel wall and run. To scrub my hands clean of his sin. But if this is what it's gonna take to protect Mama. I'm gonna have to play my part.

"Morning." Rogue stands in front of me, my T-shirt only just covering her hips and her long legs on full view.

"Morning." I scrub my hand over my face, that smile she's wearing does weird shit to me.

"So... I'm all caught up with work at the garage, and far as I'm aware, no one got killed yesterday. You wanna hang out today?" She's enthusiastic, and as appealing as it sounds, there's no chance I can be around her for an entire day without losing my head.

Especially if she's planning on being dressed like that.

"I got somewhere I need to be." Standing up, I squeeze

through the space she's left between her and the door, and she does a real shit job of hiding the disappointment from her face.

I head straight down to the club to find Jessie. I need some kinda time frame on how long I'm gonna have to tolerate my house guest.

"Any news?" I ask when I find him.

"Prez got an informer, someone who's a regular at the bar where they all hang. Apparently, they can get loose-lipped after a few." I nod, hoping to hell whoever this informer is will come through.

Once the threat is gone, everything can go back to how it was.

"You look like shit," Jessie tells me.

"I'm tired."

"Bitch too much for you to handle?" He grins at me.

"I got things covered, but the sooner all this shit is over and I can go back to dealing with the dead, the better."

"Won't be long, club wants to clear this shit up quick."

"Soon as you get something, you let me know," I tell him before getting back on my bike and heading away from the compound. I don't know where I'm heading, just that staying away from her will make things easier.

CHAPTER 20

1% MC

ROGUE

"Come on in." Maddy is balancing Nyx and Ella's brat on her hip when she opens the door to me. "What can I do for you?" She looks like she's got her hands full.

"I was just wondering if you wanted to hang out?"

God, how desperate has my life become?

"Um sure," Maddy looks as surprised as I'd been when I came up with the idea. But I'm gonna get cabin fever if I don't find some way to occupy myself.

"Ella had a rough night last night so I'm watching the little guy for her." Maddy places him down in the playpen she's got set up beside her couch, and I stick out my tongue at the little thing when he smiles at me.

"I'm kinda backed up here looking into all this stuff for Skid. I doubt I'll be much fun," she admits, taking a seat at the table and blowing the stray strand of hair that's fallen over her eyes away.

"So put it off for a few hours, I was thinking maybe we could go down to the lake and do some daytime drinking. Grimm's bound to have some blow stashed at the cabin."

"As fun as that sounds..." Miss goody-two shoes clears her throat nervously, "...I really need to work, and Dylan isn't gonna take care of himself."

"Okay, so how about you put the kid in his wheels and we

take a walk down to the clubhouse. You look like you could use the break and fresh air is good for kids, right?"

"Are you gonna take no for an answer?" Maddy sighs, defeated

"Absolutely not." I grin back at her.

"Fine, let me grab a spare diaper and we'll go for a walk, but just for an hour. Skid really wants this taken care of." Maddy leaps up and sets to work, packing up a bag for the kid. Curiosity forces me to quickly scan the screen and see what she's been working on for Skid, and when I see the names she's got scribbled on her desk pad, I feel my bones shiver.

"You okay?" she checks, once she's got the little guy strapped inside his stroller.

"Fine." I quickly pull myself back together, standing up and making my way toward the door.

"You know, if you ever want to help me with my research. I'm always grateful to have another set of eyes."

"Don't push it, Maddy sunshine." I take the kid's little rucksack from her hand and sling it over my shoulder.

Jessie looks surprised to see us when we rock up at the clubhouse, and he rushes over to give Maddy a kiss, before making a fuss of the kid and ruffling up his hair. "What brings you down here, darlin'? Thought you were working on that job?"

"I was, but Rogue here wanted to hang out," she answers him back with a tight smile.

"Oh. That's... nice." Jessie looks at me and nods his head, trying to act enthusiastic instead of confused. "Me and Troj are just waiting on Prez, then we'll be riding out to Pueblo. We should only—"

"What business you got in Pueblo?" I interrupt. Those names on the paper, now this. The club must be on to something.

"Crystal meth, apparently that guy you butchered and his friends are running a lab out there," he tells me, his eyes scrutinizing me for a reaction.

"That's out of your jurisdiction, ain't it?"

"We've been picking up some of the Bastards' slack just lately. Pueblo is close enough to become our problem if a meth situation gets out of control."

"Whatever helps you sleep at night, I'm just looking to have some fun today, anyone around here remember how to do that?" I ask.

The door opens and soon as Sheriff Roswell comes through it, I can tell from the look on his face that there's something wrong. My thoughts immediately go to Grimm.

"What's up?" Jessie must sense the old guy's unease too, because he's suddenly on his guard and quickly clicks over to the girl serving behind the bar to fix the old man a drink.

"Here, take a seat." Maddy rushes to pull out a chair for him.

"I'll get you some water." She scurries toward the bar, but the redheaded girl who lives up at the cabins is already coming over with something much stronger.

He nods his gratitude at her and before she can step away, he grabs her wrist.

"It's actually you I've come to see." His words come out a little shaky, I can tell from his tone that he's about to give the girl bad news.

"You might wanna pour one of those for yourself, sweetheart."

"I'm on it." Troj gets up and heads to the bar, grabbing a tumbler and half-filling it with the first bottle his hand lands on, while we all wait on the Sheriff to speak again.

"I got a call earlier this morning, there was a body discovered in the parking lot behind Dillon's bar in town."

Jessie immediately has his hackles up, and I don't miss the look that passes between him and Troj.

"Is this a club problem, Roswell?"

"No, son, it isn't a club problem." He takes his eyes off the girl for a few moments to assure him.

"Abby," he turns back to her. "The body they found... it was Danny." Tears are welling up in his eyes as he delivers his blow, and the confused look on her face instantly drops into devastation, her hand slipping out of his.

"It can't be." She shakes her head in disbelief. "He's coming back for me, he promised."

"Abby." Maddy kneels beside the girl to comfort her.

"It's not true. Danny wouldn't die. He made me a promise. He loved me. I've been clean all this time, ready for when he comes back."

I think I might actually feel a tiny prickle in my empty chest for the girl.

"It can't be him, it's someone else. There's no way Danny would be in town and not have come for me. We'll clear this up right now. I can come identify the body. It won't be his."

"Darlin', I identified the body myself. It's Danny," Roswell tells her, his voice cracking as he closes his eyes.

Abby takes some time to let his words sink in. Reality hitting her like a fucking car crash in slow motion.

"I'm gonna get the person that did this," Roswell assures her.

"Wait, someone did this to him?" Her eyes widen, and her shaking hand lifts to cover her mouth.

"Come on, we should get you back to your cabin. I'll call Ella." Maddy rubs Abby's back.

"No." She pushes her away, and Jessie subtly shakes his head at Maddy, warning her to back down.

"Listen, darlin', you're in shock," Jessie takes over.

"You've come a long way these past few weeks, and I ain't gonna have you ruin your recovery by being in the wrong place right now. Let Maddy take you home, her and Ella will take care of you. I'll have Storm go pick up Gracie too if you want. We're all here for you."

"I want Danny." She stands up, suddenly marching to the bar and snatches up her purse.

"Where ya think you're goin'?" Troj stands up and blocks her path to the door.

"To numb out the pain."

"Not a chance." He stands firm in front of her.

"Out of my way. You can't stop me from leaving. It's against my human rights for you to keep me here." I can't help wanting to give the girl a hail fucking Mary for that one, but I sense the seriousness of the situation would make that inappropriate.

"If you're thinking of picking yourself up a fix…" I head over, nudging Troj out the way. "…You don't need to leave the compound to do that. There's heaps of shit around here."

"Rogue." Maddy bleats out my name like a nagging goat.

"If you think that getting high is gonna make all this go away then have at it." I've got the girl's attention now, her eyes seem a little less manic and her fingers have stopped scratching at her arm.

"But, there will still be a time when you crawl down from that high. Danny will still be dead, and the reality of that is gonna hit ya all over again," I assure her, watching as her bottom lip starts to tremble.

"I love him. He loved me. He told me. He promised he was gonna come back for me. That's why I've been straight. It's been hard, I've had to fight *so* damn hard, but I did it for him." She drops to her knees and sobs. Then I glance up at Troj hoping he'll take over, but all he does is shrug back at me helplessly. I guess I have to take care of it myself.

"But you did it. You did, because you're strong. Now stand up," I order, grabbing her arm and forcing her back onto her feet. "Danny is fucking dead. He's gone."

"Jesus Christ, Rogue." Troj runs his hand through his hair awkwardly.

"That's the reality of this situation, one that ain't gonna change no matter how high you get. Now you can put having to deal with it off for a few hours, maybe even a few days. Or you can let the people who care about you take care of you and help you heal."

The girl breaks into tears, throwing her arms around my neck, and I lightly tap my palm on her back when I've decided I've had enough. She still doesn't get the hint.

"Can you call Ella?" she mumbles weakly at Maddy, who finally comes over and relieves me.

"Take her on up to the cabin, we'll keep the kid with us 'til Nyx gets here," Jessie whispers to Maddy, handing her a set of keys, and as Maddy and Abby slowly walk toward the exit, Jessie looks at me with a real smug look on that pretty boy face of his.

"That was some real sound advice you just gave out. Maybe you should take it up yourself some time." He raises his eyebrows at me before straddling the chair beside Roswell and getting into a real serious conversation with him.

"Good work, Rogue." Troj slaps me on my back, the same way he would one of his brothers, before joining them at the table.

My cabin's empty when I get home, and with the news about Deputy Dan spreading around the club like wildfire, and since she ain't at the garage, I wonder if maybe Rogue is with the other girls over at Abby's cabin.

I seriously doubt it.

I go to my room to grab a fresh shirt and when I realize she's left the bed unmade, I can't leave without putting it straight. Tucking the sheet around the mattress on her side of the bed, I scowl when my hand slides over something hard and cool, and when I pull out the white revolver she's been concealing from me, I feel the rage inside me swell.

I don't know what's got me more scared. The fact that I know the girl's unhinged and has been sleeping beside me with a fully loaded weapon beneath her, or the fact she clearly doesn't trust that I'm capable of taking care of her.

I place the gun on the coffee table, then sit staring at it while I wait for her to come home. I want to see her reaction when she realizes I've found it and that she can't keep secrets from me.

She bustles through the door about an hour later, and if I wasn't so mad I'd be impressed by the fact she hangs up her jacket, rather than tossing it on the couch.

"Hey, wanna beer?" She heads straight for the fridge, failing to notice what I got laid out in front of me.

I hear the refrigerator rattle when she swings the door shut.

"You hear about that Deputy guy? Abby's pretty cut up about it." She makes four paces toward me before I hear her footsteps stop dead.

"Grimm." The way she speaks my name nervously has me twisting my head and giving her my attention.

"Why did you hide it?" I ask, seeing how she's staring at the gun and looking guilty. A lot like someone who's just been caught the fuck out.

"Why did you hide it?" I growl the question at her again.

"Everyone carries around here. I don't see what the big deal is." Trying to shrug it off as unimportant, she swipes the gun up off the table into her delicate little hand.

The thing fucking suits her perfectly. White casing with intricate detail etched into the chrome. Pretty, but fucking deadly.

"The big deal is you hiding it from me," I point out, the words almost getting trapped behind my teeth.

"What's the matter, Grimmy?" she giggles. "Worried I might put a bullet in your brain while you sleep?"

She takes a step closer to me and crouches her body over mine. "'Cause let me tell you, if I wanted you dead. You'd already be dead."

Satisfied that she's made her point she moves to walk away from me, but I'm far from done with this conversation. Standing up, my arm automatically reaches out and grabs at the waistband of her shorts, hauling her back to me.

Rogue moves just as fast, slamming her palm hard enough into my chest to force me back onto the couch and before I have the chance to protest, she fucking mounts me.

"You ever wonder what it would be like if your mind was silent?" she asks me, pulling the clip out from the base of the gun to check it's still loaded, and when she sees that it is, she snaps it back into place with the heel of her palm.

"Ever wish that all the bad shit up here would disappear?" She taps a finger to her temple at the same time that I feel the gun she's holding in her other hand press against mine.

"One bullet could take all that away. Set you free from all the pain and darkness."

I don't flinch, all I can focus on is Rogue's denim-covered pussy and how it's hovering above my painfully solid cock.

Bitch got every right to blow the brains out my skull for the things I'm thinking about doing to her.

She drags the cool metal down over my cheek and searches my face for a hint of emotion. But I deny her every single one of them. It isn't until she twists the weapon round on herself that I lose face and grip at the handle. Beneath my hand, hers is steady as a rock, and she keeps her eyes fixed on mine, holding me like a fucking prisoner as she reaches her mouth forward and slides her perfect pink tongue over the entire length of the barrel.

Bitch is gonna destroy me, slowly and fucking painfully.

"Now, imagine how good it would feel to take all that away for someone else." Her big, blue eyes glisten with thrill instead of fear as she guides the tip of the loaded gun to touch at her lips.

"You think it'd be easier to end someone else's suffering than it would be to end your own?" she asks. She slips her lips over the tip of the gun, stretching her mouth around the barrel as she guides my finger to the trigger before slowly releasing her hand from mine.

I hold the full weight of the gun in my hand now, and I swear her eyes are daring me to pull the trigger.

She's testing me, more than I'd ever dare to test myself, and my heart beats out of my chest while my cock grows thicker beneath her.

Her groin rests firmly on top of mine now, and it isn't until I take my eyes off hers to look between us, that I realize her hand has slipped inside the front of her jeans.

Sick bitch is getting herself off, while I'm holding a fuckin' gun to her mouth.

When I look back up at her, her lips frame a smirk around the gun.

I should fuck her already damned soul all the way to hell for what she's doing to me.

She takes more of the gun inside her mouth until I feel it touch the back of her throat, and it takes all my strength to keep my finger steady on the trigger.

Closing my eyes, I can't help imagining that it's my dick slipping between her lips and filling up her mouth, and when the vision gets too much I quickly snap them back open again.

I'm immediately greeted with Rogue's eyes. Wide. Tempting. Luring, and fucking begging.

I've pictured her in plenty of sick situations while I've watched her sleep beside me, but none of them ever resulted in her brains decorating the ceiling of my cabin.

Her hips wriggle against me, while her life balances on the tip of my index finger, and if there was ever a time for me to doubt my self-control, this is it. With her finger fucking her cunt on top of me.

Pulling the gun out of her mouth, I push it up under her chin. I'm in control now and the sadistic little bitch just laughs at me, grinding herself deeper into my lap. She knows what she's doing, she can feel me beneath her. Hard and coating the inside of my pants for her. I'd guess that she's imagining how my cock would feel inside her almost as vividly as I am.

"Do it." I force the words out of my mouth, taking another glance down to where she's working herself. "Come all over your fingers for me, Rogue."

My hand coils around her throat. Squeezing tight as I slide the gun up to touch her temple.

My lips are close enough to catch each one of her exasperated breaths.

And I'm so tempted to take her mouth with mine, to taste her fear, and lap up her pleasure all while her cunt sucks at her fingers.

"I need you to save me, Grimm," she whispers, just as her body tremors and her thighs clench each side of mine. I could pull the trigger, send her away from this world on a fucking high. But I keep my finger steady. I keep her with me because I don't think I can give her up.

When she moans out in pleasure, my grip on her neck intensifies, and she rides out her fucked up orgasm on my lap while I press the tip of the gun deeper into her temple.

I want to bite the pink out of her lips when they whisper my name, and suddenly her body stills, her lips trembling as the thrill inside her eyes become sedated with relief.

The hand she's just used to fuck herself with slowly slides up between us and soaked, quivering fingers touch my lips, coating them with the sweet taste of her pleasure.

I lose all my restraint. Dragging her closer with the hand I've got clenched around her neck and smashing my mouth onto hers because I need her to taste herself on me.

I've never kissed anyone before. The thought of someone else's lips touching mine has always repulsed me.

But I'm not kissing Rogue.

I'm fucking tasting her.

Tormenting myself by sampling how good the inside of her would feel, and as her tongue rolls against mine, coaxing me, I need so much more. So much more that the handle of the gun rattles inside the arch of my hand and I fear I might actually shatter her pretty little face to pieces.

"Don't fucking tempt me," I growl the warning against her lips, pulling together enough strength to throw the fucking gun across the room.

I could stay on this couch and explore each fragment of her broken pieces. But I have to do the right thing and get the fuck out of here. Even if the lone tear that strays from her eye makes me feel like an asshole as I force her away from me.

One of us has to do the right thing.

One of us has to walk away.

Because together we're toxic.

Two damaged souls that eventually will destroy each other.

I'm halfway to the door before she speaks.

"It's not for protection... it's my last resort," she speaks so timidly that I barely recognize her voice.

I looking back over my shoulder, and she looks so weak and helpless, crawling on her hands and knees to get to the gun and pick it up from the floor.

"I keep this gun because if another bad thing happens to me, Grimm..." she pauses, her eyes falling onto the gun in her hands. "...I think I'll be done wanting to survive."

I can tell she's holding back a stream of tears and I wish she'd let them free. Rogue doesn't have to be strong for me, she can't shelter me from her agony the way she does everyone else, because somehow when we're together, I feel every ounce of her suffering.

"Why didn't you just tell me that, why did you hide it from me?" I take a few steps forward, needing to be closer, then I crouch down in front of her. She drops the gun to the floor and fists the lapels of my cut, clinging to me.

"Because..." she looks up at me through her lashes and smirks through her sadness. "I think you might care enough about me to take my last resort away from me."

CHAPTER 22

G rimm surprises me after my confession, I thought he'd be angry at me, that he'd storm out on me again, but instead, he stares back at me. How can a man turn every single emotion into something beautiful?

"You need to get some sleep." He stands up, dragging me with him.

"Don't leave me." God, I sound pathetic, but I can't have him go, not after what I've just told him. I've never admitted that to anyone before, *hell* I haven't ever really admitted it to myself.

"Who said I was going anywhere?" Grimm's lips remain straight, his eyes focused on mine like my tears are fascinating him. I sense that he wants to touch them as they slip onto my cheek, and right now there's nothing I'd like more. Grimm could be the collector of all my tears now, he's the only person who could ever truly hurt me. He does it every time he rejects me. Why does he have to punish himself?

He picks up my gun and pulls my body onto his, my head rests on his chest and the hand he's holding the gun with strokes through my hair slowly. For a second I wonder if he's going to do it. If this is him calming me, the way owners pet their animals before they have them put down. Is this Grimm caressing me, making me feel loved before he takes me out? Proving to me and himself that he's capable of overcoming his emotions.

"I never want to hear you talk like that again." His warning sets a relief inside me that scares me, he sounds angry now, and the tension in his fingers tighten against me. I'm clinging to him, needy and desperate. I don't recognize myself anymore and I can't decide if that's a good or bad thing.

"Just being honest with ya." I find the strength to look up at him.

He's been asleep for hours, his hair roughed out of place and his long eyelashes touching his cheek. I take the time to study him, to appreciate him without that cold glare of his forcing me away. He actually looks adorable sleeping, innocent and untroubled, like blood has never touched his hands or tainted his skin. It takes me a while to realize that I'm touching myself. My finger slowly slipping through my pussy lips and stroking gently. I wonder how it would feel to have him touch me there, or if he's ever even touched a girl there before. I don't understand how Grimm gets his kicks out of just watching, he doesn't even touch himself, and the need to feel his hands on me grows painful while I stroke myself harder.

"Grimm," I whisper his name, but he doesn't stir, so I push my panties off my hips then slowly reach out and take the hand he's got resting on the mattress beside me. I guide it over my thigh, his limp fingertips brushing over my skin and setting it on fire. Then I make it cover my clit, pulsing against him, begging to feel movement, tension, anything. I rub myself against his hand, holding him firm against me, and keeping my eyes on him, scared for him to wake up and catch me.

I need to come before he realizes what I'm doing. Even without his response, his skin feels good against my sensitive flesh, and I close my eyes and imagine how good it would be to feel him inside me.

"Rogue." His whisper sounds rugged and raw and when I quickly open my eyes back up, he's watching me. He looks unimpressed, one of his eyebrows raising, but giving no indication of how he'll react. He moves his glance down his nose to where I'm using his hand to touch myself, and when his teeth graze over his bottom lips, a shudder of my pleasure sparks straight to where his fingertips touch. He props his head up in his other hand, bringing his face closer to mine so we're almost touching. I can feel his breath on my skin and I swear I hear a low growl escape his throat

He must feel how wet I am, I'm practically soaking his finger, and when I feel him apply a little pressure against me, my toes curl into the mattress. He's staring at me now. His eyes so intensely holding mine that I feel like he's crawling inside me. Grimm says nothing, but his long slippery finger rubs against me and my hips buck for more of it.

He's in control, he'll decide if I come or not, and it's hot as sin. I have to remind myself to breathe when his thumb takes over rubbing my clit and two of his fingers curl inside me. He watches, intrigued as I come apart for him, the same way he'd watched me in the truck a few nights ago. Only this time he's the one coaxing me to the brink, his hand moves so slowly that I get to savor him. I feel like I'm gonna detonate and as he pushes deeper inside me, I feel myself tighten around him.

His expression remains unmoved, and I wonder if he'll kiss me again. It feels weird that he isn't kissing me. God, I want him to kiss me. I want to...

"Holy shit." I come hard, my whole body tensing and my thighs closing to clutch him inside me. I'm not ready to lose him yet. I like the feel of him there, it's as if he has the power to cleanse all the bad that came before him.

His thumb continues to rub circles into my clit, and I pulse against him as he slowly winds me back down to earth until I relax enough to loosen my legs.

Tearing my eyes away from his, I watch his tattooed hand as it travels up my body, his fingers leaving a wet sticky trail over my skin as he moves under my shirt, sliding between my tits and making me want to come all over again.

Then I feel him under my chin, his thumb and hand holding my jaw while he feeds the two fingers he fucked me with between my lips.

I suck them hard and watch his jawline tense as I lap the taste of myself off him, hoping that there will be more. He draws me closer, taking up that small amount of space between us. His lips touch mine and his tongue invades my mouth, stealing the last traces of my orgasm for himself.

"Now sleep," he whispers, pulling his soaked fingers from my mouth and tapping them against my jaw.

"There's a storm coming in, town's been hit with a red alert, high ground is looking set to get hit hard. I want everyone in, bitches and family included." Prez's eyes home in on Nyx in particular as we sit around the club table and take in his instruction. While all I can think about is Rogue coming on my fingers last night.

"Everyone stays at the clubhouse tonight, the place is on lockdown until the bad weather passes."

"Already sent Marilyn out with the Prospect to get supplies, let's just hope this storm doesn't cause too much damage," Jessie adds.

It ain't often we get hit with a red alert, but that doesn't mean I'm prepared to spend a whole evening holed up with this lot. Just the thought of it has my palms feeling clammy. Prez ends church and we all filter outside. I light up a smoke and look across to the garage. Rogue is talking to the guy who owns the abattoir on the outskirts of town, and I notice how he checks out her ass as she reaches up to grab the keys to his truck off the hook. It makes me want to punch his teeth into the back of his skull.

Rogue's reason for keeping a gun in my cabin has haunted me ever since she confessed. I've always known she had issues. I can't judge her on that one, but to think about ending her life, that shit makes me angry. Skid would never cope if he lost her. I don't know what I'd do either. And that's the part that fucking petrifies me.

I charge over to the garage and eyeball the sick bastard who's stripping her of her clothes with his eyes. I swear I'll scoop them out of his head and squash 'em if he keeps it up.

"Oh hey, honey," Rogue greets me with a wide smile. The guy probably thinks we're a couple. Good. I want him to.

"Terrible thing what happened to the deputy," he nods his head at me, trying to make polite conversation, but I give him no response. He quickly retreats, smiling at Rogue before he raises his bushy eyebrows and hops into his truck.

"You really aren't a people person, are you?" Rogue giggles, throwing an oily rag at me. I watch it drop to the floor and fight the urge to pick it up. This isn't my space, this is hers, and judging from the disorganization and mess, she likes it this way.

"So, what's going down? I saw you all coming out of church." She pulls open a drawer from her toolbox and takes out a sizable wrench, swinging the thing in her hand as she moves toward the open hood of the car she's working on.

"We were just preparing for the storm." I clear my throat when I recall her riding my fingers last night. There's nothing more perfect than the sound of Rogue coming.

"Pass me the rag." She holds out an oily hand, keeping her head buried into the job. I ignore her, remaining still. How the fuck can the girl make something dirty so appealing.

"Grimm, pass me the damn rag." She looks up at me impatiently. There's no way I'm gonna pick up a dirty rag off the floor, especially since she threw it at me in the first place.

"Christ." She rolls her eyes and abandons what she's working on to come toward me, and when she crouches on her knees to pick it up, I feel the urge to fist her hair and force her mouth onto my cock. Rogue's hot mouth taking me inside it would be incredible.

She takes the rag in her hand and slides back up so her face is aligned with mine, her eyes aren't sad like they were last night. Now they're daring and so enchanting that I don't notice her other hand move to my face, not until it's too late and I feel the long greasy swipe of her finger against my jawline.

"Imperfection looks good on you." She cocks a smirk on her lips and I step forward, grabbing a fist of her blonde hair and slamming her back into the car she's working on.

It would be so easy to take what I want, to pull down those jeans and fuck her into the chaise of the car. The garage doors are open, half the club could see us and know that she belongs to me. No one would think about touching her then.

Here we have a code, rules we live by, you don't touch another member's property and I really wish Rogue could be mine.

She hums like a needy kitten, rubbing her hips into my pelvis and feeling how desperate I am for her.

"You should loosen up a little, Grimmy, take what you want. Who knows, you might enjoy it," she taunts, batting her lashes at me innocently.

I want to make her cry again.

"I'd ruin you," I threaten.

"And I'd love it," she promises me, placing another dirty touch of her fingers on my skin, this time against my neck. It makes me twitchy, but I don't want to wash it away. I want to keep Rogue's imperfection on my skin, even if it stings.

"Last night you gave in, you should do it again sometime." She purposely licks her lips and my cock strains for release, but instead of backing away from her, I grind against her, pressing solid into her stomach. My fingers creep up to her face and clasp at her chin, pushing her hot pink lips together between my thumb and finger. I could kiss her, force my tongue in her mouth and taste her like I did last night. I can feel the tension in my fingers, almost shaking with the desire to.

"Be careful what you wish for." I release her, ignoring the sparkle in her eyes as I get the fuck away from her.

"Hey, wanna book a spot?" Ella smiles at me when I head upstairs into the dining hall. Her and Grace are laying out the spare bedding that we keep stored specially for these kinds of occasions.

"I'm not staying here tonight," I answer.

"Yeah, about that," Ella smiles at me in a way that suggests she's gonna ask me for a favor.

"I was wondering if maybe you'd give it up for me and Nyx for the night. It's gonna be kinda crowded out here and I'm sure the others won't appreciate a baby crying through the night. I really don't think he's gonna settle around all these people. Plus it's the only rutting room I can guarantee is clean," she adds awkwardly.

I can hardly say no to Prez's daughter, and it would be selfish of me to not give it up when I have no intentions of using it myself.

"Sure." I reach inside my pocket and take the key off my chain. She goes to hug me but holds back.

"That's real kind of you, and as a thank you, I'll set you up on the opposite side of the room to Squealer."

"No need. I'm staying at my cabin."

"You can't, Daddy's orders." She shoots me a warning look. "He wants everyone here, one big happy family."

I eyeball her back doubtfully.

"Come on, be a team player, Grimm," Brax's old lady, Grace chimes in. "It might be fun."

"I'm a team player, I gave up my room, didn't I?" I point out, and neither of them can argue that.

Prez comes storming out the kitchen looking stressed. I'll bet Marilyn's flapping is driving him crazy.

"Grimm, you're giving up that private room of yours to Ella tonight."

"Already done." She shakes my key at him.

"I take it you won't be joining us?" He looks at me sternly. Me and Prez have an understanding, he may not get me but he doesn't doubt me, and that suits me fine. It's been that way since the day I first met him…

AGED 18

"I'm heading out, you think you can handle shit around here?" Old man Rogers puts on his jacket and picks up the keys to his truck.

I nod back at him, we only got three guests in and there's just a room left to clean, ain't nothing I can't handle.

"Any problems… don't try callin'." He laughs at his own humor, pulling himself up into his truck, slamming the door, and then driving out onto the freeway.

I stick in my headphones and rest my feet up on the desk. Then start flicking through the job ads in the paper. There's got to be something out there that pays better than this shithole.

I'm dragging my ass on the floor, the savings account is running out, and once it's gone I don't know how I'll keep her safe.

I can feel the anxiety building more and more every day, the weight on my shoulders so fucking heavy that I'm exhausted from it.

A black van pulls up outside and I immediately straighten myself up. Mr. Rogers has already warned me about my customer service skills and I can't afford to lose this job, even if the paycheck's shit.

"Evenin'." The middle-aged man who steps through the door tips his head at me, he's followed closely by two others, both of

them looking like trouble, especially the bald one who's covered in ink.

"Can I help?" I flick out one of my headphones.

"Hope so." The guy in front smiles darkly.

"We're looking for someone." He slams a photograph onto the desk in front of me. "You got anyone here looking like that, kid?"

"Sorry, ain't allowed to disclose guest information." I sit back in my seat and fold my arms.

"You hear that, boys? He ain't allowed to disclose information." The man looks over his shoulder and chuckles at the huge guy on his left, he's even bigger and has a thick black beard. His hands are filthy, covered in grease, he must be the one who's making the office stink of oil.

He turns his stare back to me, and things suddenly turn serious. He watches my reaction as he pulls a wad of cash from his back pocket, then slams a fifty-dollar bill on the counter in front of me.

"That's for the information… and this is for your silence." He places down another two fifties.

I swallow back the urge to reach out and take it. These guys look dangerous, last thing I need is for shit to go down while Rodgers has left me in charge.

"Sorry, sir," I tell him, resisting the temptation and hoping they'll move on.

"Listen, kid, it's been a real long assed night, and I ain't in the mood for making negotiations." Reaching around to the back of his pants he pulls out a pistol, cocks it, and aims it directly in front of my nose.

"So, you either tell me what room that guy's staying in or, I blow off your face and search through every damn room myself.

I stare down the barrel of the gun, and surprisingly I don't feel the fear I expect I should, instead I wonder how it would feel to be relieved of everything. At this range, death would be *instant. There'd be no time to feel pain. The burden weighing me down would be lifted… but then she'd have no one.*

"Room eleven." I reach behind me, lifting the spare key off the hook and slam it on the counter for the silver-haired man.

He nods at me, letting me know I've made the right choice, then tucks away his gun, leaving the money on the counter and backing out of the office.

"You never saw us," the bald one points his finger at me, before following the others out and pulling the door closed behind him.

The men aren't in room eleven for long and they leave just as coolly as they arrived.

Something inside me is curious to find out what they wanted with the man, I assume that he's dead, and this place will be crawling with cops come morning.

I wait for a couple more minutes before loading up the maintenance trolley and heading toward room five to clean up after the couple that checked out earlier.

Cleaning rooms is the only part of this job I excel at, Mr. Rogers says I'm the best he's ever had. Shame the tight asshole can't reflect that shit in my paycheck.

I strip off the beds, and just as I'm about to clean the bathroom I hear the sound of a vehicle pull up outside, followed by low voices and car doors slamming. I peel down the blind to check out who it is.

"All I'm saying, Screw, is that I'm fed up to shit of this. Us, cleaning shit up after they've had all the fun. That's not what we signed up for," one guy says to another as he starts unloading the trunk of the car.

There's two of them, both big, and so alike that I can't tell them apart. The other one shrugs his shoulders in response and pulls his hood up over his head as they both head toward room eleven.

I look at what they're equipped with, a couple bottles of industrial-sized bleach, coveralls, and shoe protectors.

Amateurs.

What I'm looking at here is an opportunity, one I'd be an idiot not to act on. I've already made 150 dollars tonight. I'll bet I could easily double it. Opening the door of room five, I step outside and release the brake on the trolley, pushing it along the decking toward the room I know they plan on entering. They both eyeball me cautiously as I pass them and, despite being desperate to get a peek inside the room, I do a good job of remaining cool.

"What you staring at?" the mouthy one of the two calls out, while the other nudges him, reminding him that they need to keep a low profile.

"I was just wondering what you think you're gonna achieve with that?" I look at the bleach container in his hand.

"Ain't none of your concern what I'ma do, take a hike, Scissorhands." He goes to come at me but gets held back by the guy who looks identical to him.

"It'll be my problem when this place is crawling with cops, all because you didn't do the job right."

The guy looks pissed as fuck, and after shrugging off the other guy, he makes a few long strides toward me, wraps his hand around my throat, and slams my head hard into the wall behind me.

"You got quite the imagination there," he hisses at me.

I take a breath, trying my best to ignore the fact his hands are on me and reminding myself to stay cool. Dealing with people with this level of intelligence requires some tact.

"If you wanna clean up whatever's in that room, you're gonna need more than what you got there." I glance back down at the bleach bottle he's holding in the hand that isn't threatening to choke the life outta me.

"Yeah, and what the fuck would you know about what I'm here to clean up?"

"I know that only an oxidant is gonna strip out blood and that the shit you got in your hand will barely wipe the surface. The room will light up like a town square in December if anyone puts a UV light on it." His hand quickly releases me and he narrows his eyes at me.

"Who you work for?" Suddenly he's suspicious but I can tell he's impressed at the same time.

"I work for myself. You should call up your boss, tell him I'll make that room cleaner than a nun's cunt... But I want 500 dollars for it."

The guy laughs, then looks over his shoulder at the other one.

"You hearing this, Screw?" he snorts at his brother, and is still smiling when he faces back to me.

"No one tells my boss jack shit," he warns

"Well then," I hold my hands up in defeat. *"I'll leave you to it."* I'm about to walk away when his hand grips at my shoulder and wrenches me back. This guy's far too fucking touchy for my liking.

"Wait up, you're telling me that you can make whatever it is in there look like it never happened?"

"I'll have to evaluate first, but I can't see why not."

"And how do I know I can trust you?"

"You don't, but you don't want to risk whatever's in that room blowing back on you people. See, what your friends never asked me earlier, when they stormed in like The Sopranos, was if anyone else knew who was in that room. If they had, I'd have told them that an agent checked him in, and that agent only paid for a two-night stay. This is his second night. So I'm guessing someone will be back for him in the morning." I tip my head toward the door.

"Fuck." The guy kicks at one of the porch pillars, then

crouches down to rest his hands on his knees and take some deep breaths. He straightens up again, shakes his head at his brother, and pulls out his cell.

"Prez, it's Squeal. Yeah, we're here, and we got a serious problem."

Both guys wait with me in the office for their boss to arrive, watching the clock on the wall like it's a bomb about to detonate.

When the same van from earlier pulls up and the silver-haired guy charges in, he looks pissed as hell.

"Tell me what you know." He slams his fist on the counter.

"What I said, your guy was checked in by an agent," I answer him calmly.

"And how can you be sure."

"Because that same agent came and scouted the place out the day before he was brought here."

"Shit… has the room been bugged?"

"Hell if I know, I could tell you once I'm in there," I assure him, already feeling the anticipation building inside me. It's been so long since I've had to clean anything up. It's almost sickening that the thought's giving me a head rush.

"And if there is?"

"Then I guess you're fucked. But if it ain't, and you let me take care of it, when they come back and find him gone, there will be no traces that you were ever in there with him."

"Who the fuck are you?" He shakes his head, his eyes checking over me like I'm some kinda freak.

"I'm just a kid who needs some cash." I give him the simple version, this guy doesn't need to know my life story.

He points his head toward the door, gesturing for me to follow him and we make our way over to room eleven.

I pull a pair of gloves from the trolley and stretch them onto my hands before opening the door. At face value, the room looks normal, but the scent in the air is unmistakable.

"Through there," he tips his head toward the bathroom door

and when I open it, I see the man slumped in the bath with a bullet wedged between his eyes. Blood and brain matter splattered over the tiles that just 48 hours ago, I'd taken the time to scrub to perfection.

I move closer to the body and drag my finger over one of blood smeared tiles, checking its texture between my thumb and finger. "Relatively thin," I think out loud, taking another look around the room and assessing what I'll need.

"I can get the job done in about five hours, with help and the right supplies," I tell him confidently.

"Make a list," he tells me before turning to the mouthy one. "Squeal, you stay behind and do as he says."

"That's just great. This kid ain't even a fuckin' member and he gets to bitch me," Squeal protests, but after a look of warning from his boss, he drops his head. "You got it, Prez." His tone changes, making him sound like a scalded schoolboy.

"You'll get your 500, kid, once you've made this place exactly how it was before we came."

"What you want me to do with him?" I look toward the stiff.

"We can take care of him, unless you got any suggestions?"

"I know a place remote enough for a fire, ground's easy enough to dig. There are three-ton machines under the water, I'll bet he wouldn't be alone down there. Or with more time, I could dismember him, chop him up real small and turn him to pulp."

"Jeez, kid, you're real fucking grim," the tattooed guy tells me, his face turning a few shades lighter.

"Get to work, kid." The older guy scratches his beard thoughtfully, and something tells me that this won't be the last mess I clear up for him. And as long as his cash keeps coming, that suits me just fine.

CHAPTER 24

1% MC

ROGUE

"Pack a bag," Grimm orders, storming through the door and heading straight for the bedroom. I follow him through, watching as he pulls my duffel bag down from the top of the wardrobe and throws it on the bed.

"Where we goin'?"

"Not we. You," he tells me coldly, and instantly my stomach flips. I've finally pushed him too far.

"I'm sorry." Unfamiliar words spill from my mouth. I never apologize, and you'd think Grimm would be more grateful for it.

Still, his face doesn't change and I feel my heart beat faster with panic when I think about having to leave.

"You can't make me leave. Skid said..."

"There's a storm coming in, Prez wants everyone to stay down at the club tonight," he cuts me off.

"And what about you?" I put my hand on my hip and stare at him, already knowing exactly what he's gonna say next.

"I ain't being trapped inside a room full of people. I'll be fine up here."

"Then so will I." Taking the duffel bag, I attempt to put it back on top of the wardrobe. Grimm snatches my arm then stares at where his fingers indent my skin. I watch his jaw tense, the same way it always does when he puts his hands on me. It gets me wet every fucking time.

"Don't argue with me, Rogue, for once, just don't fucking argue."

"I'll only go if you go. I ain't leaving you up here." I stand my ground.

Grimm blows out a frustrated breath and barges past me, and I follow him out onto the decking, where the rain has already started falling heavily onto the lake's surface. The temperature in the air has plummeted and the wind is picking up. Grimm keeps his back to me, staring out at the disrupted lake, and he flinches when I place my hand on his shoulder.

"Why can't you just understand?" His voice sounds weak and when he turns around, I can see how distraught he is. "People are trying to protect you, and keep you safe." I can sense the frustration in his tone, he can't even look at me right now, and it seems like I'm causing him physical pain.

A twisted-up part of me likes that.

"And who's gonna protect you?" I slide my hand down his arm and link my fingers between his, I'm pleasantly surprised when his fingers separate and he accepts them. Relief swarms my chest and despite his face still looking angry, I feel victorious.

"Let me stay with you, we can take care of each other," I whisper, bracing myself for the harsh blow of his rejection, but the small defeated nod he gives me back puts a smile on my face instead. I forget myself for just a moment and plant a celebratory kiss against his cheek.

"I'll cook us something now before the power goes out," I tell him, almost skipping back into the kitchen. When I glance back out at him, I notice how his fingers trace over the spot where my lips had pressed.

"So, what's your magic number?" I ask, settling beside him and curling up my legs on the couch. We've eaten, the kitchen is tidy and we're ready to ride out a storm together. At the moment we still have power, but if the storm's as bad as they say it'll be, there will come a point where we'll have to make our own entertainment.

"I ain't telling you that," he shakes his head, keeping his eyes fixed on the TV. It's constantly lagging with interference from outside. Only a matter of time before we lose signal all together.

"Come on, don't be boring, I'll tell you mine if you tell me yours," I nudge at his ribs playfully.

"Rogue…" he warns

"Mine's stuck on two for now, but I can't promise there won't be more." Winking, I try to pick up the mood. Grimm seems surprised but irritated at my answer, and I prepare for him to put my total to shame.

"I don't keep count of the women I fuck," he bites back sharply, making me throw my head back and laugh.

"Relax, I wasn't talking about your conquests, Casa fuckin' Nova. I wanna know how many you've…" Drawing a line across my throat with my finger, I fake a choking noise.

Grimm shakes his head, shifting off the couch, and making his way over to the refrigerator.

"Come on, I told you mine, you gotta tell me yours now, that's the rule of the game."

"I never agreed to play no game," he points out, grabbing a beer and slamming the door shut.

"Tell me, please," I beg, turning my body round to face his. I then sit up on my knees and rest my stomach against the back of the couch.

"Okay, you wanna play truth?" He twists the lid off his bottle and tosses it expertly into the trash. "Why are you lying about knowing those men?"

I chew my lip while I try to come up with a response. I really wasn't expecting this.

"Come on, Rogue, play the game. What's so important that you'd risk your life?"

"Those men are nobodies, I don't know anything about them," I lie.

"Bullshit." Grimm points the neck of his bottle at me before he drinks from it, then steps up to the back of the couch so his chest is flush with mine.

"I don't play games, Rogue, and I don't tolerate lies. So unless you want to turn me into someone you won't like, I suggest you quit."

I got no come back to that, and I turn back around to face the TV again. It's gone completely blank now, all signal lost to the storm.

I don't want to lie to Grimm, but I can't tell him the truth.

Spending time with Anita has taught me how to pretend too. I get to be the girl that I might have become if all the nasty shit hadn't happened to me when I'm with her. It's kinda like therapy I guess, I always feel a little lighter after living in her world for a few hours, even after I come back to the real world.

As the night draws in, so does the silence. The storm grows stronger outside, and so does the intensity between me and Grimm. I play some lame assed game on my phone to distract myself, while Grimm just stares at the blank TV screen.

Living with Grimm has turned me into some kinda freak, just him holding my hand earlier had sent my pussy into overdrive. I want him when we're apart, and I want him even more when we're together.

I don't know how long I can go on getting nothing back from him. Especially when I know that deep down he wants it too.

I sense him watching me sometimes, feel how tight he clings to me whenever I get a bad dream, and tonight, I see the perfect opportunity to push his limits and ensure I get what I want.

CHAPTER 25

GRIMM

A rguing with Rogue is a pointless exercise. Rogue does what Rogue wants to do. But at least being up here with me means she isn't down there with them.

That's why I let her stay, despite knowing that she's doing it out of torment.

She thinks she's being sly when her leg gradually stretches out toward mine, and from the corner of my eye, I see her watching, waiting for my reaction. I'm not about to let her see that what she's doing to me is driving me fucking insane.

"So what's your favorite childhood memory?" she asks, trying to distract me with more small talk.

"I don't have any," I answer bluntly. It's the truth, all my memories as a child are plagued, and I hate the way she looks back at me so pitifully.

Her dainty foot slides over my leg and touches over my groin. I should shift away from her, but I remain still. Testing myself as her foot rotates small agonizing circles, that make me grow rigid beneath it. She thinks she's winning, I can tell from the wicked smile she shoots me when I turn my head to face her.

Denim is all that separates my cock from the delicate soles of her feet, and trying to stop myself from rocking back against her is like trying to hold back the force of a tsunami.

"Why don't you play along, Grimm?" She purposely takes

one of her fingernails between her teeth and stares me straight in the eye. "Just once," she whispers.

My fingers grip tight around her ankle, and I torture myself a little further by pressing it tighter against my solid cock... just for a second.

She's wrong to think it could ever be just once with her.

Take her now, take her forever. I'd never want to let her go.

I look down to where my tattooed fingers squeeze into her pale skin, and I don't know who the fuck I am anymore. Not when all my mind is thinking about is raising her foot to my mouth and sucking at each one of her perfectly set toes.

"Don't," I warn, tensing my grip, she feels so fragile in my hand. I could so easily make it snap.

She'd never be able to run from me then.

I shake that thought away before it can progress, this is why I can't let her get close. I've already gone too far with her. I shouldn't have kissed her. I definitely shouldn't have done it a second time, but the temptation to taste her was too much, especially after she'd come so beautifully for me.

Pushing her foot away, I go to stand up, but Rogue moves quicker. Placing her body between my legs, her tight stomach now occupying the spot her foot had left. I flick my eyes down to where her fingers skim across the hem of my T-shirt, I can't help but suck in a breath as they slowly creep lower to tease the skin beneath my waistband.

I'm giving her too much, letting her push too far. But her skin on mine feels too fucking good to reject.

"Rogue," I warn, shutting my eyes. Maybe if I don't look at her, I'll find more strength.

"You want me." She slides her body up over mine until her lips touch my ear. It's not a question, it's a statement, a fucking accurate one. I feel her hand dip lower into my jeans. "Your cock tells me so." Her voice sounds so sweet, almost fucking innocent, but I know better. Rogue knows exactly what she's doing and she won't stop until she gets what she wants.

It shocks me when her fingers grip my shaft, and I snap my eyes open and stand up with such force that it causes her to fall backward. She quickly recovers, resting on her knees. The way she looks up at me, her eyes on mine, so wide and so desperate makes me want to give up the fight and make her mine.

Rogue offering herself out to me like this, being so submissive, it's dangerous for her. And it's lethal for me. How easy would it be to let her have her way? To take out my cock and fill her mouth, feel it touch the back of her throat, and make her gag while my hand cradles her pretty little throat.

She thinks she's so tough, but in reality, she's exquisitely fragile. She's showing me that I have the power to ruin her, to break her spirit and turn her into a groveling wreck. The thought churns my stomach, but at the same time it stiffens my cock, and that's the evidence that he's still here, living inside me.

"No." I find the willpower to slam my hand over hers, and at that moment all innocence vanishes from her eyes, hatred settling in its place.

"Then I'm done here," she snarls, scrambling up from her knees and looking at me like I've suddenly become her enemy.

"What do you mean you're done here?" I snigger back at her. She's got no place else to go. She's trapped at the club because of her own rebellious actions, and tonight, courtesy of the storm outside, she's trapped in my cabin too.

"I mean, I'm done with you. I've been trying, Grimm… trying so hard to figure out what the fuck this is between us. But there's only so many times you can knock a girl down before she stops bouncing back at ya."

She starts heading for the door. Outside, the wind has really picked up, and when she pulls it open the thing swings open with such force that it hits the wall as the storm blows inside.

The wind feels even stronger than it sounds. It whips around the cabin and blows rain inside, creating a small puddle at her feet.

"Don't be ridiculous, get back here." I reach out to her but she throws my hand away.

"Don't fucking touch me, you think I'm scared of a little storm, Grimm? I'm not afraid of anything. I'd rather take my chances out there than stay here a second longer with you." Her words bite worse than the chill she's letting in, and before I have a chance to try and form any kinda response, she disappears out the door into the night.

There's no doubt that I'm gonna run after her. Storms like this one are dangerous, especially up here on the mountain. Wind speeds are fast, and there's no shortage of trees around to be brought down by them. Just the thought of her getting hurt makes something dig sharp in my chest.

I struggle to see more than inches in front of my face as the rain pelts unforgivingly against my eyes, and soaks through the flimsy T-shirt I'm wearing.

"Rogue, get back here," I yell against the wind, and despite the fact it makes my throat raw, I can barely hear myself.

Branches crack and scrape against the cabin roofs and the ground beneath my feet gushes with water.

"Rogue," I call out again, then I spot her figure, running along the tree line.

Chasing her into the woods, my heart beats out of my chest. My body is heavy from the weight of my wet clothes, and rain blurs my vision, but I don't let that slow me down. I manage to catch up with her when she's finally forced to stop and catch her breath.

She's barefoot, mud squelching between her toes, her legs cut and bleeding from where she must have tripped. Her blonde hair sticks to her face and her lips tremble from the cold, but she still looks fearless.

It terrifies me.

"What's holding you back, Grimm?" she screams out at me over the chaos of the storm. "I'm...I'm not used to trying..."

"What are you talking about?" I take a steady step forward, petrified that she'll bolt on me again. But I need to have my hands on her, to hold her in my arms and know she's safe.

"You look at me like you want to touch me, I see your lips twitch when you think about kissing me. I've made it about as obvious as I can that I want you but something's holding you back, Grimm. What is it?" The rain drenches her T-shirt, sucking it against her skin while she waits for answers. But I haven't got any words for her. I couldn't begin to explain. She'd hate me if I did.

"Come on, out with it, do you want me or not? Because if you do, I'm here..." The wind catches her voice and a branch falls from the tree, so close to her that it makes my heart leap into my throat, but Rogue doesn't even flinch. "I'm telling you I want you. I want your hands and lips to touch me the way your eyes do. And I'm not afraid of the darkness you got inside you, Grimm. I'm drawn to it. So if you want me, come over here and fucking take me..."

Fuck, I want to take her, more than I want to breathe.

I don't want to feel this way. It's a sickness. One that I'm trying to save her from. I don't want to crave the control I need over her. I'm so scared that I'll picture her looking like them when I'm inside her, seeing her face in one of my father's polaroid pictures, lifeless and broken.

What if she's the test I fail? What if I hurt her, or worse, what if I can't stop?

"Come on, Grimm. What you so afraid of, scared you won't get me off? Is that why you like to watch?" Her hand skims over her stomach and disappears inside the front of her pants, and I squint to stop the rain running into my eyes.

Rogue knows what she does to me, she's testing me, and in doing that she's awakening the beast inside me. Of course, I don't want to just fucking watch. I want to be her only form of pleasure, her only fucking anything.

I want her to need me.

Only me.

It's un-fuckin-healthy.

"See that's what I figured." She smiles cruelly at me. "You're scared. Go home, Grimm. I can take care of myself. Always fucking have, always fucking will." As she pulls her hands out of her waistband, for the briefest moment, her eyes show a flicker of vulnerability. And when her body turns ready to bolt again, a fear greater than anything overcomes me and drives me forward.

The fear of losing her for good.

My arm reaches out and drags her back to me. She struggles, and it's hard to keep her in my grip with the rain pounding at us, but I manage to turn her back around and slam her shoulders into the closest tree. I take one long last look at her, and with all my self-discipline obliterated, I smash my lips hard onto hers and claim that taunting little mouth again.

She summoned the monster, coaxed him out of hiding, and now she's beyond saving.

This is the kiss of fuckin' death. For her, and for me.

The ache to be inside her and make her cunt mine is so strong that even her soaked, muddy hands reaching up and touching my face don't distract me.

Out here, it's just me and her. The storm swirls around us, protecting us from all the shit that should keep us apart. Here, with our rain-soaked bodies shivering against each other, everything else is irrelevant.

Rogue's hands move down my body, tugging at my T-shirt and pulling it up over my head. Even the harsh wind and chill of the rain don't stop the fire I feel in her touch.

I rip open the buttons on the flimsy top she's wearing, grasping at the black lace that's keeping her tits hidden from me and pressing my soaked body tighter into hers. I consume her mouth with my tongue, her blue-tinged lips trembling against mine from the cold while I devour her.

My fingers slide up under her bra, fisting one of her tits and pinching her nipple between my finger and thumb. She responds by biting down on my lip, punishing me with a euphoric pain that I want more of.

How did I ever manage to hold out for so long when she's so agonizingly perfect? We fit together in the most fucked up of ways, and I won't deny myself of her for a moment longer.

My soaked fingers slide up her neck and grasp at her jaw, my tongue following its trail all the way to her ear. "I want to fucking own you," I warn, feeling the breath she sucks in against my chest. "I want to possess every part of you, Rogue. Your body, your soul, and your fucking spirit. Once I've had you, I'll never let you leave me." My threat is real, and she responds to it by grinding her hips and rubbing her pussy against my solid cock.

"I mean it. I'll ruin you."

"I'm already ruined," she tells me, her eyes wild as they peer deep inside my soul.

Why do her words hurt me? Why do I want to put this girl back together so bad that I'm prepared to give up all my broken pieces to do it?

Tightening the grip I have on her with the arch of my hand, I push her into the thick trunk behind her, dragging my head back enough to appreciate how beautiful she looks. Thick drops of water trickle over her pale skin, wisps of hair stick to her face, and the makeup she always wears so immaculately is smudged and ruined.

"Me too," I whisper because this... us, it's gonna happen, and it's gonna happen right here with this storm battling against us.

Rogue ignores all my warnings, her fingers already working the buckle of my belt. She's clumsy in her desperateness to release me, and it makes me all the more fucking determined to take her.

I speed things up, ripping open my jeans while she works against the elements to peel her own off her legs. When she stands in front of me naked and shivering, I know it's now or never.

Reaching both my hands around her body, I clutch at her ass and lift her off the ground, lining her pussy up with my hard cock and slamming into her without warning. A devilish scream tears from her mouth as I fill her and her fingers fist at my hair, nearly tearing it out from the root. I take her to the hilt, and being surrounded by her heat suddenly makes it impossible for me to move.

Rogue is too impatient to let me savor the moment, her greedy pussy wriggling for me to give her more. So I pull out of her slowly, then push back hard, grabbing her pretty face in my hand and pinning her body to the tree using only my thrusts. I take so much pleasure in watching her pupils dilate every time I fill her.

Rogue fucks with my head, she twists up every single one of my emotions, and I hate it and love it all at the same time.

There's no denying that I've become addicted to her. Rogue owns every fuck I have left to give now, and that will be a curse for her.

It's the choice she made, and now she's mine. Curses and all.

My name tears out of her mouth, echoing through the trees and getting drowned out by the storm as her pussy spasms around my cock.

Her fingernails drag through my skin, tearing open my flesh and embedding into me. And as she jerks and thrashes her body against mine, she howls out a wild laugh.

I pull our bodies away from the tree, dragging us down onto the slippery earth beneath us. My hands pin her wrists above her head, and my knees slip against the earth as I find my place back inside her again. Our surroundings are insignificant, even to me, and her mud-soaked fingers squeezing between mine as I pound relentlessly inside her don't trigger me. It's freeing.

When she struggles against my restraint, I hold her down tighter and she retaliates by lifting her knees, gripping them around my hips, and forcing me deeper into her body.

I manage to grasp both her wrists in one hand so my other can touch her, the dirt and mud on her body don't repulse me the way it should. I don't need Rogue to be clean, in fact, I like that she isn't. It gives me a purpose. I'm fully aware of the fact that I'm bare inside her, that this isn't who I am, but Rogue seems to be exempt from all my usual compulsions.

Rogue *is* my fuckin' compulsion.

I slide my filthy hand over her face, marking her skin with streaks of mud that should make me shudder, but I embrace the freedom of it. She looks so fucking beautiful dirty. When my fingers drag over her neck, I tense them a little as I pass, wondering if I could make her hurt, if I would get pleasure from watching her panic for air. But this is different from all the times before, this doesn't need to be a test. I know now that hurting Rogue would only bring pain to myself.

I could never end her. She's bound to me now, and that will be her punishment for pushing me so damn hard.

I feel myself getting close, my balls slamming hard against her ass cheeks and ready to offload any second. I want so much to stay buried in her tight little snatch, to come deep inside her and then watch it drip out of her.

I've fantasied for weeks about all the different ways I'd like to own the body beneath me. Ever since I found her waiting in my bed for me that first night.

Each time I've jacked myself into my palm, I've thought about decorating her skin with it.

Heat rushes to my tip, and I manage to tear myself out, just before I spill inside her. Releasing my long, hot jets onto her stomach,

I tarnish her with my mark, then use my muddy palm to rub it into her skin.

I look at her face while I taint her body, trying to recall a time when I've ever seen such a beautiful mess.

I expect confusion, horror, disgust. But there's a satisfied smile as her eyes follow the hand that I massage into her skin, she's enjoying watching me claim her.

I collapse on top of her, the wind whipping around us and our bodies shivering against each another's while we try to catch our breath back. I kiss her hard and possessively, knowing I'm way out of my depth, but happy to fucking drown if it means I get to keep her.

I like Grimm a lot more when he loses control. He's finally given up on whatever's been holding him back and the man who's knelt between my legs, covered in mud, with rain thrashing around him, isn't the Grimm I've come to know.

He's been rough and punishing. I feel sore inside and out. But I've never felt more alive.

My heart beats wild and my pussy throbs to have him again, and I silently pray that we don't have to ever go back from this.

When he said he'd never let me leave him, it sounded a lot like a promise but past experience has taught me that a promise is only as good as the man who gives it. I can't have Grimm let me down.

He stands up and holds out his hand for me. He looks so serious, I wish I could read his thoughts. Gripping hold of him, I let him pull me to my feet before we quickly gather up our clothes and run back through the trees toward his cabin. Something is freeing about running naked through a storm, and the sound of my laughter coaxes a tiny laugh out of him too. One that warms my whole body and makes me desperate to hear it again.

When we get inside, Grimm battles against the door to make it shut, and as soon as he turns around he puts his lips back on me. His tattooed hand smothering my cheek while he kisses my mouth, as his other hand scrunches a fistful of my hair. It's dominating and, possessive, and it gives me hope that this is us now.

"You're gonna let me clean you up," he whispers against my lips. I nod back, excited by the idea as I allow his body to back me up toward the bathroom. Once we're inside, he reaches his arm out to turn on the shower, then guides me to stand in the bathtub.

The warm water crackles against my freezing skin, but the discomfort eases when Grimm steps in beside me. He works his hands into my hair first, shampooing it with care and attention. When he tips back my head to rinse it, the dirt from my body drips onto his, but he doesn't seem freaked out about it.

After he's finished with my hair, he takes a clean sponge and starts to soothe it over my skin. I watch his intense level of focus as he covers me in suds and takes his time to cleanse every inch of me. I throw my head back and moan when he slides the sponge between my leg and squeezes his hand, the lather spilling between my thighs making me desperate to have him inside me again.

He kneels in front of me to wash my legs, and I press my palm into the tiles when I feel his lips press gently against my pussy. He doesn't linger there long before he gets back to work, continuing to make me clean, being thorough as he makes his way down to my feet and washes all the mud and blood away.

When he stands back up again, he looks satisfied and I take the sponge out of his hands, load it with more soap and then start to do the same to him. He closes his eyes and freezes, and for a second I think he's gonna stop me. But then he lets out a breath and places his hand over mine, guiding me to move over his body to make him clean again too.

When we're finished, he turns my body so my back presses against him and then pulls me down to sit in the base of the tub with him. His back is against the tiles and his chin resting on my shoulder, and his arms clutch around my waist, holding me tight.

We stay silent under the warm water until we're spotless and our skin starts to wrinkle. I can't remember ever feeling so content, and I'm petrified that I'm gonna have to come down from the high. When we eventually climb out, he wraps a towel around my body, takes my hand, and leads me into the bedroom.

Grimm is well equipped and he hadn't taken that into consideration when he'd pounded me into the tree out in the storm. I'm sore but I still crave him.

"You need to get some sleep," he tells me, like he can actually read the thoughts in my fucking head. I want to argue back, but at the same time, I don't want to ruin his mood. So I don't, instead, I snuggle in beside him, taking comfort in the way his arms show no hesitation to wrap around my body and pull me in tight. We lie and listen to the sound of the rain drumming on the roof and I can't help but break the silence.

"Are things gonna change between us now?" I ask, knowing that his answer has the potential to shatter me.

How have I let this happen?

"Everything's fuckin' changed, Rogue," he whispers, sounding like he's mad at himself, the kiss he places on top of my head reassures me that even if he is, it won't change anything.

Grimm may hate that he's crossed the line and given into his desires, but it would be impossible to deny ourselves each other now.

"In that case, good luck tellin' Skid." I smile to myself before closing my eyes. I swear I feel his lips smirk against my temple before I drift off, and I already know there will be no nightmares tonight. Not while he's holding me.

I stretch my arms out wide when I wake up and quickly panic when I realize he isn't beside me.

Rushing out of bed, I pull one of his shirts on, then make my way into the kitchen to find the space empty. The storm outside has calmed to nothing now, and I go out on the decking to look at the damage it's left behind, where hopefully I'll find Grimm.

Sun breaks through the clouds now, and the only sign of last night's storm is the debris that bobs on the lake surface. Grimm is nowhere to be seen.

I waste a whole torturous hour staring at my phone, wondering if I should call him before the door opens and there he is.

He moves straight toward me and kisses my lips, and the relief it gives me makes me suddenly realize how vulnerable I am. I don't let myself rely on anyone, not even Skid. I always figured it was the best way to protect myself from being hurt again. Since being here, I've opened up so much of myself to Grimm. And now he has the power to crush me.

"I was worried," I admit, my damn mouth, not being fucking cool.

"Then why didn't you call?" he asks like it's the simplest solution in the world. Now I feel stupid. I don't have the first clue how to handle all the emotions inside me.

"I've just been helping repair some of the damage around the club," he explains, giving off a slightly different vibe than usual. He seems more positive, like he's been relieved of a burden. It feels a little strange. A good kinda strange.

"I did something stupid last night," he says, his tone turning serious and suddenly making me feel like I've been doused with fuckin' acid.

This is the part where he tells me that last night was a one-time thing and he doesn't do commitment. I'll bet he's rehearsed it enough times with all the sluts at the club.

"Last night when we... It distracted me from things that

usually trouble me." He seems confused by his own words, and all I can do is recall the vision of our bodies slipping against the muddy earth. "I shouldn't have... without a rubber."

And he must hear the sigh of relief I make hearing that.

"That's it?" I chuckle back at him.

"That's not *it*, Rogue, that shit's pretty fuckin' serious. It's never happened to me before, and of course, I know I'm clean, but it was still a real stupid thing to do." He isn't making eye contact anymore and the way he's chewing at his fingernails shows how big a deal this is for him. "If you need me to, I can speak to Doc, he'll get ya something to cover the other issue." Grimm getting shy over discussing birth control has to be the cutest thing I've ever seen in my life.

"Already covered." I put him out of his misery, and when his chest sags with relief and his eyes finally raise to mine again, his lips are wearing the hint of a devilish smile.

"That's real fucking good news." He edges closer to me "Because all morning I've been thinking about how good it would feel making that same mistake all over again with you." He pulls me up off the chair and buries his head into my neck. His teeth scraping over my skin and setting my core on fire.

"I thought you were the kinda guy who left nothing to chance." I giggle, enjoying how his tongue soothes over his fresh bite mark. He pulls away from me, just enough to make sure his eyes meet mine again.

"You do something to me," he confesses, his pupils stabbing into mine as his hands fist my ass cheek. "Something that makes me forget who I am. You distract me from all the things that usually send me crazy."

He lifts me off the ground, and my thighs automatically straddle his waist.

I grip his chin in my hand and crush his lips together.

"You hurt me, and I swear to Satan, I will fuck you up," I

warn, before sliding my tongue over his perfectly structured jawline all the way to the cross under his left eye.

"I won't hurt you." His dark, haunting eyes make the words impossible not to believe.

Carrying me through to the living area, he lays me onto the couch and opens the front of his jeans, already stroking his cock through his colorful fist as he guides it toward me. I hook my panties over to the side to allow him access.

Grimm's thick tip glides between my pussy lips, and I grip at the plastic on the couch as he pushes himself inside me.

"It feels good inside you, Rogue," he tells me, his fingers now entwined in my hair and tugging me back enough to give his mouth access to my neck. His hips rock into mine and I gasp at the sensation of being full of him again.

"Everything feels so fucking different now, it scares me," he admits.

And I nod my head back at him because I get it. Everything with Grimm is different. He's the only person whose touch I've actually welcomed. The first person other than myself to make me orgasm. I wish I could tell him that, but I'm too ashamed of everything in my life that came before him.

Now feels different to last night, still desperate, still intense but not rushed. It gives me the chance to admire him. Grimm seems to look at me like the world could collapse around us and he wouldn't notice. The way he touches me is possessive and commanding and I know how much he needs that control. But surprisingly it doesn't bother me. Call it fucked up, but with him, I kinda like giving the power over to him.

He slides in and out of me so easily, and as I feel every inch of him possess me deeper, I can't help taking a thrill in the thought of him not ever being inside anyone else without using protection.

"Don't pull out this time," I breathe, wrapping my thighs around his hips tighter and holding him inside me. "I want to feel you come inside me." He nods his head and the arch of his hand slides higher up my throat. He doesn't squeeze like I expect him to though. Instead, he strokes his thumb over my pulse, feeling it quicken as he fucks me agonizingly slowly.

I feel the same pressure in my stomach that I remember from the night before. One different from the relief I give myself, this is far more overwhelming. It needs to release and takes over my senses, forcing me to grind against him desperately.

"Did you mean what you said, about never letting me go?" I ask breathlessly, remembering his words from last night and wanting to hear them from him again. Yes, it's fucking needy, but it's what he does to me.

Grimm nods, and I see the flash of guilt in his expression as his fingers dig deeper into my skin. I bite my lip trying to stop the gleeful smile from spreading onto my lips. Then I throw my head back and let the pleasure consume me.

"Fuck." He drops his head, the muscles in his arms strain when he braces them over my shoulders, his body leaning over mine as he thrusts into me deeper. I scratch my fingers over his ribs as I feel him tense, and one of his hands slide down to clutch at my hip.

He holds me steady, crushing me between his fingers as he spills his cum into me. It hurts a little but I don't want him to let me go. Not ever.

I don't care how fucked up he is, he makes everything right in this wicked world.

He makes me forget.

Grimm is gonna be my cure, I can already feel it happening, and now all I wanna do is be the antidote to his misery too.

CHAPTER 27

1% MC

GRIMM

This girl will undoubtedly be my ruin.

The world I thought I knew feels like it's crumbled, and that all remains standing is her and me.

I pull out of her, wondering what the hell's happened to me. I'm not repulsed after being inside her. My body doesn't feel dirty. In fact, I want the scent of her to linger on my skin, and I like that I can still taste her in my mouth.

Resting back on the couch, I give my head a chance to catch up with itself, but Rogue has other ideas. I feel her straddling my lap as she fiddles with the buttons on my shirt.

"I missed you while you were gone. Is that weird?" she asks me, with a cute little frown that could almost make you forget the devastation the girl's capable of. I shake my head back at her, maybe it's weird for other people, but not for us. The whole time I was helping out with the others, all I could think about was getting back to her.

I like her like this, relaxed enough to show me her vulnerable side. Now that she's mine I don't want her to hide any part of herself away from me.

"I want you to come down the club later, with me," I tell her, shifting some hair away from her eyes and tucking it behind her ear. I can't take hearing how the brothers talk about her anymore.

Once I've claimed her, they'll at least have the respect to keep their filthy thoughts to themselves.

"You mean together, like…"

"Exactly like that. I need everyone around here to know you're mine"

"Wow, never let it be said that Richie Carter doesn't know how to treat a lady." Her fake enthusiasm comes with a smirk that has my cock twitching to be inside her again.

"How do you even know my… you know what, I don't want to know." I shake my head at her. No one calls me by my name around here, very few people even know what it is. The girl must have been doing her groundwork, or maybe she's worked on Maddy for information.

"I gotta get back, things are busy down there."

"Okay, darling." Rogue changes her voice to mimic a suburban housewife as she goes to shift off my lap, but I grip her hips and hold her in place. Claiming her mouth in the same way I intend to in front of everyone tonight down at the club.

"Do you have to go?" she asks when I release her.

"Wouldn't be leavin' if I didn't." My thumb soothes over her swollen bottom lip.

"And, you need to get down to the garage. I don't want to get in trouble with Skid for distracting his best mechanic."

"I think you're gonna be in enough trouble with Skid." She bites down on my thumb. "Did you call him?"

"Not yet." Truth is, I'm putting that shit off. Now I have her, I don't have a death wish, and Rogue is the closest thing to a daughter Skid has. She's the closest thing he has full stop these days and I doubt he'll appreciate her being involved with someone like me.

Not that it's gonna stop me.

"I'll call him before we make it clear to the others," I assure her.

"Promise?" she asks so sweetly, before reminding me she's

anything but 'sweet' when she fists the back of my hair and forces my head up to make eye contact.

"Promise."

She kisses me, this time it's her lips that are firm and commanding, and it feels much more like a warning than a show of affection.

"Get out of here." She shifts her hot little ass off me so I can stand up.

In any other case, I'd have to take a shower. Spend a good twenty minutes scrubbing any trace of the bitch I'd let touch me off my body. But not with her. I want to keep a little bit of Rogue with me wherever I go. A constant reminder of who she belongs to now, that will have to do until later when I show my club.

Down at the clubhouse, things are looking much clearer. Luckily there's no major damage, just stray branches and debris. It won't take long for us to be back in business.

"Anyone heard from Skid?" Troj asks, his cigarette hanging from the corner of his mouth as he drags a huge tree branch toward the firepit.

"No, I'll give him a call now, see if he's followed up the lead Maddy gave him on the crew Eddie had met with," Jessie answers

"I'll do it," I interrupt a little too hastily. "He'll wanna know how Rogue's doin' anyway."

"And how is Rogue… doin'?" Troj asks with a sneer, one that tells me exactly what his filthy mind is thinking.

"She's doin' just fine." I try not to show my frustration, but it's hard when you know the outlaw version of fuckin' Tarzan is picturing your girl in all the wrong kinda ways.

I don't care if he's king of the fuckin' ring. I'd make sure no one ever found him.

"Call Skid, tell him we got things handled here," Jessie agrees with me, and I leave the pair of them smirking at each other as I try to find a quiet space.

I could go to my basement room, but the signal down there's shit. So instead I head for my room upstairs. The door's left open with the key inside it, and I appreciate that Ella and Nyx have left everything exactly how they would have found it. I scroll to Skid's number and he answers almost immediately.

"Everything okay?" he sounds worried.

"Everything's fine."

"That's what I needed to hear, Grimm. I got to head further south, gonna stay with the Dallas Charter for a few nights."

"I'll tell the others," I assure him without asking him why, if he wanted to tell me he would.

"How's Rogue?" I swallow nervously when he asks, there's only one way I can see this going and it doesn't matter how far south he's going, it won't be far enough not to drag him back here to have it out with me.

"Yeah, I got to talk to you 'bout that."

"Jesus, what's she done now?" I hear the groan in his voice.

"It ain't so much of what she's done, it's…"

"Don't tell me you let Squealer get to her." His tone gets stern.

"Not Squealer." I scratch the back of my head, wondering how much more awkward this can get.

"Troj?" He breathes heavily.

"Try again."

"Thorne. Fuck, I knew she'd be drawn to that—"

"It's none of them, actually," I interrupt him hastily, and it must give me away.

"No…" I take the low chuckle he makes as a good sign. "You gotta be kidding me."

"You're not mad?" I check because I never saw this coming.

"I knew one of you would fuck up eventually," he admits.

"So that's it? No warning, no threats?" This all seems way too fucking easy.

"Grimm, that girl comes with her own warning, you saw

what happened to the last guy who pissed her off. If you're brave enough to take that shit on, then you don't need to worry about me."

"I like her, Skid." I don't know why, but I feel the need to tell him that. I want him to know that this isn't something I gave in to easily. That I, at least, tried to resist. I did all I could to prevent it from happening, but now it has, there's no going back. Deep down, I've always known it would be that way.

"*Like* her, like her? or like her, like you like the others?" he asks, sounding a lot more serious now.

"Like her, like I never knew I was capable of liking anyone." I hear the weakness in my voice and it makes me so angry at myself. "She ain't like the others, not at all. She's been staying in my cabin since she came here, I even let her touch me."

"Okay, cool it, I may be okay about it, but I don't want the fuckin' deets. Grimm, you know what the girl means to me. She's hard fuckin' work but I'll always be looking out for her. Way I see it, now I got someone else invested in her welfare who will help me do that."

He's right about that much. I've never really bought into the whole brothers, not by blood thing, but I feel like me and Skid have something that binds us together now.

"I appreciate you understanding." I'm still shocked at how okay with this he's being.

"Grimm, if the last few years have proved anything to me, it's that if something feels right you have to go for it. I wouldn't have let anyone tell me I couldn't be with Carly. How could I expect you to be any different?"

Hearing him say his dead wife's name reminds me of everything he's been through. It's understandable why he avoids this place now.

"You focus on Chop, I'm taking care of Rogue," I assure him.

"Don't get distracted, Grimm, there's a shit storm brewing, I can feel it. She may seem like she's invincible but these friends of Eddie's are the kind of people who are gonna want her to pay for her actions."

When I get off the phone I sit in silence for a while, I can see my father looking at me now. Watching, waiting, willing for me to fuck up and lose control. My chest feels like it's tied up in knots and that he's the one pulling at the ropes. He wants me to self-destruct. But I'll keep a handle on it all. I'll protect Rogue from the part of him that festers inside me.

AGED 16

"Good, Richie. This is good." Father looks at the space around him, impressed. It's been six months since he brought me here. He's been teaching me how to clean up efficiently and now that I've scrubbed down the storage container and all traces of his latest victim is gone, I hate myself for taking pride in his praise.

"We'll take her to the special place." He looks down at the body on the floor. I took more time to wrap the body this time. After what happened last time with the blood in the trunk, I don't want to take any risks.

Mama had suffered for my mistake that night with twelve thrashes of his belt, and I won't let that happen again.

I nod before I set to work putting all my products away in the other lock up.

Then when I'm done, I help Father load the body into the trunk.

Sinnerman's Quarry is a beautiful spot. It's also miles away from any civilization. Surrounded by an open plain. The track the trucks must have traveled years ago has long grown over, and I look at my father confused when he parks close to the water's edge.

"You can't dispose of each body the same, Richie," he explains, staring out over the edge. *"This water is deep, there are three-ton machines down there,"* he explains as we get out of the car and open the trunk. *I slide on a fresh pair of gloves and help him lift the dead weight out.*

"We'll tie some of those rocks to her and send her over," he instructs, and I do as he says. Picking out some rocks and tying them to the plastic smothered body. When I'm finished, he checks my work, and nods when he tests my knots.

"What did she do?" I'd never asked him this question with the other four. I don't really ask anything. I stay quiet because I'm learning his skill. I'm protecting Mama.

The more he teaches me, the closer I get to ensuring when the time comes and he needs to disappear, that no one will ever find him. I've already decided it won't be here. This place is far too pretty, and he'd probably get a sick satisfaction from being so close to them. These women, despite their sins, deserve to rest in peace.

"She was a mother. But not a good one. She chose to use her body for money, and instead of feeding her children, she fed her habit." He grabs the bottom half of her body and I take the top, without any more words we launch her from the edge and I watch her fall into the water, slowly sinking, lower and lower to join whoever else my father has judged.

"Why do you fuck them before you kill them?" I ask, I'm curious. He claims this is God's work, but if that's the case, why does he need to take pleasure in them?

"Control. It comes with the rage, Richie. When you're older you'll understand. There is nothing more powerful than consuming a woman's body. To hold the power to decide if she lives or dies. Drawing pleasure from their fear is our reward for what we do." He stares down at the water, numb to his words.

"I'll let you come with me, once you have mastered this. I

saw the way you looked at those photographs. You can make ones for yourself."

The thought sparks panic inside me. I can't let that happen. I can't become the monster that he is. He's wrong, this isn't a gift. It's a sickness. A curse. And I can already feel it spreading inside me.

"You look real nice," Grimm tells me when I step out of the bedroom. I'm wearing white jeans and a black lace top that shows off my tattoo sleeves. I've spent extra time getting ready, and it feels a little pathetic that I'm so nervous to go hang with a bunch of people who I've been working around for years.

The club atmosphere isn't new to me, but I've never had to worry about belonging here before. I've always kept myself private and helped out when needed. But I've never worried about anyone here liking me. Now I want to be liked, I want to be accepted, because he may not show it all too well, but I know these people mean something to Grimm.

We ride down to the club on Grimm's bike together and although it isn't my first ride with him, I feel every eye drawn to us when he parks up his bike beside all the others.

Some hangouts are crowded around the huge fire that's been made up from the storm debris, and Grimm must sense my sudden discomfort because he slides his hand into mine as he leads me past them into the clubhouse.

Inside is busy too, most club members have chosen to hang in here rather than out by the fire, and I know it's only a matter of time before Grimm does something to show them all that I came here with him.

What I don't expect is for him to lift me up, land my ass on the bar, and kiss the fuck out of me within seconds of us being in the room.

The stares and dead silence all vanish from my conscience. Grimm's lips on mine are a distraction from everything around me. I kiss him back, and when I feel his fingers digging into my thighs, I wonder how far he's prepared to take this little claiming ritual.

When he pulls away from me, his face is so fuckin' serious it's almost threatening. A silent warning, that this is it, there's no going back even if I want to. I let my eyes skim around me to see the effect of his actions. Nyx and Troj are the first people I get a glimpse of, they're sitting on stools at the bar, and both of them look equally as shocked.

"Skid knows about this?" Troj narrows his eyes, seeming unsure.

"Yeah," Grimm answers him without moving his eyes from mine.

"And he's okay with it?" Troj checks.

"Yeah," Grimm repeats, seeming a little lost.

"Nyx," a loud female voice shouts over the music. I feel a huge relief when all the attention shifts from me and Grimm onto Prez's daughter, Ella, who's marching toward Nyx like she's gonna knock him clean off the stool he's sitting on.

"What's up, baby?" Nyx looks calm considering the murderous glare his wife's giving him, and he takes a sip of his beer before he swivels his body round to face her. Crack… her fist smashes into his jaw, and he shakes his head, dazed, before sliding his hand over where she just hit him.

Maybe me and her could get along after all.

"You've knocked me up again." She keeps her voice low, but her tone harsh, and I swear she's gonna swing for him a second time.

"What?" Nyx's eyes expand even more. "Ell, that's awesome." He pulls the dopiest smile I've ever seen on anyone with a dick, and it must be fake because he can't seriously be happy about this fucking disaster.

When he reaches out his hand to pull her close, she shoves it away.

"Dylan isn't even one yet." Her eyes start to fill with tears, and Nyx reaches out for her again, and this time she doesn't stop him. She lets him pull her against his body and take her head in his hands.

"You know this time's gonna be different, right? I get to take care of you." He kisses her forehead and his words seem to soften her a little.

"It's just scary," she admits. "I feel like I'm starting to get things right with Dylan and now this... You're really happy about this?" she checks.

"Another little Carson running around and kicking up hell, what could be bad about it?" His thumb wipes her tears away and his boyish charm manages to draw a smile out of her.

"You're right." She snorts a little laugh, "I'll leave it up to you to tell Daddy the good news." She smiles at him sweetly before turning her back and heading back out. His wide smile and all the color in his face suddenly fades and after shooting Grimm and Troj a worried look, he quickly jumps off his stool.

"Hey, baby, wait up..." he chases after her.

Troj shakes his head and laughs, tapping his palm on the bar to summon one of the club sluts over. "Paige, get pouring, we got some celebrating to do."

Suddenly we're surrounded. Squealer, Screwy, Jessie, Maddy, and Brax's girlfriend Grace all seem to appear out of nowhere.

Paige lays out the shot glasses and pours the bottle of bourbon straight across the top.

Everyone grabs one and Troj raises his long arm above us all.

"To Grimm and Rogue, the most fucked up couple in club history... Oh, and to Nyx's balls, cause Prez is gonna have 'em."

I join in with the whoops and wails around us, clinking my glass against everyone else's, and when I look at Grimm, he's staring at me like he's in a different place to everyone else.

I smile at him, and he smiles back in a way that assures me he's happy, and it warms my body before the bourbon even touches my lips. I don't hold back, because I don't have to anymore. Grimm just made me his. So I lean forward and kiss him like we're alone in his cabin, not caring who sees or fearing his rejection.

Grimm stays by my side, and kudos to Maddy and Grace, who really go to an effort to make conversation with me. They even ask about cars.

Tonight, given the circumstances, I decide to tolerate them, and having a conversation without Maddy prying into my past turns out to almost be enjoyable.

Grace tells me all about the counseling course she's doing, and the foundation she set up with her family's fortune to help the kids who have been affected by corporations like the Agency. And Maddy invites me over to her cabin for the girls' night she's having on Wednesday...

Brax arrives not long after and when he rests his arm on the bar, I immediately notice the blood on his knuckles. Grace goes to him, and he pushes her blonde hair behind her ear with his stained fingers, kissing her mouth like they've been parted for months before he gestures over to Grimm for a private word.

Doesn't take a fucking genius to figure what that's gonna be about.

Grace comes back over with a huge smile on her face, and I watch Grimm nodding as he takes instruction from Brax. Shit looks kinda serious.

"Storm." Grimm takes the box of bottles he's about to top the fridge up with and hands them to Tommy.

"Me and you got somewhere to be."

The look on Storm's face proves he isn't keen on the idea.

"I could come instead," Tommy suggests, puffing out his chest.

"This is club business, grunt," Grimm swipes back at him, and I notice the way it pisses Tommy off. Everyone around here treats him like shit after what his father did, the only reason he gets to stick around is because Skid sees the good in people.

"Take it you have to leave?" I shrug when Grimm comes to me a few minutes later.

"Yeah, you want me to give you a ride back up to the cabin?"

"I think I'm okay down here." My words must surprise him because they surprise me. Strange as it is to admit it, I'm actually starting to feel comfortable around these people. There's an unspoken trust between everyone and for the first time ever, I kinda feel like I'm a part of it.

"Stay out of trouble, I'll be a few hours." Grimm grabs my throat and pulls me in for another pussy punishing kiss before he tips his chin at the others and leaves.

"I've been claimed now, that means best behavior, right?" I call out after him and wink.

"Damn fucking straight," he warns, looking back over his shoulder at me sinisterly before he walks out the door.

I don't want him to go, but this is what Grimm does. These are his people and I can't have him to myself 24-7 despite how much I want to.

A few hours pass and the girls become more fun once they've had a few shots. Maddy even shares some kinky shit about Jessie, which I fully intend to use against him next time we work together.

Nyx and Ella came back to join us eventually, both looking a little flushed, and a lot less tense.

Squealer isn't such a sex pest now he knows that I'm

Grimm's, and even Brax is friendly toward me once he gets himself cleaned up to rejoin us.

"Did I hear that right?" Brax checks, after his brother tells him he's gonna be an uncle again and when a nod from them both confirms it, he buries his head in his hand.

"I got a little freaked out by it all at first, but now that we've talked about it..." Ella looks across at Nyx and smirks. "It's gonna be exciting."

"Can you imagine how cute Dylan's gonna be with a little brother or sister?" Grace gushes.

"Or a cousin," Nyx suggests, grinning at his brother and earning himself a scowl.

"We're enjoying it just being us." Brax looks up at Grace who's perched on his lap looking all dreamy.

"For now..." she warns. "You're on borrowed time, Marshall. Once I'm done studying and setting up the foundation, I'm gonna have a lot of time on my hands." Brax rolls his eyes at her, but I see the hint of a smile in them when they settle back on her.

"I should get back, Marilyn only came to sit with Dylan so we could tell Dad, I don't want to take advantage." Ella gets up ready to leave.

"I'll come too." Nyx finishes what's left of his beer before standing up beside her.

"WHITISH," Squealer lashes out his arm and cracks an imaginary whip.

"Fuck off, Squeal." Nyx uses the hand he's got resting over Ella's shoulders to flip him off.

"I don't know what's happening to you all, these bitches even got our dark prince all tied up in knots now." Squealer taps his toothpick on the table.

"Might happen to you someday, Squeal." Brax reaches forward, grabbing a handful of peanuts and emptying them into his mouth, and Grace laughs at his comeback as she tucks herself back under his arm.

"The day you catch me leavin' this clubhouse before midnight to go home and play happy families, is the day you can put a bullet in my skull. Put me down, brother, my life won't be worth living." Squealer slouches back in his chair, placing his feet on the table and folding his arms.

"Your mother must be so proud," Grace sighs.

"Brax, hush your bitch she's giving me a headac—" Squealer doesn't get to finish his sentence before Brax reaches across to grab his leg, lifting it up and tipping him backward in his chair. Carefully sliding Grace off his lap, he stands up and places his boot into Squealer's throat, the smug asshole doesn't even look worried.

"I've warned you about disrespecting Gracie." I wait for a reaction from Squealer, this has the potential to turn into a full-blown fistfight, but instead, he just laughs.

"Cool it," Jessie warns them both, and Brax retracts his foot and snarls before Squealer gets up and dusts off his cut.

"See what happens to 'em?" He shrugs at Troj. "Cunt struck. These bitches are taking us out one by one. Grimm's just the latest man to fall."

"Why do you have such a problem with people being happy with each other?" I ask, because I'm curious and I can't keep my mouth shut.

"Ain't got a problem, darlin', just think it's a shame these boys ain't embracing the facilities we got here anymore."

"Facilities?" I sit back and get ready to judge this asshole.

"Us single brothers get variety, we get performance, and with none of the drama."

"Here we go again." Jessie slouches back and sighs, this must be a speech he's heard before.

"I just don't get why you'd tie yourself to one woman when you can have a whole heap of them. Last night I had sweet little

Laurie's mouth wrapped around my cock, tonight I might decide to work a shift out of Paige." His eyes move over to the bar where the pretty girl with a pink bob is serving Tac and Thorne.

"And that satisfies you? Treating women like playthings that you can throw away when you're done with them."

"The women that hang around here use us just the same way, darlin'. They use us to get high, they ride our dicks to forget about their problems. Some stay a few weeks, others stick around for the long haul. It's all a fair game, Rogue. Let's see how long you can ride it out."

"She ain't a fucking whore." I spin my neck round when I recognize Grimm's voice behind me.

"Never said she was." Squealer picks up his glass and winks at me before making his way over to the bar to join Tac and Thorne.

"We really ought to go," Ella says, awkwardly tugging at Nyx's shirt.

"All good?" Brax nods at Grimm, who's wearing the same baseball cap that he had on when he came to scrape Eddie up off my floor, it's pulled backward and he's still got the black bandana tied around his neck that I know he would have used covering the lower half of his face while he dealt with Brax's problem.

"It's taken care of." He nods back at him, looking hot as hell.

"Didn't take you long?" I point out, I know how thorough Grimm is with these things.

"It helps when Brax makes them dig their own graves." He smirks across the table at Brax.

"Just because I know about this shit doesn't mean I need to hear details." Grace wrinkles up her nose like she's offended, and Brax sniggers as he shares a dark look with Jessie.

"I thought things had calmed down around here," I point out. The club has been working hard to take down a local pedophile ring, I guess you could look at them as vigilantes rather than bad guys, but I thought all that shit was dealt with.

"Nah, this one was a private job for an old friend of mine." Brax turns his attention back to Grimm. "I'll make sure you get your cut."

"I'm getting a drink then I'm taking you home." Grimm's hand slides over my shoulder and he bends down to kiss my cheek before moving over to the bar.

"That's gonna take some getting used to," Jessie smiles at Maddy.

I can't help being cautious about what Squealer said, and I watch how the sluts here look at Grimm. They all see the appeal in him, same as I do. And they get off on the darkness in his eyes that screams danger.

The nasty little bitch who fingered her pussy for him the other week blushes when he walks past her, and the bitch Squealer was eying earlier is leaning over the bar, her arms pushing her tiny tits together, desperate to get him to notice them.

She's playing a dangerous game with those flirtatious eyes of hers, especially if she wants to keep them. I wonder how many of the girls here have pleasured themselves for him in the past.

It makes me crazy just thinking about it.

Rage builds up inside me when I imagine them flirting with him, and I don't know how the other couples work things, but I want to make damn sure everyone here knows how it's gonna work for me and Grimm.

Getting up from the table, I strut my way over to the bar, and placing both my index fingers between my lips, I whistle loudly over the music. Someone cuts it, and suddenly I have the attention of everyone in the room.

"Just a heads up for any bitch here that thinks it's okay to look, touch or even think about Grimm. This will be the only warning you get…" Reaching out my hand, I grab Grimm's crotch, feeling it harden in my hands.

"This is mine, it's claimed, and I will fuck any bitch up that doesn't heed my warning."

Everyone in the room looks shocked, apart from Squealer who's trying really hard not to laugh. One day he might understand. But for now, his low-life opinion doesn't count.

When Grimm snatches my wrist and pulls me tight against his body, the tension in his grip has me worried I might have taken things too far. I didn't intend to embarrass him, I just needed to set things straight.

"Outside, now." He speaks harshly, downing the shot that's been placed in front of him.

He's mad. Crazy fucking mad.

"I'm not gonna apol—"

His hand slams over my mouth to silence me and I can taste the bleach from them on my lips.

"Outside, now. Unless you want me to fuck you right here with the entire club watching."

This has to be a club first, a bitch claiming a member. Rogue feeling the need to warn the club whores off me may be about to get me some serious shit from the brothers. But I also find it fucking hot.

Her warning proves to me that she feels the same fierce agony inside her that I do.

Dragging her into the foyer, I figure I'm gonna have to take her up to my room because I haven't got the patience to get her back to the cabin.

"Where we goin'?" she pulls me to a stop, then wetting her lips with her tongue, her bright eyes glisten back at me daringly.

"I told you I need to be inside you," I explain, tugging her to move, but she resists, refusing to budge.

"Then be inside me." She has that look on her face, one that hints trouble as her hands grab my cut and she pull me onto her lips. She catches my tongue between her teeth and laughs.

"Fuck me here," she dares when she releases it.

"Here?" I pull back.

She's got to be kidding.

"Yeah, here."

"But…"

Rogue has already loosened my belt and is busy hitching her skirt up over her thighs.

"Rogue, that's not how things work with…"

"I've seen it myself, you guys ain't shy. Fuck me here where everyone can see us."

"It's different with an old lady," I tell her, hissing a breath through my teeth when her fingers coil around my shaft.

"So I'm your old lady now?" The huge smirk on her face tells me that she likes the sound of that. And it's a good job since I have no intention of asking her.

This is me telling her.

"I want everyone to know that I belong to you and that you're mine too. The whole fucking club can come out here and watch if that's what it takes."

I can't say the thought doesn't appeal to me.

I spin our bodies so she's the one pressed into the wall now, then slam my mouth over her lips, rolling my tongue around hers. I lift her skirt higher over her hips with one hand while my other one slides up her throat and clasps under her jaw. She feels so fuckin' good in my hands, and as I trail my nose over her cheek, I inhale her scent.

I've missed her in the few hours I've been away from her, it's unhealthy, but since when has anything that gives you a buzz been good for you? While her hand works me desperately from inside my jeans, I slide my hand between her legs and stroke her pussy. She's wet, primed, and ready for me to remind her needy little cunt who it belongs to.

Pumping me through her palm, she guides me closer to where she wants me. When I drag her panties out my way with my finger and push inside her, she lets out the cutest delighted squeal.

Her grip scrunches into my cut as I slam her into the wall, thrusting fast and hard as I claim what's mine.

My fingers press into her neck, controlling the pace that she moves against me, her wet pussy clutching for more each time I pull my thick cock away from her. The door behind me opens and when I hear people passing through the foyer, I don't stop. I don't care, and neither does she. They can stand and fuckin' watch if they want to. Because when I'm connected like this with Rogue, nothing else seems to matter.

"I meant what I said," she tells me, her long fingernails gripping at my hair and forcing me to look at her. "You ever touch one of those sluts again, I'll make you watch while I cut their throat. I think I'd enjoy watching you clear up another one of my victims." Her warning is possessive, it's fierce, and it makes me slam into her harder.

I use my grip on her throat to pull her onto my lips.

"You're a fucking psycho," I tell her, unable to stop myself smiling against her mouth. Yeah, she's a fucking psycho, but now she's *my* fucking psycho.

"Say's the demon to the devil," she whispers back at me, biting down hard on my bottom lip again and making me taste my own blood.

I offload inside her at the exact same time that her pussy clamps me tight. This girl is gonna be the end of me. This is exactly how I predicted it would be, nothing is enough with her. I can feel the obsession growing inside me and there's nothing I can do to stop it. Going back from this isn't an option, not now that I know how good it feels to own her.

Then after kissing her one more time before pulling out of her, I tuck myself away. I wait while she straightens herself out, admiring how flustered and freshly fucked she looks. And the sweet as sin smile she gives me to tell me she's ready is irresistible.

"Come on, I'm taking ya home. It's been a long night."

"And I ain't finished with ya yet," she promises as I lead her outside to my bike and sit her on the saddle.

"Never knew ya had it in ya, kid," Tac calls over from the other side of the fire pit where he's chatting to some hangouts. I shoot him a serious look back, but when Rogue's devilish giggle tickles the skin between my neck and shoulder, I can't help smiling myself before starting up my engine to take my old lady home.

I leave her sleeping and make myself a coffee before stepping out onto the decking. The lake is calm, and so are the cabins surrounding me but it's still early.

The job I did for Vex last night will have earned me enough money for a month of living support for Mama. The place costs a fortune, but the caregivers are the best in the state, they keep Mama happy and cater to her needs. I can't think about how hard it would be to take care of her myself, and I feel guilty for the dread that puts inside me.

But pretense is a hard thing to keep up, even harder when all the bad shit still festers inside your head and can't be forgotten. Still, I'd rather be plagued with memories than oblivious to reality.

It feels kinda strange having something to feel positive about. Things seem to be going right for me and Rogue. We have the support of the club and from Skid. Being around her surprisingly helps keep my compulsions under control.

When I reach for my cigarettes, I notice a stain on the shirt I'm wearing, I actually can't remember the last time I did any laundry.

Pulling the shirt off over my head, I head back inside. Quietly lifting the clothes out of the laundry basket ready to wash. I roll my eyes when I notice a pair of Rogue's jeans thrown on the floor over on her side of the bed. They're smeared with oil so I pick them up and add them to my pile. She looks so angelic when she sleeps. No attitude, no makeup, just a content expression on her face as she lays out on my pillows, dreamin'.

Once I've set these clothes to be cleaned, I'm gonna speak to

Jessie. See if someone can take care of the garage so I can get her away from here for a day. I know she's feeling trapped, and a little freedom from the club will do us both some good. I also need to ask him what kinda stuff bitches like to do, cause hell if I got a clue on that shit.

I go through the pockets of my jeans, pulling out some dollar bills, and the baggy Tac gave me a few days ago. That's another thing I haven't done in some time, I can't remember the last time I got high.

I can't resist pulling Rogue's jeans to my face and inhaling them, they smell like oil, rubber, and peaches. I may have only had her for a few weeks but I'd know my girl's scent anywhere. I'm fucking addicted to it.

I check Rogue's pockets too and when I pull out a folded envelope and recognize the postmark, it's impossible to resist the temptation to open it.

It's a visiting order, one for Florence. Rogue has kept this from me, like she did the gun. I just can't understand why.

Scrunching the letter in my fist, I tuck it inside my cut, I'll deal with it later. Right now, I need to do laundry and put some space between me and her before I pin her down and fuck some answers out of her.

Bile builds in my throat when I start relating to my father's need to know where Mama was every minute of the day. It's only a matter of time before he starts taking over my head. I want to fight him away, usually, I can. But it's getting harder and harder, especially when all I want to do is protect Rogue.

She isn't leaving this club without me, and if whoever this order is from is important enough for her to want to go visit, I'll be going with her.

I leave the cabin and head down to my basement at the club. The place couldn't be any cleaner, but I need a distraction so I set to work reorganizing the cleaning products and scrubbing off the shelves. I put my headphones in and clean my equipment. Then using a scouring pad, I scrub my hands until they feel raw.

When I come back up the stairs and cross the yard to the garage, Rogue is hard at work, her music pumping loudly and her out-of-tune voice killing all the high notes. I stand and watch her for a while, with all the rage inside me pumping straight to my cock. She doesn't know I'm watching her, and she looks so fucking happy. Now I'm gonna have to stamp all over her good mood.

Why have I got to be such an asshole?

"Shit..." she clutches at her chest when she spins around. Her overalls are open at the front and she's wearing one of my T-shirts. Her hair is tied up with my black bandana and she's got a grease mark under her right eye. I stalk toward her and swipe away the imperfection from her skin with my thumb. I don't care that I carry the mark of it now, just so long as she's perfect.

"You shouldn't creep up on people like that." She grabs at my cut with her filthy hands and pulls me onto her lips. Now isn't the time to press her on the visiting order that's burning a hole through my pocket. I've got it counted as at least nine hours since I'd last been inside her. So lifting her up by her thighs, I kiss her lips and walk us into the office. I kick the door shut with my foot, ready to punish her for all her sins on the desk.

CHAPTER 30

1% MC

ROGUE

"Wake up, wake up." I shake his shoulders relentlessly and when he peeps open one eye, I look down at him with a huge playful smile.

"Come on, get up." I know he's tired but all work and no play makes Grimm a dull boy.

"Come back to bed," he moans, dragging me on top of him, then rolling over to trap me between his body and the mattress. Will I ever tire of wanting him?

"Nah ah. I'm in charge today. I want to give you something," I tell him, resisting the temptation to let him have his way.

"Sounds intriguing." His nose slides up my neck and he sucks my skin through his teeth. Him leaving his mark on me has become my new favorite thing and I crave so much more of it.

"Not that." I reach between us and grab his dick. "I'll be giving you my undivided attention later, big boy." I talk directly to his junk and love the way it makes him laugh.

"Get dressed, I've already made breakfast." I manage to wiggle my way out from under him, and his palm stings my ass as I make my way back out to the kitchen.

"So where are we goin'?" Grimm asks after we've eaten and I'm leading him out to his bike.

"We're going to the park," I announce, watching his expression turn horrified.

"The park?" he checks, looking confused as he climbs on and takes his handlebars.

"Yes, Grimm, the park," I confirm, hopping on the saddle behind him and clinging to his waist.

When we arrive at the park, I'll admit Grimm looks a little out of place, but with his hands tight in his pockets and a scowl on his face, he follows me through the gates until I find us the perfect spot.

Some families look like they're set up for the day and there's a group of older kids playing soccer, but it's not too busy. Luckily the grass is dry, so I lie out flat on my back and pat the space beside me.

"Lay down." Grimm looks around us, and his cheeks flush with color.

"Rogue, there are kids here, I don't think we should be…"

I interrupt him with a loud giggle.

"Just lay down. You'll see what I mean." I sit up and drag on his arm, forcing him down beside me, and when his head is resting beside mine, I loop my fingers through his and stare up at the sky.

"Tell me what you see." I suck the fresh air into my lungs. It feels good to be away from the compound, just the two of us.

"I see the sky… Rogue, what is this all about?"

"You're not looking properly, look again."

Grimm makes an impatient huff before focusing his attention above us.

"Okay, I see blue sky and clouds."

"Yes, you do." I smile. "And that's because you have no imagination."

"Did Squealer or Tac give you something this morning?" Grimm turns his head to me, and I roll my eyes at his accusation.

"Let me tell you what I see." I look back up at the sky. "Over there, I see an elephant." I point to the fluffy cloud that's floating above us.

"A what?"

"An elephant. Look closer."

"That's not an elephant. It's a… Well, I don't know what it is, but it ain't a fucking elephant," he argues.

"Now that over there…" Grimm points to the cloud above it. "That's a pterodactyl."

"You're getting it." I nudge him in the ribs. "Though I'd argue that's more like a Concorde."

"Check out ya elephant, it's shifted into some kinda demon, you see the horns?" he sniggers at me, and I roll on to my side so I can watch him.

"Trust you to find the devil in cloud watching." I laugh, and he laughs too. It feels fucking warm inside me, and for the first time in my life, I want to cry over something that makes me happy.

"Check out that one, it looks like a side profile of Marilyn." Grimm lifts up the hand that's holding mine so he can point.

"She would not love you for that."

I press a kiss on his cheek because I can't resist. Then after I snuggle under his arm, we carry on watching the clouds pass over our heads.

I buy us a hotdog from the vendor, loading them up with onions and hot sauce. We people watch, making up crazy stories about the ordinary people who pass us. Then we get ice-cream and look for more images in the sky. I fall asleep with my head on his lap, the sun heating my face, and his fingers stroking through my hair.

I don't know how long I'm out for before he stirs me awake, but when I open my eyes, the park is almost empty and the vendors are packing away.

"We should get back to the club," he whispers, pulling me up onto his lips. "Thank you for this, I didn't know it, but I needed it."

"I'm glad you enjoyed your gift," I tell him, watching his face crease up in confusion.

"You said the other day that you had no happy memories from when you were a kid. So I gave you mine. The only one I got," I explain. "My mom took me to the park a few months before she left. We watched the clouds together and got hotdogs. We fell asleep in the sun and felt the grass between our toes. Everyone deserves one happy memory, Grimm." I smile at him and feel one of those damn tears creeping up on me again.

"That's the nicest thing anyone's ever done for me," he whispers, the sincerity in his expression so intense it breaks my heart.

But I shrug like it's no big deal.

"Thank you for my gift. I'll treasure it forever." He slowly moves his lips back onto mine and kisses me so softly that I feel my whole body tingle. I have to break the moment before I do something stupid and tell him I'm falling in love with him.

"Come on, you better get me back to the club so you can show me how grateful you are." I hop up onto my feet and pull him up.

"I'm driving back." I snatch up his keys from the grass beside him and race off toward his bike.

Of course, Grimm caught up with me, and of course, I don't get to drive home, but none of that matters when I'm resting my cheek against his back with my arms clung around his waist as he rides us back to the compound.

It's getting dark when we arrive at his cabin, and I can tell Grimm's deep in thought when we're sitting at the table eating the mushroom risotto he cooked for us.

I don't ask him what he's thinking about. I don't want to ruin our day by prying. But when he grabs a hoodie and heads for the door a few hours later, I feel my heart sink.

"I'll be back real soon," he promises before rushing out, and I'm far too stubborn to give in and ask him where he's going.

I wait around for over an hour, flicking through the TV stations and watching stupid videos on my phone. I get bored of staring at my screen so I roll myself a spliff and take it out on the deck, hoping it will chill me out.

"Miss me?" When I spin my head around, Grimm's standing in the doorway, holding a lantern in his hands. I'm sure it's one of the ones that Maddy puts a candle in to make her porch look pretty at night. I can see the tiny flickers of light inside it now.

"I had to get you something. It's not as good as what you got me, but here." He places the lantern on the table in front of me and I lean closer to get a better look.

"Fireflies." I look up at him from the lantern where the bright flickers are dancing against the glass.

"I used to sneak out at night and catch them when I was younger. I always wanted to bring them back and show my mama, but couldn't risk getting in trouble. They'd have made her smile. She liked pretty things." He looks back at me a little awkwardly, like he suddenly feels stupid. "Now I wanna make you smile."

I leap off my chair and fling my arms around his neck.

"I love them." I squeeze him so tight, hoping that he feels how much. And the words are all there, right on the tip of my tongue. I want to tell him that I love him. But I'm too scared of it to say it out loud.

So I remain silent, and we sit together sharing a joint and watching the fireflies dance.

"I should stop marking you." The thoughts in my head come out loud as we lie in bed and my finger circles the purple bruises I made on her thigh last night.

"I like them," she tells me, looking up at me with her big blue eyes and making me want to give her more of them.

"Grimm," she stops me, her dainty hand pulling at my wrist.

"Do you ever think about making more marks on me?"

I close my eyes and take a deep breath. If I could scrape the thoughts out of my head I would.

"Yes," I admit, because I have to be honest with her, even if I hate myself for it.

"I want to try it."

"No." I shake my head firmly, I'm not fucking playing games, especially when I can't guarantee the consequences of them. I'll never test myself with Rogue that way.

"Hear me out." She shifts her body up mine and holds my eyes with hers. "When I was younger, I used to hurt inside so much that sometimes I had to release it…" I want to ask her what hurt her so I can do something about it, but I don't want to interrupt whatever she's opening up to me about. So I swallow down the pain I feel, tuck her hair behind her ear, and listen.

"I'd sit for hours and think about how to make it stop. Then one day I found a way." Her head drops like she's ashamed, and I force her chin back up with my finger.

"My pain felt like a poison, slowly leaking into my bloodstream. On bad days it itched so bad under my skin that I found it impossible to focus," she explains, and I can relate to every word.

"I knew it was wrong, but I did it anyway because it felt too good to spill a little of that poison out of me."

"Rogue, what are you talking about?" I ask, trying to make sense out of what she's saying.

She takes my hand, guiding it so my fingers slip over the inside of her arm, and beneath her colorful tattoos, I feel bumps and ridges that I've never noticed before.

"It's easy to mask pain, you just need to find a distraction," she whispers.

"You did that to yourself?" I check, feeling all my muscles tense.

"For a while, when things got really bad," she admits. "But I stopped when Skid started to notice."

"And did it make the pain go away?" I ask her, curious.

"For a little while, but it always came back."

"So what are you saying, Rogue?" I look at her fiercely, I want to make whoever made her do that to herself fucking suffer.

"I feel that same release when you're inside me," she tells me. "And I wonder how it would feel if you maybe…"

"No, absolutely not." I pull back from her, this is too much. She doesn't know what she's doing.

"Grimm, I want to test us. We need to know each other's limits. I want you to cut my skin, and bleed some of the pain out of me."

I scrub my hand over my face when my dick gets hard at the idea.

"Rogue, you don't know what you're asking me to do." I shake my head.

"I'm asking you to give in to your desires. I'm giving you my permission and trusting you," she explains calmly.

Her hand slides over my torso on its path to the bedside table where the knife I took off my belt last night is resting. I grab her throat in the arch of my hand to stop her and she smiles at me darkly.

"You don't scare me. You won't hurt me. I can't be hurt anymore. She takes my wrist in her hand and pulls it slowly away from her skin and in replacement of her slender throat, she presses the handle of the knife into my palm, before shifting her hot little body to straddle me.

I trail the tip of the knife over her skin, starting at her collarbone and finishing at her waistband and as I slide it across her pelvic bone, she throws her head back and grinds against my hard cock.

"You really want this?" I check, my voice coming out weak.

Can I trust myself? What if I like watching her bleed too much to stop?

"Yeah." She nods back at me, taking my wrist again and guiding my hand back up to her collar bone. "Here," she instructs, and I hesitate before I act. I know I'm gonna enjoy this far too much but I promised myself I wouldn't test myself with her.

"Do it." Her eyes flare at me.

I press the tip of the knife into her skin and drag it slowly through her flesh, and she sighs so beautifully I couldn't regret it even if I wanted to. Her blood drips onto my knife, and the tiny rotations her hips make against me have me desperate to be inside her. So I thrust her up with my hips, slide my free hand between us to grab my cock, and slowly edge it inside her. Rogue takes the knife from my hand and licks herself off my blade, her tongue sliding flat against its metal while her pussy clenches around me.

"Fuck, I wanna taste you." I grab her throat, dragging her

onto my mouth and tasting the copper tinge from her lips and tongue.

She's holding the knife now. She could slit my fucking throat if she wanted to. I pull back and watch the small streams of blood weep from the slit I put in her skin, mesmerized as it slowly trickles over her chest and drips onto her nipple.

There's more than I expected there to be. I purposely didn't cut too deep so I wouldn't scar her, and I give into temptation, fisting her blood-streaked tit in my palm and watching her blood stain me. I find it fascinating how she can counteract all my triggers. I'm craving more of her blood on my skin, and the taste of her in my mouth feels like it belongs there.

"Again, here," Rogue presses the blade against her lower belly, digging its point into her skin. And with her sticky blood coating my hand, I slide my fingers down her body and take control of the knife again.

Her life is in my hands and it feels so fucking precious.

I stare into her eyes as I make another incision and her finger trails through the gash, collecting more blood that she coats my lips with. I snatch her fingertip between my teeth and narrow my eyes at her. How can it be possible to worship something and hate it at the same time?

I hate what she does to me. I hate that she triggers every demon inside me, raising them to the surface and calling out to them to wreak havoc. I cut her again, this time just above her belly button. This time the cut is bigger, but it's still controlled and as soon as I feel the loss of that control start to slip, I toss the knife out of my hand onto the floor. I roll my hips, stirring myself deeper inside her pussy while I slide my hand through the mess I've made of her skin.

I smear her blood all over her hot little body, pushing my hand up between her tits, slipping over her neck, before I wrap my hand around her jaw.

"You look divine when you bleed." I tense my fingers,

admiring the bloody prints they leave on her cheek. Her thrusts against me become more erratic, and I'm gonna fucking come if I don't act fast. Using my strength, I flip her onto her back, and keeping her in the arch of my hand, I look down at her body and admire every inch of it.

I lower my body down hers so I can taste her tainted skin, my tongue working through the mess I've made of her. She fists at my hair, holding my face to her body while I lick and kiss her all the way back up again.

"You're fucking perfection," I hiss at her when my eyes find hers. Then I bite her lip and make her moan before finding my place inside her again and fucking her slow.

I savor every inch inside her blood-slick skin slipping against mine. I don't care about the mess it's gonna make. I'll make us both clean after. I'll soothe her wounds and I'll take care of her. No one will ever hurt her again.

And if it's pain she wants, I'll be the one to give her it.

Something inside me tells me that I'd give her anything.

I t's just past 2pm when I finish up in the garage. Grimm stopped by earlier to fuck me on the desk again before he rode out with Jessie and Nyx, and now I'm left with nothing to do.

I have no idea how long Skid expects me to stay at the club. But I'm not angry about that anymore… I'm not gonna leave now, not with things working out so well with me and Grimm.

But I do want to get out of here for a few hours, and I know just the place to go to pass some time until he gets back.

The thought of seeing Anita excites me, and the more I find out about Richie Carter, the closer I feel to Grimm. Since me and him are a thing now, I figure I deserve to know everything. That, and I'm actually growing to like the woman.

I sign in at reception and make my way toward her room, knocking before I let myself in.

"Evangeline." Anita looks pleased to see me when she greets me with one of her warm maternal hugs.

"I wasn't expecting to see you so soon. Is everything okay?"

She looks worried all of a sudden.

"Everything's fine, I was just passing and thought I'd stop by."

"Well, I'm so glad that you did."

"Peter's away with work and it gets so boring with no one

here to take care of... Good gracious." Anita looks horrified when her eyes fall to my hands. They're a little stained from oil, but they've been much worse.

"Come with me," she ushers me into the bathroom. It's even cleaner than Grimm's, if that's even possible. Leading me to the basin, she runs the warm water and pumps the aromatic hand wash onto my hands. Then she focuses all her attention on getting the black stains off my skin. Her fingers scrubbing until they make me sore and the water almost scalding me.

When she's satisfied that they're clean, she empties the basin and rinses them off with cooler water before carefully patting them dry with a towel.

"There, that's better, we can't have you getting into trouble, can we?" Her smile is warm and, doing my best to hide my confusion, I follow her back to the couch.

She seems calm again now, and it explains where Grimm gets his obsession with cleanliness from.

"You must tell me, did you speak to that boy you're fond of?" she asks with a newfound excitement in her tone.

"I did," I admit, feeling a little strange talking to Anita about her own son, even if she is oblivious.

"And...?" Her eyes widen and I can tell she's genuinely excited.

"It went well, we're kind of a thing now."

"Well that's fantastic. See, I told you he would like you..." She pauses to read my expression. "Why do you look so worried?" she asks with concern in her voice.

"We're complicated. Both of us have issues, we've got pasts that neither of us are prepared to share. It makes it difficult."

"I see." Anita places her hands on her lap and thinks for a moment.

"You do realize that you're in love with him, don't you?"

I immediately shake my head.

"That's not possible."

"Of course it is." She giggles playfully. "And whoever he is, he's such a lucky boy to be the recipient of it. Love is a strange thing, Evangeline."

"And do you love your husband?" I ask, wondering where he is, I've already figured that he doesn't live here with her.

"Very, very much." Her eyes glisten differently when she thinks about him, and I notice a tiny tear developing in the corner of her eye.

"Let's take a walk in the gardens." She stands up, shaking away her sadness, and I let her take my hand and lead me outside.

"Well, that was a waste of time." Jessie's frustrated when he gets back on his bike. Me, him, and Nyx came to the address Skid asked us to check out, but the place is empty and it's fucking clean too.

"This is gonna piss Prez off. He wanted this issue stamped on." Nyx lights up a cigarette.

"Maybe he'd be in a better fucking mood if you hadn't just knocked up his daughter again," Jessie sniggers at him, and I can't help smirk at the scowl Nyx gives him back.

"Come on, we'll ride back to the club and call Skid." Jessie goes to start up his bike.

"You guys ride on. I got somewhere I need to be," I tell them, and they both nod back at me before tearing off.

I turn my bike around and head for Forestbank.

It hasn't been that long since I last went to visit Mama, but spending time around Rogue makes me think about her more. My mother is the victim that I refuse to let Rogue become. Spending more time with her will help me remember how vital it is that I don't let myself slip.

I've never lied to my mama about who I am or what I do. I've just never told her. I allow her to make up her own version of the man I've grown into.

It's the only way she'll ever get the dedicated, hard-working son she always dreamed she'd raise.

Visiting her is always tough, especially when she talks about Father like he's the perfect fucking husband. And playing along with that is draining, but I continue to do it out of guilt.

I park my bike up outside the care home. The rates here are expensive, especially with all the extra handouts I pay to the staff in order for them to play their part in mother's charade. But it's all I can do for her now, and as frustrated as it gets me, sometimes, I find myself wishing that I could live inside her hollowed-out head just for a fuckin' day.

I walk straight past the reception toward Mama's room. It's rare for me to visit on a weekday. I usually show my face on the last Sunday of every month. Mama won't be expecting me, but I'm sure she'll be happy to see me. She smiles continuously when I visit her and tells me endlessly how proud I make her. It makes me feel like shit. But never as much as I do when she tells me how much like Dad I am.

I let myself in and find her room spotless as usual. The patio door is open, so I figure she'll be outside, either reading one of her books or admiring the roses she prides herself in growing. And as I brace myself to step outside into her imaginary world, I see something that stops me.

Rogue... She's here, and she's talking with my mother. The pair of them are laughing, and look so content in each other's company.

Quickly, I step back out of sight, managing to keep my eye on them from behind one of the thickly lined curtains.

Rogue is crouching down now, smelling the bloom that Mama is proudly holding between her fingers. The outside breeze carries the sound of her giggle toward me, and instead of the burning rage I should be feeling, I feel a smile hook on my lips.

I have no fucking clue how she found out about this place or how she's managed to uncover one of my biggest secrets, but I get a strange kinda comfort outta seeing her here. And so I watch them both for a while longer.

They sit down to rest on one of the benches and seem comfortable talking to one another. Mama doesn't stop touching her, stroking at her hair, and holding her hand in hers while they speak. And the more I watch, the more I realize that Rogue doesn't seem like herself. There's nothing sarcastic or fake about the way she beams back at my mama. She's lapping up her attention and accepting all her affection welcomingly.

"Mr. Carter it's good to see you." A female voice distracts me from the unlikely scene in front of me, and when I look over my shoulder, one of the carers is watching them too.

"Your mom will be delighted to have two visitors today." She beams brightly.

"You didn't see me." I try not to make that sound like a threat.

"But..."

"The girl, how often does she visit?" I interrupt, needing answers.

"You mean your cousin? She comes maybe once a week. Is there a problem?" She looks confused.

"No," I snap back. "No problem."

"I'm glad, Evangeline has made a very positive impression on your mother." She gets back to watching them with a fond smile on her face, and reaching inside my back pocket, I pull out a hundred dollar bill and tuck it inside the pocket of her tunic so I don't have to make skin contact.

"I want to know when she visits, text me on the number you have for me whenever she arrives and then again when she leaves."

"Sure," she agrees. I don't know the woman's name but I've always found her cooperative.

I leave them to it when the warm feeling that seeing Rogue

puts in my chest starts to spread to the rest of my body. Then jumping on my bike, I head back to the club.

AGED 16

His body weighs a lot more than I calculated. It's dark and I can't see where I'm stepping as I drag him through the yard.

This is not how I had this planned out.

The rain falls hard, and despite it being a nuisance I figure it'll make clearing any blood trails easier. My arms ache already, despite me working out after school for months. I've lifted logs and sandbags. Repped paint tins and anything else I could get my hands on. But I'm nowhere near as strong as I need to be. I don't know how I'm gonna make it all the way to the woods at the bottom of our field. And I wish I could just leave him out there to rot.

Mama is finally asleep, and I'm determined to have this taken care of before she wakes up. I'd sat and thought about how, and this is my only option. I have to bury him, somewhere where no one will ever find him.

I head to his shed to find a shovel, Father still hates me being in here, even though I know all his secrets now. And when he caught me in here the other week, he'd pounded me every night for a fortnight.

The fucker can't pound me now,

I leave his blood-dripping body on the ground and head through the door. Inside is a lot messier than it was the first time I came in, there's no order in here anymore. Different sized screws and bolts are tipped out on the workbench. Wood shavings litter the floor. It smells bad in here too, like stale cigarettes and paint stripper, and as soon as I locate the shovel I get the hell out of there.

I last remember him using it to turn over Mrs. Draper's rose bed for her. Father always did a good job at playing the good Samaritan around town. But I wonder if Mrs. Draper would still think he was so wonderful if she knew that the ashes of the young woman, who went missing from Durango last month, were turned over with the very same shovel.

There's poetic justice in the fact I'm going to use it to bury him in the ground, and that all the skills he taught me haven't gone to waste.

They'll be used to make sure that no one ever finds him.

I get an idea when I see the wheelbarrow on my way back to him, and I tip out all the leaves I'd raked up before school this morning and wheel it to where his body is waiting, wearing the same empty expression I'd left him with.

I don't know why I'd expected it to have changed while I'd been gone, perhaps it's because I know how mad he'd be at me for entering his sacred shed.

His body feels cold against mine when I lift him up and throw him into the wheelbarrow, pushing him across the field, into the woods.

This land is owned by us. No one ever ventures out there, but still, I'll have to dig deep. I can't risk a wild animal turfing him up.

It's hard pushing such a dead weight and the uneven ground doesn't help. But eventually, I get to a spot where there are fewer trees, and the ground is soft enough for easy digging. Then taking the shovel, I force it into the earth and bring out the first heap.

It's gonna take me all night to get deep enough but I don't stop, even when my muscles beg me to. The rain comes down hard, making the mud slide around me, and it's so much harder to keep going. But knowing that there's so much more work to be done back at the house keeps me moving.

Now that he's gone, I'm gonna take care of Mama the way

she should be taken care of. She won't have to worry anymore. She won't live in fear.

When the hole is past my shoulders, I pull myself out and give myself some time to get my breath back. It seems fitting that I'm laying him to rest in such a filth-ridden hole. I can't remember much of what the Bible says about life after death, but if the rumors are true, Father's soul will be terrorized for all his sins.

Taking his ankles, I pull him from the barrow and tug his body until it rolls into the hole.

His body hits the earth with a hard thump, and I stare down at him. This is how I want to remember him. He doesn't look quite so threatening with his body sliced to pieces, and the crisp white shirt Mama hung on his wardrobe door for him this morning drenched in blood.

I spit on his body before I kick some dirt over him. We're free of him now, and while his body rots away out here, I'll make Mama well again. We'll visit the beach and swim in the ocean. Then we'll stop for a burger at a roadside café. Mama will smile, and if I spill burger sauce on my shirt we'll laugh about it.

When the hole's completely filled, I pull some branches over the fresh grave, put the shovel back in the wheelbarrow, and make my way back home.

The first thing I do is scrub the pool of blood from the garage floor. It's gonna stain but I already have an idea how to cover it up. Father passed a lot of his knowledge on to me and I've adapted some ideas of my own just lately.

Heading back to his shed, I take a tin of paint, some sandpaper and some wood varnish. I pour the paint over the bloodstain, before cleaning it up again, and instead of a red tinge on the floor, what's left is a blue one that no one would suspect.

If only my next job could be so easy.

The living room is a blood bath, the hardwood floor's coated with blood, and red handprints are all up the wall from where he tried to fight back. The carving knife is still where I dropped it, his blood dripping from its tip. I take it to the kitchen and place it in the sink, letting the cold water run from the faucet over my stinging hands and the blade. The water turns red, and I watch it disappear down the drain until it turns clear. The walls are first, and I scrub them with bleach before I use the tin of white paint, that Mama keeps in the basement to touch up the walls, to cover over the now pinkish stains.

The coffee table is broken, so I take that out to the garage. I roll the rug up from the fireplace and take that out too. Then filling up a bowl, I get to work on the floors. Scrubbing them to the best of my ability, and then sanding the places that need attention with the sandpaper I took from the shed. The new varnish in here will still match. It's only been a few weeks since he made Mama re-varnish downstairs.

I step back to assess the area. Aside from the wet paint marks on the wall, and the slightly shinier patches on the floor, you would never know what had happened here tonight.

No one will, ever.

I turn out the lights and head upstairs, stopping when I pass their bedroom to check in on Mama. She's sound asleep, The bruise on her cheek purple and angry looking. I go to her wash basket and take out the clothes that she'd been wearing today. Tomorrow I'll burn them, along with what I'm wearing now and the rug.

"He can't hurt us now," I whisper to her as I kiss her on the cheek. Then I go for a shower to wash the final traces of him out of our lives.

It's been a week since we put the point out to everyone that me and Grimm are only for each other now. My little speech must have worked because all the little hoes down here seem petrified of me. They should be.

I'm locking up the garage when Grimm's bike pulls up in the yard, he looks so damn hot when he rides, and before he has the chance to dismount, I run across the yard, jump on his tank and wrap my legs around him.

"Pleased to see me?" I whisper, looking down between our bodies at the bulge in his jeans. He answers me by grabbing my waist and forcing me to grind against it.

"Put her down, Grimm." Thorne shakes his head as he passes us to head inside.

"Take me home and fuck me." I readjust Grimm's fringe to the way I like it.

"Got to speak to Prez first, you wanna grab a drink while you wait for me?"

"Sure," I shrug, leaping off him. I forget Grimm has club commitments sometimes, and that his world doesn't just revolve around me.

He tugs me back and kisses me, before taking my hand and leading me through the foyer. "You wanna head in there?" His eyes gesture to the small bar room opposite the member's lounge.

The one that Maddy, Gracie, and Ella have claimed as their own now. I shake my head, I'd much rather throw insults at Squealer or talk engines with Storm than listen to Ella moan about decaffeinated coffee or hear Grace gush about her charity work.

"I hear ya," Grimm smirks, guiding me through to the main bar. Mel is serving today and she snarls when she sees us together. She really is a bitter bitch, anyone can see how desperate she is to be someone's old lady. So I purposely fake her a smile that says, 'eyes off what's mine, bitch'.

Grimm gives Storm a nod across the room. Which I know is a signal for him to keep an eye on me and because I'm in a good mood, I let it go and smile sweetly at Grimm when he presses a kiss to my cheek and goes to find Prez.

I roll myself a joint while I wait for him, and Paige, one of the club whores takes the stool beside me. She's a pretty girl, with a unique sense of style, and I make time for her because she isn't fake like the others.

Licking along the rizla, I admire my work before lighting the end and just as I'm about to take a long draw, Grimm snatches it from my mouth and places it between his own lips.

"Shit's bad for ya," he warns me, gripping it with his teeth.

He takes a long toke, then exhales through his nostrils, clouding my face with smoke. I stand up and take the joint from between his lips, turning it around and filling my lungs before I stretch up on my toes and release the smoke directly into Grimm's mouth.

"You guys are so fuckin' hot." Paige's voice reminds me that there are other people in the room.

"Come on, the sooner we get this over with, the sooner I can go check on El," Nyx taps Grimm on his shoulder.

"Where you going now?" I look at Grimm, wondering how much longer it's gonna take before I finally get to have him to myself.

"Church, I won't be long, and I'm taking this with me." He

takes the blunt from between my fingers and dangles it in his mouth, before following Nyx outside.

Prez isn't far behind them and I can tell from the tension in his face that something's going down. The place is suddenly a lot quieter with all the brothers gone. Only whores, hangouts and little old me left behind.

I ask Paige how Abby's doing, and she tells me she's been staying off the compound at Grace and Brax's place. It explains why she wasn't there when I called by her cabin to check in the other day. Paige chats a little about herself to me too. She doesn't feel like she fits in with the other hangouts, and I can see why. The girl is clearly intelligent. She's well-spoken and well-mannered, and I can't help wonder what brought her here. But I won't pry, I know how fuckin' irritating that can be.

I'm heading through the foyer to use the restroom, my eyes focusing on my phone while I type out a text to Skid letting him know everything is okay at the garage.

Not paying attention causes me to collide into another body, and as soon as the scent hits my nostrils the familiarity nearly knocks me off my feet.

Cattle shit, not just a waft, but an overwhelming stench, and I fear looking up and seeing who the smell belongs to.

"Evangeline... I heard you were hanging out here these days." His smug grin hasn't changed over the years, and his face is still as ugly as a bull's ball sack.

"What are you doing here?" I snarl.

"Got some business with Jimmer Carson, he's lookin' for some storage and there's plenty of room up at the farm these days." I shudder when I think back to my visits to the farm.

"Get out of here," I warn him, I can't take him being here.

"Or what, you'll do to me what you did to Eddie?" he sneers.

"I don't know what you're talkin' about," I brush him off, there's no way I'm admitting to slaughtering one of his best friends.

"We know what you're trying to do, Evangeline." His dirty hand moves into my hair and he strokes it tight to my head. It makes my bones freeze and the pit of my stomach flip. "Look at you now, a biker's bitch... and you used to be such a good little girl." The way he chuckles to himself makes me want to rip his throat out.

"I suggest you put your little revenge plot on hold, you wouldn't want these kinda people knowing what kind of a girl you really are, would ya? I imagine that if they did, things would change real quick for ya." He opens the door for me like he's some kinda gentleman and waits for me to pass.

When I come back out a few minutes later, I hope he's left, but instead, he's propped up against the bar giving Mel all his attention. I can feel myself starting to shake, and I don't know if it's out of fear or anger. I have to get out of here before I react, so I head straight for the door.

"Whoa." Grimm places both hands on my shoulders, stopping me when I get outside. The whole gang is with him, and confused faces and hard eyes watch on as my arms wrap around Grimm's waist. Clinging to him like a pathetic little girl. And when I feel his lips touch the top of my head, I breathe again.

"You okay?" He untangles my arms from around him and forces my chin up with his hand.

"I'm fine, I just need a drink that's all." I try to sound convincing.

Now that I have Grimm, I feel strong again. I won't cower out of here because of an asshole like McAlister. Seeing him here just took me off guard, and for a moment I forgot who I am.

I have to find out more about this business he has with the club and make sure it doesn't follow through.

"Come on then." Grimm takes me under his arm and leads me back inside.

I can't stop my eyes from wandering around the bar, trying to seek him out, and when I locate him, he's sharing a drink with

Troj and Prez over on the sofas. Laughing like he isn't partially responsible for ruining my innocent years.

I can't help thinking that the bottle he's drinking from would look better wedged into the back of his skull.

Grimm keeps his hand in mine while he speaks with Jessie, but all I can think about is him, that smell, and how long it used to take to rid it from my clothes and hair.

AGED 12

"You like the baby ones?" He creeps up behind where I'm standing and watching the calves in the barn. Daddy used to come here and work on the machinery, I always liked coming with him to help. There are so many places to explore and things to see.

The place has lost its appeal now, Daddy only ever comes here to drink with his friends these days and he won't leave me at home. Maybe he's scared I'll leave him too.

Since Mama went away, he hasn't done much work. And I hate his friends. I don't like Uncle Nick, Frank or Eddie and I don't like this one either.

"They're sweet," I answer politely, hoping he will go away and leave me alone. Instead, he steps closer and places his hands on my hips. When I try to wriggle away, he holds me firm.

"It must be tough since your mama up and left." He talks to me like he cares, and I nod my head, the tears are already starting to fall from my eyes because I know what comes next.

"Your daddy's not been taking proper care of you, Evangeline." He brushes my hair with his hand. "Pretty girls should always be taken care of." His wet, sloppy mouth invades my mine and he forces my body onto his. I push him away. I've grown stronger these past few months. Chop taught me how to

throw a punch when he saw the bruises on my arm. I told him I was getting bullied at school, and I'm happy for him to think that rather than have him know the truth.

McAlister's grip on me tightens, and his voice turns vicious, "You know your mama left your daddy because he couldn't take care of her. Your old man takes pleasure in things he can't afford, and unfortunately, other people have to pay the price for it."

"Please leave me alone." I try being polite, even though I know it won't work. Not with people like him.

"There are men who want to hurt your daddy, little one, you wouldn't want him to disappear like your mama did, would ya?" The thought makes me panic. Daddy isn't the best parent in the world, but he loves me, and I love him. He's just hurting, he'll get better. I know he will. He just has to get himself over losing Mama.

"I can protect him, make sure the nasty men leave him alone. I just need you to do something for me, Evangeline."

"What?" My lips tremble as I wonder what this one will want to do to me, will he be gentle like Eddie, will he want tears like Derek.

It turns out quick and rough is his style, and I prefer it that way because it's over so fast. I don't even have time to distract myself by counting all the cows in the pen as I squeeze the metal bar in my hand and McAlister makes one long final groan into my ear. Both of us twist our necks around when we hear a sound come from the other side of the barn. Daddy stands swaying against the doorframe, and my heart explodes into a million pieces. This is going to crush him, he can't lose his friends too. No matter how much I hate them. He stares back at us like he can see right through me. He's emotionless and when he turns away and stumbles back out onto the yard, I want to chase after him, explain that I'd done what I did for him so that the bad men won't hurt him now. But by the time McAlister's released me and

I get outside, he's already gone back into the house to be with the others.

The smell still surrounds me even though we're a whole room of people apart. And I want to make him hurt, the same way I did Eddie. When Grimm loosens his arm from my waist to lean across the bar, I make my escape without a word of explanation, rushing toward the door and out into the fresh air before I take the gun that I know Grimm carries in his holster and shoot that mother fucker right between the eyes.

Sucking in clean oxygen, my skin still prickles with the thought of him touching me. My hair still feels infested by his hands, and I shake my fingers through it because I can't fucking stand it.

"Rogue, what's the matter?" Grimm chases after me, and as soon as his palms touch the outside of my arms, it instantly makes it easier for me to breathe.

"Rogue, you okay?" I can hear the panic in his voice and I quickly spin myself around to rest my cheek against his chest. His heart is thumping almost as fast as mine, and I listen to it for a while, trying to remind myself that I'm not a scared little girl anymore. Somewhere along the way, I got strong. Or at least I thought I had.

"Tell me what's got you freaked?" Grimm whispers, scrunching my hair between his fingers and forcing me to look up at him.

He's so beautiful, it almost distracts me, Grimm is my very own dark angel.

"I just want to go home, you stay and hang out. We can fuck when you get back." I take a step back from him, and when he releases me he looks hurt.

"I don't wanna fuck, I wanna talk about whatever that shit

back there was about. That guy you were looking at, did he hurt you?" Grimm looks like an animal ready to tear something apart.

"No… not tonight," I say quietly, then only just manage to grab hold of his cut before he spins on his heels and starts heading back inside.

"Please, I don't want trouble tonight. I just wanna go home." Grimm freezes on my words, anger still flickering in his dark pupils, but when I beg him with my eyes, he takes a long, frustrated breath.

"Then we go home," he tells me, finding his calm. Taking my hand, he moves us over to his bike, and once he's settled on the seat, he reaches his arm behind my back and guides me on behind him.

"Rogue, is there a reason why that man shouldn't be breathing?"

"Please, Grimm, just take me home," I beg, resting my cheek on his back and feeling my body relax when he starts up the engine.

I can't let her see how fucking angry I am. Not while she's so frightened. I know my girl, she's confident, strong, and sassy. The girl that just ran out the club looking so petrified isn't her.

She heads straight for the shower without a word when we get back to the cabin, locking the door behind her. She's never, not once in the whole time she's been staying here, locked herself away from me. And I want to rip the damn thing off its hinges for the distance it puts between us.

I pace the wooden floor, pulling my fingers through my hair, and trying to think of what could have gotten her so spooked. My feet tap against the floor while my fingers stretch and curl. There's too much tension building up inside me, I can't cope with it and I have to figure a way to keep a lid on it before talking to Rogue.

She comes out of the bathroom a little while later with a towel tied around her chest and her hair soaking wet. She's been crying, I can tell that from her puffy eyes, and it makes me fuckin' savage.

She gives me an unconvincing smile and makes her way straight to the bedroom. So I quickly follow her before she can try trapping me out again.

"Rogue, you need to tell me why that man got you freaked

tonight." My voice comes out firm, despite me intending it to be soft, but I can't control my anger.

"I don't want to talk about it." Rogue continues to get ready for bed, pumping some moisturizer on her palm and rubbing it into her legs. She's refusing to look me in the eye and it makes me even more furious.

"There's a lot of shit you don't want to talk about, Rogue, but I'm fed up of you keeping that shit from me, especially when it's clearly important."

"Well, he ain't important so it don't matter."

"It matters to me." I step in front of her so she can't avoid me with her eyes anymore. Her secrets are making me feel so out of control. I can't protect her if I don't know what she needs protecting from.

"Grimm, I'm warning you." She flicks her eyes up at me.

"Tell me," I push.

"If you wanna know if he fucked me, the answer is yeah, he fucked me. Now, will you just drop it?" Her words feel like a sledgehammer to the guts, but if she thinks that trying to hurt my feelings is gonna make me back off, she's wrong?

"No, I won't fucking drop it, why you being like this?"

"You should understand better than anyone why people keep secrets, Grimm. Secrets spread like poison, you can't rid them from your blood no matter how much you cut. They travel inside wherever you go. You're already riddled with your own, why do you need mine too?"

"Did he force you?" The words taste like fucking acid on my tongue

"No," Rogue shakes her head slowly, and I try to hide my disgust, the guy has to be at least thirty years older than her and clearly doesn't take care of himself. I'd smelled him from where I was standing on the other side of the room.

"Did he pay you for it?" I try again, trying not to imagine

him with his hands on her, but it's too late, my mind is already contaminated with the vision now.

"Like I told you, I don't want to talk about it." She's warning me not to push her further, but all I can think about is the old man down at the club and Rogue willingly letting him put his hands on her.

"I got a past, Grimm, you want us to work, then you got to get over that."

"I don't think you should be worried about me getting over it," I snap, tired of her bullshit. When is she gonna realize that I need the truth? She stands up in front of me and without any warning, she slaps her palm hard against my cheek. I quickly snatch at her wrist and pull her closer. She's giving me nothing and I feel so helpless that I wanna make her pay for it.

"Fuck me." Her words send a shiver down my spine. Her eyes are being far too stubborn to release the tears they hold. "I need you to fuck me," she repeats.

I'm so fucking mad at her, it's a bad idea, what I should do is punish her by refusing. But I need to release all the tension inside of me just as much as she does. Rogue's nostrils flare when she inhales. And before I've reached a decision on what I'ma do next, she reaches out and fists my shirt. Her lips are on mine, stealing every word I want to say to her, making me forget every question and swallow every curse. She takes and takes, her tongue rolling around mine, and her lips commanding my silence.

Reaching under the waistband of my jeans, she takes my cock in her hand and starts to pump her fist, firm, fast, and controlled. Her eyes on mine, and all her vulnerability subsided. Determination is all that blazes in them now.

"Fuck me," she whispers again, letting the towel drop to the floor. I could never tire of looking at her body, every angle is perfect. It makes me crazy to think of another man's hands touching her, even if they came before me.

She pushes me onto the bed and gets on top of me, her hand still working me through her palm, and her tongue gliding over my jugular as her fingers fumble between us, ridding me of my belt and ripping open my jeans.

I hiss as she takes my whole length inside her and I grip at her thighs, but she isn't gonna let me control her rhythm. She's gonna take what she needs from me, fast and hard. Pulling my T-shirt up, I hold it between my teeth so I can watch how her sweet cunt stretches around my thick cock.

She takes all of me and holds herself still, her pelvis tight against mine as she keeps me imprisoned inside her. Then she begins to move, painfully slowly. Finding me a new angle of pleasure with every slow euphoric twist of her hips

I press my thumb between her pussy lips and stroke her while she rides me. I love hearing her purr, and she throws her head back, her long blonde hair touching my balls. She's a rare beauty.

There's nothing that compares to her, and I know that if I had to, I'd kill to keep her.

"You make me forget all the bad shit, Grimm," she whispers as I guide her body closer to orgasm.

"Tell me what fucked you up, Rogue." I squeeze her jaw in my hand so she can't avoid my question.

"Not today." She bites down on her lip, shaking her head, and the sassy bitch almost has me spilling my load. I slide my hands down to her throat and it changes the expression on her face back to pleasure.

I own her now.

I control her.

And it's a sick satisfaction that I think she gets off on too.

She calls out my name as she comes. And I release her from my grasp, freeing her body to take what it needs from me, her uncontrolled hands scratching and gripping at my skin as she slams herself harder into my lap. My fingers bury into her ass cheeks, imprinting her skin, marking her as mine.

She stills when I groan and my cock pumps deep inside her. Both of us clutching each other like we fear we'll be torn apart.

"Promise me you'll never leave me." She suddenly sounds weak again, and I lift my head up from her chest and look into her worried eyes.

"Never," I promise. It's the easiest promise I've ever had to make, because having Rogue with me feels like I've found the part of me I never realized was missing. "You could tell me anything, it wouldn't change the way I feel about you." My finger brushes over her cheek.

"I don't know how to do this shit, Grimm, being with you scares me." She guides my hand to touch over her heart and I feel it beat against my palm. "I can't lose you. If I did, I'd go back to being numb again." A stray tear falls over her cheek, landing on my hand and chilling my skin.

"You understand me, don't you?" she asks hopefully, her hand wrapping around my wrist to prevent my hand from moving.

"I understand." I nod back at her because I do. Everything has changed since she came into my life, and whether we're a blessing or a curse for each other, there's no way I'm letting her go now.

She rests her head on my shoulder and curls her arm around my waist. Both of us are shattered.

A few of us rode out to Pueblo today to check out another address Prez had got from his informer, there's no doubt it's where they're cooking meth. The location is perfect for it. I'd sat and watched from far enough away to see the people who came and went. Recognizing one of them from the picture Maddy had of the men in the bar.

After I reported it to Prez, we all took a vote and we'll be moving in on them in the next couple of days.

We'll bring in the people we need answers from. Brax and Jessie can do their thing, and depending on their victim's cooperation, I will no doubt end up doing mine.

I wait until Rogue's eyes are closed and her breathing is steady before I head back down to the club. The guy who'd freaked her out is getting his dick sucked by one of the bitches Tac likes to use, and I storm over to where he is and lift him off the couch by his collar. His cock falls out her mouth and she backs away quickly when she realizes shit's about to go down.

"Easy, brother." Troj pulls at my shoulder but I shrug him off.

"This asshole knows something about Rogue," I explain, keeping my eyes on the stinking piece of shit I've got gripped. Troj holds up his hands as he takes a step back.

"That true?" Prez shoos Haven off his lap and steps up beside me. "You know Rogue?" he asks the prick who's currently cowering in my hands.

"I didn't touch her." He shakes his head.

"See that's funny, 'cause she told me that you did." My face stands just an inch from his and I stare back at him with wild eyes.

"You know these men?" I shove the photo that I carry around in my cut into his chest. He chokes and sputters as he studies it. His head shaking some more, and I don't need a fuckin' degree in psychology to know he's a mother fuckin' liar.

"Bad shit happens to liars around here," I threaten, side glancing at Jessie whose hand is already twisting the handle of his knife.

"You start talking, or my friend here will cut that bullshitting tongue out ya mouth."

"I know them," he admits, his eyes falling to the ground. "They hang out at a bar in Pueblo."

"And what would they want with Rogue?" Prez asks, turning a chair round and straddling it.

"Hell if I know, you know what she can be like she's always getting herself in trouble." My restraint is about to snap.

We're so close to nailing those fuckers, and him turning up at the club can only mean bad news.

"You came to me and offered me storage. You ain't asking for much rent, and you know the shit we'd be keeping there ain't legal. What's in it for you?" Something is clicking in Prez's head and I don't fucking like it. The guy suddenly looks a lot like someone who's been caught out.

"Jessie." Prez flicks his head toward the guy I have pinned, and as Jessie starts moving forward, his head starts frantically shaking and he strains against me.

"Ivan! the guys work for Ivan, they run a few of his houses out in Pueblo."

"Crank or whore?" Jessie asks a question that I don't want to hear the fuckin' answer to. We know it's fuckin' Crank, we checked the place out earlier.

"Crank. Eddie was working for him too, and they know what happened to him."

Jessie presses the tip of his knife under the man's chin, causing sweat to pour out of his forehead. "You workin' for this Ivan too?" he asks, and when the man nods his head, the knife makes a dimple in his skin.

"So you came here, offering us a deal so you could take them back some information?" Prez remains cool, lighting himself up a cigar.

"What do you want to know?" he shrugs. Prez acting so calm ain't a good sign for the guy.

"Ivan wanted to know if you knew about the houses and if the girl that killed Eddie was here," he admits, and Prez nods his head, slowly taking in the information he's being given.

"Anything else?"

"He wants the girl to pay. Eye for an eye."

Jessie gives me a side glance that warns me not to react, but the rage is almost at the surface, and it's gonna unleash all over this motherfucker.

"Grimm, go be with your girl," he says, his hand taking over from mine, pinning the fucker against the wall.

"No way, I'ma make this fucker pay." There are still too many unanswered questions, like how this fucker had managed to get his dirty fucking hands on her?

Does he have anything to do with that visiting order I'd found a few days ago?

And who the fuck is Ivan? I've never heard of him, and judging by the look on Prez's face, neither has he.

"Jessie's right, Grimm. Go be with Rogue, we'll handle this." Prez looks at the man while he's speaking to me. "This man came to *my* club, he drank *my* liquor and he used *my* girls. And he intended on running his mouth back. Believe me, he's gonna pay."

"But—"

"Grimm, Rogue needs you. I ain't never seen that girl look the way she did when she ran out of here." Prez is right, this goes way beyond personal now. This guy has a death sentence laying over his head. It ain't my job to execute. That privilege belongs to Jessie or Brax. All I'll get is his cold stiff body when they're done with him.

I storm out of the club onto my bike because Rogue needs me, she needs to be protected now more than ever. That asshole just confirmed it.

The guys in the photo want her to pay, she's in just as much trouble as we suspected. I can't let her leave the club now, not even under supervision.

When I get home I check in on her, she's sleeping soundly. Watching her look so peaceful soothes a small part of me, I need it. I hate that it's Jessie who gets to make the man, who came here to taunt her, bleed.

She wakes up screaming a little while later, and I hold her

until she goes back to sleep. I kiss her and tell her she's okay, and it makes me thankful that I get to be the one who calms her. She needs me here with her now, but tomorrow while she's working in the garage with the twins, I'm gonna find out what that man did to make her so afraid.

"Looking for something?" Grimm looks smug with himself as he rests his shoulder against the door frame, he's only wearing black jeans and his hair is still ruffled from sleep. He looks disastrously delicious, but I can't tell him what I'm looking for, not without having to give him an explanation.

I can't find the visiting order Dad sent me, and I really need to find it so I can respond.

"Just squaring things up around here." Looking around the room, it's obvious to both of us that I'm lying, there's nothing to 'square up'.

"You know, if you tell me what it is you're looking for, I might help you find it." He steps closer and wraps his arms around my waist. His devilish smile reaches all the way to the cross that's tattooed beneath his eye, and I slide my hands over his biceps.

"It's nothing," I assure him, hating the way his smile instantly drops. He lets go of my waist and heads over to the door where his cut is hanging, then takes something from the inside pocket and slams it on the table beside me.

"Thanks for your honesty," he snaps, looking fucking stung as he walks out and slams the door shut behind him. Looking down at the table, I see the thing I've been looking for. Grimm had it all along and I pick it up, ramming it in my pocket as I chase after him. When I open the door, he's pulling on his white T-shirt, and he slicks back his hair as he silently steps past me, like he can't bear to be in the same room as me.

"Don't be like that, Grimm. I was just—"

"Keeping more shit from me?" he interrupts me mid-sentence. "Rogue. I've told ya, there ain't nothing from your past gonna make me not want you. But I'm starting to wonder what the fuck it is you're keeping from me. I've seen the damage you can do, hell, I've been the one to fuckin' deal with it. But you ain't invincible. And all this 'keeping shit from me' stuff… scares me."

"Scares you, what? You're not making any sense."

"It doesn't matter 'cause you ain't going to that visit." He looks at me with narrow eyes that dare me to answer him back. And I can't decide if I want to kiss him or make him bleed.

"Last I checked, I was a grown woman," I bite back.

"Yeah, a grown woman who has people out there who want her dead. And people here who need her alive. You ain't leaving this compound until shit's cleared up, and you certainly ain't goin' to no damn high category prison."

"He's my father." When the words blurt desperately out my mouth, I immediately wish I could take them back.

Grimm looks a little shocked but he still isn't backing down.

"Then he'll understand why I want to keep you where I know you're safe."

"Jesus, Grimm." I roll my eyes at him.

"Can't you see that I'm doing all I can to keep you safe?" He slams his fist into one of the wooden beams that are holding up the ceiling.

"You're trapping me, Grimm, forcing me into a corner, and I'll strike if you keep pushing me," I warn.

My words hurt him. I can tell from the way he stares back at me, and he holds me with that stare for a really long time before he speaks again.

"You ain't leaving this club," he snarls, pulling on his cut and leaving without looking back. I chase him to the door.

"I'll do what I please, Richie Carter, and if you try stopping me I'll make you regret it. Who's gonna clean up then?"

I go back inside, slamming the door and screaming out in frustration. Then I burst into tears. Grimm's only trying to protect me and he's right, there's so much he deserves to know. But I can't bring myself to tell him. He'd see me differently if he knew. Nobody wants to play with broken toys, not even Grimm. And if he thinks McAlister and the guys in that photo are the only fucked up secret I want to keep hidden. He's wrong.

AGED 18

"Happy Birthday." Skid's voice is about as enthusiastic as a husky biker can get, and the cupcake he's holding looks tiny in his huge, oily palm.

"Really?" Placing my hand on my hip, I scowl at him. He knows I don't do birthdays, I'm against sentimental shit like that.

"Come on, not every day a girl turns eighteen."

I manage a smile back at him before I snatch the damn thing out his hand. In one sharp blow, I extinguish the candle, then trail my finger through the frosting and bring it up to my mouth, sucking in the creamy goodness.

Chop sits at the desk watching me, his narrow eyes immediately causing me to pull my finger from my mouth. Suddenly the frosting doesn't taste quite so sweet.

"Here, it ain't much, but we had to get ya somethin'." Skid holds out a gift, it's clear from the way it's presented that Carly's wrapped it…

I undo the ribbon slowly, trying to remember the last time I got given a gift, then I quickly shake the dark memory that

*resurfaces away. Opening the paper, I can't help smiling when I
see the bright pink overalls, with 'Rogue' embroidered on the
chest.*

*I've been hanging out here at the club's garage for nearly ten
years now, I even dropped out of school when I was sixteen so I
could spend more time here. Of course, Skid flipped his nut when
he first found out, but I managed to talk him around eventually.*

*But today, this is their way of telling me that I'm here for
keeps. That I belonged here with them. And it means a hella lot
to me.*

"We've just about taught you everything we can. You
officially ain't the garage bitch no more," *Skid laughs, slapping
me hard on the back.*

"Thanks." *I launch myself at him, my arms not quite able to
wrap all the way around his massive shoulders. He affectionately
squeezes me back, almost taking all the air from my lungs. When
he lets me go, I slowly edge toward Chop.*

"Thanks, Chop." *I tense as I lean in and give him a hug too.
Things between me and Chop have always been a little cold, Skid
tries telling me he's that way with everyone, but I sense
differently.*

*Chop returns my hug loosely, his firm tap on my back
signaling when we're done.*

"Carly wants you to come by the cabin tonight for dinner,
that's unless you got any other plans of course?" *Skid picks up
the clipboard and slides a pen behind his ear.*

*I've never been one for socializing around the club. I show
up, I work, I go home. Skid and Carly are good people. They are
kind to me, but they aren't my family.*

*Still, the thought of spending my birthday alone isn't all that
appealing.*

"Sure," *I nod, and I can tell Skid is pleased with my answer.
How hard will it be to hang out around theirs for a few hours
after work, eat some food? I enjoy their company.*

"Dinner will be at eight." Skid winks, before leaving the office to get stuck into the day's jobs. I give Chop an awkward smile before following Skid out into the workshop.

Chop may look similar to his brother, but he's very different in nature. He's never mentioned anything about how I'd come to be here, not since the day he caught me stealing, but I know he doesn't trust me, and the feeling is mutual.

By late afternoon, Chop has done his usual and gone AWOL, leaving Skid and me up to our necks. The silence out on the yard quickly turns into chaos, and Jessie charges into the garage like a bull.

"Skid, we got to ride out." His hand slams his against the bonnet of the car Skid's working on. Rolling out from under the chassis, Skid is up on his feet and stripped of his overalls in seconds.

"You're gonna have to manage things till me or Chop get back," he instructs, pulling his cut over his shoulders. Whatever shit the club has going on sounds pretty serious, and it's likely that's where Chop is occupied too.

"I'm a big girl now, remember?" I tease, shooing him away.

"See you back at mine later," he says, before rushing out the door and leaving me with a stack of jobs to do by myself. So, I crank up the stereo, pick up my wrench and get back to work.

Being busy is something I never take for granted. My mind only ever seems clear when I have tasks to put my energy into. I continue to work past dusk, and curse myself when I check the time and realize it's already past 7. There's no way I'll have time to go home and change before dinner now, and with no sign of Skid or Chop, it looks like I'm gonna have to lock up by myself too.

Struggling out of my overalls, I do a quick check of myself in the mirror. Almost all my make-up from this morning has worn off. So I quickly touch up, pull my hair out of the messy bun on top of my head and try my best to smooth it out.

The low rumble of the roller door closing causes me to jump, and I spin around ready to curse Skid for damn nearly giving me a heart attack. Instead, I freeze when a very pissed-looking Chop is standing in front of me. His arms hanging at his sides and his fists clenched tight. He's breathing real heavy, like there's something he needs to get off his chest, and I quickly scroll my head for reasons for his anger to be directed at me.

"Did I scare ya, darlin'?" Chop moves a few paces toward me, and I step backward until the metal filing cabinet prevents me from going any further. I recognize the look his eyes hold, have seen it more times than I like to remember, and when he rubs his lips together like a hungry predator, gut instinct tells me exactly what's coming.

"You look worried, Rogue," he taunts, hanging his head to the side as his body presses into mine. Judging from the reek on his breath, he's drunk enough to ignite.

"And here was me thinking you were fearless." He chuckles at me like he's letting me in on a private joke.

"I gotta get goin'." Faking him a smile I attempt to pass him, but his huge hand blocks me, meeting with my chest and slamming me hard into the metal behind me.

"You ain't goin' nowhere. You see, I've been talkin' to some folk." One of his thick fingers twists itself around a few strands of my hair, and my stomach threatens to empty. "Turns out you ain't quite the helpless little innocent my brother thinks you are," he sniggers.

"I don't know who you been talkin' to, Chop, but you got me all wrong." I do my best not to show him any fear, assholes like him feed off that kinda shit.

"Eddie," he whispers the name, hitting me with more liquor-laced fumes as he speaks against my cheek. Just the sound of his name makes me shudder, and Chop's reaction proves he knows it, the gruesome smirk he watches me with tells it all.

"Turns out all these years I've been missing out on something."

I shove his body as hard as I can, just about managing to jerk him away. I try not to panic as I rush toward the exit. The shutters are down but they aren't locked, and though it's heavy I know I'll find the strength to lift it if it means getting away.

But I don't get far enough away from him to worry about that, Chop's forceful arm wraps around my waist, wrenching me back onto him, and his breath is hot against my ear as he speaks.

"I'll make this real quick for ya, Rogue." *He lifts my body from the ground as if I'm weightless, and I use every attempt I can to get away.*

When I scream he silences me, squashing my lips and cheeks in his sour-tasting palm. I fight like hell, my elbows jabbing his body and my legs kicking. Yet he still manages to maneuver me like a ragdoll, forcing the front of my body over the hood of the Sedan that I've been working on for most of the day.

His belt rattles and his low desperate grunts muffle into my hair as I feel his cock hit against my back.

"You think you got me and my bitch brother wrapped right around your pretty little finger, don't ya?" *He forces the jeans off my hips with his free hand, pressing his body hard into my back. His weight crushes me into the car, and tears pinch between my eyes when I feel him hard and strained pushing against my entrance.*

"You may have him fooled, but I see ya for exactly for what you are... Slut." *His warm, wet tongue slides over my cheek, and when I fidget to get away from it, his cock presses even tighter against me.*

My stomach clenches as he pushes a little more of himself inside me, a low moan of relief escaping from his throat as he invades.

"Please stop," *I whisper, already feeling all my strength*

draining from my body. This can't be happening, not here, not when this has been my safe place for so long.

Chop ignores me, rutting me hard against the car, the grill on the front chassis digging deeper into my shins with each thrust he forces inside me.

The pain is unbearable and when my body refuses to respond to him, Chop spits into his palm and rubs his saliva between my legs.

I refuse to release my screams for him, I'd sooner choke to death on them before I give him the thrill of my terror.

I count each thrust, willing for him to burn out, and it feels like hours before his body finally stiffens and his massive hand grips at my hip, squeezing into my skin as he empties himself.

Released from his hold I topple forward, my cheek resting against the cool metal of the hood while my breath comes back to me.

Chop flops out of me, and I feel a tiny sense of relief when I hear what sounds a lot like a condom snapping off his dick.

I gasp when I feel his hands back on me, reaching around and grabbing at my throat before spinning me to face him.

"Don't think for one minute you got me in the palm of that pretty little hand, Evangeline." He smiles at me cruelly, letting me go and taking a step back. My legs fail to hold me, and I slide off the car landing in a heap on my ass. Chop tosses the filthy used condom at me and it lands between my legs.

"Best we don't tell Skid about our little secret, darlin'. Hell, if that fucker gives up on ya, you ain't got nothin' left." His words are harsh, and the fact they're accurate feels like acid eroding through my chest.

Chop makes his way to the door, rolling it up just enough for him to duck underneath. I pray for the thing to fall down and crush him for what he's done to me, for making me feel like this again after feeling freedom for so long.

"Oh, I almost forgot…" He pokes his head back under, giving me a glimpse of evil one last time before he leaves.

"Happy Birthday, Rogue," he sneers.

I don't know how long I sit on that floor, staring at the discarded condom as it leaks out onto the concrete. My limbs are sore, my skin bruised and the inside of me empty of anything other than hate.

I think about running, of never coming back here. But the fact that it's exactly what Chop wants gives me the determination not to. For what he's just done to me, I'm prepared to make it my life's work to make sure that I stay.

Eventually, the feeling finally comes back to my legs, and my head stops spinning. I scramble onto my feet, grabbing my purse and trying to ignore the raw feeling between my legs as I hobble toward my car.

"Happy Birthday, darlin'." The male voice startles me, and when I spin around I find Squealer's eyes dancing over my body greedily.

"You okay?" he asks, squinting his eyes like he can sense something's off. "You look kinda freaked."

"I'm just tired." I pull everything together so I can smile at him.

"I got somethin for ya if you wanna come back to mine?" Squealer fists his junk, and when his cut moves slightly I catch a glimpse of the dagger he's got strapped to his belt.

It sparks a little bit of life back inside me.

"That's sweet of you, Squeal." I pace closer and rest my palm on his solid chest. I watch his lips curve up into a smirk as I slide it down over his impressive abs, all the way to his belt. Then stretching high up on my toes, I allow my lips to touch the skin just below his ear.

"But ya ain't my type," I whisper. Turning my back on him, I head back toward my car, taking a quick glance down into my hand and smirking to myself. I managed to retrieve it so

smoothly he didn't even notice. But then, I always did have swift hands.

"Never had you down as a cock tease, Rogue," Squealer shouts after me.

"There's a lot of things you don't know about me, sweet cheeks," I call over my shoulder, before sliding into my car and tucking Squealer's little weapon into my boot.

And the next time Chop or any other fucker thinks they can hurt me, I promise myself that I'll teach them a lesson that will be their last.

There's only one way to bury this shit for good, and that's to bury them.

I'm done looking over my shoulder, I won't be this club's latest problem. I'm not sinless and innocent like the other girls are. I don't need protection.

I'm fucking Rogue.

I protect myself.

Always have and always will.

I can work on forgetting them… when I know they're all destroyed.

Rushing back to the bedroom, I open the underwear drawer and take out my gun. I tuck it into the back of my jeans before I check myself in the mirror. My make-up is on point today and it seems I'm having a good hair day too. I'm ready to do the world a fuckin' favor and rid it of some assholes.

I leave the cabin, crossing the yard and getting in Skid's car, then I speed out of the club knowing exactly where I can start my hunt.

The bar out at Pueblo is quiet, but it's still early. Stevo is sitting at his usual spot at the end of the bar and he doesn't even look up from his paper as I strut in. Not until I pull the gun from my jeans and press it against his temple, anyway.

"They ain't here," he tells me, without even flinching.

Stevo never touched me himself, but he knew that they did and he'd never tried to stop them. He let them use his bar to drink and brag about it. He fed me chips and supplied me with sodas when Daddy brought me here with them.

I wonder if he was ever sick enough to have wanted to cross the line with me too.

Maybe I should blow his brains out against the wall just in case.

"Tell me where I can find them," I ask him calmly, I've got to stay cool and think straight.

"Let me think about this, you already sent one of them on a one-way trip, so that just leaves Nick, Derek, and McAlister."

"Start speaking, Stevo." I press the gun deeper into his skull and he rolls his eyes. He probably thinks this is an empty threat, and I fire a shot into the floor to prove there's nothing empty about my barrel.

"They've been spending a lot of their time out at McAlister's farm, you know it?"

"I know it," I tell him, getting ready to leave.

"Rogue, you ain't thinking about doing anything stupid, are ya?" he asks me, almost sounding like he's concerned for me. He's about ten years too fuckin' late on that one.

"Nothing that shouldn't have been done a long time ago."

He yelps out in pain when I put a bullet in his knee cap, and I leave him rolling around on the floor in agony to go in pursuit of justice.

I park up on a hill that looks down over the farm, making sure I'm sheltered by the tree line. The first guy that I see come out, pulls the white mask off his face, and sits on the bottom step of the porch to light up a cigarette. He's young, probably around my age but I don't recognize him. This must be where they work from these days, and it's only a matter of time before one of the raping bastards stop by. I'll wait it out and I'll take them down one by one. Then I'll go back to Grimm and I'll tell him the truth.

He may not think of me as the same person after, but if it's honesty he wants, he'll get it. Every ugly part of it. And he'll see how strong I can be when he realizes I took care of my business.

I wait for the guy to go back inside the house before I get out of the car and go to the trunk. I stopped by the hardware store and got a few supplies on the way out here. A bullet to the head is far too courteous for these sons of bitches. I want them to scream like Eddie did. But I've learned from living with Grimm how vital it is to be through.

I take out the crowbar so I can keep it on the front seat beside me. I may have to move fast and I want to be prepared.

A rustle in the bush behind me distracts me and when I turn back to the trunk I'm met with a solid fist to the face, one so strong that it knocks me on my back and makes the sunlight, that pours through the trees, turn black.

I had to get out of there, I had to fucking breathe. Rogue just doesn't get that all I want to do is protect her. To keep her fucking safe, and now I'm starting to wonder if I'm gonna be able to do this. I got angry back there. I threw my fist at a fucking beam because I wanted her to feel the pain inside me.

I just need her to understand and let me take care of her.

I've spent every day since I was fourteen years old telling myself that I won't become him, that the power he used to preach about doesn't exist. But I'm feeling it inside me, now more than ever. Rogue draws it out of me, she plays with it between her dainty little fingers like it's a fucking game, and she doesn't realize how close to destruction she's getting.

I pull back my throttle and ride. I let the wind blow against my face, and the pain sinks deeper into my chest as I realize that the biggest threat there is to Rogue, is me.

"You haven't got a choice. This is God's gift."

I hear his voice in my head and try so fucking hard to blank him out.

I pull my bike up outside the church and I race inside, pushing through the doors and storming up the aisle. When I reach the top of the alter, I drop onto my knees, staring up at the stained-glass window that shines down on me and let it heat up my skin.

"Take it," I speak out loud, the shake in my voice becoming uncontrollable. "If it's true and you put it inside me, you take it away right now. Or fucking take me." I draw the knife from my boot and place it on the altar. "I will not live with your curse inside me. I will not become him."

Picking the knife back up, I scrape its blade through my palm and squeeze my hand together, the blood drips through my fist and onto the tiled floor beneath me. I want to drain the rage from my blood and expel all the compulsions I battle with.

"I hate you," I yell, feeling an invisible belt tighten around my chest. "I hate him." I slam my palm hard onto the floor.

"Richie Carter." I hear my name and I wonder if it's the devil summoning me.

"Is that you?" I hear the clipping footsteps getting closer and when I turn around, I see Mrs. Dwight.

"I thought I saw you come in here." The pastor's wife smiles at me warmly, her eyes swelling with concern when she sees blood dripping from my left hand and a knife in my right.

"Richie, are you okay?"

"I didn't come here to hurt anyone," I tuck the knife away. This woman was friends with my mama, she showed her warmth and kindness every Sunday. I won't have her scared. I wipe the tears from my eyes with the back of my hand and feel the blood from it streak my face.

"You're hurt. Let me take a look," she moves toward me and when she reaches out to me, I pull away from her.

"Take a seat," she points to the front pew, then disappears behind one of the curtains and brings back out a first aid box.

"It's been a while since we've seen a Carter in our town." She sits beside me, very carefully taking my cut hand in hers and assessing the damage.

"You came here angry. Did yelling at His Lord Father make you feel better?" she asks me, with such a calm tone that I wonder if I'm imagining her.

"It's okay, people get mad at Him all the time..." She leans forward and whispers, "Even I do."

"I'm mad at myself." The admission comes out of nowhere. "I made myself a promise and I don't think I can keep it."

"Oh." She nods understandingly, as she swipes an alcohol wipe through the gash I made in my palm.

"So once you were done yelling at Him, you were going to ask Him for His strength?" she smirks.

"I don't want His strength, I don't want anything from Him," I bite back.

She nods her head contently at my answer, and I can feel myself thawing to her calm.

"Do you think He calls upon people to do His work?" My eyes glance up at the ceiling.

I'm not an idiot, I know my father used God as his reasoning to do bad. But since Rogue, I've felt the power inside me grow. I'm starting to doubt my logic.

"You mean people like my husband?" Mrs. Dwight chuckles.

"My husband spends every Sunday here preaching from that book," her head points over to the stand where his huge Bible lays open in preparation for his next sermon. "I find humor in the fact it was written thousands of years ago and we still use it as our guide. We've evolved. Times are different now. The Lord's book needs an update," she sniggers, who knew the old woman has had a sense of humor for all these years.

"So what brings you back into town?" She places a pad over my cut, then carefully binds my hand with a bandage.

"I don't know. Anger, resentment. Forgiveness."

"Oh, so you want His forgiveness too?" she chuckles. "You realize that in order to get that, you have to forgive yourself first. We can't seek the approval of just one man. We have to find it in ourselves and in the people around us. We have to accept ourselves as the person He created."

"And what if that person has evil inside them?"

275

"If you came here a sinner, Richie…" her finger touches the badge that's sewn onto my cut. "…only you get to decide what man leaves."

"I want to be the man she deserves. I don't want to hurt her. I want to heal her," I confess, and it feels freeing to say the words that have been plaguing me out loud. "I'm scared of what's inside me. She's already been broken and she won't tell me how. Whatever it is that hurt her so badly, I feel the force of it inside me whenever I'm with her. And the pain it causes me makes it impossible for me to imagine what it does to her. How can my damaged soul be any good for hers?"

"People fix each other all the time, they pull strength from each other… *that* is God's work." She looks at me cleverly before snapping the lid shut on the first aid box and smiling at me. She places it back where she got it from and then pauses in front of me.

"He sends things to try us, and when we overcome them, the rewards are great." I freeze when she places a kiss on the top of my head.

"Be great, Richie." She smiles at me one more time before she leaves me alone, and her heels clip against the tiny white and red tiles that line the church aisle.

I sit for a while and evaluate what she's said. I want to believe it's true, I want to believe in the good. But I haven't seen much of it in this world.

No one will ever know until their judgment day if all this is real, and pulling my fingers through my hair, I decide that I have to take the risk.

I'll believe in the higher power until I'm proven otherwise. I'll have faith that He has work for me to do. My work is to heal Rogue, to guide her forward, and protect her. And when my judgment day comes, I'll just pray that He forgives me for the things I did in order to make that happen.

I dip my hand into the stoup on the way out of the door,

wetting my fingers and feeling the holy water singe my skin as I touch the sign of the cross from my forehead, to each shoulder.

I'll save Rogue's soul, even if it means sacrificing mine.

Turns out, my father was right all along.

The power is strong. So strong that it can strike at any time, and *this* is how *I* control it.

AGED 18

"Hello, Evangeline." *Frank's voice makes me shudder. It's been a long time since one of Dad's friends turned up here. I knew that Dad was meeting them all tonight at the bar, and this one reeks of alcohol as he sways into my room and sits on the edge of my mattress. Him getting in here proves they still have a key, and I wonder if any of the others have come with him as he starts removing his boots.*

I've been doing a lot of reflecting since Chop raped me at the garage last week. I like the person I get to be when I'm there too much to let him take her from me.

Rogue is the girl who doesn't give a shit, nobody or nothing can hurt her.

Chop looked surprised when I showed up for work the morning after my eighteenth birthday. On the inside, I may have been aching but on the outside, there wasn't a chink in my armor.

I smiled at him when he turned up for his shift. I made him his coffee, same as I did every other morning, and I carried on as normal. As the day moved on, I started to feel more and more powerful.

Every step I took made me sore, but I never let him see it. I giggled with Skid when he sent Tommy over to the club to ask

Prez for a tub of elbow grease, and I sang at the top of my lungs when a song I knew came on the radio. I blanked out all the bad and worked my ass off to show the fucker that he had no effect on me.

It's been a long time since one of Dad's friends have touched me, I guess I lost my appeal to them when I started to develop, or perhaps they got scared when I dropped out of high school and started working full time at the club. So, as Frank wipes his mouth with the back of his hand and then slides it up my thigh, I wonder what brought him here tonight.

"You wanna play a game?" he whispers, his dirty thumb swiping over my lip. No, I don't want to play his game. His games always used to hurt.

"I know it's been a while since I stopped by, but that doesn't mean I don't think about you." Taking my wrist, he forces my hand onto his crotch, and I feel him hard beneath my palm.

"You see what you can do to me, Evangeline," he tells me proudly,

"I want to make you happy too, you gonna let me make you happy, sweetheart?"

I want to laugh at him. How in the hell does he expect to make a girl happy with what he's got packing?

I remain silent and let him climb on top of me, and I think about them all, Nick, Eddie, Derek, McAlister. All those men stole my childhood from me. Chop was just another name on the list, but I vowed he would be the last.

And as I feel Frank's wet, sloppy lips touch mine, and smell the acidic stench of his breath... I decide that the time has come to make them pay.

"You're going to really enjoy this next part, Evangeline." He flashes me a yellow-toothed snigger as he reaches his hands into the front of his pants to release himself, and I smile because I reach for something too. Something that I've kept under my mattress since the night Chop thought he could break my spirit.

And this time, I really am gonna enjoy the next part...

"What the fuck did you do?" My father stands at the entrance to my room with his eyes bulging out his head.

"I killed him because I can't do this anymore. I can't let them hurt me. You need to know what's been happening. You're friends, they—"

"You killed him, Evangeline," he interrupts, his stare focused on Frank's body, and the knife I used to slit his throat laying on the bed beside him.

"Yeah," I answer, surprised at how calm I'm feeling. I just took a man's life and I feel no remorse. Maybe I really am invincible.

"What were you thinking, are you out of your mind?" He starts to pace the carpet at the foot of my bed.

"No, none of this is right, Dad, it all ends now. I picked up some leaflets. I've been saving the money that I've earned from working at the garage. I can get you into a program that will help with your addiction."

"Ahhh, the club, this is their doing. I knew no good could come from you hanging around them."

This only proves that for all these years, he's been too high to realize. He has no idea what I've endured for him and now he's angry at me for taking my life back.

"This isn't the club's fault, this is your fault. I waited for so long after Mama left for you to get over it. I needed you to be my dad, and I wanted you to be happy so much that I let them all touch me. Him, Eddie, Derek, even McAlister and—"

"Stop it, shut your mouth!" He rubs his hand over his face and looks back at me furiously.

"No, I won't shut my mouth. I'm taking control."

"You go to the bathroom and clean yourself up while I think

about what to do with this." He glances at the mess I've made of Frank again.

"Dad..."

"Do as you're fucking told, Evangeline!" he yells at me, and I feel the tears forming in my eyes as I run for the bathroom.

I scrub Frank's blood off my skin and wash my hair, waiting for the guilt to come. Then I get out of the shower and wrap myself in a towel.

When I step out into the hall, Dad's waiting for me, he looks so scared. I guess any parent would after seeing the body of the man their kid just murdered.

"The police are on their way, they are gonna wanna speak to you so we have to get our story straight."

"The police." I panic, this can't be happening, he can't have handed me in.

"Frank came here drunk and I caught him trying to rape you. I killed him. Okay? I did this."

"I won't let you do that. I killed him, I'll own it. The club can help, I'll call Skid."

"No, no club. You keep them out of this." He slams my shoulders into the wall behind me. "When the police question you, you don't mention the others, this is the first time anything happened to you. Do you understand?"

"No, I don't understand, they are bad men. They rape little girls. They all need to suffer." I hate how he closes his eyes and his muscles tighten. This can't be easy for him.

"They are dangerous men who will come after you if they know what you did here. I'm taking the blame on this, you just have to keep your mouth shut. If you tell anyone what they did to you, they will hurt you, and they will hurt me. Do you understand me?"

"Please, don't," I shake my head. This is everything I've been fearing since Mama left. This is what they held over me with. I can't lose him.

"You remember what I said, Evangeline." He shakes my body to bring me back to him and the sirens that are approaching get louder. "You stick to the story, you don't mention the others. Promise me."

"I promise," I whisper, tears making my vision blurry as three armed officers storm in through the door and grab hold of him. I sink to the floor and wrap my arms around my knees as they drag him away.

"I love you, Evangeline," he calls out before they take him from me.

Fingers pat against my cheek, bringing me back around, and I jolt when I realize I'm in a room I don't recognize. The back of my head aches like a bitch and when I raise my hand to touch the wound, I realize my wrists are bound together.

"Welcome back." The voice that speaks to me brings back more dark memories, and when I look up at the man standing over me it takes everything in my power not to shudder.

"I'm disappointed in you." He crosses his arms over his chest and stares down at me. His hair is long and greasy now and he's lost a little of his bulk since I last saw him.

"Nick," I speak his name venomously. I've been waiting to come face to face with this fucker again, and now that I finally have he's got me tied to a damn chair.

"After all I did for you, Evangeline." He shakes his head at me disappointedly. "Why couldn't you just keep your pretty little nose out of our business?"

Because you hurt me, is what I want to scream at him. But I stay quiet, and I forbid the tears from my eyes because, to get out of this, I'm gonna have to be strong.

"Did you honestly think Stevo wouldn't alert them that you were coming?" he laughs at me.

"I guess while you were busy blowing out his knees you didn't take the time to notice how good the place is looking these days. How do you think he paid for that?"

"I don't give a fuck how he paid for it." It's my turn to laugh now.

My cheek stings when he smacks his palm against it.

"Ivan is running things now, and he's got plans, big plans."

"Who?" I've never heard of the guy.

"Ivan," Nick says the name again like I must be the only person on the planet who hasn't heard it before.

"Never heard of him," I shrug, purposely sounding unimpressed.

"Oh, you will," he threatens me, with a smug grin that I want to melt off his face with a blow torch.

"Nice as it's been to catch up and all, I suggest you untie me and let me be on my way before my friends at the club come looking for me."

Nick raises his eyebrows at me. "And how do you think they're gonna find you, sweetheart? Ivan's a clever man, he's been creeping up under their asses for some time now."

"They know where to start looking," I assure him, "and I'll bet they're there now smashing Stevo's skull into his shiny new bar." I lean forward and bat my lashes at him.

"I found you, so they'll find you. You can believe that," I promise.

"By the time they do, it'll be too late. Ivan doesn't take too kindly to people who hurt his employees. Eddie had been working for him for a long time. The boss is pissed at you."

"How can you be so sure I hurt Eddie? He might just have skipped town." I shrug.

"Ivan sent him for you, he was prepared to give you an opportunity and you fucked up, and then you proved your guilt when you decided to hide out with those bikers."

"Guess things didn't turn out so well for Eddie, huh?" I laugh, and it earns me another swipe from the back of his hand.

"If it weren't for the fact Ivan wants to speak to you, I'd slice open your throat, you smart-mouthed bitch. You were so much sweeter when you were helpless," he sniggers, and I pull against my restraints to get at him.

"You're all bunch of sick fuckers." My emotions get the better of me. "I was just a kid and you were supposed to be my dad's friends. He was crushed when he found out what you did to me…"

Nick's smile grows wider, and the nasty glint in his eye suggests what's coming next is gonna be brutal.

"You are a thick little slut, aren't ya?" The delight on his face makes me want to tear it off with my teeth.

I swear to God, if they've managed to hurt him I will make their deaths slow.

"Your daddy had a habit that he couldn't keep up with. He was always begging for one more hit that he couldn't afford. And so he gave us the only thing he had…"

I gasp in horror and Nick leans down to whisper in my ear.

"He sold you over and over for a high, sweetheart."

"That's not true," I shake my head, refusing to believe the vile spew that's coming from his mouth. My dad had a problem, there was no denying that, but he would never have used me. He loved me.

"You seem upset, it's a shame Derek ain't here to see those pretty tears, he tells me no one's taste quite as bitter as yours." I shift in the chair and try to lash out at him. But I'm bound too tight.

"You better hope whoever your friend is, gets here before the Dirty Souls do," I warn him because it's the only way I can hurt him right now. I'm tied, and helpless and I hate it.

"My dear sweet girl, you have no one to protect you here, just like you didn't have anyone back then."

He slumps down on the couch opposite me and pulls a baggy from his pocket. Then dipping his finger inside, he snorts the white powder right off his fingertip.

"You want some?" He shakes the bag at me teasingly. "You know what it'll cost ya," he chuckles, dipping in for a second helping. I think about how I might kill him. Smashing his head through the TV screen would be a good start.

I think about Grimm, and how we left each other on an argument this morning. Maybe now's the time to admit that he'd been right.

CHAPTER 39

1%

MC

GRIMM

Maddy's hands feel like heavy weights on my shoulder, and the room around me starts spinning. Rogue is in danger, most of all to herself. She's out there and I have no way of finding her. I can't even get Mads to track her damn cell phone because she's left it behind. I can hear my heartbeat thumping in my ears, feel my blood burning as it rushes under my skin, and I want to tear into it and rip out my pulse.

"Grimm, you're panicking. I need you to breathe." Maddy's right, I can feel myself losing it, and if there's any chance of me getting to Rogue I'm gonna have to pull myself together.

"Grimm, breathe…" she repeats, and I try sucking in air, but fail. "Jessie, you need to get up here now, I'm in Grimm's cabin."

Maddy crouches on the floor in front of me. "We'll find her, Grimm, but you have to calm down. I promise we're gonna find her." I try inhaling through my nostrils and find it a little easier.

"That's better. Keep breathing." She breathes with me, slowly and calmly, and I try to focus on pulling the next one in with her.

"What's goin' on?" I hear Jessie's voice as he storms through my cabin, and the way Maddy looks up at him proves that, despite her calmness, she's worried too.

"Rogue's gone," she explains, keeping her voice steady.

"Fuck!" Jessie must kick or punch something because I hear wood splinter behind me.

"Grimm." He takes Maddy's place in front of me, his hand reaching out for my shoulder before he thinks better of it and pulls it back. "Look, brother, we need you here with us if we're gonna find her. You got any idea where she might have gone?"

I shake my head, feeling worse than fuckin' useless.

"We had a fight, she took her gun," I manage, the buzzing in my head is preventing me from thinking straight.

"And you've got no idea where she might have gone?" he asks again.

"You think I'd be fuckin' sitting here if I did?" I snap.

"I'll call Storm and have him ride over to her place." Maddy leaves the room with her cell already pressed against her ear.

"I'm gonna call Prez. You get yourself together, Grimm." Jessie stands up and shuts the door after him. Leaving me alone. I focus on breathing, instead of trying to tear my hair outta my scalp. I count down from ten, and slowly all the static inside my head seems to ease up a little.

I go up to her bedside table and rip through her drawer trying to find some clue to where she might be. When I find nothing, I go through the rest of her shit, and then the rest of the cabin.

"Church... you okay to ride?" Jessie's eyes nearly bulge out his head when he comes in from the decking and takes in all the mess around me.

"I can ride." I leave him standing in shock, and rush to my bike.

Prez is already seated when I get to church, closely followed by Jessie.

Brax and Nyx are sitting side by side, and they look as if they might be able to understand a fraction of the panic I'm going through. Then Squealer and Screwy come next.

"Can't believe you let her give you the slip." Squealer shakes his head at me and I lose my shit, launching at him and fisting at his T-shirt.

"Grimm." Jessie is up and out his chair fast enough to stop me from landing one on the clever-mouthed cunt. He puts himself between me and Squealer while Brax and Nyx hold me back.

"Now ain't the time for being smart, Squeal. Rogue could be in some real danger." Hearing Prez say those words out loud slices me open and all the strain in my body weakens. Brax and Nyx release me and I slump into my chair, focusing on the table in front of me and reminding myself to breathe.

"Everyone, calm down." Prez slams his gavel. "Rogue's out there, and we don't know enough about this Ivan asshole to be squabbling. Jessie, where's everyone else?"

"Tac's on his way, Thorne took the cage with Troj and they're taking their shift watching McAlister's place."

Prez nods. "Well then that leaves just us to come up with a plan on how to get her back. And, Grimm," he looks across to me, "We're gonna get her back, brother." He's got that determined look in his eyes that gives me a little confidence. It also suggests that the old man cares a little about my girl himself.

"Rogue, she's got a gun, she told me—" Jessie's cell ringing interrupts me from explaining.

"It's Thorne… You're on speaker, brother," he answers.

"Where the fuck is Grimm?" Thorne yells down the phone, and the way he sounds panicked does nothing to help my anxiety.

"He's with us, what's up?"

"Me and Troj just pulled up at McAlister place, Carly's car's here and it looks like it's been abandoned. There's been a struggle for sure." I feel my nostrils flare as I rise up on my feet.

"I'll call my informer," Prez already has his phone pressed to his ear.

"Least we know where to start lookin'." Nyx looks over to me, and if that's his attempt to make me calm down, he's fuckin' failed at it.

I pace the room while I wait for Prez to come off the phone, cracking my knuckles and trying to keep my shit together. What the fuck was Rogue doin' there? I told her how dangerous it was for her to leave the club.

"Rogue stopped by the bar earlier, she shot out the owner's knee cap for the address... stupid bitch!" Prez chucks his phone at the table in temper.

"I gotta get out there and find her." I start making my way toward the door, I can't wait around anymore. Screwy stands in front of me, his huge body towering over mine and blocking my way. He shakes his head and gestures with his eyes for me to sit back down.

"Screwy's right, you wouldn't know where to start looking." Prez scratches at his stubble.

"I'd know where to fucking start," I tell him. "We go in now, we take the house down, I'll bet someone there will know where she is."

"We're low on numbers for that kinda operation," Brax points out, and usually that point would be valid, but not while my girl's out there in danger.

"Brax is right, taking down the place is one thing, but we don't know who we're dealing with yet, it's a risk." Nyx backs up his brother and before I can argue, Jessie stands up.

"And if it were Ella or Gracie out there, would you expect us to still be sitting on our asses discussing it?" he questions them.

"No," they both answer at the same time, without hesitation.

"Way I see it, Ivan started the war when he sent one of his men into our club for information. Taking out his house is a good start on letting him know we ain't gonna be fucked on. He's laid low this long for a reason. He fears us, now let's prove to him why he's right to." Jessie backs down and nods at Prez to confirm he's finished.

"All those in favor of taking down the cook house and bringing Rogue home?" Prez asks the table.

"In," I'm first to speak.

"In," Jessie's vote comes next. Followed by two more yes's from Nyx and Brax. Screwy nods his approval and Squealer stares me down while he thinks about his answer. His lips lift into a smirk, then his huge hand slams into my shoulder. "'Course I'm fucking in, let's go get your psycho bitch back, Scissorhands."

"Arm yourselves up, brothers, looks like we're going to war," Prez slams the gavel, and the sound of wooden chair legs scraping the floor gets my adrenaline pumping.

"It was gettin' too quiet around here anyway," Squealer adds, following the others to the vestry where we keep our weapon supply.

I rush down to the basement, grabbing a handful of face masks for the others. If we're going in, we'll need protection from the fumes. Then I meet the others in the yard and hand them out.

"What's going on?" Tac asks when he pulls up among the chaos.

"We're raiding the cookhouse," Nyx explains, handing him a semi-auto as he gets off his bike.

"Cool," he shrugs, checking that he's loaded.

Jessie throws an AK at me, and we all pile into the back of a cage that Screwy pulls up beside us. Prez rides shotgun, while Jessie calls the others to let them know what's going down.

"You good, brother?" Brax checks as we get closer, and I nod back at him, clutching the handle of the gun tight in my fist. The van comes to a stop and when Thorne opens the door and we all pile out, Nyx hands out the guns we brought for Troj and Thorne.

"Four have come out to smoke, one left not long before you arrived." Troj fills us in on the activity.

"Let's do this." Jessie slides the mag into his AK, and flicks his cigarette at the floor. He pulls up the white mask I gave him to cover his mouth and nose, and I cover mine with the black bandana that still smells like Rogue's hair.

The rest of the crew follow, separating in groups to make sure the house is surrounded and waiting for the signal.

The sound of the front door crashing open moves us into action. Squealer raiding through the back door first, then me and Nyx piling in behind him. Three pairs of shocked eyes stare back at us and Nyx moves first, smashing the handle of his gun into the face of the one closest to him. The one nearest the door tries to bolt and runs himself straight into Screwy's chest. The fucker bounces back on his ass, and Screwy pins him to the floor by his boot.

I press the barrel of my AK into the skinny prick's temple, while Squealer has his fun taking out the other guy.

"Clear," Nyx shouts.

"Clear," another voice comes back from the other side of the house and when I look down at him, the guy under Screwy's boot looks scared as hell.

It doesn't take long for us to have all six men rowed up and tied in the living room.

"We're about to offer one of you an opportunity." Prez starts pacing in front of them. "The guy you're working for has pissed off my family. This setup he's got is a little too close to my backyard, and now he's taken something that belongs to us."

I eye up the line of men, and all of them look petrified. These men are the bottom of the pack, they don't deserve to die. But they will if they don't cooperate.

"So which one of you wants to rat and walk out of here with your life?" Prez asks.

"You wanna know where the girl who killed Eddie is?" one

of them pipes up, earning him a glare from the guy sitting next to him. "Fuck this shit, man, you know who these people are? I didn't sign up for this shit. Nick and Stevo can screw themselves."

Jessie gives me a look that shares my thoughts. These monkeys in front of us have no idea what they're involved in.

"Nick got a call from Stevo to warn him that some psycho whore was on a warpath." I move forward, ready to smash the cunt's head off his shoulders but Jessie pulls me back and shakes his head at me. "So he took her."

"Took her where?" Prez crouches in front of the rat.

"Probably at the main farmhouse, about half a mile down the road."

"It's quiet out there, they can really take their time with her, I hope he makes the bitch pay for what she did to Eddie," the big guy in the middle speaks up, and I slam my fist into his jaw, causing blood to spray over the person sitting next to him.

"Let's have some respect when referring to the lady, shall we?" Prez warns him, and when Squealer snorts, I eyeball him.

"You," Prez turns his focus back to the rat, "You're coming with us."

Troj steps forward and unties him from the chair, keeping his arms behind his back and forcing him out the door.

"He'll come after you, No one fucks with Ivan and gets away with it. He won't give a shit about your pathetic club." Big guy isn't giving up, and the four other guys look at him like he's crazy.

"Oh, I'm counting on it," Prez sneers.

"Load these four assholes into the cage, we'll take them into Roswell." Prez orders and the twins, Brax and Nyx step straight into action, taking one each. Brax knocks his guy clean out when he tries to struggle, then heaves him over his shoulder.

"You're in charge here, ain't ya?" Prez asks the mouthy guy who's still tied to his chair in the middle of the room.

"You could say that," he shrugs cockily.

Prez nods his head slowly, almost looking impressed.

"Get the gas, Jessie." Prez's eyes remain focused on the guy, who suddenly doesn't seem so confident. Jessie comes back from the cage with two cans of gasoline and after he hands one to me, we douse the place and I pour what's left in mine all over the asshole's head. Fucker can choke on fumes for calling my girl a fucking whore.

Thorne passes Jessie the rope and we back out of the building. "What you doin'?" The guy's eyes are wide with panic as he starts to fight against his ropes.

"You're the one in charge," Prez reminds him.

"Ain't ya heard? A captain always goes down with his ship." Jessie salutes him on his way out the door. We leave one end of the rope dangling in a pool of gasoline, and take the other end with us to where the others are waiting at a safe distance.

"Light it up," Prez orders Jessie, who flicks his zippo and ignites the end of the rope. We stand and watch as the flame travels down the rope, burning away until it disappears inside.

Then the windows blow out and wood flies in all directions when the place goes boom. I'd love to watch the place burn, but right now all that matters is my girl.

Nick sits licking his lips at me, it's been a few hours since he took me, and I wonder if Grimm or anyone at the club has realized I'm missing.

When the door opens and a man I don't recognize steps inside, he tosses a box at Nick and scowls at me.

"What's this?" Nick asks, opening the lid. "Jesus Christ." He quickly shuts it again, almost gagging on his words.

"That's a package courtesy of our pals the Dirty Souls. They had it dropped off at the bar, it came with a note too." Reaching into his back pocket, he passes a scrunched-up piece of paper to Nick.

"See no evil," he reads it out loud and looks confused.

I smile to myself because I don't need to look inside the box to know what's inside it. McAlister showing up at the club last night and now a package being sent to the bar from the Souls is too much of a coincidence.

"And then there were two." I smile across to Nick, I may be tied up but these assholes aren't gonna break my spirit like they did Evangeline's, Rogue can't be broken.

"Shut your fuckin' mouth or I'll fill it with my dick." The guy I don't know slaps the back of his hand against my face, and I manage to smile at him.

"Remind me again why we ain't fucking this little slut?" he asks Nick.

"We ain't got time for distractions. Besides, I don't know what Ivan has planned for her."

"You boys better make sure you do as you're told now." I laugh at Nick, he's nothing but a weak, grown-assed man who rapes little girls and takes orders. I can't believe I'd ever been afraid of them. Nick grabs my face in his hands and forces me to look at him. "I'd break the fuckin' rules to take another shot inside your cunt, sweetheart," he spits at me, and I keep my brave face firmly in place, refusing to show him anything but courage.

"It could be hours before Ivan gets here." The other guy grabs my face and forces me to look at him. "I'm tempted to break them too."

"Aren't I a little old for you now, Uncle Nicky, you much prefer scared and vulnerable, don't ya?" I turn my head to him and wink seductively, hoping I can coax him close enough to rip out his throat with my teeth.

"You think I don't still have that power over you?" He stalks toward me, taking my ponytail in his hand and ripping my head back.

"I could ruin you all over again, little one," he whispers his threat into my ear, and I can't prevent the shiver it sends down my spine. "I think you'd like it, you never did fight back. Always took it like such a good girl." His free hand slides down to my chest and squeezes hard around my tit. "I like how you've changed, Evangeline." His wet tongue rolls over my cheek and I struggle against the chair I'm tied to. I can feel something building in my chest and it feels a lot like fear.

"Fuck it. Let's have one for old time's sake." Nick smiles at me, and I notice that the other guy's already got his hands inside his pants.

"Best make the most of you while you're still in one piece.

When Ivan finishes with you, you'll be the one getting boxed up and sent out in pieces." His hand travels lower, I figure that if they're gonna rape me, they'll have to untie me. That's when I will fight, and I'll fight to the death if I have to.

"I want her ass, Nick," the guy I don't know says as he jacks himself through his fist.

"You can take whatever you want once I'm finished," Nick promises, watching for my reaction as his hand slides into the front of my underwear.

I want to scream, his hand doesn't belong on me. I'm Grimm's now, he's the only one who gets to touch me.

"Your pussy's gonna get me into trouble, but I'll take the consequences," Nick tells me before a loud crash distracts him, and when I look over to the door and see Grimm, I smile.

"Now ya fucked," I whisper to Nick, just before the chaos descends. Grimm comes straight for Nick, ripping him off my body and throwing him to the wall.

Grimm's fist smashes into Nick's face over and over again, and I call out his name when I feel something cool press against my temple.

"None of you move or I'll blow the pretty little head off her shoulders," the voice comes from behind me, and when Grimm abandons Nick to turn around, I see something in his eyes that I've never seen before... fear.

"Drop your guns and back the fuck out of here," the guy with the gun to my head orders.

"Don't hurt her," Grimm's voice is desperate. He sounds weak and I hate it.

My eyes dart around the room, there are three other Souls here. Jessie, Troj, and Brax. This bastard is outnumbered and yet they all stand frozen.

Maybe these assholes like me after all.

"She killed Eddie, you killed McAlister. Tell me why I shouldn't?"

"Because the minute she dies, you ain't got anything to bargain with. We came here for her, we're leaving with her." Jessie is the voice of reason and the guy laughs at him.

"You hear that, sweetheart? The biker boys wanna bargain for ya, who'da thought you'd be so special?" I see a change in Grimm's expression. It's so slight that no one else would notice it, and the side glance he gives to Jessie tells me that something's about to happen.

I raise my eyes and look in the mirror above the fireplace, and see Squealer slowly creeping up behind the guy.

A noise comes from outside, and I assume it's Ivan and his men arriving. It distracts him, and when he glances out of the window to check, Squealer strikes.

The gun goes off, so loud that I think my ear's been blown off. I don't feel any pain but I do feel a warm spray of blood against my neck. My eyes are still open, and although I can't hear a thing, I still have my vision.

The door opens and more men pile into the room. Men I don't recognize. And when the sound rushes back to my ears, loud and constant shots make my eyes desperately seek out Grimm.

He's crouched low, coming toward me looking panicked and furious all at the same time.

Taking the knife from his boot, he works fast to cut through the ropes tying me to the chair and frees me.

"Get her out of here," Jessie shouts out over the noise, and I feel myself get dragged on to my feet. Grimm shelters my body with his and starts making for the back door and when I see Squealer lying on the floor behind me, I stop moving.

"Go, I got him." Brax shoves me on, and I'm not strong enough to stop Grimm from dragging me outside.

He immediately presses his fingers to his lips, warning me to stay quiet, and keeps us crouched low as he checks around the side of the house.

"There's two more covering the front door," he says looking back over his shoulder at me. Then before I can speak his lips are on mine, and his fingers dig into my neck like I'm slipping off a ledge. "Don't you ever fuckin' do that to me again, Rogue? Ever, you understand?"

"What are we gonna do, Grimm? They're outnumbered, we got to go back in and help them."

"I'll go back in and help them when you're safe."

"Grimm, I'm fine. Go back in and get Squealer."

Three loud gunshots fire, and this time they don't come from inside. Grimm takes another look around the side of the house.

"And here comes the fuckin' mayhem," he says, taking my hand and raising me to my feet. He pulls me around to the front of the house when he sees that the two men out front have been taken out. Prez, Thorne, Tac, and Nyx pile out the van, followed by Screwy who jumps out of the driver's seat.

"Go get in the cage, Rogue," Grimm orders as the boys hop over the two dead men to get in through the front door.

"Screw, Squeal got hit." Grimm pulls on his shoulder to warn him before he goes in, and the man's eyes blaze with fury before he charges inside the house. Grimm doesn't go with them, instead, he drags me further away toward the van.

"I ain't getting in there," I protest. "Give me a gun and I'll fight as good as any Dirty Soul." The whole reason they're here is because of me. I want to make those fuckers bleed too.

"Rogue, you get in the damn cage," Grimm warns, getting frustrated.

"No," I point blank refuse him. "I can fight, you know I can."

"Don't argue with me on this, get in the fucking cage." His grip on me tightens like he's scared I'll bolt.

"I may be female, Grimm, but…"

"It ain't got nothing to do with the fact you're a female."

"Then give me one good reason why I can't go back in there and kill those scumbags."

Grimm comes at me fiercely, pushing me so hard that my shoulders hit the back of the truck.

"'Cause, I'm in love with you and I can't fuckin' lose you!" He spits the words through his teeth like he's angry at me for it, and I feel my skin tingle, and the tears flood my eyes.

"And what if I lose you?" I bite back at him.

"You won't, not now that I got something to live for. Now *please* will you just get in the mother fuckin' cage so I can go focus on killing the people who wanna hurt you." It's the sweetest thing anyone's ever said to me, and I feel like maybe I should kiss him for it.

"I'll get in the cage," I tell him, wrapping my arms around his neck and kissing him hard. "And when we get home, I'm gonna ride the fuck out of you."

"Deal," he smirks back at me, pulling away, eager to get back inside.

"Kick some ass, baby," I call after him, jumping inside the back of the van and closing the door.

CHAPTER 41

1% MC

JESSIE

"**G**et her out of here," I call out to Grimm as more men pile through the door. Men who are fucking shooting at us.

Rogue is still in shock, it's the first time I've ever seen the girl look worried, and I somehow manage to dodge a bullet aimed at my head as I rush toward Squealer.

"Go, we got him." Brax pushes Rogue forward when she stops to stare at his body on the floor. And Grimm drags her out through the back door, hopefully to safety.

The others aren't far behind us, they were meeting Roswell to offload the guys we took from the house, and I really hope they hurry the fuck up.

"It was a bad hit." Brax covers me while I check Squeal over. He's taken a shot to his lower abdomen and there's a lot of fuckin' blood.

I grab one of the pillows from the couch and hold it tight over the wound. Flashes of Hayley bleeding out in my arms threaten to haunt me, but I push those thoughts away because I have to focus.

"Hold on, Squeal. I think it's a straight-through," I tell him trying to sound positive.

He doesn't answer me, probably because he's in too much pain. Shots are firing everywhere, ricocheting off the walls, while men drop everywhere.

The guy Grimm knocked out before he left comes to, and races straight at me. I use the hand that ain't keeping Squealer alive to lift my gun and fire at him. And a direct shot to his chest drops him onto his knees. I check on Brax, who's abandoned his gun somewhere, and is now fighting knife and fist.

"I know I can be an awkward prick sometimes, but you ain't gonna let me die are ya, VP?" Squealer's voice croaks at me.

"Tempting, but no. Stay alive," I warn him, being forced to watch as my club brothers fight off double the number of men.

"Oh, this must be killing ya." Squealer chokes out a laugh, then winces in pain.

Troj snatches the gun off the guy he's struggling with and tosses it at Brax, who catches it without hesitation and fires it straight through the jaw of the guy he's grappling with.

"Jess, I can't stay awake." Squealer clutches at my arm, he's looking pale, and his eyes are sinking and looking fearful. Shit, I've not once in all the time I've known the annoying fucker seen him look scared. And that fucking petrifies me.

"I'm losing too much blood," he groans.

"Tell me something I don't fucking know, Squeal." I press my hands into his body harder, hoping that the pressure will stop him bleeding out. He goes fucking limp on me, and finally, I hear more guns firing and Nyx charges through the door followed by Thorne and Prez.

Behind them is Screwy, who takes one look at his brother before his rage takes over. He moves toward us like a tornado, crushing anything in his path to get to his brother. He lifts up the guy who has jumped on Thorne and throws him into the wall. Then twists the neck of the one who's about to aim his gun at Tac. Kicking his gun over to me, he takes out his knife and slits the throat of a guy who's trying to get up from the floor.

I keep the pressure on Squealer's wound despite him being out cold now. I can still feel a pulse even though it's fuckin' weak.

Screwy trudges toward me, taking another guy out with a fist to the throat, before he crouches down and heaves Squealer onto his shoulder.

"He's alive but he needs to get to a hospital," I tell him, making sure he's covered as he makes his way toward the door. Grimm's here too now, but I quickly realize there isn't anyone left to fall.

Screwy made sure of that.

I race to catch up with Screwy, jumping in the driver's seat of the cage he piles Squeal into. His hands have taken position over the wound now, he must have lost the cushion somewhere on the way as the blood is seeping through his fingers.

I wonder if that pulse is still beating, the way Squealer's skin is rapidly turning grey isn't a good sign and I put all my focus into driving to the closest hospital. It's only about twenty miles, and I toe it all the way. But the drive seems to go on for hours.

When I finally get there, I skid to a halt behind an ambulance and slide open the door for Screwy, he looks murderous as he pulls his brother back onto his shoulder and I race ahead into the ER reception to get us some help. I don't give a shit that I'm covered head to foot in blood, and I ignore the shocked shrieks from the people waiting to be seen.

"We need a doctor now," my fist bangs hard on the reception counter.

"Now!" I yell at the blank-looking receptionist.

Squealer hangs limply over his brother's shoulder as Screwy steps up behind me, and remembering how quickly Hayley turned cold on me has me taking action. Squealer can't fucking leave Screwy. I won't fucking let him.

I rip some junkie off the gurney he's sitting on, and drag it to Screwy so he can lay Squealer out. The blood looks way worse now that everything's so clean and bright, and a doctor appears out of nowhere and starts cutting through his shirt.

Screwy goes to follow him but a hand presses against his

chest and some five-foot fuck all nurse tells him to stay put. Shaking his head, he presses forward and before he takes the woman off her feet, I somehow I manage to pull him back

He stares at me and growls.

"Screw, you gotta let them work on him," I explain. There's no way I can hold him back by myself if he chooses to flip.

"Blood," he forces the word out of his mouth, his eyes wild and voice so deep it vibrates through my chest.

"Yeah, there's a lot of blood, but the doctors are gonna fix him," I assure him, though the state he looked when they wheeled him away and the fact they were pumping his chest, has me struggling to believe my promise.

I sit with Screwy in the family room, the silence tense and the minutes passing slowly without any word from the doctors. Screwy is about to lose his shit. I can sense it, and I have no idea how to make him calm down.

The brothers start to come and go in small groups, all of them silent and somber and not knowing what to say to Screwy.

We may have taken down Ivan's men back at the farmhouse but we got nothing to celebrate and we can be sure of one thing now… This shit is way bigger than a fuckin' cookhouse and a vendetta against Rogue.

Whoever this slippery fucker Ivan is, he's managed to crawl in right under our noses and if it hadn't had been for Rogue, we'd still be clueless to his operation.

Eventually, a doc steps into the room and the look on his face says just about everything.

"I take it you're the next of kin?" He looks at Screwy. A nod from Screw has the doc sitting down beside him, and the sigh he releases before he speaks makes my heart drop to my stomach.

"It was a straight through, but he lost too much blood." I watch Screwy turn white and his eyes flicker with flames.

His chest is lifting up and down at such a rapid pace, that I know things are gonna start flying soon.

"We repaired the damage it caused and stitched him back up, and he's in the ICU. I wish I could make you some guarantees but…" I breathe a sigh of relief when I hear there's hope, but Screwy isn't letting up.

"Can we see him?" I ask, knowing it's what Screwy needs.

"Yes, of course, one at a time, and the police are going to want to speak to you." He looks at me suspiciously, and I can understand why considering the state of us and the nature of Squeal's injury. The cops ain't something we have to concern ourselves with, especially since we're on our own turf.

Screw disappears with the doc, and I slip back into the plastic chair and scrub my bloody hand over my face. Squeal is alive… for now… And we have that to be thankful for.

"Penny for your thoughts." Maddy's sweet voice has me looking up from the floor, and she stands in the door frame looking beautiful as always.

"How you get here?" The last thing I want is her traveling alone while all this shit's going down. and when she steps closer I wrap my arms around her waist and pull her onto my lap.

"I came with Grimm, he insisted Rogue get her head checked out," she explains, and we both look at each other and smirk. "You know what I mean."

"Any news on Squealer?" Her fingers slip through mine, gripping me tight despite the mess of them. She shouldn't be tainted with this shit, and times like these I feel like a real selfish bastard for dragging her into this life.

"It ain't looking good. He's in ICU, Screwy's with him now."

"And what about you, you doing okay?" I lift my head from where I've rested it on her chest and shake it. It's pointless lying to her, Maddy knows me inside and out.

"Brought back everything that happened with Hay," I admit. "I thought he was gonna fuckin' die."

"Rogue doesn't know how serious it is. Prez says it's best not to tell her till he's got the all-clear," Maddy whispers, stroking her fingers through my hair and making me feel calm again.

"We made a choice today, Mads, one that I didn't realize was gonna put you in so much danger." I scrub my hand over my face again, I need to fucking make someone bleed for this. And while I was playing fuckin' medic, all the others were causing pain, I've had no release.

"You did what you had to, to save Rogue, it wasn't a choice, Jessie. She's one of us. Skid loves her and it's obvious that Grimm's fond of her." She smiles at me after making the understatement of the fuckin' century.

That fucker's crazy for her.

"Let's go home," she says, and when I flick my eyes up at the clock and realize it's gone two in the morning, I agree.

"Troj is gonna hang back here and wait with Screwy. He won't be on his own," Maddy says, standing up and pulling me to join her.

"You think he'll make it?" she asks me, looking petrified. My girl cares about everyone, my brothers are her family now, just as much as they're mine.

"I hope so, Mads," I tell her, tucking her under my arm and leading us out so we can go home.

Troj is outside the front entrance having a smoke, and I smack him on his shoulder as we pass him,

"You good, brother?" he checks.

"We will be, once that fucker in there stops creamin' all the attention," I tell him, before getting into the cage and driving my girl back to the club.

CHAPTER 42

1% MC

GRIMM

Squealer's in bad shape, I owe him my girl's life and all I can do is hope he pulls through so I can show him my gratitude. Screwy and Jessie rush him outta here in one of the cages, while the rest of us all pile into the other one and head back to the club. There's silence among us, everyone's bloody. Some of us are bruised. But everyone's thoughts are in one place, and that's with Squealer. Rogue sits between my legs and I hold her tight in my arms until we've pulled up at the compound. Everyone's heads are low as they make their way inside to the bar.

We may have been victorious in ruining Ivan's enterprise but one of us has fallen in the process. And now that we've kicked the hornets' nest, it's only a matter of time before we find out how big the sting will be.

"Let's get you home." I guide Rogue toward my bike but she stands firm.

"I need to know that Squealer's okay."

"I'll get one of the boys to call me as soon as they hear. I'm gonna get the doc to come check your head out." Her blonde hair is matted at the back with blood, the gash is only small but it's fucking there and I don't like it.

Dark bruises are rising up on her skin, from where they hurt her and I want to kill every one of them again for it. My only consolation is knowing that now, those mother fuckers can't hurt her again.

"My head's fine," she protests.

"Rogue you got knocked out, and you look like you've gone twelve rounds with Troj. I should take you to hospital." I need to hear that she's okay before the nerves in my stomach go away. Thinking I'd lost her the way I did earlier is a feeling I never want to experience again, and I'll have Maddy put a fucking tracker in her arm if that's what it takes to make sure it doesn't.

"I want us to talk first." She looks at me nervously. There's a misery in her eyes that tells me whatever it is we're gonna talk about is gonna cause her pain and once this is over and she's got all this out, I'm gonna make sure nothing can hurt her again.

I give in, riding us back up to my cabin. The place is still trashed from where I flipped out earlier, and Rogue looks shocked as I guide her straight through to the bathroom. She watches in silence as I draw her a bath, and then winces as she sinks herself into the water. Her body must be aching from what they put her through, and all I can think about is how I can make her better again.

I start with her feet, soaping up my hands and cleaning her toes, and as she watches me, her teeth dig into her lip like she's holding back her words and her tears at the same time

"Talk to me, Rogue." I prepare myself for whatever it is she has to tell me, already knowing that I'm gonna fucking hate it.

"Eddie, and those men..." She swallows thickly and closes her eyes, "I've known them a long time. Since I was a little girl." I squeeze the sponge that I'm cleansing her with tight in my fist, fearing what comes next as I rotate higher up her leg.

"My mom and dad started hanging out with them just before Skid and Chop caught me stealing from their garage. They were bad people, drug dependent, and it didn't take long for Mom and Dad to become like them. Dad stopped going to work, Mom was sick all the time, and then she left us." I nod in understanding, seeing how close to breaking she is destroys me, but I have to stay strong for her.

"I knew what Dad was doing, and that it was wrong, but when he was with them he was always so happy. They hung around at our place, they gave Dad an endless supply of what he needed, and it came with a price." Her voice wobbles and she looks down into the water. "I had to keep him around, Grimm, I couldn't let him leave me too."

The tear that drips onto her cheek makes me clench her thigh a little too tightly.

"Are you tellin' me—"

"I thought those men were his friends. I'd already lost one parent and I was too scared to lose another."

"Who hurt you?" I ask, needing names.

"All of them," she says the words so feebly, like she's the one who has something to be ashamed of, and I close my eyes to shield her from the anger in them.

"How old were you?" *God, I don't think I wanna know the answer to this question, why am I fucking asking her it?*

"Eight, when it started. Around eighteen when it stopped. Something happened that pushed me over the edge. I flipped and I killed one of them. Then I let my dad take the blame for it."

I can feel the bile in my throat. It's no wonder my girl's so fucked up, she's been abused since she was fucking eight years old. Thinking about it makes me crave their blood.

"Your father let them use you like that?" I take my hands off her skin, fearing all the tension inside me could hurt her.

"I didn't think he knew, he was always high, or drunk. He didn't know which day of the week it was half the time. But I thought I was saving him, keeping him close. And in the end I lost him anyway."

I feel my heart split as I watch her bottom lip shake, and her hand reaches out for mine and moves it back on to her body.

Suddenly she seems so fuckin' fragile that my own fingers tremble as they touch her.

"Please keep touching me, Grimm, this is why I didn't want to tell you. I don't want you to look at me differently."

Sliding my hand up between her tits, I take her throat and drag her closer to me. I kiss her lips, and taste her salty tears as they stream out. They may be causing her pain but I'm glad she's choosing to give them to me. I want every single part of her, her secrets, her vulnerability, even her fucking crazy.

"Before you came to save me, Nick told me..." The words seem to lodge in her throat, like she's gonna choke on them.

"Tell me," I whisper, holding her jaw tight in my palm, and soothing her hair gently with the other. This is what she needs from me and I'll never deny her it. If there's more to this fucked up story, I need to hear it so I can fix her from it.

"He told me that my dad knew the whole time, that he offered me to them." She breaks right in front of me, her head falling heavy in my hand and her knees rising up to her chest. She wraps her arms around them and clings them tight, her sobs lifting her shoulders. And I don't know how to comfort her because all I can feel inside me is rage. Rage that I've got to keep a lid on because she needs me to be strong for her.

Sliding my hand up to her cheek, I hold her face in my hands and press my forehead against hers. I breathe with her, hoping that she can hear the words I'm saying in my head, because I can't get them out for her.

"I've been angry for so long, Grimm. I wanted them all dead. Finding this place and Skid, crazy as it sounds, showed me reality. It gave me an escape from them." And it suddenly fucking dawns on me that she was hanging out here while all that was happening to her.

"Why didn't you tell Skid?" This is gonna break the man.

"It was already a part of my life when I came here. My dad needed his drugs, he was in so deep with them and I was scared they'd hurt him. I couldn't tell Skid because I was worried he'd think my dad wasn't taking care of me properly."

"He didn't take care of you properly, Rogue... he let his friends..." I can feel my hold on her becoming too tight and when her hands press on top of mine, it feels as though she's the one soothing me.

"I need you not to be mad, Grimm," she whispers. Her tears falling between us and her shaky breaths touching my lips. "If I'm gonna tell you the next part I need you to promise me that you won't go crazy, 'cause I want you to know it all and for me to be strong enough to tell you, I need you here with me."

Fuck, there's more? And I don't know how the hell I'm gonna handle it. But I will, for her.

I'll do anything, even if it means tearing my own heart out.

"There was a time at the garage, it was my eighteenth birthday."

"Those fuckers came here?" I pull back and stare at her. They came on to our compound and did that to her?

"Not them." Her head shakes back at me and her eyes drop to her knees. "Chop."

I feel every muscle in my body stiffen.

"He found out about what was happening at home, he must have hung around with the guys that night. He threatened to tell Skid, and then he..." My finger presses over her lips 'cause I can't hear anymore.

Chop betrayed us all, none worse than his own brother Skid, but hearing this, knowing that he's hurt Rogue makes me want his head.

"Jesus, Rogue." I feel like I can't breathe. The pressure crushing my chest is too much to sustain, and the heat in my blood is scalding.

I don't give a fuck that I'm still wearing my clothes when I climb in behind her and pull her on to my chest. I gotta hold her, I have to let her know that I'm here.

We stay like that for so long, breathing each other in, and it isn't until I realise that the water's turned cold that I slide out and take a towel from the rail. I help her onto her feet and wrap it around her body. She may be broken and bruised but she's still perfect. And she's mine. As long as I'm living, no one will ever hurt her again.

"You gotta let me take care of you now, Rogue," I whisper, praying that now I'm in, she'll never shut me out again.

"Did you mean what you said before?" she asks, wrapping her dripping wet arms around my neck. "Back at the farm, when you said…" A tiny hint of a smile lifts onto her lips again.

"Rogue, I don't know what the fuck this is. What I feel for you is a physical pain, but it's one that I wanna feel for the rest of my life."

"You think two fuck ups like us got a chance?" she asks, her big blue eyes magnified with tears and looking so fucking beautiful.

"We got no other choice, Rogue."

The way her smile widens tells me she likes the sound of that.

"Now go get dressed, I'm taking you to hospital to get you checked out."

"I'm fi—" I silence her with my finger again, and she bites down hard on its tip.

"Fine… I'll come with you and get checked out, but only to stop you worrying, and because I need to check on Squealer."

Telling Grimm everything felt surprisingly relieving.

Carrying secrets is a tiring burden, and now that he knows all my ugly, I feel a little lighter. I'd seen the pain it caused him, the heat was penetrating off him. But if me and him stand any chance in making it together, we can't have secrets.

I agree to go to the hospital with him, despite knowing I'm fine, because I know that Squealer isn't. Back at the farm when I'd heard the gun go off, I'd known straight away it was serious, and if we lose him it will be all my fault.

Turns out all those sick fuckers who spent years hurting me, are all monkeys working for this Ivan guy. And now because of me, the club has a problem with him too.

Grimm calls Skid and tells him what's happened and of course, he's already on his way back to the club. The club will need all the numbers they can spare while we wait for the blowback of what happened today. But I make Grimm promise me he won't tell Skid about Chop. Skid's dying on the inside, and I won't be another issue for him to take on his shoulders.

Maddy catches a ride with us to the hospital when we leave. Jessie still hasn't come home and no one's telling me shit, so I know things aren't looking good for Squealer. As soon as we get to the ER, Maddy rushes off to find Jessie for an update, promising to find us and let us know when she's heard.

It takes forever for me to be seen and I can sense Grimm getting real pissed while we wait.

"How's ya head?" Troj asks, after I finally get the all-clear and we join him in the family room.

"They glued the gash in my scalp and gave me some pain killers but I still got one hell of a headache," I tell him, taking a seat.

"Roswell's just been in to take a statement, he's gonna have to speak to you for the record, but we're covered."

"Any more news on Squeal?" I ask, hating how worried Troj looks.

"Squeal's out of surgery, but not out of the woods. He had to have a blood transfusion and Screwy's refusing to leave him, he won't even take a fuckin' smoke."

"Stay here with Troj, I'm gonna go see if he's okay." I slide my hand out of Grimm's.

"I don't know if that's a good idea." Troj looks at Grimm nervously.

"I'm just gonna check if he needs anything, it's the least I can do." I'm not about to wait for permission from either of them and when I stand up and Grimm tries to pull me back, I show him a look that tells him exactly that, before I continue to make my way toward the room Squealer's in.

Screwy's sitting in a plastic chair beside his bed, and it looks like it's gonna buckle under his huge frame. He looks broken, staring at a spot on the floor with his hands clenched together. He doesn't even look up when I step inside the room, and I feel real fuckin' awkward about the whole situation.

"I'm sorry 'bout your brother," I croak, not really knowing where to start. He's got every right to be mad at me. Screwy's gaze doesn't lift, but his foot taps a little faster, and I wonder if he's gonna blank me out completely.

Squealer's wired up to a heap of machines, ones that keep

buzzing and beeping, but he's breathing by himself, which I'm taking as a major positive.

"You could go get a coffee or a cigarette. I can stay with him."

Screwy's head shakes, but his eyes remain unmoved and I step closer, carefully placing my hand on his shoulder.

"I know what it's like to only have one person in the whole world that matters to you," I explain. "Go get a smoke, take a slash, he'll still be here when you get back."

Screwy looks up at me, his eyes red and fierce with anger, and he shocks the hell out of me when he nods his head then stands up on his feet and makes his way to the door. I wait for him to leave before taking the seat and looking at Squealer. He looks so peaceful, and without his mouth talking shit I can almost appreciate what all the women who hang off him see in him.

"I guess I need to thank you for what you did, and you have no idea how pleased I am that you're unconscious for this, you smug bastard." I imagine him smirking, and when his lips don't move it makes me feel real fucking sad.

"I know how much you're lapping up all this attention, but I ain't having your death on my conscience so you have to pull through. If not for me, for your brother. He needs you, the club needs you, and well... I'd miss you if you weren't around." God, I can't believe I feel the need to say this.

"You'll never know because I ain't ever gonna tell ya about it, but this isn't the first time you saved me. Shit was bad for me, and then, when it got a whole lot worse, I thought I was gonna fall apart, and then you came out of nowhere with that big old smile on your face, and you made me feel normal again. Just for a tiny second, but it was long enough to make me realize I wanted to fight.

So, I owe you a knife and a life."

My eyes well up with tears and I use my sleeve to wipe them away before anyone comes in and sees them.

"You're a pain in everyone's fuckin' ass, Squealer." I lean closer and tell him in a harsh whisper, "but you make people happy when shit gets too serious. The club need that, and I need that." The thought of him not waking up makes me hurt too much to think about.

"For fuck's sake, open your eyes and say something offensive," I snap at him. I take his hand in mine and squeeze it enough to try and make him feel pain, and when he doesn't respond I close my eyes and sob.

"That was a real touching speech, darlin'," I hear his voice croak, and I wonder if I've imagined it when I look up from our hands and his eyes are still shut. Then I see that hint of a snigger pick up on his lips and I can't hold myself back

"Squealer." My arms automatically fling around his neck.

"Steady, don't want Scissorhands getting jealous." He huffs a laugh at me and then flinches with pain.

"You almost fucking died, you idiot." I slap him on the shoulder, softly of course.

"Jeez, thanks for saving my life, Squealer, I really owe you one. Do you want me to suck your cock now or later?" he says sarcastically, and it makes me want to hug him and slap him all at the same time.

"You know what I mean. You had everyone worried. Screwy's been in here with you all night. We thought..." My eyes begin to prickle with tears, happy ones.

"It'll take a lot more than a bullet to rid you guys of me. Did they get 'em all?" He lifts his hand up to rub his face and stares at all the tubes going into it.

"Every last one," I put on my brave face and smile proudly back at him. "I should get a nurse or a doctor. You in any pain?" I stand up and make my way to the door, colliding with Screwy's firm chest, and the relief I see on his face warms the pit of my stomach.

"I'll leave you guys to it and send someone in. I got to call the others to tell them you're gonna be okay." Screwy stomps his way over to his brother's bed and grabs him in a huge hug that must cause him pain.

"Chill. bro, I can't fuckin' breathe," I hear Squealer cuss his brother, and it almost has me skipping up the corridor to find Troj and Grimm.

Grimm sits on one of the plastic chairs, while Troj paces in front of him.

"He's awake," I put them both out of their misery, and I'm taken completely by surprise when Troj comes at me, lifting me off my feet and spinning me around.

Grimm growls, and Troj puts me back down again, pulling out his cell as he charges out the room to go find Squealer.

"He's gonna be okay." I step toward Grimm, who kisses me like we've been apart for days.

"I never thought I'd be so relieved to see that mother fucker talking." I giggle. "We should get back to the club and tell the others."

Grimm must agree with me because he practically drags me out of the hospital and back to the car.

Word has already reached the club when we get back, and as happy as I am that Squeal is gonna be okay, I don't feel much like celebrating.

Now that I've come down from the initial relief. I've been hit with reality. The men that hurt me might be dead, but in the process, I've caused a war between the Dirty Souls and whoever this Ivan guy is.

Grimm pours us a Jack each and lights up a smoke. He places the drink on the table, and gestures for me to take it with a tip of his head. I don't hesitate, knocking it back and hoping it will take some of the edge off.

"I know that you've been visiting my mama," he speaks so quietly, and looks hurt. Suddenly, I feel guilty, and the last thing I need after all that's happened today is an argument.

"I'm sor—"

"I ain't mad," he interrupts, swishing the amber liquid around in the glass before he knocks it back.

"You did something real brave today, and you let me in. It's only fair that I do the same for you. I promise that once we've had a decent sleep, I'll tell you everything you need to know about me."

"I'd really like that." I take his hand and lead him into the bedroom.

"I wish I could have killed them all myself," I admit as he slides into the bed beside me.

"No more killing, Rogue," Grimm tells me sleepily, and I watch his eyes close and his body relax.

CHAPTER 44

The sound of my cell phone buzzing disturbs me, and I quickly grab it before it disturbs Rogue. It's the care home and for them to be calling this late at night, it has to be something bad.

"Mr. Carter, it's your mother, she isn't having a very good night. We thought it best you come in and try and stabilize her before we give her any medication."

"No, no medication, I'm on my way." Hanging up the phone, I quickly throw on some pants and a shirt.

"Where you goin'?" Rogue stirs, her voice all cute and sleepy as she stretches out her body.

"I got something I need to take care of, I'll be back in a few hours, and then we're gonna spend the day together."

"Anything I can help with?" she yawns, and for a second I think about taking her with me, but I can't, not until I've explained everything to her properly.

"No, darlin', but I do need you to stay here."

"Cross my heart." She rises to her knees, climbing up my body and kissing my neck. "Come back to me," she whispers, assuming that it's club shit I'm going to deal with.

I ride my bike to the care home as fast as I can, knowing that when Mama gets like this, there's only one person who can calm her down. The nurse that meets me at the entrance looks worn out.

"She's been up all night asking for your father," she explains, leading me briskly to Mama's door. "We can't calm her down and we didn't want to try sedation until you'd had a chance to calm her yourself." I nod back at her gratefully then wait until she's turned her back before I open up the door into my very own version of hell.

Mama looks wired, her hair unruly and her nightdress clutched in her fists as she paces the room.

"Richie, my dear boy." She runs at me and crushes me between her arms. "It's your father, he hasn't visited in days, something's happened to him, I know it has. I can feel it." I take a deep breath that I hope will help me find strength. Then taking her shoulders, I hold her steady in front of me.

"I'm sure he's fine, Mama, he'll be home soon." Playing her game breaks my heart. But I do it for all she's suffered. Over the years it's become more and more difficult. The longer I do it for, the more it drains out of me, and I've been doing this ever since the day I buried my dad's body in the woods.

I'll never forget waking up that next morning and finding her pressing his shirt. She'd made him his breakfast, and done his lunch bag for work. She acted as if nothing happened, spending the day making sure the house was spotless, ready for his inspection when he got home, and that evening she laid the table for him and served him up a plate.

At first, I thought it was out of habit. When you've had things drilled into your head the way she had for all those years I figure it's hard to stop. But as time progressed and she'd talk about him like he was expected home any moment, I started to realize I had a real problem on my hands.

I put it down to shock, hoping that this was her way of dealing with everything. But as she got progressively worse, I had to accept that the issue was way more serious. Mama had erased that night from her memories.

Her head invented its own story about him working away on business. I was only sixteen back then and I had no idea how to deal with her, so I'd played along.

She made herself ill keeping the house tidy to his standard. It wasn't just her mental state that forced me to get help. I somehow managed to keep her alive for a year but it was becoming harder. She'd leave the iron on, take dishes out of the oven without using mitts. I had to watch her deteriorate, slowly losing more and more of her every day. And there was nothing I could do about it.

"Richie, look at you, your shirt's all creased and your hair's all over the place." Her eyes fall onto my hands and her mouth drops open. "What's this, tattoos?" She reaches out to grab my arms, forcing my shirt up to my elbows and studying my ink as if it's the first time she's ever seen it. I usually cover my arms when I visit her, but I've never been able to hide the ink on my hands. I always figured she chose to blank it out, same way she does all the other things she hates.

"You know what your father thinks of tattoos, they're the devil's markings. Why would you do this to your body...? If he comes home now and see's you like this..."

I don't know what it is that makes me snap. Maybe it's because I've had one hell of a long-assed fucking day, or perhaps I'm just fucking exhausted from all this shit, but suddenly I lose patience.

"But he isn't coming home, is he, Mama? He's not coming home because he's fucking dead." She gasps, stepping away from me, her tired eyes suddenly widening to full capacity.

"Why would you say such a thing?" she shakes her head at me, looking disgusted.

"Dad ain't ever coming back, Mama. Ever... you made fucking sure of that when you stabbed him twenty-five times."

Thwack. Her palm stings my cheek as it connects.

"What a cruel, evil thing to say, Richie, I should wash your mouth out," she scolds.

"It's the cruel and evil truth, and I've been playing along with whatever this is for too many years now."

She stumbles back and drops into her chair as recollection battles through the walls she's built in her head. And suddenly her expression turns horrified, and her hands cover her mouth when reality sinks in.

"And do you know why I do this, Mama?" I crouch in front of her and take her hands in mine.

"I do it out of guilt because I should have been the one to stop him from hurting us, I should have been the one who stopped him hurting them... way before you had to find out. But I was scared of him. I believed all the shit he told me about him being part of God's plan because I was too fucking scared to end him myself. *I* should be the one who killed him. It was meant to be me."

AGED 16

Dad's car is parked outside the house when the bus drops me at the end of our lane. It can only mean trouble, Dad never comes home early. His routine is regimental.

As I walk closer toward the house, I think of all the reasons that might have brought him home early, perhaps Mama is sick. Or maybe someone's found out about the bodies that are hidden up at Sinnerman's Quarry.

When I step onto the porch, the door creaks open. I'm greeted with an eerie silence, and as I walk into the living room, my feet freeze on the perfectly polished wood beneath them. There's blood everywhere, soaking into the floorboards, smeared onto the wall, and all trails of it lead to the lifeless body of my father that's sitting propped up against the wall.

His white shirt is red from blood, slashes and holes punctured through the fabric. Turning my head, I see Mama sitting up straight in her chair, her usually immaculate dress stained red, and her hands soaked to her elbow in thick red blood. When she turns her head and looks at me, her eyes are vacant and unapologetic, and I slowly step toward her and pry the carving knife out of her hand, dropping it to the floor.

Slowly and with her normal elegance, she rises to her feet, ignoring the blood on her hands and the mess surrounding us as she moves closer to me. Her hand brushes through my hair, setting it in place before her tacky fingers straighten up my tie.

I notice the red toolbox beside her chair and close my eyes. She knows, I can't protect her from it anymore.

"That's better, Richie." She smiles at me.

"I'm quite tired, I think I should lay down for a while." She's robotic as she turns away from me and starts heading up the stairs, her hand leaving a bloody trail on the banister.

"Mama, he killed innocent women, he beat you almost every day. And I've had to listen to you tell me I'm like him for over ten years. I'm nothing fucking like him. I fight every day to battle those demons. But that doesn't mean I'm good. I'm in a biker gang called the Dirty Souls, my family out there consists of ruthless, dangerous men, who fight and kill for what they want and the people they love. But I've only ever cleaned up for them. Like I did for him, and the same way I did for you."

"You're lying, and when your father gets home he's going to be furious with you for upsetting me." She shakes her head, refusing to accept what's coming back to her.

"I never blamed you for what you did to him. I only ever

blamed myself. You found out who he was that day, and you were hurt. You did what I should have done the day I found those pictures. I took care of it though, I used what he taught me to make sure no one ever finds him. And that's the sick part of me, Mama. I have his compulsions too, I need to control everything around me and I exhaust myself trying to keep it in, but I can do it. I've been doing it for all these years."

I can see that my words are sinking in as she looks sadder.

"You're safe. To everyone else, Dad will always be the guy that skipped town and left his family. Just another missing person. But not to us. We know the truth, we know what he did to those girls and you stopped him from hurting any more."

When her eyes find mine, they're crammed with tears and somehow she looks older.

"I love you, Richie," she tells me, her hands gripping at my shirt and pulling me close.

"I'm sick, aren't I?" she whispers

"You're gonna be fine, Mama," I assure her, we've had this conversation before, she'll have forgotten it in a few hours, and her mind will reset. But I'll stay with her and I'll hold her for the short time I have her back. At least this time I have something to tell her, that I hope she'll store with the memories she keeps.

"I'm tired, Richie, will I forget all this again before I wake up?" she asks, her drained voice sounding a little hopeful.

"Yes." I pick her up and carry her over to her bed, gently laying her out on the mattress and she smiles at me sleepily.

"I wish you could forget too," she whispers, stroking her frail hand against my cheek, and I lay down beside her and take it in mine. "I'm not sad anymore. I have someone now. Someone who takes care of me and helps me drown out the monsters in my head. She makes me forget too," I admit, and the smile Mama gives me makes all the pain of being here worth it.

"And I already know you're really gonna like her." I smile back.

"That's such good news, darling," she breathes, her lids flickering. "Tell me about her."

"Well, her name's Evangeline…"

"Okay, okay. I'm coming. I throw on one of Grimm's T-shirts and rush to answer the door. Whoever it is ain't giving up. And when I fling the door open with my usual attitude, my heart breaks when I see Skid standing in front of me.

He looks shattered, angry, and sad all at the same time and I throw my arms around his neck and take comfort in him being back.

"Why didn't you tell me?" he asks me sternly, his hold on me almost crushing.

"I didn't want Grimm to tell you." I pull back and look down at my shoes like I'm being scolded.

"I knew you had it rough, but if I'd have known..."

"I know, and I love you for that, but I didn't want it. I was trying to keep my family together. I realize now how foolish I was now, but I can't take it back, and neither can you. So we just have to heal. Both of us."

"My god, girl, you're a pain in my ass." He tugs me back in for another hug, and I feel him wipe his eyes with the hand that's wrapped around my shoulder.

I knew Grimm would have to tell him and the others about what happened to me as a kid. But that doesn't make it any easier. I'm gonna hate the way everyone around here is gonna look at me from now on. I just want to go back to being me.

Forget all the nasty shit. I just hope Grimm's stuck to his word and hasn't told Skid about Chop. That one, I want to be taken to the grave.

"I'm coming home. I'm gonna help Grimm take care of you, and start pulling my weight at the garage again. Hell, Rogue, if you can get over what's happened to you, I've sure as hell gotta try too." I feel the huge smile lift my cheeks and I don't even try to hide it from him. "But you gotta promise me something…" he looks at me sternly. "No more shutting me out. You're more than just the crazy girl that works in the garage, now. You're family and you gotta start embracing that shit."

"Did ya hear that I'm Grimm's old lady now?" I can't believe how pathetically proud I sound saying that.

"Yeah, I heard."

"And did you make him suffer the 'hurt her and I kill you' lecture?" I ask intrigued.

"Do I need to?" He cocks one of his thick, dark brows at me and it feels so good to have him back.

"Everyone here's gonna hate me. I kinda caused a war. I've put their old ladies at risk, and you know how touchy they get about that shit." I roll my eyes like it doesn't matter, when in reality it really does. If I've learned anything over the past few weeks it's that these people are good. Maddy, Ella, and Gracie may all be a little square for my liking, but they tolerate me and for that, I have to give them some credit.

"Nah, I just come outta church, you didn't cause a war, Rogue, you alerted us to something that would have become a huge problem if it had flown under the radar for much longer. Ivan has a much bigger crew than just the assholes we put out. He's clever and, more worrying, he's got a good legitimate profile under his belt. Now I ain't saying that they're all too happy about how you handled the situation, but they won't hold no grudge."

"Was Grimm at church? He got called out last night and hasn't come home yet."

"Yeah, he's just talking with Prez and Roswell, they're figuring out how to handle the mess at the farm."

"So we have time for some breakfast?" I relax, knowing that Grimm's okay.

"Yeah, we got time." Skid smiles at me.

It's a whole hour before Grimm comes home, and I don't give a shit if it makes Skid feel uncomfortable when I run to him and leap onto his body, wrapping my legs around his waist. He clearly doesn't care either, because he kisses me the same way he does when he's fucking me.

A fake cough from Skid pulls us apart.

"Where were you? I got worried," I ask Grimm before he gets mad at Skid.

"There was some shit at the home last night with my mama," he explains, and I note how Skid looks confused. Grimm doesn't talk about his mama to anyone.

"It's dealt with now. Roswell's taking care of the farm situation. But this Ivan's a sly fucker. I don't like it one bit, Skid." Grimm places me back onto my feet and throws Skid a worried look.

"So what you're saying is that I'm still not safe." I sigh.

"What we're saying is, you're gonna keep low for a while until we figure out what this guy's about, and then run him out of town. It shouldn't be a problem for ya. You got him and the garage all on your doorstep," Skid smirks

"And now I got you too. How lucky can one girl get?" I kiss Grimm on the cheek then skip over to plant one on Skid too.

"You're taking a few days off," he orders, picking up his keys from the table and passing Grimm on his way to let himself out; he slaps him in the back.

"Look after our girl," he tells him.

"How's your mama?" I ask Grimm, last night he told me that

he knew I visited her, and I can't believe he's not mad at me for the invasion of his privacy. "She's good now, just had one of her breaks, it's normal for her condition."

"And what is her condition?" I ask him, hoping that he's finally gonna let me in.

"Before I can tell you that, I gotta take you somewhere and I got to ask you to keep a secret."

"You have my word," I draw a cross over my chest.

We ride for about twenty miles, passing through a town that looks like it's living fifty years behind time, and when Grimm pulls off onto a dirt track, he stops in front of a huge detached house.

It's run down and in serious need of repair, but even I can imagine that it used to be beautiful.

"What is this place?" I ask, unsaddling the bike and stepping toward the front door.

"Don't go inside." Grimm snatches my arm and pulls me back. I can feel him shaking as he holds on to me with a firm grip, and he snarls at himself like he's regretting this.

"This is where I grew up," he explains, resting his ass back on his saddle and placing me in between his legs. I wait patiently for him to tell me more, knowing how hard it is to unearth the things that you fight every day to keep buried.

"My dad was particular about stuff. He liked to control shit," he starts, his eyes fixed on where his fingers are fiddling with the hem of my shirt. "He'd beat on me and my mama if things weren't kept right, everything had to be perfect, not a thing out of its place."

Things slowly start to make a lot of sense.

"That really sucks." I stroke my hand through his hair, while I wait until he's ready to tell me more.

"He had another compulsion too… When I was about twelve, I found out that he liked to hurt women. I don't know how many victims there were, but I know he killed a lot of innocent ones.

He claimed he had the strength of God inside him and what he was doing was all part of God's plan but…"

Grimm clenches the cotton in his fist so tight I notice his knuckles turning white, and I wish he'd look up at me.

"When I was fifteen, when he showed me how to get rid of them, he told me that I had the power inside me too and that I'd have to be smart if I was gonna carry out God's work."

"Jesus Christ." I slam my hand over my mouth because I don't know what to say. No wonder Grimm and his mama are so fucked up.

"I was scared of him, and because of that, I helped him get rid of them, Rogue. That's how I got good at what I do for the club. Because he taught me."

"I…" For once in my life I'm speechless.

"You don't have to say anything, I know I should have done things differently. But he told me that hurting those other women stopped him from hurting Mama, and I had to protect her."

I can feel my heart breaking, and now I know how he must have felt last night when I poured out my heart to him, because I'm so angry right now that I could move the earth but I need to be here for him.

"I hated him back then and I hate him more now, because sometimes…" Grimm's eyes flick up to mine and he looks ashamed. "I can feel that part of him inside me."

"Sure you like things in their place, but you'd never…"

"I want to control you," he interrupts me. "When I'm with you, sometimes it's all I think about. If I had my way, I'd keep you locked inside my cabin day and night. It's an illness, Rogue, and I'm really fucking sick with it." He watches for my reaction like he's ashamed, and when I smile back at him he looks confused.

"Well, if that's the case, I'm sick with it too, 'cause given the chance I'd do the same to you," I admit.

"You killed him, didn't you?" I guess this is why he never

wanted to speak about killing people. It can't be easy to take the life of the person who gave you yours. I can be so insensitive sometimes. I really need to work on that if I'm gonna be accepted by these people. And the past twenty-four hours have proven to me how much I want to be.

"I've never killed anyone," he confesses, and I can tell that hurts him by the way his brow furrows.

"But you're so… Grimm, how is that even possible?"

"I've thought about it plenty, but I'm too fucking scared to do it. I've got enough of that man's evil inside me, I got his OCD, I got his need for control. What if that part of him comes out of me too? What if I hurt you?" Seeing tears in his eyes, triggers mine, and his hurt feels like a knife tearing through my insides.

"I don't want to turn into him and lose you, Rogue."

"That ain't gonna happen, men like you get possessive over their women. Look at the way Brax is with Grace and Jessie is with Maddy. They love them fiercely but they'd never beat on them. You would never hurt me, Grimm. I trust that and you have to, too," I assure him, taking his hand and kissing his knuckles.

"Tell me what happened to your father, did he get caught? Is he in prison too?" Grimm shakes his head back at me.

"I buried him in those woods when I was sixteen." His eyes glance toward the tree line about half a mile behind the house. I can't hide my shock, and the way he's looking back at me proves he isn't surprised by it.

"I thought you said you never killed him?"

"I didn't kill him. Mama killed him."

"Your Mama!" My voice lifts a few decimals. I can't believe what I'm hearing, the sweet woman who I sit drinking lemonade with and talk to about flowers being capable of murder seems too far-fetched.

"I came home from school one day and found her with a

knife in her hand. She'd found out about the women he killed and I guess she just lost her shit."

"That's kinda kick-ass," I snigger, before realizing how incredibly insensitive I'm being, *again.*

"Sorry." I lower my head, but Grimm quickly lifts it back up again with his finger.

"Never apologize for being you." He stares back at me intensely with those dark punishing eyes. And I realize that regardless of what happened to bring us here, me and him were created for each other.

"Mama doesn't remember anything about that day, she's got some form of dissociative amnesia, and it seems to have triggered some Alzheimer's traits too, she forgets silly things that could cause her harm. I've never had her diagnosed professionally, but I've spent a lot of time researching it. I pay the home for their silence, so she can stay in the world that she's created for herself. She had a bad day yesterday, I went in and I said some shit I shouldn't have." Grimm looks disappointed in himself.

"You need to stop beating yourself up about stuff. What your father did to those women, and to your Mama, you were a victim of it too. Look at all you've done to protect her, none of this is your fault. And you're doing the best you can for her."

"I should have been the one who killed him, I look back and think about how many times I thought about doing it. But I wasn't strong enough, I was too scared. If I'd have just been brave enough, I'd still have Mama with me."

"You were sixteen years old, you shouldn't be blaming yourself, you were a child." I can hear my tone changing because all this is making me so angry. I could stomp into those woods, dig up that motherfucker and spit on his skeleton for what he's done to Grimm.

"So were you. You were just a kid when your dad let his

friends hurt you," he growls at me. "And yet you protect him, I already know you're not gonna let me hurt him."

"I can't argue that right now. I haven't figured out how I feel about it myself yet. And if I think about it for too long I know I'll fall apart." It makes me feel weak and helpless to admit that, but with Grimm, I'm not scared to let my guard down anymore.

"So what we gonna do with this place? It's riddled with shit memories. If your mama still owns it, you should sell it."

"I tell myself every time I come here that I should burn the place to the fucking ground." He kicks up some dirt with his boot, and makes a sad laugh.

"That's exactly what you should do." I take his hand in mine. "Set fire to your past right here, and we'll move on together."

"You're crazy, you know that?" He looks up at me, and despite all the heavy shit he's just told me, he's smiling, and I nod back at him before I kiss him.

"Come on, there should be some gasoline in the shed." Grimm takes my hand and leads me around the back of the house. I wait outside while he fumbles around, then eventually comes out with a can in one hand and retakes my hand with the other.

Marching us back to the front of the house, he starts to douse the front porch. His face holding such a strong determination as he shakes the can, pouring it over the broken swing chair and covering as much space as he can before it runs out.

"You know you could probably sell this place for a fortune, this location, and all this land." I check he's sure before he strikes the match.

"I got everything I need at the club, and I got you. This place can fall to ash." He takes one last look at the house before he flicks the lit match at the porch. It doesn't take long for the flames to grow, spreading rapidly around the house and giving off so much heat that we have to take a few more paces back.

Grimm looks tranced as he stares into the flames, and I watch the orange and red flares brighten his dark pupils before I rest my head on his shoulder and watch them destroy.

"You think you'll go for that visit and ask your father for the truth?" he asks, lighting himself a cigarette, then placing his hand over where mine rests on his chest. And I realize that I have all I need now too. I've let Grimm into my life, I've even let his club in a little too. Skid's come back, and I got a real chance of being happy if I wanna be.

I don't need to know the truth, it's not gonna change the past.

Reaching into my back pocket, I take out the visiting order that I've been carrying with me since Grimm gave it back to me. And moving forward, I feel the heat of the fire warm my face as I toss it toward the house. Then I step back and watch the paper crumple, and disappear into flames.

Grimm pulls me back and snatches a fist of my hair, his mouth consuming mine in that way that makes me forget anything bad ever existed.

"Let's get out of here," he says with the most perfect fuckin' smile I've ever seen.

"Yeah." I smile back at him, letting him lead me back to his bike. The engine rumbles, and I hold on to him tight as we leave the blaze behind us and head back to the compound.

CHAPTER 46

1% MC

GRIMM

M y cell vibrates, and when I see it's Jessie I step outside to answer it.

"Grimm, where are ya?"

"Had a private issue to take care of," I answer, unwilling to give any more away than that. My club brothers don't know anything about my mama, and that's the way I intend things to stay.

"Me, Brax and Skid are gonna ride back out to the bar in Pueblo, we wanna talk to the owner who Rogue shot, and we ain't sure how shit's gonna pan out. Figured as it's Rogue related, you'd want in?" He's damn fucking right on that one.

"I'll be back at the club in thirty, don't go without me," I tell him, hanging up the phone.

"Anything important?" Mama looks up from the photo album that she's flicking through with Rogue when I step back inside.

"That was work. I got a job come through." Rogue looks up at me and smiles mischievously.

"Oh that's a shame, Richie, but you mustn't let me keep you. Are you going to visit again next week?"

"Of course we will," Rogue responds. "And in the meantime, I'll practice that stitch you taught me." She smiles so sweetly that it's almost impossible to imagine the dirty things I did to her just hours ago at the cabin.

"Who died?" she asks as we climb onto my bike.

"No one. Skid and Jessie are riding out to Pueblo to speak to the guy you shot."

"You want me to come too? Maybe I could shoot out his other knee." She wraps her hands around my waist and kisses my neck.

"Ain't you got some stitching to be working on?" I tease, looking over my shoulder and smirking.

"You keep throwing that dirty smirk over your shoulder at me, Richie Carter, and I'ma fuck you right here in this parking lot."

"You know, Mama remembers things that aren't related to her trauma. She will ask you next week to show her what you've been practicing."

"And I'll distract her by telling her how insanely in love with her son I am."

I shake my head at my crazy girl, before kick-starting my bike and heading for the club.

Jessie leads the ride out to Pueblo, and when we get there, there's someone already waiting for us by the door. The guy's around Skid's build and I'm guessing he's our informer since he nods at Jessie as we pass him.

The bar's near enough empty and as soon as we step inside, the two women working behind the bar scurry outback. Two men are sitting around a small table, and I snigger when I see one of them has his leg in a cast. He must be the one Rogue shot. There's a box set on the table between them, that I also recognize.

"See you got the last part of your friend," Jessie gestures his head to the box that contains McAlister's tongue.

"Ivan is gonna want blood for what happened." The older guy swipes under his nose like he's thirsty for a fix.

"Ivan won't be getting jack shit from us," Brax says, and when the younger of the two stands up like he's gonna do something, Brax quickly steps up into his space and stares him back down onto his ass again.

"Prez wants a meeting, on neutral ground. We ain't interested in what he's doing so long as it doesn't involve our family and it don't get brought into our town." Jessie puts it simply and the older guy laughs at him.

"You think it's gonna be that simple? You boys have been running shit your way for too long, you haven't come up against someone like him before. He's a different level of power. One that'll wipe you clean out."

"Well he didn't do such a good job of that the other week, *us* on the other hand... What was the body count, Brax?" Jessie looks over to Brax, whose eyes are still blazing into the younger guy, daring him to move.

"I got it at nine," he answers.

"You're making a mistake." He shakes his head.

"We hear he owns this place too, maybe we should let him know we ain't fucking around." Skid moves behind the bar and helps himself to a shot from the optics.

"Here's how he can contact us," Jessie places a card on the table with a cell number scribbled on the back. Then with a nod, we all leave the bar.

On the way out, Jessie shakes hands with the guy on the door, slipping him a hundred dollar bill through his fingers. And when the cuff of his jacket shifts up, I notice something that makes me stop in my tracks.

I see the tiny individual tears tattooed onto the arch of his left hand, and instantly I recall how Rogue shattered telling me about the man who stole her tears and marked himself with them to torment her.

My feet are moving toward him before my head even plays out what I'm gonna do about it. My fist snatching at his shirt and shoving him into the wall behind him.

"What's with the tats?" I look down at his hand and snarl at him.

"Nothing of any significance." He turns his bottom lip down and shrugs, remaining calm.

"Grimm, chill. He's good." I ignore the voice that comes from behind me and slam his body harder when he tries to move.

"You tell me what those tattoos mean right now or I'll slit your damn throat." I mean every word, I may have spent a lot of years doubting myself, but there's nothing in question when it comes to Rogue.

"You really wanna know?" He looks down at me with a snigger.

"They belong to the whore you got working at your club," he tells me. "That little bitch was playing with my dick way before she started fiddling with your engines."

"Holy shit!" I hear Jessie's voice and catch Skid stepping forward in the corner of my eye. The guy starts to struggle, and although he's much bigger than me, I find the strength to hold him.

I guess God put that power in me after all.

I use my thumb to press his eyeball into the back of his head, and the fucker screams, fighting hard to push me off. But I don't let up, not until I hear a pop, followed by an agonized cry.

"Leave him," I hear Skid growl from beside me, and when I check over my shoulder he's stepped in front of Brax and Jessie. Neither of them attempts to fight him off, so I get back to work. Pounding the sick fuck's skull into the brick wall behind him, my hands and face become filthy with the bastard's blood, but my arms don't tire.

I keep on pounding until he stops fighting and his limp body slumps down the wall.

"What the fuck was that?" Jessie asks, moving around Skid and standing over the body. I look down at the lifeless figure and stand in shock. Taking his life had been easy, no hesitation, no remorse. He'd hurt Rogue, he made her cry. And I'd do it all over again, as many times as I have to, to protect her.

"He hurt Rogue," I explain.

"We better load him up before any of us get seen." Brax takes a look around us, it's the middle of the day, and although it's in a quieter part of town, this ain't a good situation for me to have put us in.

Skid is already shifting him into the side alley while Brax calls Storm to bring out a cage. Meanwhile, Jessie looks at me shocked.

"Come on, Grimm, let's get back to the club, yeah?" He speaks slowly to me as if he doesn't trust that I'm stable. Which I find ironic considering the things I know he's capable of.

This is my first, and something tells me he senses that. I don't give a shit about who's gonna deal with the mess when I start making my way to my bike and start it up. I'm covered in the fucker's blood, but all I can think about is getting home to Rogue. I want to hold her in my arms and promise her that he'll never take a single one of her tears ever again.

I'll deal with this body later, the others must understand because no one tries to stop me from leaving, and I ride full throttle all the way back to the club, heading straight up to my cabin when I see that the shutter door is shut on the garage.

"Hey," she greets me in that same way that always makes my chest feel warm as I storm through the door, then she looks shocked when she sees me. I'm a mess. My skin and clothes, contaminated with his blood, but it doesn't stop me from going to her and grabbing her cheeks in my blood-stained hands. I force my tongue between her lips, owning her mouth, and it seems to calm all the anger inside me.

"He's dead," I tell her when I stop to take a breath. "The guy who took your tears, the one who gives you nightmares. I ended him."

"Grimm…" I don't give her a chance to finish what she

wants to say. Instead, I kiss her again and push her body against the pillar in the middle of the room. She smells so clean and fresh, she must have just showered, and I'm spoiling her with the sweat and blood of my sins. It doesn't feel the slightest bit wrong, Rogue has awakened something inside me that overrides all my compulsions.

Right now it feels like she's the only thing that can cleanse me. Rogue is my cure, and by ridding her of him, I can be hers too.

"That's the kinda romantic shit I'm talking about," she teases, and I actually laugh along with her, my lips pressing deeper into hers so she doesn't just hear it, but feels it too.

"Fuck me, Grimm." She pushes my cut off my shoulders and pulls at my T-shirt, and I lift her up so she's straddling my waist. Because I don't care if that asshole's blood is still on my skin, I'm gonna give her what she wants, and I won't make her wait for it.

N ame something sexier than your man coming home covered in blood and telling you he just killed for you?

Grimm has me in his arms, but he doesn't throw me on the bed and fuck me like I expect him to. Instead, he sits me on his lap and lays back against the mattress.

He's looking sexier than I've ever seen him with his body streaked red and his eyes alive with desire. He slides his body between my legs, placing my knees on either side of his shoulders, and his hands aren't gentle when they fist my skirt and push it up over my stomach.

He rips at my panties, leaving a burn mark on my hip from the friction of the fabric, before his mouth attacks me savagely. He licks and nips through my center, while his fingers grip at my ass cheeks and keep me tight to his mouth.

His tongue magically rotating inside me, is like nothing I've ever felt before, creating little sparks of thrill in my stomach that build into something that feels like it's going to erupt. It's almost scary, like it'll be too much to sustain.

My whole body threatens to burst into flames as I wriggle against his mouth, trying to push myself over the edge. But his hands keep me seated, forcing me to feel every flick and roll of his tongue. Taking control, just the way I like him to.

I give in to him, relaxing my body and letting myself get swept away in his pleasure. I feel his bruises setting into my skin, I love it when Grimm leaves his mark on me. I climb higher and higher, riding his face, pushing myself for more, and screaming his name. Then my legs get taken from beneath me when Grimm flips me over.

He climbs on top of me and when I look up at him, his lips are swollen and flushed from devouring my pussy, and the streaks of blood on his face make my pussy throb to feel him inside me

"You taste like fuckin' sin," he growls at me, reaching over his back with one arm and pulling his T-shirt over his head before he invades my mouth with his tongue, forcing me to taste some of that sin for myself.

His hand fists at my hair as he leans his arm over me, and frees his stiff cock with his other one.

I feel him fall hard against my thigh and he takes both my hands in his bloody ones, squeezing me tight between his fingers as he pushes them behind my head and pins me into the mattress. His eyes peer into mine so intensely as he sinks himself inside me, and both of us moan at the contact.

He rotates his hips over and over into me, keeping himself rooted deep and holding me with his glare. It causes pain deep in my chest when I think about losing him, and I quickly dash those kinda thoughts away.

Surely the world has been cruel enough to us. It would never place us together and then tear us apart.

His teeth sink into my collarbone, and I come again when his thrusts quicken. I mess his hair up between my fingers. But he's too far gone to care. Since being with me, Grimm has loosened up on a lot of things, and I look forward to seeing how far I can push him.

"Tell me you're mine," he groans.

"I'm yours," I promise, watching as the satisfaction in my

words send him over the edge. His cock pulses hot spurts inside me as one of his hand's release mine so he can wrap it around my throat, squeezing me while his teeth sink into my earlobe.

"And I'm fucking yours, Rogue," he warns, "every fucked up part of me."

CHAPTER 48

1% MC

GRIMM

Maddy managed to hook me up with a visiting order. So I'm here waiting along with all the other friends and family members at Florence for the prisoners to come into the visitor room.

The door opens and they spill through, greeting their wives, mothers, and kids. The asshole must sense that I'm here for him because he automatically comes across and takes the seat opposite me.

"You know who I am?" I ask him coolly.

"I know where you're from." His purple-ringed eyes look down to my arm where the tattoo all my brothers have is etched onto my skin.

"I'm guessing you're the one I need to thank for this?" he holds up his arm, revealing a hand that's bandaged tightly.

Skid's buddy, Dodger, took a finger off for each friend he let fuck his daughter.

I nod, staring down the fucker sitting in front of me. He's balding, overweight, and he sees himself as a fucking Soprano, but any guy who spent as many years as he did using a little girl isn't gonna do fuck all to intimidate me.

"I came to tell you that I'm responsible for Rogue now." The smuggest of smiles finds its way to his face and it makes me want to rip it off.

"Ahhhh my little Evangeline." He sits back in his chair and looks above him as if drawing memory of her in his head.

"Yeah well, she's my business now. And fuck all to do with you."

"Business," he scoffs at me. "That crazy little bitch is good fuckin' business alright." I shoot up ready to launch at him. But the guard on duty eyeballs me, forcing me to find my cool again and sit back down.

It's vital that I finish what I came here to say, and getting kicked out of here before that happens is only gonna make me the loser.

"You are the lowest form of scum I've ever laid my eyes on," I growl at him under my breath as I lean forward, and he laughs back at me through his black eroding teeth.

"It bothers you, don't it?" He crosses his arms over his potbelly. "You can't stand to think of all the men who got inside her before you did." I shake my head in disgust. This man is going to suffer, I'd decided that before I came here, but now he's forcing me to up my game.

"You did the right thing taking the rap for what she did because if you were on the outside, you'd already be dead."

"You think I did that for her?" He throws his head back and laughs at me.

"The girl had lost her mind, it was only a matter of time before she ratted them out. I was coming in here anyway. Rather come in a murderer of a nonce than a supplier to one." He looks me dead in the eye as he speaks. "And now I'll always have that on her."

My fists clench under the table. How I haven't rammed his face into the steel by now is a miracle beyond mystery.

"I could lean over this table and kill you, right now," I hiss at him through my teeth.

"Go ahead. If it bothers you enough, you'd be doing me a favor. I'm serving a life sentence for what that fucked up little whore did to Frank." He holds his arms out. Tempting me. The room is full of guards and visitors. There would be no getting out of it. No clean-up in the world could erase me killing him in front of these many people.

I'm not a rash person, I'm smart and I know exactly how I'm gonna make him suffer. I release my fists, bringing them up and crossing them in front of me on the table, cooling myself off before I speak.

"Nah, it doesn't bother me. You wanna know why?" I don't give him the chance to answer. "'Cause I'm gonna spend the rest of my life sinking my cock into your daughter's sweet little pussy. I'm gonna take care of her, and love her with everything I got. I'm gonna do all the things you never did. And as much pleasure as it would give me to snap your neck right here, I ain't gonna. Because I can't do any of those things for her from inside these walls." I lean even closer to him. "So I'll kill you every night in my sleep. While your little Evangeline is tucked up safe under my arms. Where no one can hurt her. Not even her sick cunt of a daddy." I watch his face drop and know I've won. But I'm not done yet, not even close.

"You see that guy over there," my eyes roll over to a big brute of a man two tables over. His long ginger hair is pulled tight in a ponytail, and he has tattoos covering every inch of his muscle-strained arms. I know that when he stands he's almost seven-foot tall. "That's—"

"I know who he is," Rogue's dad interrupts me, and the fear that sets in his eyes cools the blood beneath my skin a little.

"Buzz watches over Dodge and some of the other brothers in here as a favor for the club. And in return, we take care of his wife on the outside. We also pay the guards to give him what he needs here…"

I watch his skin turn white

"You know he likes ass. Right?" I keep my hard face fixed

346

on him as he looks back across at the tower of a man, who's being visited by his wife.

"Apparently he put his last bitch in the infirmary, something to do with internal tearing." I watch the lump disappear from his throat as fear swallows it back.

"He gets real grouchy when he hasn't got a play thing. Guards struggle to keep him in check. Guess it's a good thing we got him hooked up for the foreseeable." The man's timing couldn't be any more perfect when he looks over at me from the other side of the room and winks the eye with the large scar running through the middle of it.

"Please," Rogue's pathetic excuse of a father begs.

Now it's my turn to laugh, but not for long. I want to eat up all his fear before I leave, take it home with me and remember what it looks like on him during the times I have to comfort my girl from one of her nightmares.

I get so close to his face that my nose almost touches his. Sweat is pouring from his pores as his eyes flick between me and his new bunkmate. And I tap his cheek with my hand.

"Save the pleading for Buzz, I hear he likes it…" I whisper, standing up and raising my chin at Buzz before I leave the room.

When I get back to the club, Rogue is sitting playing poker with Squealer, her feet propped up on the table with a beer in one hand and her cards fanned out in the other.

"Hey." She smiles over at me, and I go straight to her and kiss those pretty painted lips. I check her hand before I make my way over to the bar for a drink, and Squeal is gonna have to have a good one to beat it.

He's been out of hospital for a week now, and not being able to ride is killing him. He'll be back on his feet soon enough, but until then, Rogue has taken it as her responsibility to keep him entertained.

"How did the visit go?" Skid asks under his breath, smacking his palm into my shoulder, I look at it and he quickly moves it. A lot has changed since Rogue set my life into a whirlwind but I'm still me, and human contact that doesn't come from her still ain't all that welcomed.

"Could have killed the fucker," I admit.

"Yeah well, that would be giving him the easy road," Skid seethes. I've promised Rogue I'll never tell him about what Chop did to her, and I won't. The man doesn't need anything else to hurt him. I'm just pleased that he's sticking around for her.

We both watch her take Squeal's money, looking pretty smug with herself as Squeal throws his cards down in a strop and tells her he ain't gonna play with her anymore. Grabbing up her money, she leaves the table, fanning the bills in front of her face as she approaches us.

"Good work." Skid balances his huge arm across her shoulder,

He's the only guy around here who can touch her without sending me crazy.

"I gotta head out on a run to Utah, I'll only be gone a few days," he explains to her. "This fight with Ivan ain't over, you gotta lie low and do what the brothers tell ya until it passes, you hear me?"

"Scout's honor." Rogue lifts up her hands and rolls her eyes at him.

"I mean it, Rogue, you're one of us now, you let us protect you."

The tiny smile that Rogue gives him back is enough to tell us that despite her protests, she enjoys being a part of our fucked up family.

"You feelin' happy, darlin'?" I shift her between my legs and force her chin up so her eyes look into mine, they could never lie to me. And after being with that man today, I need to know that she's got everything she wants.

"The happiest I've ever been," she tells me reassuringly.

Looking at her, I wonder how anyone could have ever hurt her, especially her own father. I cup my hand between her legs and give her some friction, those big bright eyes of hers sparkle for me and her lips pull up into a teasing smirk.

"Get a fucking room," Squealer calls over from the table where he's sitting.

Rogue takes her attention away from me for a second to give him the finger.

"Come on, let's go back to our cabin. I ain't giving him a private show." She practically drags me away from the bar and toward the door.

"And that's the thanks I get for taking a bullet for you," Squealer calls out after us.

"Fuck off," we both shout over our shoulders in unison, as we walk out into the yard.

I'll never tell Rogue that I visited her father today, or that I'm gonna make sure he suffers every day that he remains on this earth for what he did to her. But that will be the only secret I ever keep from her.

Rogue accepts all the fucked up parts of me, in fact, she embraces them. She's taught me how to live.

I don't fear what comes next for us, because our damaged souls are already broken, and what's already broken can't break.

"**A**pologies for dragging you all here so early." I light up a smoke, toss the match, and look at all the tired faces in front of me as I take a long drawback. "Something's been brought to my attention that requires some urgency."

Jessie knows what I'm about to share, and I can tell by the look on his face that he's worried about it.

"We all know about the new threat." My eyes fall on Squealer, who's still healing, he's pissed that his injury has been slowing him down around here.

"Turns out, Ivan's silence over the past few weeks hasn't been a sign of him backing off.

He's been scheming, lying low, and coming up with a legitimate way to screw us... Looks like he's found it." I reach under the table and grab the cardboard tube before slamming it on the table. Troj is the first one to grab it. He pops the top off and pulls out the plans from inside, before he lays them out and starts to check them out.

What he's looking at is a building proposal for over a hundred houses.

"What's this got to do with us?" He looks up to ask me. And I slap another piece of paper on top. Then watch my Sergeant in Arms, the calmest guy I got, tense up with anger.

"That's Cheyanne land," he points out, his eyes shifting around the table to check the reaction of his brothers.

"Maddy's been keeping track of anything that's got Ivan's name attached to it. He's proposing that the state own the land, not the Indians, and he wants to buy it and build on it. He knows what that would mean for the club."

"The Cheyenne have lived there for hundreds of years, he can't just roll into town and tell them that land ain't theirs," Troj intervenes, seeming to get more and more irate with the evidence in front of him. Since when was he so fucking cultured on Native American history?

"Turns out he's got a solid case, Mads hacked his lawyer's IP. There ain't no written evidence of the land ever belonging to them. The state could claim it if they see it as being profitable," Jessie adds, stubbing out his smoke and slumping back in his chair, my VP is usually the one with all the answers but he ain't got shit on this.

"We gotta stop this from happening," Troj slams his palm hard on the table, making me wonder what the hell's gotten into him. Troj is known around here for his laid-back attitude. Even when he's got a fight coming up, he never loses his shit like this.

"Well if anyone's got any ideas, now's the time to speak the fuck up." I reach forward to put out my smoke.

"Supposing he proves the land is the state's, what's to stop us going in with a higher offer? We've wanted passage through the land for years. Surely someone can be bribed?" Nyx suggests, and all eyes go immediately to Thorne. He's the money man, he deals with club profits and all our businesses.

Thorne shakes his head gravely. "Funds are stable but ain't no way we could afford that amount of land, not when we're up against Ivan and money ain't an issue for him."

"Then have Jessie's bitch get her hands dirty, she can tap into some accounts, move some money around. She proved that when she worked for the Bastards, right?" Squealer's clever mouth runs off again and Jessie is already up and on his feet, rounding the table to get to him.

Troj stands up and manages to block him.

"Calm down, man, we need your head in this," he tells him sternly.

"Mads ain't doing anything that's gonna get her put in jail, and don't you ever mention Bastards and her name in the same sentence again." Jessie pushes against Troj's shoulder and points his finger at Squealer. I glance over to Brax, who I know will be thinking the same as me. Maddy got deeper connections with the Bastards than anyone else here knows about. Maddy herself doesn't know that the Bastards' ex-president was her father and if Jessie's got anything to do with it, that's exactly how it's gonna stay.

Standing up, I move to rest my hand on Jessie's shoulder.

"And the club wouldn't expect her to," I assure him calmly.

"One day, your cunt smart mouth is gonna drown itself in all the shit it spills," Jessie warns Squealer, slowly backing down and retaking his seat.

"There is one thing we could do," Brax says, twisting the tip of his knife into his wooden armrest and focusing on the blade.

"Speak up," I encourage him,

"We could make peace with the Indians, offer them our resources, and help them fight for their land. A legal battle would come off better if it was them appealing it. Who knows, we may even get out of them what we've been trying for since we moved here."

Brax has a good head on his shoulders, it's the reason he's been filling Skid's boots as Road Captain. Skid didn't want to reclaim his role after he returned from being nomad, he's gonna focus his attention on working at the garage and healing. Whatever it takes, we're just happy to have him back.

"You've got to be kidding," Tac chuckles. "Those stubborn

savages wouldn't understand a fucking peace treaty if it slapped 'em on their asses."

"And what would you know about 'em, Tac? You talked to any of them lately?" Troj tosses some attitude across the table, cracking his knuckles the way he does before a fight.

"Guess we won't know till we ask." Skid shrugs, looking like he's impressed with Brax's idea.

"Brax might be onto something." Thorne sits forward and leans his arms on the table. "We could get enough funds to help them with the legal side of stuff, Maddy could put some evidence together to back up their claim, even if we gotta plant it."

"There's just one fault in that plan, Thorne," Tac reaches in his cut for a smoke. "Those cunts fuckin' hate us."

Tac has a point, that Chief of theirs got a real grudge against the club. I've tried being polite on more than one occasion and he's thrown that shit right back in my face

"I say we put it to a vote," Jessie suggests, his eyes still narrow and zoned in on Squealer as he releases a steady stream of smoke from his lips.

"Okay, all those in favor of making nice with the Indians?" I put the question to the table. Jessie nods, and the same response follows from Nyx and Brax.

"I can't fuckin' believe I'm agreeing to this." Tac sighs before nodding his head. Thorne agrees too. Screwy and Squealer nod in unison, and Grimm gives his approval. "We gotta do what we gotta do," Skid points out. And when my eyes fall to Troj, I can see that something's troubling him. "I'm in," he says with the same determined look he gets on his face before he steps into the ring to kick ass. This whole Ivan thing has got him seriously riled.

"Then it's done, it's time to pay our neighbors a visit. Jessie, you're coming with," I instruct, and then wait until everyone has piled out before I stand up and follow after them. Troj is hanging around waiting for me by the door when I step outside.

"I'm coming too," he tells me abruptly. It ain't Troj's style and I'm surer than shit, now, that there's something he ain't telling me.

"I wasn't gonna head down there without my Sergeant, it goes without saying that you're coming." I smack him on his shoulder, deciding not to press him on it. When Troj wants to tell me what's got him bent out of shape, I'll be back ready to listen. But until then, I got a war on my hands that needs dealing with.

Ivan and his crew are showing their cards, they mean business. And the fact I'm gonna have to make nice with the Natives, who hate us, to give us an upper hand on it, pisses me off. But these days I lead by example, and if eating a slice of humble pie is what's gonna protect my club and my family, then I'm ready to swallow it.

ACKNOWLEDGMENTS

Thank you so much to everyone who has read this far, getting to the fourth book in the series feels like such a big achievement and I wouldn't have been able to do it without the love and support from all my readers, bloggers, and author buddies. There is so much more to come from these Dirty boys and I can't wait to bring it all to you.

Sharon, thank you for listening to all my crazy ideas, for being my alpha reader, talking to me for hours, and living the Dirty Souls fantasy with me. It's been a long road for both of us and I'm so proud of all we have achieved this year.

Lucy, thank you for loving Grimm since you first heard his name, and staking your claim on him from day one.

Andrea, you are such a beautiful person inside and out, I feel so grateful to have you as a friend. Whether you're proofreading my latest work, sending me pictures of hot men to keep me inspired, or rolling out the plastic sheeting you never fail to make me giggle.

My amazing Arc readers and street team…Girls, you're all crazy, but I wouldn't have you any other way. Your endless support, your playlists, and our amazing group chat give me so much motivation, and I love every one of you. I have also have to give a massive cheer to my PA Leanne, who does a fantastic job of keeping us all in check.

Angela, Karen, and Aliana thank you for being my first readers and forever having my back. You guys are like the three musketeers and have been there for me so much this year. I can't wait to finally hug you all.

Huge thanks to Erin, JJ and Emily, my amazing author friends who I couldn't be without.

To my incredible editor Sarah, who by some miracle is still putting up with me, and to Kerry at Rebel ink for helping me bring these Dirty Soul boys to life.

And to Apryle and Kate, my amazing friends who are always there to drink wine with me and make me laugh.

Finally, I want to say a massive thank you to my husband and our little tribe. I'm so proud of each and every one of you, I'm so lucky to have you all support me the way you do. I love you with all my heart.

ALSO BY EMMA CREED

His Captive

US: https://amzn.to/35GxYDf

UK: https://amzn.to/3klppSc

CA: https://amzn.to/33CXPJr

DIRTY SOULS MC SERIES

Lost soul

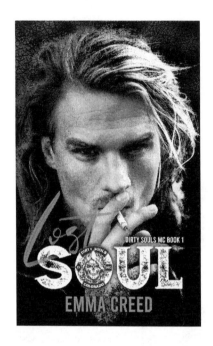

US: https://amzn.to/3rxkPF5

UK: https://amzn.to/3aOKenS

CA: https://amzn.to/2KVeoL7

AU: https://amzn.to/2JtMPbw

Reckless Soul

US: https://amzn.to/39rUnFL

UK: https://amzn.to/36mXbC0

CA: https://amzn.to/3pveo3O

AU: https://amzn.to/39xNCm1

Vengeful Soul

US: https://amzn.to/3xq7K34

UK: https://amzn.to/3sT9Epw

CA: https://amzn.to/3gzuKa4

AU: https://amzn.to/3aBs3Rs

ABOUT THE AUTHOR

Come find/stalk me on the following social media platforms.